night music

jenn marie thorne

Dial Books

Dial Books
An imprint of Penguin Random House LLC, New York

Copyright © 2019 by Jenn Marie Thorne

Visit us online at penguinrandomhouse.com

Printed in the United States of America
ISBN 9780735228771

10 9 8 7 6 5 4 3 2 1

Design by Cerise Steel
Text set in Legacy Serif ITC

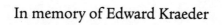

In memory of Edward Kraeder

1.

a stranger was playing my piano. *My* piano, untouched for months, purring under his fingers like a stray cat. More than purring . . . singing, leaping, laughing, dying, all in the time it took me to stumble-run downstairs.

I stared into the dusty living room from the bottom step, not trusting my eyes—my ears even less. But there he was, half standing while he played, one knee on the bench, like this was a quick errand he'd needed to run.

A boy. Tall, lean, angular, skin rich brown, hair a supernova of spirals backlit by afternoon sun.

I couldn't see his fingers, but I could feel them skipping over the keys, tiny pings in my chest, arms, spine. *So many notes.* It was contrapuntal, insanely complex, cogs and gears—which piece? I couldn't pick out the key, let alone the composer, but here *he* was, commanding my piano, smiling at some private joke. He wasn't even looking at the keyboard as he played.

He was staring at me.

"Do you like it?" he called.

Was this a hallucination? A musical one?

"You play really well," I got out.

Nobody was supposed to touch my piano. Not me, not anybody. Not anymore.

Not a *stranger in my house.*

He was still going—softly now, relentless, the key shifting. "But the piece?"

My eyes darted to our tall many-paned windows, the big oak doors—open to the stoop. How had he gotten in? "I—I'm trying to figure out what it is. I know it's Bach, but . . ."

He hopped with delight, not missing a single note. "Not Bach. But oh my God, that you thought so . . ."

He grinned, so relaxed and weirdly familiar that everything seemed to readjust like it does in a dream, making me wonder if *he* lived here and *I* was visiting. He had a single dimple, an easy smile—what was *happening*?

Chatter from West Seventy-first Street filtered into the living room and away. I took a step closer. A better look.

My age—seventeen, eighteen?—dressed like an August issue of *GQ*. Short-sleeved striped button-down, royal-blue bow tie, neatly pressed chinos, a canvas belt. He was definitely real. Hyperreal.

This couldn't be an intervention. Nobody could have been tone-deaf enough to send a brilliant pianist here to tempt me to change my mind. Could he be some stalker fan of Dad's or Mom's, or Win's or—was it pure coincidence? Had I just . . . left the door open behind me and he'd seen the piano? *Or, or, or . . .*

My staring must finally have gotten to him, because he bobbled the first note in twelve thousand. He took his hands off the keyboard, a magician before the reveal.

"Want another try?" His bright eyes locked on mine.

I didn't. I didn't want to talk about music at all. But I didn't want to lose whatever game this was either.

"Frescobaldi."

His eyebrows rose. "Damn, going for the deep cuts." Then he rubbed his cheek, relaxing his shoulders, falling marginally mortal. "It's *Bell*."

"Bell?" I eyed him warily. "Elizabeth? Or . . . it really doesn't sound like Iain Be—"

"*Oscar* Bell." He closed the distance, extending his hand. "Nice to—"

I edged away. "You composed that."

He shrugged. Cocky.

"That's *your* fugue." A snort burst out of me. "Okay."

"I could sketch it out for you." He glanced around, miming scribbling. "I should start writing this shit down anyway."

Before he even finished saying it, his knee was back on the bench, fingers back on the keys, repeating the first movement, adding another voice, another and another as if it were as simple as breathing.

I didn't realize I'd been backing up until I hit Mom's Steinway across the room. I flinched away like her piano was a hot pipe. "You couldn't have improvised that. There's no—"

"Course not." His eyes danced up to meet mine, teasing. "I came up with it on the ride over."

Now that I looked out through the front bay windows, I saw an SUV taxi idling at the curb, back hatch open.

"Sorry if I surprised you." The boy's voice dropped into a different register. "Mr.—uh, Marty just said to come say hi to Ruby."

I closed my eyes, letting out a slow breath. He knew Dad. Of *course*.

"I'm *hoping* you're Ruby? But right now I'm thinking you're not."

"What? I'm her. Me," I said as Dad's voice bellowed from the street, "*Carry it down there and put it by the door, that's good!*"

This guy—"it's *Bell*"—was still staring at me.

I shrugged, flustered. "Why wouldn't I be Ruby?"

"I don't know. You seem older, so I thought maybe you were another of his students. And . . ."

Another of his students? Since when did Dad have his own students?

"The way he talked about you—I thought you'd be short?"

I let out a startled laugh, then glanced down. All five foot eight of me was draped in black—black ballet flats, black yoga pants, black sleep top, black cardigan, its black sleeves covering my hands to the fingertips. With my pasty face and long dark hair frizzing loose, I must have looked like something out of a micro-budget horror movie.

But Oscar extended his hand again. "Sorry. Let's . . . I mean—I'm Oscar Bell. Nice to meet you."

"Ruby. Chertok," I said, sliding my palm into his. "Pleasure to . . . um . . ."

He smiled, lips parted as if he wanted to finish my sentence for me. His hand was sturdier than most pianists'—warm and smooth, except for his rough fingertips.

"You've met! Fantastic!" Dad filled the doorway, six foot two, wild white hair, pink forehead, nose, cheeks, gray beard, arms and legs and trunk like an oak. He strode forward with his hands out and I thought for a second he wanted a hug before he zigged left and clapped Oscar on the shoulders. "This is our prodigy."

"Ah, I don't know about that." Oscar looked at the floor—smiling.

He knew about that. He knew *all* about that.

"Found him on YouTube," Dad said, leaning against Mom's piano like it didn't burn his skin at all. "Can you believe it? I love the Internet, *love* it."

Outside, the scrawniest kids I'd ever seen were lugging furniture into our basement apartment from the trunks of what now looked to be a line of taxis. A desk, twin bed, chair, low bookshelf, all of it the same dorm-room pine.

Dad laughed. "What are the odds of somebody like you going to the same school as Nora Visser's niece?"

Oscar's body wavered like a struck string.

Dad whapped him. "A once in a lifetime musical prodigy with a family connection to our board chair! Uncanny."

"Yes! I mean, thank you." Oscar beamed back, height restored. "But yeah, pretty wild."

I tapped the window. "Dad, are those Amberley kids? Why are they—what's with the bed?"

Dad glanced over his shoulder. "They're moving Oscar in. I found them lazing around the common room and they volunteered to help."

Of course they did. They'd go dumpster diving if the great Martin Chertok asked them to.

Then I turned. "Wait—what? Moving Oscar . . . ?"

"He'll stay in the basement apartment this summer. The dorms were full and we're between tenants—it's kismet!"

We'd been "between tenants" for eight years, since my brother Leo got his spot with the Boston Symphony. We stored our luggage down there now. And here it was, coming back up the stone steps, one empty roller bag at a time being hauled by a bespectacled teenager wearing a T-shirt that said: *Oboe You Di'int.*

"Thank you again for this, sir." Oscar's voice was suddenly neutral, the light drawl I'd noticed gone. "I'm so honored to have the chance to study with you. The New City Symphony completely changed my—"

"The honor's mine." Dad waved away the compliment, turning so that all I could see was his wall of a back. "I love new talent, it's what keeps me going." He pointed to the piano. "What was it I heard you playing a second ago?"

"What we were talking about in the car," Oscar said, scratching his hair so it bent like a crown and sprang back up. "The baroqueness of the bridge, you know? I wanted to try it out."

The baroqueness. Of the bridge.

Oscar traced the keys and then started the melody again, lightly, carelessly. Perfectly.

Even without seeing Dad's face, I could sense the reverence on it. He tapped the piano lid. "This is going to be a good summer."

This summer. In my house. The summer I was supposed to find solace, clarity, a series of days that had nothing to do with music.

Mr. Prodigy—Oscar—was still playing, oblivious to all damage. His song surrounded me, a trap, one strand slipping around the other—

I was in motion. To the coat-tree. The porcelain key bowl. Bag, keys, ponytail holder into hair, me into the sweltering street. The music trailed me out, Oscar Bell's voice following after.

"Oh. Hey, sorry if . . . It was nice to meet you, Ruby!"

Never missing a note.

2.

behind me, I heard Amberley students arguing over which way to tilt the bed through our basement door—the city din, the slam of the back of a delivery truck, a distant jackhammer, none of it enough to drown out the sound of my piano—until I reached the stoop two buildings down, where a blond girl in running gear was tying her sneaker, screaming into her cell phone.

"That's how you want to do this? *Really?* I don't know, you could be *supportive?*"

For the first time, I glanced back. Not because Julie Russo was yelling. Because she was wearing *running gear.*

Her eyes drifted to mine. She blinked slowly, a challenge, just as Dad stepped back onto the street behind me, shaking hands with the Amberley kids—all those brilliant musicians hauling *dorm furniture,* what a travesty—and I had to walk faster.

I could go to the courtyard. God knew it was quiet. But I didn't want to pollute it with how I felt right now.

Central Park swayed across the street, a border to cross. I sprinted through the crosswalk as the light stopped flashing, then past a watercolorist's easel, a pretzel stand, a busker playing the flute, "Danse de la Chèvre," so clear, I could practically feel ice crunching on grass, wind surging down—

I kept going until I couldn't hear the flute anymore. Just bikes ticking along the path behind me. Ducks squabbling on the lake. My wool cardigan, hot. Itchy.

I found a bench and sat, watching the world spin on.

Was this the plan? *No,* it was *not.*

Dad was supposed to be doing his "in residence" thing, presiding over the Amberley School of Music's prestigious teen summer program, preparing the upcoming Met season, being the human mascot for Lincoln Center. *I* was supposed to cover the pianos in our living room with tasteful dust sheets, enjoy the silence, smother every mope, hide from prying questions, take the opportunity to . . .

To . . .

No idea.

When I reached the shadow-dappled edge of the park again, the honk-clamor-shriek of Central Park West splashed me like a puddle. I checked my phone for the time.

4:07. Still a few hours left in the day to accomplish . . . something?

A taxi stopped a few feet ahead and a petite forty-something stepped out, sunglasses sliding low as if to avoid detection. The sun reflected off a high-rise window like an arrow onto her copper bob.

"Nora?" My step slowed. She didn't hear me.

Nora Visser, Amberley's board chair. Family friend since before forever. My godmother. *Not* a musical genius—she just had this weird gift for living. She could trip over a curb and make it look like the happiest thing that had ever happened. And here she was, stumbling onto the same stretch of concrete as me while the taxi she was in sped away with someone else still sitting in the back.

I felt like a sailor spotting land. "Nora!"

She turned—and the look on her face made me wish she hadn't.

Her first reaction was close to horror, such an alien expression that I thought for a second I'd confused her for someone else. But I stepped back, and there she was again, the real Nora, tickled to confetti bits to see me.

"Ruby!" Nora extended her arms like a net and I walked in, noticing as I did how flushed her cheeks were. "You have just made my day, I can't even *tell* you!"

"What are you doing here?" By *here,* I really meant the taxi. Nora never took cabs.

"Oh, lord . . ." She shook her cell phone like she was trying to strangle it. "One appointment to the next. You know how I am, I overbook. I just can't seem to say no! How are you, sweetheart?"

She adjusted a frizz of my hair, and something about the small touch made my eyes go tingly.

I smiled to cover. "Good. Great! What's next, then?"

"Oh!" She slumped daintily. "A reception for the Central Park Conservancy. A tea . . . sort of . . . thing?"

"Tea sounds nice," I said, mostly to unfrazzle her.

"Would you like to come?" The instant she said it, I knew that it was a formality, *the done thing,* but—

"I'd love to!" My skin went from hot to scalding. Taking someone up on an empty invitation was the opposite of *the done thing.* Even so, I wanted it. Tea. Park. Distraction. "Would you mind?"

"Oh my goodness, please do!" Nora squeezed both my hands and bounced on her low heels. "You would be *saving* me."

I laughed. "From what?"

"Boredom!" Her eyes flitted to my all-black outfit, smile unwavering.

"Oh. When does it start? Do I have time to—?"

"Absolutely!" She swiveled toward my block. "We're close, and it's a pop-in kind of thing . . ."

We linked arms and hurried to the crosswalk.

"Don't you dare spruce too much. A light dress is fine, especially in this heat. *How* is it July already? You don't even need any makeup. You're just"—Nora framed my face with her hands, eyes proud, like she'd painted me—"charmed!"

Charmed. That wasn't a word I heard much, especially from someone as sparkly as Nora. I was stupidly pleased by the compliment.

We got to the stoop and I found to my relief that all the Amberley students had disappeared back through their prodigy portals. The front room was silent, but I could hear Dad pacing the floor up in his study.

"I won't be long," I called over my shoulder.

"No rush!" Nora was already absorbed in her cell phone, pushing buttons with the tip of one finger like she wasn't sure how to work it.

I took the stairs to my fourth-floor bedroom two at a time, passing dusty-framed black-and-white photos—a recent pic of Alice playing the viola, Win at the podium, Leo with his oboe, me at ten holding that ridiculous piccolo.

Then I confronted my closet, every hanging garment blurring into a smear.

Dress. A light dress.

I pictured Nora's outfit—knee-length pink and orange, heels—and picked the most similar dress I could find—pale blue, starchy. I hadn't worn it for a few years. It was tight against my armpits, shorter than I remembered, but whatever, it would work.

I kicked on some lace flats and scooted down to the third-floor bath for a quick splash of water to help with the death-pallor thing, and—

I turned the handle and the door slammed back in my face. "Oh."

"Just a sec!" Oscar's voice rang out. Then the sound of the toilet flushing. And a zipper.

"Oh. No. Take your . . ." I paced away, heart pounding. Then I fled to my room, staring out my window at the white-washed walls of the apartment building across the street until I was sure I could hear the bathroom door open and his steps moving down the creaking stairs.

Why was I embarrassed? This was my home. *Mine.*

I threw open my door to prove it, and thundered down two narrow flights, only to come to a halt at the sight of Nora, Dad, Oscar all standing around the dining area—Nora perched on her tiptoes, trying to touch Oscar's hair, murmuring, "You are *so* lucky, mine just sits there!"

What in the no.

Oscar's laughing eyes darted to mine, one blink flashing *mayday.*

"There's a lock," I blurted. First thing to pop into my head.

Nora pulled her hand back to gawk at me, and Oscar shifted out of reach.

"On the bathroom door."

Oscar imitated sheepishness. "I noticed a second too late. Sorry."

I shrugged, so very breezy. "I didn't see anything. So."

Thus descended the heaviest silence in the history of Manhattan Island.

Dad clapped a hand on Oscar's shoulder. "Shall we get to work?"

And the tableau churned back into motion.

"I'm abducting your daughter for a fundraiser tea," Nora shouted. "Hope that's all right!"

"As long as all she drinks is tea." Dad shot me a wink over his shoulder.

I forced a smile back, deflated by his non-reaction. This was a *thing*, after all, wasn't it? After months of stasis—me, switching lanes. But I knew better than to take it personally. Martin Chertok, Greatest Living American Composer, presided over the realm of music, not park teas. If it didn't involve instruments, it didn't warrant more than a passing wink.

Nora squeezed Oscar's wrist as he followed Dad's slow trudge upstairs. "So glad we nabbed you, Oscar. Can't wait to see what you dazzle us with next!"

"Great to finally meet you, Ms. Visser," he called back, his brown eyes meeting mine for the briefest second before he disappeared up the stairs.

I followed Nora out, turning the name "Ms. Visser" over in my head. She'd only been a "Visser" for six years. I'd gone to the wedding, but couldn't remember what her last name was before that.

"Our newest recruit," Nora said as a Bentley glided to the curb. "He's young!"

"Is that a surprise?"

She waved to her driver and hopped in the back, patting the open seat for me to join her.

"Not at all." She pulled out a lighted compact as we pulled away. "He just seems older in the video, don't you think? Maybe because he's got the baton. That does something to conductors. Gives them a little . . . what's the word . . . ?"

"What video?"

"You haven't seen it. *Stop.* Tell me you've seen it!"

I winced an apology.

"Ha! So there *are* limits to Nancy's magic." She dropped the compact into her purse and pulled out her phone.

"Nancy?"

"Wait, I've got to find this for you . . ." She started feverishly typing, then beamed up at me. "Gravitas!"

"Gravi—?"

"The word I was thinking of." Her face was buried in her phone again. "Let me see if I can . . ."

We pulled onto the Seventy-ninth Street crossing. Traffic was at a standstill.

"Thank you so much for bringing me," I put in, strangely jittery. "I haven't gone to anything like this in forever."

Nora squinted up. "Not the Cloisters. It can't have been that long."

"Two years, I think?"

"Anna kept twirling you, do you remember? Calling you her 'miniature.' God, she was so proud of you."

I didn't remember it—not like that. I remembered Mom fuming at Dad for not wanting to go out. Her too-sharp smile as she dropped a dress in my lap and told me to forget homework and Hanon, she needed a date. I'd been out of place, gawky and confused all evening, and it had still been a starlit blur of happiness. Our last hurrah.

"I've missed you, you know," Nora said. "Your whole family."

My throat went tight. "You see Dad, like, every day."

"I know, and I adore Marty beyond words, but . . . I haven't heard from your mom in almost a year, can you believe it? How is she doing?"

"She's . . ." I smoothed my hem. Over and over. "Really good! Busy. Her tour is going well." All facts that could be easily googled.

"Well, *that's* great. She deserves it. Such a talent."

Nora watched me with taut eyes, like she wanted to go on . . .

But then she shifted, bless her, into a playful wink. "People have been asking about you."

Oh God. "*Me.*"

"They want godmother gossip. Whether you're going to follow in your family's footsteps, carve your own path."

Your own path. My body loosened into those words. To do that, to have the option . . .

"Whether you're seeing anyone." She nudged me.

I coughed on my laugh. "I'm not. At all."

"Hmmm." Nora swiped her phone screen. "Who do I know? Charlie Weatherby's starting at Yale in the fall. Might be too short for you."

"It's really okay—"

"I'll keep thinking. Oh—voilà." She handed me her phone, a video already playing on its glossy screen. "Now, come on, you *must* have seen this. It was trending on Twitter last month!"

I don't Twitter, I thought, watching as what looked like a school orchestra performance began on screen, shot on a shaky cell phone camera.

"He's really got something." Nora leaned against me to watch.

"Who—?" I started to ask, and then I saw him, tossing his head back to grin at the audience, the video finally focusing on his face.

Of course. Oscar Bell.

3.

The camera was moving closer. What were they playing? It sounded like Vivaldi, but . . .

The key shifted, the violins did a funny leap that made my breath hitch, and—it was the same theme, but now it sounded like Haydn . . . or Mozart? Elegant, silvery, impossibly clever.

"What is this?" I asked, but Nora was leaning into the front seat, saying something to her driver, so I pulled my focus back to the screen.

A teensy diminuendo and the arrangement shifted again fearlessly, swelled into a twentieth-century Romantic. Shostakovich? Stravinsky? My brain couldn't catch up with my ears. It sounded like a storm on the ocean.

"Do you recognize it?" Nora smiled over her shoulder. "This is more your generation."

"A . . . medley? Different periods of classical music . . ."

"It's Kudzu Giants!" She bounced back into her seat as the traffic started moving again. "I don't follow hip-hop either, but it's a song called 'Sparkler' that's very of the moment. And he's done it in the style of—"

"Everyone." I stared.

Nora took the phone and tapped the screen so the title of the video appeared: *Variations on a Kudzu Giants Theme. By Oscar Bell.*

One point eight million views.

I understood why. It was the quality of the music, the inventive-ness, but the audio wasn't the only reason this had gone viral. It was the visual.

Oscar Bell, jaunty shirtsleeves and a loosened polka-dot tie, natural hair haloing an ecstatic face as he conducted with passionate strokes. His baton wasn't tidy. He looked like he wasn't sure what to do with his left hand. He needed work.

But Nora was right. He was *music*. No separation between him and the piece. It flowed from him, flooding the orchestra, the audience, me in this backseat, staring at a tiny screen—wishing I could grasp it somehow, that invisible element, that perfect confidence. That *joy*. I wanted to steal it for just an hour, a minute, a heartbeat . . .

"*Finally*." The car stopped with a jolt and Nora took back her phone. "Tea time for me time!"

I got out of the car a little shakily, thanking the driver before step-ping out onto familiar red bricks. We'd arrived at Bethesda Terrace—a vast, sweeping patio bustling with tea-goers in sundresses, sprinkles on a red velvet cupcake.

Nora pulled one side of her dress straight, nearly falling over in the process. "I should warn you—there are *always* photographers at these things. *Vanity Fair, Vogue,* city papers. You don't mind having your pic-ture taken, do you? It can be a little much."

"Oh." I was suddenly mortified by my dress. "Do I look all right?"

"Ruby! You could wear a potato sack!" She winked at a young man holding a clipboard, then cut a line for us through the clustered crowd. "That's an expression, of course, but do you *know*—I tagged along to the spring Chanel show and what do you think I saw com-ing down the runway? Lydia!" she hollered into the distance. A tall woman with buttercup-blond hair swiveled to wave back. "There's someone you've *got* to meet."

Lydia's eyes widened into perfect circles, a little girl spotting a fairy. "That's *not*."

"It *is*!" Nora beamed, then stood on her tiptoes to whisper to me, "See? Everyone likes you already. Sarah?" She pirouetted to touch the wrist of someone passing. "I thought you were in Malta! Don't tell me that fell *through*?"

A glance around the party as Nora's many friends descended was all it took to explain Dad's comment about drinking. For a tea party, there sure was a lot of champagne being passed around. A huge banner of sun-dappled oaks competed with the park itself, Bethesda Fountain splashing happily, the mossy lake napping beyond. Everyone here was laughing or on the verge of it, languid bodies, cheery cheeks, like today was the first day of a long-awaited vacation. Conversation rose in waves and—

Someone somewhere was playing the harp. I strained to hear it. It sounded like rain on the roof of my grandparents' porch . . . and yet the second I tried to pick out the piece, that cozy feeling evaporated. It turned into laughter. Tittering behind hands, a mocking sound.

I stared at the toes of my shoes.

Dad would know which piece it was. I had a ludicrous flash-image of him standing here listening. No wonder he'd ditched that Cloisters party way back when.

No wonder it all turned out the way it did.

A beat of silence fell around me and, looking back up to a wall of expectant faces, I realized someone must have asked me a question.

"Ruby's studying the piano," Nora answered, to a chorus of "Ooh!"

"I . . . ah . . ." Pain sparked in my chest. *Please don't ask. Please . . .*

That thirty-something woman, Sarah, leaned in. "When can we expect a performance? At *Amberley,* maybe?"

My eyes lassoed Nora's. The tiniest line formed between her brows. She pulled me into a squeeze. "I'm secretly hoping I can talk Ruby into joining *our* ranks."

"*That* would be a treat," Lydia said. "For us, I mean."

I breathed out.

"Are you interested in philanthropy?" Sarah asked me.

"Very!" The *done thing.* Still, it didn't feel like a lie. "I want to make myself useful. If that makes any sense?"

They glanced at each other as if I'd recited their secret password.

"Quick smiles, ladies?" I turned to see a bald man lifting a camera to his face while everyone drew themselves sideways and taller. Two snaps and done. He asked Nora a question and she pointed to me and murmured something back that made him raise his eyebrows.

My name, I realized. *All she's done is tell him my name.*

I was a person of note here. I had a gravity field, lovely things orbiting, glances and chitchat and tiny cakes on trays and everything nice. And why yes, I *will* have an oolong, thank you very much!

A clinking noise sounded behind us, and a short man in seersucker stepped out of the crowd to give a speech on the organization and everyone's support and something about "legacy" directed at the older ladies in the crowd. It lasted two minutes, then the party resumed.

"That's it?" I asked Nora quietly.

"That's it." She shrugged. "A reminder of why we're here, and the river flows." She floated her purse like a canoe. Then, abruptly, she called out, "If we reach fifty thousand dollars today, Stephen and I will be happy to match!"

A cry rippled through the crowd, then applause, the party's chatter taking on a new pitch. The seersucker man looked like he was about to pass out from relief.

Nora linked arms with me. "And *that* is how you get it flowing faster!"

"You're good at this."

She laughed. "I am! Just takes practice. When I started, I barely made a peep. But you have to think about the cause. It really is everything."

She beamed around us, like she had an ownership stake in the park, knew every tree by name.

We rode home as the light dimmed over the park, casting boughs and benches and bicyclists in the same golden glimmer. I was catching the sunset through the open window, feeling like maybe I was starting to own it too.

"You really are a natural." Nora patted my knee. "If you're interested, start thinking about what your passions are. Where you can have the most impact."

She couldn't have meant it, nobody even knew about it, but my mind immediately landed on my trust. I'd always planned to use that money as a down payment on an apartment once my piano career ignited. Now that that future lay dead in the ground, I could find something else to take its place.

I could have an *impact*.

Hope dug into me, but my hair blew gently in the hot breeze, softening its edges.

"Do you know of any organizations that could use volunteers over the summer? Anything with a teen council, or . . . I don't even know what you'd call it."

"*Absolutely!*" Nora perked up even more. "Well, of course—there's Amberley."

My shoulders clenched against the feeling of an elevator plummeting.

"We're having an event at Wing Club in a few weeks, a young donors' gala. Everyone there would *love* to meet the youngest Chertok, all grown up."

They'd be sorely disappointed. "I think maybe . . . not music."

Nora's face fell. "No?"

"Just . . ." I stared at my locked fingers. "Anything else. I'm open."

"You've really given it up."

"Taking a break," I lied.

"I understand," she said quietly. "I do."

She'd been entwined with my family since before I was born. She'd been privy to everything that happened with Amberley. She had to understand.

"So how do you feel about the environment? Art?"

"Um, yes!"

"I know everybody at the Met." She winked. "*Museum,* not opera, don't worry. Let me think . . ." She scrolled through her phone, then her head jolted up. "Aha! There's an event, Monday, early evening, nothing fancy—are you free? *Please* say you're free."

She put her hands together, pleading. I couldn't nod fast enough.

"Nora," I sputtered as I stepped onto the sidewalk. "This has been so—"

Nora shushed me through the window. "Thank *you* for coming. Nice to have some company for a change!"

I watched her roll away. She'd known everyone at that party, kept chatting with them about dinner plans.

She misses Mom.

I crumpled that thought and left it on the sidewalk as I stepped onto the stoop.

The house was dark, upstairs and down. Dad must have been out being Dad and who knew where Oscar Bell was. Probably getting to know the other Amberley geniuses—sparks swirling, earth cracking beneath their feet.

But none of it happened without people like Nora. People to make the river flow.

The house was so still I could hear a clock ticking on the third-floor landing. I climbed the stairs, running my fingers along the built-in bookshelves crammed with first-edition novels and fraying scores and bric-a-brac ceramics, past Alice's old room that still smelled like her hand lotion, Dad's study, messier than it should be, Win's old room, now crammed with empty luggage, all of it quiet, quiet, quiet, until I got to my tidy little bedroom at the top.

The sunset clinging to my skin had faded by the time I changed into pajamas, but I still went to sleep feeling like there was gold in my veins.

Then, at one in the morning—music.

Faint, a trickle of a melody, loud enough to have invaded my sleep. I swung my feet out from the covers, held on to the cracked window-sill, and listened.

The tune was sweet, lyrical. Sad, spiked with hope, straining upward. Like it wanted *so badly* to be heard.

It couldn't have been Dad. He was a nine-to-five creative and slave to his sleep schedule. Besides, this was coming from outside. The instrument was tinny . . . a synthesizer? I leaned my head out the window far enough to see a light on in the basement apartment.

The music stopped mid-phrase. The light in the basement turned off.

I slunk back into bed. The house was quiet again, the city broadcasting its usual midnight programming. But that melody wouldn't leave me alone.

And I dreamed about his stupid YouTube video.

4.

my body felt wired from the second I woke up, but it took sitting and stretching to remember why.

Tea parties. Possibilities.

A boy downstairs.

As I got out of bed, my grandparents smiled from the digital picture frame, sitting on the dock with their terrier who'd died two years ago. Every time Grandma Jean called, we sketched out plans to visit—Christmas, spring break—but time had flown by until April, when my days ground to a screeching halt, and I still hadn't made it.

Maybe I could visit this summer. I had a life span of free time now.

Dad was in the kitchen, whistling *Don Giovanni*. He'd conducted it at the Met last season and I'd watched it twice from the pit. The ovation orchestrated itself in my head as I plodded downstairs.

"Morning," I croaked, drowning it out.

"Coffee?" Dad offered.

I nodded, sliding past him to make it myself—black, one sugar, in one of our glass mugs so I could see the steam swirl and settle—then poured him a refill too.

"What do you think of Alban Berg?"

"Um." I blew a black ripple across my cup. The steam retreated, came back.

"Would young people know him?"

"I am not the person to ask what young people would know." I sipped. Too hot. "But . . . no. Young people would not know Alban Berg."

"Eh. I figured." Dad sighed, sitting next to me at the kitchen table—a slab of oak, the bottom etched with all our initials. "We need something fresh. Young."

"Wasn't Berg, like, early twentieth century?"

Dad waved his hand. "The aesthetic, though. You know what I'm saying."

"Something to break up Mozart and Verdi."

"*Shake* up. Nora's words."

I frowned. "I thought you were planning the opera season."

"No, that's all set, this is . . ." Dad's voice drifted as he stood and shuffled away, head cocked.

I swirled my coffee and waited. This was Dad—as much as his beard or tuna melts or meandering pep talks. He was hearing Berg right now, trying to imagine how *young* it might feel to someone who wasn't seventy-two.

Nora's words from yesterday came to mind: *of the moment.* Amberley was trying to shake things up. Why? I could ask, but talking about Amberley hurt. Better to change the subject.

"What's the deal with this Oscar kid?"

Dad leaned against the archway to the kitchen. "Incredible, right?"

"No, I mean . . . sure, but—what's he doing here? What's the plan, what's he studying?" I swallowed my coffee. It burned my throat. "Piano, or . . . ?"

"No, no, no." Dad chuckled. "Conducting. Composition."

"But Amberley doesn't have a summer program for—"

"He'll study with me." Dad knocked on the wall. "This is an exceptional case."

"Is he really that exceptional?"

My voice sounded caustic. I hadn't meant it to.

But Dad's eyes had gone distant, like when he was conducting. "We popped by campus on the way from the airport."

You picked him up from the airport. Yourself.

"We found Arnie, Cooper, and Li Chun all in the recital hall . . ."

Piano chair, violin professor, cello chair.

"And Oscar sat right down at the piano." Dad laughed. "Like he wanted a place to sit, so why not there? And Arnie, you know Arnie . . ."

Dad made thunderclouds with his hands while I tried not to think about the last time I saw Arnold Rombauer, Saturday, April 12, 4:25 p.m., a stern silhouette on the other side of an audition screen.

"He said, 'You gonna play that thing or just warm the bench?' And Oscar started riffing, a fake polonaise. Pretty soon, everybody's shouting requests. Mahler, Vivaldi, Shostakovich, Philip Glass, and by God, he nailed them all. *Skewered* them. A seventeen-year-old! I've never seen anything like it in my life."

"But *you* were like that, Dad. You were composing at fifteen—"

"Not like that." He waved it off, picking up a pile of mail from the kitchen counter. "It was work for me. I had to sit down and figure it out—still do. Music bubbles out of that kid. This summer, we're gonna figure out how to channel it, get it down, get it heard."

"I saw him on YouTube," I admitted. "Nora played it for me."

"She does like that video," he said, sifting through the mail. I made a mental note to go through the stack again once he'd finished. He had a habit of mistaking bills for junk mail and fan letters for personal correspondence.

"For you, my dear."

He tossed a postcard onto the table. I slid it closer, taking in the familiar photo of a lantern-lit forest full of young musicians before turning the card over. No phones or email allowed at Wildwood, but my friends had promised to write.

"How's our Farrah?" Dad sat. "Enjoying camp?"

"I assume so," I mumbled, deciphering her messy writing.

. . . *Wally and Max miss you desperately, their words verbatim . . . finally a new kid this year, a violinist from Texas, but alas he's super awkward, not as hot as you might hope . . .*

"You sure you don't want to head up?" Dad put his hands behind his neck, voice carefully bored. "They won't mind you skipping a week. It's no Amberley, but it's a solid program."

I picked at a scuff in the wood. "Bit too solid for the likes of me."

"Why would you say that?" He leaned forward. "This is the first year you've missed since you were—what? Twelve?"

"Dad." I stared at him. "Come on."

He let out a long sigh—as close to a confession as I was going to get. "It's not as simple as you're making it out to be, Ruby. What selection committees are looking for is potential, and legacy's a damn strong indicator of—"

"I'm seventeen." Lang Lang had been performing professionally since fourteen. Even Mom, a famous late bloomer, made her competition debut when she was younger than me. "Wouldn't my potential have shown up by now?"

He didn't have an answer. I didn't expect him to. It was time to move on.

I got dressed while Dad was in his study, grabbed a notebook and a pen, shoved them in a canvas bag, and headed for the door.

"Popping out?" Dad shouted from the stairwell. "Wake up Oscar, would you? Tell him to come on in when he's ready."

I froze. "Um."

"Thanks, doll."

I tiptoed to the doorstep of the basement studio apartment, wary of vermin, but it looked like somebody had swept.

I knocked. My stomach tightened in the silence that followed. He was still asleep. I was lifting my hand to deliver a louder knock when the door swung open and there he was, YouTube sensation *Oscar Bell, 1.8 million views.* Wearing boxer briefs.

"Hey," he said blearily, rubbing his eyes with one hand, leaning against the doorframe with the other.

I looked down, avoiding eye contact, but then there was his chest and his bare, broad shoulders, and, frantically avoiding that, there was his stomach, a light line of fuzz leading to the waistband of his underwear and *oh my God, just look at his face.*

His eyes widened slowly, like he'd only now regained consciousness.

"Morning," I said, concierge-neutral. "Dad says to join him upstairs. Whenever you're ready. No rush . . ."

"Ah great. Thanks. What, um, time is it?"

"Seven."

"Right. Wow. Guess I need to stop staying out so late." He grinned, like he would never *dream* of doing something so ludicrous.

"How late?" I had to ask.

"I actually have no idea. Before dawn."

"So like . . . an hour ago."

"Possibly." He seemed awake now. Alert. And not one bit concerned that he was mostly naked to the street—to *me*. He'd even opened the door wider.

His boxer briefs were bright blue. And tight.

"What time did *you* go to bed?"

I blinked. Upward. "What?"

He smiled. "What time . . . ?"

"Ten twenty-seven."

"That is *specific*."

"I checked the clock before I fell asleep. It's digital. So. Big numbers."

Big! Numbers!

He was grinning at me like a kid on a carnival ride.

"Did you go out with Amberley kids, then?" I leaned against the stoop rail, super breezy, I talked to half-naked guys all the time, occupational hazard, NBD.

"Um? No." He frowned, thought. "I went out . . . wandering. I mean, it's New York, right?"

His eyes landed on mine, piercing, *joyous*—like that video. Which reminded me what he was doing here in the first place.

"Right, well . . ." I motioned to the street. "I'm gonna *wander* right now? I'll see you around."

I'd made it to the sidewalk when he called out, "Thank you, Ruby!"

I turned back with a wary wave and watched as his eyes, shoulders, lips, everything about him sort of . . . loosened.

"Thank you for waking me up."

A wince flickered over his face, and I wondered if that wasn't quite what he'd meant to say.

"No problem." I spun away, then called behind me. "You might want to set your alarm. Dad does his best work in the mornings."

The crosswalk light started flashing. I jogged to catch it before either of us could expose anything else.

On the other side of the avenue, I pulled myself together, as Mom would say. It took effort.

A droplet of sweat trickled down my back. My breath felt funny, like my veins were full of ginger ale. And I was overdressed *again* in a long-sleeved cotton dress, looking like a shut-in who got locked out of her apartment.

The truth was, apart from commuting, my life till now had rolled out inside the confines of my air-conditioned house, school, rehearsal rooms, performance spaces. I got cold easily, I bundled up. But this real-life air was sticky-hot and the sun hadn't even reached the skyline yet.

The park felt cooler, at least, dew dampening my bare ankles as I walked the green path toward the sheep meadow, where there hadn't been sheep for a good eighty-five years. The smell of grass here was heady and strong. I sat against a tree, pulled out my notebook, clicked a fresh pen, and thought about my next big step toward making an impact.

And thought. And zoned out. And pictured Oscar in the doorway, stopped myself, refocused. Wrote:

Buy clothes.

And couldn't think of anything else.

Not, *stretch, morning scales, Czerny, Brahms, battle with Liszt, wind-down with Schumann*—just . . . shopping? To go to fundraisers, be a part of that world, I needed new clothes. Still. How empty. How . . . surface.

I shut my eyes for a second, blotting out the thought of what Mom would say, then scribbled:

Follow up with Nora re: possibilities at the Met—*museum, NOT opera*

There. New life. New interests. It wasn't a lie. It was a pivot.

As I was sinking into images of dusting off some gilded antiquity, wearing glasses I didn't need, a real image jostled me back—a recognizable blur. She passed at a light clip without so much as a nod, our standard non-greeting for the past six years.

I usually looked away. Today, I gawked.

Julie Russo had the outfit, new-looking sneakers, the almost crisp blond ponytail, music gear, the whole thing. She didn't look like a runner, though. She traced a zigzag down the footpath and her lips were clenched like she hadn't figured out how to exhale and run at the same time. Not that I was any expert. I only ran for buses and didn't even catch them most of the time.

The Julie I used to know was a loud talker, sporadic baker, collector of plastic horses—and later, I'd surmised from down-the-street observation, a late-night partier, attractor of boys, winner of screaming matches. But a *runner*?

I stared at the two items in my transformation notebook. I stared at Julie's retreating ponytail. And then I sprinted after her.

"Julie! Hey!" She didn't look back.

A full turn around the volleyball courts and skate park before she *finally* stopped to tie her shoe, but when I caught her, I found to my surprise that she was as winded as I was, and *oh my God* was I winded.

She jumped with a low scream at the sight of me, her face hydrant red.

"Am I that scary?" I tried to laugh through my labored breathing but wound up hacking a cough.

"Depends," she panted. "Are you stalking me?"

She straightened, hands on hips, the blood in her face receding into two cheek circles, like a little Dutch girl in an illustration.

I wasn't sure what I looked like right now, but not Dutch, and sweatier than any picture they'd put in a book. "I wanted to ask you how long you've been running?"

"Seriously."

It seemed like a fair question to me. "It doesn't strike me as very Julie-ish."

"Oh! *Doesn't* it?" Her blue eyes sharpened even as she moved away. "First of all, I haven't been Julie since the seventh grade. It's *Jules*."

"Oh." How was I supposed to know? We weren't exactly Facebook friends.

"Second . . ." She laughed up at the sky. "*That's* what you want to ask me? We haven't spoken for six years and you want to know how long I've been running?"

"We've talked," I tried feebly.

"No."

"We say hi, or . . ."

"No."

"In six years—?"

"No."

I opened my mouth. Shut it. God *damn,* I was dying of sweat. I pried my dress off my midriff and held it out so I could draw a breath.

"I just thought it was interesting that you're doing something that, to outward appearances, seems brand-new for you. Whoever you are now. And I guess I found that interesting because I've quit piano—"

"You . . ." Julie's smirk dropped away.

"And I don't know what that leaves me with now, as, like, a human being, or what I have to offer the world or even what to do with my day and I can't even be at home because there's this kid there studying with my dad and he's straight out of my fantasies—"

Her eyebrows shot up.

"*Not* like that." *Sort of like that.* I swallowed. "I fantasized about *being* him, all my life, but I'm so *far* from being him that his presence is . . ."

I couldn't think of the right words, so I made a weird disintegrating gesture, and she nodded like she got it.

"And so now I'm avoiding my house. And I'm thinking about getting into philanthropy but I'm worried if I'm going to stretch that far, I might as well become, like, a cowgirl. An astronaut? Um."

Julie—*Jules* looked at me. Then she wiped sweat off her forehead and shifted her weight with a sigh. "Yeah, so, two weeks. I started running right after school got out."

That explained the zigzag. "You just decided—"

"Ty, my . . . ugh, my *boyfriend*"—she said it like it was the worst thing you could call someone—"made some joke about me running the marathon. Like, who do I know who would be the absolute worst at running? Oh, obviously my girlfriend, she's so lazy, hahaha! And then he did this run." She imitated it—wrists high, hands flapping. "And everybody died laughing, *so funny,* so I threw my drink in his lap and started training the next morning because *fuck* him if he thinks he knows what I'm capable of."

If I'd been embarrassed about my own rant, I wasn't anymore. "And this Ty person is still your boyfriend?"

"Tyler," she groaned. "Yes. Pending probation."

I wasn't sure if she meant relationship probation or legal trouble, so I mirrored her knowing nod.

"You *wanted* to be a cowgirl. Do you remember?" Jules squinted at me. "They asked us at Bridge to Learning so they could put it on a poster."

"I don't—"

"Doesn't matter." She scratched her head. "Listen, I can't help you with the philanthropist-socialite thing . . ."

Socialite? I winced. I wouldn't say they were the same thing at all.

"But if you want to run with me, that's fine."

"Oh, I wasn't—"

"It's not, like, life-changing so far, so don't get your hopes up, but it's . . . I don't know. It's something different." She shrugged. "For me anyway. You might be some fitness nut, I don't even know you anymore."

I glanced at myself.

She burst out laughing, then smothered it. "Sorry. I . . . that wasn't cool."

"It's fine." I knew what I looked like. I was skinny, but not in a *Self* magazine way. More of an "all my exercises involve sitting on a piano bench" way.

"I'm starting earlier tomorrow," she said, her voice a warning. "Before it gets stupid hot."

"Early's good!" I shot her two thumbs-up.

"Like six. In the morning."

"I'm up then anyway!"

She snorted. "Course you are. All right, then. Meet you on the corner."

And she jogged clumsily away.

I pulled out my notepad and, next to *Buy clothes*, wrote: *Buy exercise clothes.*

I had no idea why, but that felt a million times better.

5.

triumphantly homeward I marched, arms laden with bags bearing swooshes, bold colors, feet with wings. I would try running! I would see where it led! If I could become a runner, I could become anything!

Almost. I turned the key to the house, met with a sound that lifted my heart only to pummel it—my Baldwin, happy at last.

Oscar still wasn't using the bench, just composing upright with the same concentration level other people used to send a text. When I came in, he let the melody trickle away. He was fully dressed now, to my disappointed relief, wearing the same chinos as yesterday with a fuchsia polo shirt, its collar extra crisp against the deep brown of his skin.

"Hey," he said.

"I'm gonna go take a shower." *Totally* something you tell a guy you barely know.

He grinned slowly. "Okay."

I turned away so he couldn't see my slow self-immolation. "Where's Dad? Um, my dad. Obviously he's not your . . . yeah."

"He's out with your brother."

I whipped back around. "Leo's in town?"

"No, um, Winston? Win?"

Win was here? And they were having lunch together? I fumbled in my bag for my phone. No missed calls. "Oh."

"I think it was a business lunch," Oscar said quickly. "Something about the philharmonic."

"Huh. Maybe they want him for a guest conductor spot."

"Or more than guest." At my blink, Oscar grinned. "They didn't say anything to me! I'm just piecing it together. From bits of conversation."

"Whoa there, detective."

He tipped an invisible hat. "Inspector Bell."

It wasn't bad investigative work. Win was only twenty-nine, but he'd made a splash in Philly, and his contract was up in January. Music Director at the New York Philharmonic—that would be incredible. No wonder they hadn't invited me to lunch. It made sense, it was fine.

"You'll see him tonight," Oscar said, sliding out from behind the piano. "He and Alice are coming for dinner."

"How do you *know* all this?"

I felt a stab of guilt for my lack of filter. But he just shrugged, smiling bigger.

"I'm invited too."

"Awesome!" I started up the steps with my bags, then poked my head over the railing. "So are you here practicing? Or hanging out, or . . . ?"

"I only have a keyboard in the apartment. Do you need your piano? I can—"

"No!" I coughed. "No."

"Your dad said I should keep working."

"Yeah, that's great!"

Working. Not practicing, not writing, *working.* Like he'd already arrived, fully formed, planting flags on continents far out of—

"Do you need anything?" I shouted, tracing the curve of the ban-ister. "Water, tea? Dad usually drinks coffee when he's, um, working, but I could grab you a soda? An iced . . . something? Something with ice in it?"

Oscar looked amused. "I'm good for beverages. But thank you."

"Okay." I restarted my climb, backward. "Anything you need, just—"

"Hey actually," Oscar called out. "Marty thought maybe you could show me around town? I've hit a mental lull, so . . ."

You and me both, buddy. I leaned against the wall. "I can do that. After—"

"After your shower." He smirked. Shook his head.

I sprinted up the steps.

This isn't anything, I told myself, grabbing fresh clothes, stepping into the hall bath, lifting my dress over my head, and disappearing into the stream of water. I'd walk him around the block. I'd print him a map, send him to Times Square, come home, get on with my own life.

Drying off, I searched for my reflection in the mirror, but it was too blurred to make out. *Ruby Chertok: A Portrait in Steam.*

I swiped it clear and hurried to my room before vanity could seize hold. Still, I rebraided my wet hair three times, telling myself it was because I needed to practice looking presentable, dammit, not because of the first, second, and third impressions I must have made on Oscar Bell.

Hearing the living room so unmusical as I tromped down the steps, I wondered if I'd spruced myself up for nothing. But there he was, holding the door open to the street, gazing out dizzy-eyed, like he was trying to inhale the city.

It was my turn to smirk. *Tourist.*

Then he turned and saw me, and I could swear, his whole body ignited, a machine revving to life. Genius or no, the guy had excellent manners.

He motioned gallantly out. "Shall we?"

Case in point.

I led the way down the stoop.

"So what do I need to know?" He parked himself in the middle of the sidewalk, arms spread wide, summoning the seven winds.

"Can you give me a category?" I asked, instead of suggesting he tuck in his hands to avoid getting them smacked down by passersby. "Geopolitics? How to make soups and stews?"

"Category . . . ah, Day-to-Day Awesomeness." He glanced back at the stoop. "I'm gonna be living here for two months."

Six weeks, three days. I knew how long the summer program lasted.

"I need to know what's good." He clapped. "Where do I get my toothpaste, what's the best place for a cheap lunch, where do you go for inspiration?"

I started us walking west. "Duane Reade on Columbus, for toothpaste. But who knows? You might find it inspirational."

Oscar let out an easy laugh and I adjusted my bag to hide the thrill that shot through me.

"Seriously, though. What are your go-to places?"

"They pretty much all involve baked goods."

"*Yes.*" Oscar gave an awkward sideways gallop. "This. Nobody tells you these things."

"There's literally an app for bakeries in New York."

"Really?"

"All the apps have now been invented."

He nodded solemnly. "We've reached the singularity."

"We'll need pastries to help stave off madness. Um, so, SweetStreets— the app—it's pretty exhaustive, but I can, like, curate, if—"

"That would be great. I'm more of an analog person than an app person."

I'd sort of guessed. Oscar never seemed to have a cell phone in his hand. He was totally present, peering at every building we passed—the brownstone with the eagle keystone over the door, the burnt-umber apartment building with scaffolding attached to it for the past three years, the pink house where three tiny dogs always barked through the first-floor window.

We turned onto Columbus, straight into the spiced scent from the Turkish corner restaurant, but Oscar didn't seem to notice.

He started drifting into the Top Cat Deli. "Want lunch? I haven't had anything since—"

I pulled him to safety.

Oscar looked at my hand, his arm, with a surprised smile. I let my fingers slip away, the feel of his biceps lingering. Kept walking— assertively, so oncoming foot traffic would part for us.

"Not that place."

He glanced backward, galloping to catch up. "Why not?"

"It smells weird. They leave the buffet out too long." I pointed to a shop across the street. "That's the one you want."

"The Three-Star Deli? They couldn't name themselves the Four- Star Deli?"

"They're honest." I shrugged. "I respect that."

The light was changing and he wasn't following quickly enough, so I pulled him across, gently this time. "Sorry. I hate missing lights."

"Is this . . . a New York thing?"

"Don't know. Never lived anywhere else."

"I live in the suburbs," he said, following me into the deli. "I've been known to miss a light or two."

"The suburbs?" I snorted. "Do you even walk anywhere?"

"Of course we do. All the way from our cars to our houses."

"Apologies. Sounds exhausting."

"The struggle is real." Oscar squinted up at the endless deli menu.

I cooled off against the ice cream freezer, watching as Oscar ordered his lunch in such a roundabout way, it became a weird kind of performance art.

"I like all types of meat. And toppings. If you could only have one sandwich for the rest of your life, what would that sandwich be? That's what I would like to try."

I wondered whether to stop him, to tip him off about how to "when in Rome" when in New York. But even more mind-boggling was that this surly, middle-aged Russian dude, who had never once smiled while ringing me up, was leaning on the counter with a big grin, tickled pink to have been asked.

Oscar ate his sandwich—corned beef, coleslaw on rye—while walking. I averted my eyes, but so far, he was making an art of it. No mess, no smacking . . . as elegant as eating a sandwich in the middle of Columbus could be. Every time a passerby gawked at him, he gave a jaunty nod like he was the mayor of an old-time village out for a stroll.

"How is it?" I asked.

He let out a low moan. "You have to try it."

"I had two slices of pizza like an hour ago. But thank you kindly."

"*New York City pizza.*" He turned to me, electrified, like he'd just woken up from a nightmare in which pizza did not exist. "Is there a—"

I laughed. "Of *course* there's an app."

A blast of arctic air hit me from the open doorway of a boutique and I closed my eyes in rapture. When I opened them, the building ahead—cherry-red brick, green awnings—made my throat go dry. The corner studio on the second floor had musical notes plastered on its windows. A plump figure moved past, clapping her hands in time with a metronome. As much as the sight of her stung, I kept staring.

I hadn't seen Mrs. Swenson since the afternoon in April when I'd turned up to our Monday lesson and told her I was done. She'd seemed sad—*actually* regretful, not "put on a good show for the sake of my famous dad" sad. I'd promised to keep in touch, but so far, I hadn't. I lived in vague dread of bumping into her on the street.

Oscar was looking up into Mrs. Swenson's window now too. His eyes drifted to mine. "Friend of yours?"

"Yes, Oscar, everyone in New York knows each other."

He looked away, laughing, subject avoided. But I could still feel him taking mental photographs of everything we passed. He swiveled to read the curlicued name of a florist, then turned to nod at a guy loading beer kegs into the cellar of a sports bar. His fascination was a floodlight—illuminating a purple bike chained to a rack, the blue fence of a sidewalk café, two kids on scooters with stickers on their helmets, chatter peppering the air, engines purring, doors opening, pigeons coasting, the wind lifting my braid, rushing past my legs . . .

Oscar was watching *me* now. Probably because I looked as touristy as he did.

"Sooooo," I said. "How does a kid from the suburbs get into classical music?"

"Same way as a city kid. I listened to it."

I raised my eyebrows, challenge accepted. "Who's your favorite composer?"

A grin shot across his face, then he shut his mouth like he was talking himself out of answering.

"*Holy* crap." I stopped walking. "You were going to say yourself, weren't you?"

His eyes lit up. He looked away.

I pointed at him. "Admit it!"

"You've got to be your own favorite!" He shrugged, still smiling wolfishly. "It's what keeps you interested. But if we're talking real composers, there's no way I could pick just one. In terms of inspiration, I've got Coleridge-Taylor, Florence B. Price, Joseph Boulogne, *so* many others. If you mean who I admire most on a technical level, that's complicated—everybody's got that little something you can pick out and marvel at. And for who I like to, you know, *listen* to—that depends on my mood."

"Okay, let's put it the way you did with your lunch order. If you could only pick *one* piece of music to listen to for the rest of your life . . . ?"

"Cruelest question in the world," he said, blithely biting into his sandwich. "*Evil* question."

"*Cop-out,*" I coughed.

He laughed. Still didn't answer.

I tapped my lips. "Schoenberg?"

"Heady stuff," he answered, chewing. "But you've gotta love any composer so forward-thinking that his music manages to start a riot."

"Cage?"

He walked next to me in confused silence for almost a block, and I was beginning to thrill with victory when he turned to me with a grin and I realized he was imitating Cage's "*4'33"*," in which the pianist sits in silence for the length of the piece's title.

"Eh?" He put his arms out.

I didn't want to laugh. "It's the *eh* that really sold it."

"You should always explain your jokes. It makes them extra funny."

"I like to end my jokes with '*get it?*' In case, you know, people don't get it."

"That's just good manners." He took another bite, smiled around it.

"So, where are you from, exactly?" I asked as he chewed. "I thought I'd heard an accent."

"Exactly? 5320 Falmouth Road, Bethesda, Maryland. Upstairs, first bedroom on the right." He peered up at the leafy ironwork on the building we were passing. "Not sure about an accent . . ."

I glanced at him. He stared ahead. I took the hint.

Finishing his sandwich, he crumpled up the paper, tossed it at a corner trash can. Missed. As he veered to retrieve it, I kept walking so he couldn't see my smirk.

He jogged to catch up. "So what about inspiration?"

"You want me to tell you a place where you can be inspired?"

"I want to know where you, *Ruby Chertok*"—he stroked his chin as we waited for the next light, then laughed, breaking pose—"I was going to use your middle name but I don't know it."

"Anna," I answered. *Don't mention my mom.*

"Where you, Ruby *Anna* Chertok, find your inspiration."

"I'm more of a mundane person than an inspiration person."

"Doubtful," he said, and before I could figure that out: "Your dad said you study piano."

"I don't play anymore." I watched the sunlight strobe between rooftops as we walked. "I don't know why he told you that."

"Have you gone back to wind instruments?" His face dropped at my blank reaction. "I saw the photo. In your house. The piccolo . . . ?"

"*Oh.*" I groaned. "Ha. No. That was just for the, um . . . it was an ad campaign for Lincoln Center. They had a bunch of kids for different areas of the arts. Shakespeare, ballet. Like we were *the future,* la-la-la. Most of the models were actually studying, but for my shoot, they just handed me random instruments. Violin, French horn. I never played a note. So . . . yeah."

Where were we even going? A light was changing—I veered us randomly left.

"You're a model. Whoa."

"For two hours when I was ten. I'm retired now."

"Congratulations on your retirement. Are you embarking on a twilight career?" Oscar asked. "Golf? Mahjong?"

His voice was light, but I sensed sincerity in the question. What could I answer? *I'm going shopping for party clothes later this week!*

"I'm going to be an arborist."

"Word!" Oscar skipped ahead and walked backward. "You're *branching* out, then."

A laugh caught in my throat. "*Wow.*"

"What's your favorite tree?"

I stared.

"If you had one tree to look at for the rest of your life, what would it be?" He squinted, thinking. "I'd pick the dogwood."

"Oak. The mighty . . . oak, I was kidding about the whole arborist—"

Oscar fell into step to stage-whisper, "I got that."

"Although, who knows? I don't *not* like trees?" I wasn't ready to talk about the park and Nora and parties for the greater good. "I'm just . . . between passions right now."

"So what you're saying is you've got free time."

I blinked up at him.

His eyes flashed as he nodded. "Good to know."

I wasn't sure how much to read into that, how much to react, what to do with my arms, so I crossed them and started blabbering, "So hey, I think I should lay this out there—I'm not like the rest of my family? They're wizards, I'm a squib. I tried to be magical. It didn't work out. I'm not complaining! Just the way it is. So now all I know is . . . I'm going to try something different. And, like, *tackle* it. So."

"I like that."

"You like what?" I glanced at him, cheeks burning.

"Different. Tackling." He shrugged. "You."

"You hardly know me."

"Okay, yes, true." He stopped walking, turned to face me. "I guess I mean I like you as a thing."

"A *thing!*" I burst out laughing. It couldn't have been what he meant. Then my gaze drifted past him to the hectic intersection where we were standing.

"I like that someone like you exists," he went on. "You are . . . an object of interest."

I stopped smiling. Froze in place, staring. Of all places, I'd walked us here.

I'd been on autopilot and my system was still set to Lincoln Center.

"Wow. Um, *why?*" Oscar closed his eyes. "I . . . if my sister were here, she would be full-on slapping me. Just, like, Feminism 101: Don't Call Somebody an Object. And I've made you totally uncomfortable—"

"I'm not uncomfortable," I said, my fists balling. Not because of him. Because of *here*.

"I apologize." His eyes were intent on mine now. "We just met, but that's not what I'm about. I just . . . I can't always control my mouth."

Which made me look at his mouth. Full lips, creased charmingly at the corners. I looked away, thawing, trying to remember what he was apologizing for.

Then he glanced behind him and hopped in the air. "Hey! Where it all happens."

I stared across four lanes of stopped traffic, taking it in, Dad's office, his fiefdom, home of the philharmonic, the Metropolitan Opera, the American Ballet Theatre, the Amberley School of Music. Once, it was just my playground, a place with walls to climb and benches to do coloring and flat tiles to bounce my pink sparkle ball. And I remembered when it changed, shifted, lodged itself in the exact center of the universe—the night of Alice's professional debut, right here at the phil, an absolute triumph.

She'd been my age.

Someone bumped me from behind.

"Sorry," a short kid mumbled, holding his cello case at arm's length as he bustled past. I gave way, a few seconds too late. Halfway down the crosswalk, he glanced back, mouth falling slack like he recognized me. It did happen from time to time.

My heart thumped. I could hear it. Probably everyone could.

The kid continued away.

Oscar motioned after him. "Shall we?"

"*You* shall, should." One more step back. "Definitely. I would show you around, but you were here yesterday, right? And I'm supposed to meet up with my friend"—I pulled out my phone as if checking the time—"and she's having a personal issue, so I can't invite you, but, um, I'll see you at the big family dinner." I waved like I was on parade. "Have fun, make good . . . choices!"

I turned and sprinted away, marking the fastest possible route—one long, noisy block to another world.

Safely inside Central Park, breathing green, I secured a boulder to sit on, a fenced-off vista to peer at bleakly.

Okay. I needed to pull in the damn reins. He thought I was somebody. A Chertok. He'd blank me once he knew.

But it *was* flirting, wasn't it? I wasn't that clueless.

After way too long replaying the sound of Oscar's words—*I like you*—low, clear, direct—I got up and bought myself a pretzel from a cart. As I sat down to eat it, a park squirrel came to join me, scrawny, a section of tail-fur missing. He perched next to me on the bench and stared.

If you give them food, you're making them bold, which isn't safe for them—they could get hurt—but the thing was, it felt off to be alone right now, like an omen of things to come. I *needed* to share this meal with somebody, even just symbolically, so I tore off a chunk and handed it over. I'd fully expected him to scamper away, shouting "Sucker!" in his squirrel-tut language, but he stayed put. We sat eating our pretzels together, two city-dwellers with nowhere to be, nothing to do but sustain ourselves with park food and stare at strangers.

This was easy. I understood this interaction. Maybe I could get a pet. Mom's allergies didn't matter anymore.

A dude raced past on a bike, blasting eighties music out of a built-in speaker. The squirrel stood and fled into the greenery behind me.

I finished the pretzel alone.

6.

I was drafting a Very Important Action Item email to Nora, stuck on increasingly desperate subject lines—*"The event we discussed"* . . . *"Dress code for Monday?"* . . . *"Metropolitan Museum, not Opera, hahasomeonehelpme"*—when I heard voices downstairs, the front door slamming like somebody had kicked it behind him.

Win's kick.

I ran downstairs so fast, my heels skidded ahead of me on the carpet. Win was there, I heard his glittering chuckle. Then I realized who he was talking to and slowed down to give a glance at my outfit, a cursory tug, a silent groan.

Win was laughing again. "How do you know all this?"

"I got stuck in a tour group!" Oscar sounded dazed. "I looked up and couldn't get out. It wasn't bad, actually, so I just went with it?"

"Were they foreign?"

I rounded the corner to see my brother with his shoes already off, feet kicked up on our dining table, candy-striped socks on display.

Oscar's back was turned. "I don't think so. Some of them looked Amish, maybe?"

"Now I want to crash a Lincoln Center tour."

"You'd get recognized."

"Not if they were Amish." Win leaned over to whap Oscar's shoulder, like he was tagging him in a schoolyard game. "Enjoy your anonymity. Won't last forever."

Nobody had noticed me. If Win had been alone, I would have charged over, but I just waved feebly and said, "Hey."

He startled like he had no idea I was going to be here. Coming from Win, it felt incongruously flattering. "Rooster!"

He swung his feet off the table and jumped up for a hug, trying to lift me and failing—he wasn't tall. I laughed as he gave up with a theatrical cough.

"I mean, greetings, young sister. Pleasure to see you again."

I shoved him. "Why didn't you text me you were coming?"

"Watch it," he laughed, looking down at his arm. "I need these things. Yeah, this was a last-minute deal. And aren't you usually at Wildwood?"

Nobody had told him. It wasn't exactly newsworthy. But Oscar looked positively fascinated.

I shrugged. "Not this year."

Win's eyes went glassy. "Huh. Yeah. Breaks are good. What am I saying, you're a kid, you've got plenty of—"

The doorbell rang, automatic subject change, thank Christ. Dad barreled down the steps to answer it. Before he reached the front door, keys jangled against the lock, and Alice slid inside holding bags of stacked containers from Citarella. Her black hair was pinned in a bun, curls spilling loose like ribbons.

"Did you just . . . *ring* the *doorbell*?" Win cocked his head.

Alice stopped and looked at us. "I don't live here anymore."

"This will always be your home." Dad kissed her on the head while he pried the food from her arms.

"Especially since your place is, what, four blocks away?" Win chuckled. "Miss Independent."

"*Seventy* blocks, thank you, I moved downtown." Alice threw her hands in the air. "And lovely to see you too, nice to get the third degree the second I step inside! It's been a *day,* I'll have you know. We're saddled with this crazy Frenchman as a guest conductor, we can't make out a word he says, so rehearsal was like a Pinter play, and then the line at Citarella nearly made me turn straight around and give up. But I *didn't,* because you *requested it specifically.*"

I glanced back at Oscar, his face carefully expressionless, and tried to telepathically communicate that, unlike Winston, my sister was not usually this extra—but then I processed what she'd said. Win's visit wasn't a surprise to her. He'd even put in a dinner order.

"Aw, you've missed me." Win opened his arms.

She shoved him before hugging him tight.

"Obnoxious." She turned to kiss me absently on the cheek. "Hey, Roo."

Then she saw Oscar—and went bug-eyed. I hoped to God that wasn't how I looked when I first met him.

She extended her hand. "Hello there, I'm Alice."

"Oscar Bell," he said quickly. "Such an honor to meet you. I have your recording of the Brandenburg Concerto No. 6, it's one of my all-time favorites."

"Oh! Well. Thank you very much. It's *lovely* to meet you too."

Then she turned to me with this weird, pointed look. I just as pointedly ignored her, gliding into the kitchen to ladle the takeout into ceramic bowls.

Dad grabbed a bottle of wine from the chilled cabinet, then tugged on my braid as he passed me with a wink. I joined them at the table with the last of the dishes. Win mouthed *thank you* to me, and I smiled back.

"So, Oscar," Alice said. "Tell me about yourself."

Now *this* was legitimately the cruelest question in the world, but Oscar considered it while he scooped wild rice onto his plate. "I am a work in development."

I glanced up to see his eyes glint and had to stop myself from snorting.

"What an interesting answer." My sister nodded, the very picture of politeness.

I had to hand it to her—if you hadn't known Alice for years, you'd never guess she was interrogating you. Clearly she was as thrown that Dad had taken on a student as I'd been.

"I'm gonna start saying that in interviews," Win said. "'Tell us about the upcoming season, maestro?' 'It's a work in development. *As are we all.*'" He stroked his chin pretentiously.

Oscar laughed. "Ah, you know, I'm a standard American seventeen-year-old."

In no universe did he believe that.

"Makes the question hard to answer."

"We're gonna work on answering it this summer," Dad said, breaking out of whatever mental orchestration he'd been listening to. "The composer part. The human part too. They go hand in hand."

Alice leaned toward Oscar. "You'd like to be a composer?"

She glanced at me and I glanced back, conveying all the "Yes, can I *help* you?" I could in one slow blink.

"Well . . . yeah," he said. "Not sure I can call myself that yet, but—"

"Course you can," Dad said, clapping him on the shoulder. "Wear that badge with pride."

"There's a badge?" Win frowned. "If I'd known there was a *badge*, I would have started composing years ago."

"Do you compose?" Oscar asked eagerly. "Is that something you're—"

"*No.*" Win waved his hand in an elegant arc. "I'm an interpreter of genius, not one myself."

"That's not what the *Philadelphia Inquirer* says," Dad said, beaming.

"They just want my body," Win said, and I burst out laughing. Win was kind of a playboy—tousled hair, young for a maestro, out on the scene, loving it too much.

I looked back at Alice to see if I could catch one of her classic eye-rolls, but she was still staring at Oscar, squinting. *Um.*

"You'll be interpreting *this* guy one day, Winston. Mark my words."

"I've marked them!" Win said, shoveling sprouts into his mouth with gusto.

Dad grabbed Oscar's shoulder again, shaking him proudly.

I squinted. Why was everybody so handsy with Oscar? It was friendly, yeah. But strange.

I recrossed my legs under the table so that my foot bumped Dad's knee. He dropped his arm, glanced at me.

"When did you and Ruby meet?" Alice asked.

"Um." Oscar peered over at me. I scooped some vegan loaf. "Yesterday? I was playing her piano and I don't think she was too thrilled about it . . ."

I coughed. He grinned.

"Wait, what?" Alice asked. "You . . . ?"

"Oscar is my student," Dad said, fighting a smile. "He's in the Amberley program but living here so we can work more closely."

"He's *living* here?" Alice scooted her chair back like she needed some air. Then her eyes widened even more and she burst out laughing. "Oh my God!" She put her hand to her curly hair. "I thought he was Ruby's boyfriend!"

A forkful of vegan loaf tumbled off my fork and onto my lap. I scrambled to wet a napkin in my water glass and dab the stain, my cheeks a nuclear wasteland.

"Well, that explains the . . . how did you put it . . . *third degree*?" Win giggled, holding his stomach.

I looked up. Oscar was watching me, showing absolutely no sign of embarrassment.

"Ruby's . . . boyfriend?" Dad repeated, as if those two words didn't belong together in any context.

"I was *surprised*, but . . ." Alice blanched. "Oh. Jesus. Not because of anything . . ." She waved at Oscar. "Because she's *Ruby*."

Okeydoke. I stood from the table and started upstairs.

"Rooster," Win groaned. "Don't get sensitive."

"Bathroom," I called back, and la-la-la'ed my way up the stairs until I was in the hall bath with the door locked and the vent on, so I couldn't hear them laughing anymore.

I sat on the closed toilet lid and stared at my fingernails, avoiding my reflection in the shower glass. Okay. Maybe I hadn't been the type "boyfriend" went with, but I was in a transformational period. Was it so far-fetched? Nora didn't think so. Maybe I *would* go full socialite and bring home a different guy every week, starting with Charlie-whatever at Yale, and see how funny they thought *that* was.

My eyes dragged themselves upward and there I was, scowling back. Wide-set eyes. Nose, cheekbones, chin.

She looks the part, doesn't she?

In my head, Mom laughed.

All you have to do is put her on mute.

I covered my eyes with my hands. Counted to three.

Okay. I pressed against the mirror and stood, ready to face the canned laugh track again. Maybe by the time I got downstairs, they'd have gotten it out of their systems. If I sat still enough, quiet, maybe they would forget I was there.

But when I opened the door, Alice was inches away, fingers pressed to her eyes like she'd been crying.

"Al," I said, touching her shoulder. "Oh no, what's the matter? I didn't mean to—"

"Dry lens." She pushed past me to get to her drawer—still full of her toiletries, deodorant, hairbrush, contact solution. "I'm sorry about that, downstairs."

"Oh. No." I leaned against the countertop. "It's just we met yesterday. Like he said. So it was . . . awkward, I guess, but it's not a big deal." *At all, at all, at all.*

"Well." Alice looked at herself in the mirror, slipping her contact lens back in. "*I* for one am mortified. He's got to think I'm some monster racist now. In hindsight, it's completely obvious that he's Dad's student! I just, I don't know, it didn't connect at first. And you two seemed . . . cozy."

"We weren't even next to each other."

"It was a *vibe*. I did think it was unprecedented. You bringing a guy home."

"Like you're one to talk."

Since her "Unhealthy Obsession with Young Gustavo Dudamel" stage at age sixteen, I'd never known Alice to even crush on anyone. As far as I knew, she was married to her viola.

"Touché," she said. But a flush was creeping up her neck.

"Oh my God," I breathed. "You *have* somebody. Alice! Who is it?"

"Nobody!" Her cheeks were now practically purple. "It's . . . well, it's not a thing."

"Who?" I grabbed her, scooting the bathroom door shut to give us privacy.

Alice reached past me to open it again. "Seriously, it's . . . no."

Clamped lips, glassy eyes, conversation over. We'd time-warped to a decade ago, when she was a teenager and I was tiny, permitted to talk to her while she did her makeup—but only to a point.

She scooted into the hall, and looked back, softening. "If it *becomes* a thing, I promise to fill you in."

I knew not to take it personally. We all had our roles to play. Leo was the zealot, Win was the prince, and Alice was the secret agent. Given her near-clinical caginess, I was surprised anyone had gotten close enough to prompt a blush.

Still, as she walked down ahead of me, I felt myself hollowing.

What was my role again? I'd somehow forgotten.

When we got back to the table, Win and Oscar were locked in laughing conversation, Dad typing on his phone—tweeting, probably; the man was J. K. Rowling levels of addicted.

I started clearing plates, letting my hair curtain my face.

"Bear in mind, this woman is *six years* older than him," Win said, knocking on the table to punctuate his words. "She's an adult."

I knew this story. He was making fun of Leo's first date, with a famous violinist when he was nineteen. Was this Win's way of making me feel better or worse?

"And he's in agony, like, sweating. He comes to my room with this huge bouquet and wants my opinion on the flowers."

Alice sat, shushing Win halfheartedly. I thought of poor Leo, hardly my closest sibling, but *still*—not even here to defend himself.

"Flowers! On a first date!"

"I hate this story." I let the stacked plates fall onto the table with a clang. "What's wrong with flowers? For fuck's sake! It was *nice,* he was being nice!"

Everyone stared at me—even Dad, who looked like he'd just arrived from Alpha Centauri. "You want some flowers, Rooster?"

Win covered his mouth with his fist, a snort bursting through.

Oscar started to stand, the careless smile he'd been wearing dropping away.

I gathered the plates and hurried into the kitchen, blinking away my anger as I kicked open the dishwasher.

The air behind me shifted.

"Let me do that," Oscar said softly.

"No, I'm . . ." I looked up at him. "I'm good."

"What's next, then? Dessert?"

A new smile hovered—an unasked question.

Was he asking me to prepare dessert for everybody? Or if I wanted to go *out* for dessert? Or did "dessert" have a *double meaning*?

Through the doorway, I could see Alice and Win pretending not to spy, waiting for the next joke they could regale near-strangers with. *Remember that night fifty-four years ago when Rooster was too awkward to talk to Dad's composition student? We cry from the laughing! Haha—!*

"Dessert. Let's do it."

"Pastries?" He offered me his arm.

I took it. "Pastries."

We crossed the living room, wind in our sails. I grabbed my bag from the rack, gave a cursory wave, and shut the door behind us, drowning out Win's "Um . . . good-bye?" with a satisfying clunk.

7.

Oscar waited on the sidewalk while I adjusted my sandal with a clumsy hop, so unruffled that my own mental wrinkles started to smooth. "I feel like we just had dinner in front of a live studio audience."

I winced. "I should have warned you."

"It's the same at my house. But our show is . . ." He smiled slowly. "Maybe on a different network."

"There is no demographic interested in my family."

We started down the street.

Oscar laughed. "If you go to the library, there are, what? Six biographies about your dad?"

"Oh. Yeah."

"I have to admit—it's weird." Oscar stuck his hands in his pockets. "Meeting them. I had this idea of what the Chertok family would be and . . ." He went quiet.

"*What?*" I nearly whapped him, but stopped myself.

"I was wrong! You're all . . . human."

"Sorry to disappoint."

"You know what I mean."

I did. And I liked it. And there was something about that one word, *human,* that leveled us out. I only wished it were that easy.

Oscar's phone rang from his pocket—a classical piece I didn't recognize, overloaded with strings. Instead of answering the call, he texted with his thumb while we walked.

"What was that ringtone?" I asked, the safest question.

"Oh." He glanced up, looking embarrassed. "It's . . . um . . . Farzone?"

I blinked. "Is that a composer?"

He laughed, a sudden blast. "No. It's a PlayStation game. It's kind of old but my friend TJ is hardcore into it, so . . ."

He held up his phone. It looked like it had been dropped on hard floors a few hundred times.

I smiled. "Hi, TJ."

Oscar wiggled his phone like it was saying hi back. Then he pocketed it.

"He, ah, calls a lot, on his headset thing . . . So, where are you taking me?"

I skipped a little at the question. "Only to the best-reviewed patisserie on the Upper West Side."

He clapped, delighted. "That has got to be the whitest thing I've heard you say."

A laugh burst out of me. "What if I'd said '*most exclusive*'?"

"Ooh, that's whiter."

"'Upper *East* Side . . .'"

"Throw in something about how they sell treats for your goldendoodle—"

"How did you know? We go there every week after Barkley's massage!"

"You win. Stop or my head will explode."

L'Orangerie was open until nine on Saturdays, so we made it by two minutes. The girl behind the counter avoided eye contact, clearing out the display counters, when the owner walked in from the back of the shop, polite-face curdling at the sight of us.

Not *us,* exactly. She was squinting at Oscar. And my jokes about white people no longer seemed so funny.

"Closed," she said in her light Parisian accent. I gave a grudging wave and watched as recognition bloomed. "Oh! Yes, come in, we can serve one more."

"Two more," I corrected.

"How is your father? *Please* tell him I say hello."

I bit back a knee-jerk "I will" and turned away. I didn't even know this woman's name, just that with Mom gone, half the ladies-of-a-certain-age in Manhattan thought they had a shot with *the* Martin Chertok. But I didn't like how it felt knowing that my face was what turned this woman's expression into artificial sweetener, like we were in the same noxious club. I wouldn't tell Dad a thing.

Oscar was whistling Grieg, scrutinizing what remained in the display case. He glanced at me. I kept my eyes on the food. Tarte au citron, petit gateaux chocolate, a couple of sagging croissants, and—

"Those fruit tarts, please!" I chirped to the shop girl, pointing into the glass. "And a lemonade."

"Two fruit tarts?" Oscar side-eyed me. "You mean business."

"One's for you, you have to try it."

"Your face right now!" He laughed. "You're taking this pastry thing *seriously*."

"I take everything seriously," I said, but cracked a smile. "Get whatever else, it's my treat."

"No, let me—"

"I've got it."

I usually hated these arguments, but this one felt like a dance.

"Okay." He nudged me. "Next time."

I slid into an iron table on the sidewalk while Oscar finagled an elaborate macchiato drink with a heart-shaped swirl on the top—nothing compared to the glory of this tart. Round and creamy with pops of color, green, red, piercing blue.

Across the table, Oscar tilted his back and forth.

"I can get into French pastries. French entrées on the other hand . . ." He puffed his cheeks like he was going to be sick.

"French food is amazing!"

"I have sampled it firsthand, *ma chérie,*" he said. "I went to Paris with my school freshman year and the first night, we had this pre-pared menu at a corner bistro, all of us piled in—to this day I don't know if we all caught a virus or if it was the soufflé we ate, but the hotel that night and the next two days . . . holy Lord above. Stuff of nightmares."

"Oh my God."

"It kind of bonded my class. We speak excellent French but none of us will ever eat anything Gallic again. Like . . . even the smell of thyme . . ." He raised the tart and looked at me over it. "This I can do. I've come so close to getting one of these at Whole Foods, but if I buy one, my mom'll give me her four-hour Sugar Is a *Drug* speech. So how do you do it? Not a one-bite deal."

"Too big," I agreed. "I have a method."

"I'm shocked."

I glared across the table. "Do you want to know? Or—"

"Sorry! I do. Please . . ." He grinned. "Go ahead."

"The polite thing is probably to take dainty bites from the side, but I eat it"—I plucked a blueberry from the center to demonstrate—"one at a time."

The blueberry burst in my mouth, sour and tangy. Then the next blueberry and the third. Then I moved on to the strawberry, sweeter even than the custard, bright like sunshine. Then the kiwi, its faint grittiness tickling my teeth. The apple came next, thin sliced, flat against my tongue before that satisfying crunch. All that was left was that gorgeous piecrust and a generous layer of custard.

I hesitated, but then . . . *screw it.*

I closed my eyes and licked the custard out of the crust with the tip of my tongue, a spiral from the edge inward, until there was nothing left but to fold the tart in half and finish it off in two floury bites.

Oscar let out a slow breath. "*Damn.*"

He looked like he was taking mental photographs, locking me into his memory.

"I'm going in. I'll try it your way," he said, closing his eyes and eating a single blueberry. "This is . . . an education."

"Happy to help."

I *was* happy. I felt new. Primary colored.

He'd moved on to the strawberry, nodding thoughtfully as he tasted it. Wind swept down the avenue, touching awnings and café umbrellas and cars, whispering under the city din.

I stretched my legs, hands resting on my happy stomach while I let my head loll back. It was easy to forget how three-dimensional the city was until you had the chance to sit and take it in. By day, the buildings looked like castle walls—now, with their windows lit gold, it felt like we were being cradled by stars.

I glanced back at Oscar. He'd finished his tart and was looking at me like he'd been waiting to say something, trying to find the right words.

"You really do . . . *tackle* things, don't you?"

Heat shot up from my ankles—but it didn't sound like an accusation. More of a compliment. "I do. When they matter. The trick is finding something that matters."

"Like, say . . ." Oscar held up his empty paper wrapper. "Fruit tarts."

"Exactly. So what do you think? Worth it?" At his confused expression, I added, "Worth hearing your mom's lecture, or—?"

"She doesn't know what she's missing."

"No sugar? At all?"

"Apart from national holidays? Nope." He swirled his coffee. "Obviously, we eat what we want when she's out of range, but . . . let's just say we had a lot of kale growing up. Not greens. Kale."

"Kale's okay!"

"In extreme moderation." He leaned back, stretching. "I don't mean to act like she's some tyrant. She's a hospital administrator, so it's more about 'best practices.' Like, we were all born exactly two and a half years apart, because that's supposed to be the best gap. I . . . don't even want to think about how they managed that."

Like Leo and Win and Alice. Thirty-two, twenty-nine, twenty-six . . . then me, nine years later. Surprise!

"She played Mozart for all of us in the womb to make us smart, that kind of thing." Oscar sipped his coffee. He tilted it, offering me some.

I swiped cinnamon off the foam with my pinkie. "Hasn't that been debunked?"

He pointed at me. "That's what they say! I don't know, though. We all came out sharp. I was the only one who started kicking every time she put on the *Jupiter Symphony*. Mom said we all liked it, but I seemed to *recognize* it."

The *Jupiter Symphony* played in my mind, grief rumbling under it like static.

I smoothed my hair back. "So who is 'we all'? What's your sitcom cast?"

He fumbled in his pocket and pulled out his phone. "Two sisters. One older, one younger." Then he handed it across the table—a photo of two grinning girls piled onto a pink sofa. He leaned over to point, his face inches from mine. "Etta, Bri. They're crazy, I love them a lot."

I peeked up at him. I loved my family but I never *talked* about loving my family. It wasn't how we worked. And here was this boy, just throwing the word out there . . . *love* . . . so comfortably.

"What's your brother's name, the older one?" he asked, leaning back to pocket his phone. "I can't believe I'm blanking. He's an amazing oboist . . ."

"Leonard. Leo. He's got two little kids, Aaron and Matilda, so I'm an aunt." *Sort of.* I'd only met them once.

"What about your mom?"

My mouth went dry. I sipped my lemonade.

"She's touring, right? That's what your dad said."

"Well, yeah." I peered over at him, confused. "I mean, she's not with Dad anymore. They split up last year. Amicable. Totally fine, no drama."

"That's ideal."

"Yeah, it was really . . . evolved. They're still friends, it's just the way it is."

Another swig.

Oscar smiled. "But she's been on tour?"

"Yeah! The last . . . eleven months? She's doing great, getting tons of high-profile bookings, it's awesome. You know, for so long it was all about Dad, and now *her* name is getting out there. I really admire that."

I finished off my lemonade and capped the bottle, turning it over in my hand.

"Do you get to see her much?"

"She's taking a break soon. So. We'll catch up then. I mean, it's not like I'm five, right?"

"No," he said softly. "Well, I hope I get to meet her while I'm here. She's an incredible artist."

I stood, jaw tight. "She is. You ready to—?"

"Oh. Yes." He tossed his trash into the bin by the door and followed me to the intersection.

As he drew level, I glanced over at him and caught him staring. Instead of looking away, he shot me a brazen, single-dimpled grin, and it edged out all thoughts of my mother.

We strolled around to the park, passing high-rises with their doormen waiting in pools of lobby light, carriages clip-clopping back to the park stables, taxis, vans, buses skidding past, taillights cutting a red streak through the darkness.

Normal life, summer in the city. It had been here this whole time, year after year, and now I was in it.

We looked at each other again, briefly this time, and our steps took on a different beat, like gravity wasn't working as well as a second ago. Oscar started humming to the rhythm. I recognized the tune.

"Is that something you've been working on?"

"Yeah, I can't . . ." He reached out, fighting with something invisible. "I can't get rid of it, so I'm trying to figure it out."

"You act like you've got cholera."

"That's what it feels like!" He walked backward to face me. "I've come down with a melody. But the only way to get rid of it is to make it music, find it friends."

"Friends?"

"Harmony. You know, you have the theme . . . bah-dum-dum, deedly-dum. Dumdum." He sang the tune—clumsily; thank *God* there was something he wasn't good at—while clapping the rhythm like a dance. "And then you could do an undercurrent, vrum-vrum-vrum-vrum progression, a Haydn kind of deal. Or you could ornament it even more, like my boy Wolfgang. Undermine it, make it an abstraction, there's a million ways you could go."

He fell silent.

I glanced over. "Why are you looking at *me*?"

"I want to know what you think!"

I shrugged, laughing, but he still seemed to expect some insight. "You need to write what *you* want to write. There's no, like, absolute correct answer."

"That's what Marty—um, your dad says. I've got to find my own voice. I've kind of never thought of it that way. I was always playing around. It's like, what are those people who write extra chapters of books online . . . ?"

"Fan fiction?"

"Yes! Bri's into that. And it's what I've always done—I write symphonies in the style of Mozart because I *love* Mozart symphonies and I want there to be more of them."

"There are *forty-one*!"

"Fifty if you count mine." He rubbed his palms together. "Fan *composition*. That's my thing."

"Time. Out." I stopped. "You've written *nine* symphonies. Full—?"

"In the style of *Mozart*," he corrected, walking backward again. "Couple of Beethoven symphonies, pieces for piano and violin—Chopin, Schumann, easy stuff—singspiels, a Joplin rag, a Strauss waltz . . ." He beamed. "That one was tough! You need a hook or it's not danceable."

I was so thrown that it took me a second to realize we were back at the house. Half the lights were off upstairs. Win and Alice must have left already.

"This was . . ." Oscar looked like he was searching for the right word, but gave up with an exhalation. He motioned to the basement apartment and I felt an almost physical tug toward it. "I've got this keyboard, that's it, but I could play you some of the stuff I was working through last night . . ."

"Oh." I stepped back. "I've got an early morning. I'm going jogging. And . . ."

And nothing.

"Wow. Jogging."

"Yeah. Jogging? Running?" I leaned against the stoop rail. "Running. It's new. We'll see. But I've got to get out super—"

"I should wind down too," Oscar cut in.

"Dad does like to work early, so . . ."

"I have to rewire myself. I'm not great at sleeping when I'm supposed to be sleeping, working when I'm supposed to . . . you get it."

I did, sort of. I wondered how he got through high school, but if I asked him, it would extend tonight even further and I would absolutely find myself going downstairs and sitting on his dorm bed and . . . not . . . sleeping . . .

"Good night," I said, not firmly at all.

He leaned in for a side-hug and . . . *goodness*. I could feel his hipbone slip perfectly against my own, the length of his rib cage running all the way up my torso, my face in line with his. When I inched away, I smelled boy—warm, salty, unfamiliar.

"I'm gonna dream about that fruit tart." He stepped away, eyes sparkling like he'd said something scandalous.

I replayed it in my head all night long.

8.

All Jules said when she saw me on the sidewalk in the sickly pre-dawn light wearing the ridiculously short shorts and synthetic top I'd bought yesterday was, "Let's go."

No "Hi." No "Here are the basics of jogging technique." No "I'm glad we have this chance to catch up." She got going and I trailed her, frantic, like she'd stolen my phone.

"How long have you been with your boyfriend?" My voice was shrill from trying to keep it level as I ran, but I still felt a shiver of glee saying the word *boyfriend*. Like maybe, possibly, it could belong on my lips.

Jules blinked hard at me. "What?"

"Your . . . boyfriend?" I smiled, polite.

It had become hard to smile, though, let alone talk. We'd crossed the road, onto the park paths where runners go and I was now one of them, and it had felt weird and loose and awkward at first, but now it was starting to *hurt*. My ankles were wobbling, my throat raw, and I could feel everything—knee joints, rib bones, the skin on my face. I'd run before, of course, in gym, but only the bare minimum, and I didn't do sports, I did orchestra, used to, anyway, and this was a million times more excruciating because I was in public and trying to keep pace with Jules and she wasn't even *sweating* yet.

"If you want to catch up on all the time we've missed, that's completely cool," she huffed, in rhythm with her stride. "Just not . . . right . . . now . . ."

"Right," I said. "Good idea." But my breath felt like lava, so it came out, "Gun . . . duh . . . I can't."

I stopped. I had to. Spots were gathering.

She glanced over her shoulder with a thumbs-up. "Good start!"

I couldn't tell if she was being sarcastic.

Falling onto a park bench, I retied one squeaky new sneaker, tugged up the sock, and looked at my watch. It was 6:09. I'd been jogging for four minutes.

The park felt weird this early in the morning, like if you weren't exercising, you didn't have permission to be here—until dawn, it belonged to animals and homeless New Yorkers. Right on cue, I looked at the treetops and saw a hawk swoop by on his way to his aerie in one of the high-rises bordering the park, the luxury apartment buildings where Sarahs and Lydias and Noras lived.

What did that hawk do all day? Did he have a mate? What was my squirrel up to? Were they mulling their destinies, their talent, their impact, or were they just watching the sunrise?

What was Oscar—?

Stop. I stood and brushed myself off, trying my best to plod home, not skip.

The lights were on at the house, so Oscar and Dad were up and working. I smoothed my hair and pulled down my sweaty jogging shirt before unlocking the front door. But the music greeting me was muffled—they were in the study, noodling music on Dad's upright. I recognized the snippet Oscar had hummed last night and felt like I was in on a secret.

Then I glanced at Mom's Steinway. She was supposed to have collected it months ago for her "new place," which she hadn't even started looking for yet, as far as I knew. The piano had stayed put, along with a box of other bits and pieces—an antique hand mirror, a copy of *The Goldfinch* with a bookmark stuck fifty pages in, the tea mug I'd bought her for Mother's Day when I was seven.

I wondered what she was doing right now. But the answer was obvious. Wherever Mom was, she was practicing. She played every morning for two hours, took a break, played again in the afternoon for two more.

I'd done it too, every day.

My fingers were resting on my own piano's keys. I'd walked to it without realizing. I looked at my hands, slowly pressing, gently enough not to make any sound but a near-silent thump. There was something kind about the curve of the instrument, an old friend welcoming me back—but the keys beneath my fingers were as indifferent as ever. I pulled away, feeling tricked.

There came a shock of furious playing upstairs—gorgeous, dazzling flurries raging into a snowstorm. I couldn't tell if it was Dad or Oscar. It didn't matter.

I shut the lid and walked away.

"Re: Met tmw—no dress code! Business casual, no fuss. Museum not Opera, YES, buuuuuut I do have a table for that other Met's gala(!) tonight if interested in making an appearance? Might need a stylist for this one so let me know asap. xoxoxo nora"

My stomach clenched until the second I hit send. *"Thank you SO MUCH, but I already have plans tonight. Excited for tomorrow! xo Ruby."*

I did not, in fact, have plans beyond writing back to Farrah, running around with the vacuum, giving the bathroom a quick clean, showering the Lysol smell off my skin.

Back in my room, my hair still dripping, I gazed at the dusky sidewalk below—and saw Oscar leave the basement apartment wearing a tuxedo. It fit him loosely in the shoulders, but still looked as natural as a T-shirt on him. I pulled my soft robe tighter in case he happened to look up. Then I felt the front door shut downstairs, seconds before Dad joined him on the curb, dressed to the nines himself.

A black sedan pulled up and Nora got out, auburn bob and LEGO posture telltale even at this distance. She lightly touched Oscar's shoulder, smoothed the sides of her little black dress, and motioned to the car.

I rested my head against the glass. Dad was the Met's musical director and Oscar was his pet protégé. Why hadn't it occurred to me that they would be going to the gala?

Because Dad didn't invite me.

Nora glanced up at my window. I stepped back, feeling caught in my lie. By the time I dared look, the car was gone, leaving me in an empty house.

Empty's good. Empty's the plan. I stretched my arms over my head—but the silence didn't feel like a balm. It was heavy, dusty, full. The house sounded like it had the night after Mom left. Like we were all in the process of moving out.

I dropped my arms. I'd said I had plans.

I was going to get some.

I tugged on clothes, knotted my hair into a bun, grabbed my bag, and hurried down the block—two stoops away, Jules's building.

I scanned the row of buzzers for the name Russo, to no avail. Which apartment was hers? She lived with her grandmother, who must have had a different last name . . . which, of course, I couldn't remember. I hadn't even been this close to her building's front door since I was ten.

Just as I was about to give up, I saw Jules tromping down the stairs inside and waved.

She cocked her head, frowning as she came out. "Are you looking for me?"

"You said we should catch up later. So I thought I'd give you a try." I kept smiling, feeling more like a stalker than ever.

"That's sweet," she said sourly. Her eyes dropped down my body. "You don't look terrible."

"I *don't* look terrible. Um." Black leggings, gray silk flats, random, ill-fitting T-shirt. "I didn't even look at these when I put them on."

"That explains it." Jules pressed her cherry-red lips together as if in concentration, and I took the awkward beat to check out her outfit—blousy short-shorts, black ankle boots, a floppy T-shirt bearing the image of a fishing lure under a paper-thin blue leather jacket. Her hair was loose, jagged at the edges like a craft project, and she appeared to be wearing no makeup except for those lips. And yet it worked. She was art.

She blinked like she was clicking her face out of safe mode. "Listen, I'm going out. With some friends."

"Oh, okay." I started to back up.

"I don't have anything remotely in your size, but let me grab you something . . ." She waved at me, squinting. "Yeah. And then we'll go, okay? I'll be two seconds."

"Oh." *We.*

She was already back inside her brownstone, taking the steps three at a time. In what felt like no more than the two seconds she'd promised, she was back downstairs, holding a drapey red tank dress out to me.

"Um . . ."

"It goes over . . ." She glanced wistfully over her shoulder at a passing taxi. "Let me do it."

Before I could protest, she was shoving this thing over my head and I was pushing my arms through like a toddler and blinking down at my getup and . . . holy hell, it worked. I looked like someone who went out at night.

She flagged the next taxi and waggled the door until I joined her inside.

"Fifty-first and Eleventh," she said, then pulled out her phone to text as we glided away.

"Where are we—?"

"My friend's brother tends bar at this club in Midtown, so we get to sneak in. It's terrible but we've made it our own. The music is *awful*."

She beamed like that was a selling point.

My heart hammered louder the farther west we drove. *Out. To a club. With strangers.* I knew this was normal, this was what everybody did at all the schools around me—this was a real-life experience—but it felt jarringly like a dream where you've woken up in Spain with no shoes on.

We got out of the taxi in front of a nondescript bar with a bored-looking bouncer manning the steel-gray door. My outfit gave me a burst of courage. This was a costume. I was someone else. I drew a breath and started toward the door.

Jules grabbed me from behind and steered me away, face frozen casual.

"Oh." I glanced back. "Is that not—?"

"Do you have a fake ID? Didn't think so. We go in the *VIP* entrance."

She made air-quotes around *VIP*. I soon realized why. We got into the bar through the back alley, walking past an overflowing dumpster to squeak open a staff door kept open by a bent MetroCard someone had slipped into the lock-catch. Jules motioned me inside, carefully replaced the card as she shut the door, then strode ahead with renewed bounce.

The evening had begun.

9.

The hallway was dark and the floor was sticky. Music thumped in a distant room and Jules was right—it was terrible! I followed her past a vacant bar to a windowless room lined with ugly velvet banquettes, where a guy and girl sat sprawled in opposite corners.

I edged in behind Jules, straightening my dress strap as they jumped to their feet. The girl was intimidatingly pretty—Asian, model-tall, with a perfect purple ballerina bun. The guy was on the short side, olive-skinned, wearing an untucked dress shirt with the sleeves rolled up, like he'd just gotten off work on Wall Street.

He's trying to look older, I realized, but then he smiled, totally affable, and I felt bad for noticing.

Jules glanced back at me, almost shyly. "Yeah, this is Sam and Joey."

I couldn't figure out whose name was whose, so I gave a general wave. "Hey."

Jules whipped back around, sculptural hair flying. "Meet Ruby."

"Hey Ruby," Joey/Sam said in unison.

"Her dad is Martin Chertok," Jules added.

They stared blankly at us—and a thrill shot through me.

"Martin *Chertok*," Jules said again, louder, like she hadn't been heard over the thump-thump-thump of Top 40 in the next room. "The classical composer?"

"Cool!" the tall girl said, but it was obvious she was pretending.

"Ugh." Jules threw herself onto one of the sofas. "Heathens. Sorry, Ruby."

"Not at all," I chirped, too enthusiastically. But oh my God, I *meant* it. I was outside the gates of Musiclandia, and the air was so heady and clean! Actually, it smelled like beer stains in here, but *still*.

Joey/Sam—I was leaning toward him being Joey—scooted closer. "Where do you go to school?"

What a delightfully ordinary question! "Exton?"

Everybody groaned.

Jules slung her arm around me. "Don't mind us. We're victims of the public school system."

A boy walked in with his arms spread wide and, again, apart from Jules, everybody rose to greet him.

She turned to me instead. "So! Tell me what you've been up to for the past six years."

Tyler, then. Still on probation.

"A lot of piano," I said.

"Yes, I figured."

"But now I've quit."

"*Why?*" Jules leaned in, unblinking.

"Because I suck."

"Hmmm, dubious reason." She stood, presenting her cheek for Tyler to kiss.

"You didn't answer my texts," he said. He was handsome, in a high school production of *Grease* kind of way. "I didn't know if you were hanging out tonight."

"Oh, is that a problem?" She sat again, crossing her legs coquettishly. "Did you invite another girl?"

"No! *Jesus.*" He motioned to the door. "Do you want something?"

"Water," she said. "Ruby?"

"You're still not drinking?" Tyler sounded amused.

"Nope." She examined her thumbnail.

"I make one comment—"

"Ruby, do you want a drink?" she asked, louder.

"I'll have a Shirley Temple," I answered, and immediately wanted to bury my head in these disgusting cushions till I passed out from shame.

But the model clapped. "Oh my God, I love those! I'll have one too. But put some vodka in mine."

The dance floor in the other room had started filling up in the time it took to get our drinks. As I wobble-walked out with them, I found myself matching step with the bass beat whether I wanted to or not. My Shirley Temple had tasted slightly off, so I was guessing I'd also gotten the Sam upgrade. It felt . . . interesting.

We bobbed around the side of the room, making fun of the music—dancing with exaggerated enthusiasm. Ironic dancing? This was new.

Then Jules pointed to the front door. "I have to eat."

Out on the street, everybody headed north, like they were psychically linked and had already decided on a destination.

Joey hung back. "Are you a senior?"

"Yeah, next year."

"Us too. Do you know where you're applying for college?"

Normal. I loved normal. I could *totally* normal. I wobbled and Joey caught my elbow.

"Um, not yet." I jogged to catch up with the others, crossing the street past dark office buildings to a glowing diner. "I need to pick a life direction first. Where I can make the most impact."

"Oh, right," Joey said, but he looked confused.

We followed everybody inside to a corner booth the waitress was still clearing. The place was packed—our timing had been impeccable.

Joey slid in beside me. "Are you going to stay in the city? I applied to Northwestern, but there's no way I'll get in."

"You'll get in!" Sam turned to me. "He's a math genius."

I coughed, abruptly on the spot, like Joey and I were on a blind date.

Joey flushed. "I get good grades, that doesn't mean I'm a math genius."

Genius. I pictured tuxedoed Oscar sitting at Nora's table at the Met gala tonight, smiling under the ballroom lights, the set of his jaw, fingers idly tracing a tune against the edge of the tablecloth . . .

"You calculate derivatives faster than me." Sam opened her menu. "And I'm *totally* a genius, so."

"Have you decided on Binghamton yet?" Tyler asked Jules. The subject hadn't changed, exactly, but this had the tone of a private conversation.

Jules sipped her water as her boyfriend kissed her shoulder. "Nope."

He straightened. "Nope, you're not applying, or nope, haven't thought about it."

"I haven't had time to think about it."

"With all your training." He said it flatly, no sarcasm, but her face went cartoon red.

"Yes, with my training and my life, which you are barely a part of."

"Whoa." He raised his hands.

"Anyway, I'm staying in the city, so you need to come to terms with that. I'm not moving out of my apartment until they forcibly evict me."

I squinted at her. "Why would you get kicked out of your apartment? You're not, like, squatting—"

"It's rent controlled," she said. "How else do you think we could afford it? Grandma's a social worker, but she's been there since the Dutch bought Manhattan, and she's the only name on the lease. As soon as she dies, the rent goes nuclear, I'm out on my ass."

"Is she sick?" I asked. "I didn't—"

"No, Jesus, we are out of touch, aren't we? She's fine! Everything's fine."

Everyone in the booth was frowning at Jules and me now, queasy with confusion. They snapped out of it long enough for us to all order dinner, then Joey asked, "How do you and Jules know each other?"

"We're neighbors," I started, sipping from my water as Jules cut in—

"We don't. We used to be best friends, *awww*, but then Ruby here went off to Exton and I stayed in public school and she pretended not to know me anymore."

"Excuse me?" My mouth fell open, the straw sticking to my lip. "That is not what happened at all."

"Okay, cool, I'd love to hear your version. After all these years."

"We just . . . didn't have the same interests anymore."

"Oh, this is classic. Go on."

"I started to get serious about my practice schedule."

"She plays the piano," she explained to the table. "Or is it 'played' now that you've quit?"

I jabbed my straw into the bottom of my cup. "And you weren't serious about *anything*, so we drifted apart."

"I wasn't . . . ?" She sputtered soundlessly. "Newsflash, Chertok, you're not *supposed* to be serious about anything when you're ten. I was a kid. You were a robot."

"What?"

"A robot." She jerked her arms. "'*Must not hang out, must do scales.*'"

"Only in the afternoons," I snapped. "You could have hung out after that. We could have had sleepovers."

"I'd made new friends," she said snootily.

I had too. But I still hit the table. "So you admit it."

"Admit what?"

"You dropped me."

She blinked. "Let's call it mutual."

I fumed a breath. Everybody was staring.

Jules reached across the booth and grabbed my hands. "But now we're friends again, yay!"

I wasn't sure how offended to be, but she squeezed one more time and her face relaxed into a real smile and I realized . . . she was being sincere.

I laughed. "Yay."

The night was easier after that. We slipped back into the club and after another sneaky Shirley Temple—Sam started calling them Shirley Temple Blacks, the actress' grown-up name—I even attempted to dance for like three minutes.

After a mysterious argument with Tyler in the corner of the club that ended with a public make-out session, Jules grabbed my hand, waved good-bye to the others, and marched us back outside to hail a taxi home.

"This was fun," I said, getting out at her building.

"This was the usual." She sounded strangely sad about it. But her face lightened as she extended her hand. "Give me your cell phone." She typed something in and passed it back. "Text me if you feel like coming over. I'm skipping the run tomorrow, but if you want to join me Tuesday—"

"Yes! See you then."

New friends. New topics of conversation. The new and awesome normal.

The light was off in the basement apartment. Oscar was probably out, not that it was any of my business. I glanced at the time on my phone as I fumbled for my keys—and nearly dropped my bag.

One in the morning. I did not do this. Ever. My dad must have filed a missing person report. I held my breath, tiptoeing into the house, primed for yells, "young lady"s, the sound of the door being blow-torched shut behind me.

But I hadn't gotten any frantic calls on my cell. No texts, nothing.

All the lights were off. I had to fumble my way to the steps to my bedroom. I saw a scribbled note resting against my closed door, Dad's handwriting.

Working with Oscar at Lincoln Center tomorrow. Lilly Hall. Be a doll and bring us some of those pastries I like? 9am or so. xo Dad.

I sat on the top step, staring at the note. I let out an empty laugh. Then I crumpled it and threw it at the ceiling.

10.

my stomach clenched as I reached the Amberley campus. I trod on, swinging the bag of pastries like a wrecking ball.

Colossal gleaming walls, iconic fountain dancing in the middle of the dizzying plaza, banners waving for performances to come, tourists snapping pics—and just around the corner, Lilly Hall. *This is okay, this is fine.*

I dared a look around the school's side courtyard, playing Spot the Musician, which took me all of ten seconds. Two skinny white guys sat on the edge of a planter eating bagel sandwiches, talking animatedly while their feet idly tapped a steady rhythm. *Percussionists.* Two whispering girls passed me on their way to the dorms, cradling hot venti Starbucks cups. *Vocal program.* A gangly South Asian kid nearly ran smack into me, his expression fuzzy, fingers frantically tapping the straps of his enormous backpack.

Keyboard program. He's working on a piece in his head.

I stopped walking for a second. Shoved it all down and kept going.

Music surged as soon as I stepped from the lobby into the hall—"Mercury" from *The Planets.* The full orchestra was up on the stage, and the players were clearly my age. Summer program kids. Dad was conducting, talking to them . . . a real honor. He swished his baton, motioning for them to stop, which they did, messily. It was their first day together, everybody slightly out of synch, but Dad seemed pleased to bits. He shouted, "Yes!" then waved for someone else to fill his place.

Oscar? I paused in my step to watch him, dizzy from the vertigo of spotting someone you've just met in a completely new context. He nodded, clearly nervous as he took the baton from Dad with a bow. Then, as Dad walked away, he straightened, gesturing grandly toward the wing Dad had disappeared into, and the orchestra burst into applause, as if Oscar had compelled them to do so.

I blinked hard, trying to figure out what I'd seen.

Something happened the instant Oscar touched that baton. His energy changed, becoming visible, *palpable,* even from here. His posture was perfect, arms primed and ready as he took to the podium. Then he lifted the baton—and began.

They played. At his command. Yeah, this was what orchestras did, but he looked like an actual sorcerer. He shushed the woodwinds, drew them out louder, cracked a beat to ignite the strings, and kept the pulse of the piece pounding like his own heart. The entire hall was crackling with power, filling with sparks.

And he was doing it.

"He's talented. No wonder Kat was talking about him."

I whipped around, my eyes adjusting slowly to the darkened hall. There were two girls in the back row in slouchy dresses, hair pinned up tight. Ballet students, from next door. Why were they taking their break here?

"How old?" one murmured to the other.

"Don't know. Old enough. He's hot."

"Kat was totally right."

Who the hell was Kat? Was she another dancer? Why did I hate her so much?

I hurried to the side of the stage where Dad stood watching the podium like Oscar was juggling knives.

"Dad." I held out the bag of pastries. He kept bobbing his head with the music, eyebrows knotted as he made mental notes. "*Dad.*"

He startled. "Oh! Thank you!"

I waved, hoping for a quick good-bye, but he leaned in to kiss my cheek, which made me smile despite myself.

Then he whispered, "See?" and motioned to the stage.

I wasn't even sure why Oscar was here. Was this a conducting clinic? Was he taking the helm of the school's orchestra? Listening, I realized it amounted to the same thing. Day one, *this* assured. He knew the music like he was thinking it up, breathing it out. And the orchestra fell in line, totally in his thrall.

When I closed my eyes and listened, I went sunburst bright. Watching Oscar, it intensified, but then I took in the full orchestra—ninety-seven of them, my age, impossibly brilliant—and the light sputtered.

I needed to go.

Quick lean-hug good-bye into Dad's arm, then away. Mid-house, a flash of red hair made me turn—Nora, standing beside William Rustig, Amberley's president.

William—*Bill,* to Dad—was sleek, silver-blond, possibly an android. Win used to call him "Bill's Rusting" when Dad wasn't around, joking that everything he said was "*Programmed. For. Minimal. Controversy.*" Right now, Bill wasn't saying anything, and neither was Nora, both loitering in the aisle, staring at Oscar like they were waiting for him to levitate the timpani with his baton.

I half waved to Nora as I slipped past, but she didn't notice—a relief. I'd see her at the museum event tonight. I wanted her to find me at my best, summer lit, not here, a shadow.

I glanced back in the hope that Oscar had somehow noticed me come and go, but his entire world right now was "Mercury" and I was not even here, just passing through.

Even with my eyes focused on the path out, the glimpses of Lincoln Center that crept in were enough to make my rib cage ache. Was this how people felt after they sold their house and watched other people move in?

Don't mope, silly girl. You were only ever visiting.

I was rummaging through the kitchen, typing a grocery list on my phone, when Oscar and Dad came back.

"We've got to home in," Dad was saying. "You can do everything, that's what got you here, but what do you *need*? What *compels* you?"

"Need," Oscar murmured—and that one word was enough to conjure images of him up at that podium. "So . . . does it have to be something that strong? Can it be—"

"If you want the music to be strong, then yes, the impulse behind it has to be a cannon blast."

"Okay, yeah."

I forced myself to move. Added baby carrots and hummus to the list and shut the fridge, loud, so they'd know I was home.

"Do you know why I wrote *The Sleeping Variations*?" Dad asked.

"I've been wanting to ask." Oscar poked his head into the kitchen with a quick wave hello.

I jumped, startled. By the time I recovered, he'd already reversed around the corner.

"It was the winter *The House Guest* closed," Dad went on. "Nobody knew what to do with it, was it Broadway, was it an opera? I was a little lost . . ."

Muesli, tangerines, bananas, pasta went on the list. I wrestled down a grin, Oscar's face—*so* excited to say hi—lingering like a mirage. Basmati, almonds . . .

"Then I met Anna."

The phone wobbled.

"She was sitting at a café, annotating music. I fell in love with her before I even said a word to her."

I shut my eyes, breathing.

"She wasn't impressed with me. Not at first. Not even after I told her my name—she wasn't such a fan of the New City Symphony." Dad laughed, delighted, like it had just happened, like they weren't divorced, like he'd seen her at all in the past year. "But I won her over. And I wrote in a fever. I burned . . ." There was a sound, he was thumping something—his heart? "And so I set fire to the orchestra. That's how that piece came about."

"Ruby too."

Dad didn't respond.

"How Ruby came about," Oscar went on. "And . . . Alice, Leo, Winston . . ."

"Oh!" Dad let out a booming laugh. "Right, sure. Is she here, Ruby, you around?"

He was shouting up the stairs.

"Yep!" I walked out of the kitchen, eyes locked on my phone. "Anything you want from the store?"

I peeked up to see Oscar stare at his shoes, at me, away again.

"Coffee!" Dad dug in his tweed jacket. "I've got a coupon for

Fairway. French . . . roast, Oscar, what do you need?"

"Me?" Oscar startled alert, glancing between us. "No, I can handle getting my own groceries. Probably. If you show me where the supermarket is."

I grinned. "*Supermarket*. Ha. Suburbanite."

"You don't have supermarkets?"

"We say grocery store."

"It's like another planet." Oscar clutched his forehead. "How will I ever adapt?"

Dad passed me a silky envelope. "Nearly forgot. Nora sends her apologies, etcetera, can't make it to the museum tonight, says you should go in her place."

I turned the envelope over, panic rising. "Did she say why—?"

But Dad was talking over me, one hand on Oscar's shoulder. "*You* go."

Oscar's face went slack. "Um. What are . . . ?"

"I'm out of pocket tonight. Erich Fuller's in town, I've got to ferry him to Jean Georges, and . . . what is it, an exhibit preview?"

I frowned. "I think so. It's at six . . ."

Dad turned to Oscar, decision made. "You'll enjoy that. And Ruby won't mind having a plus one, will you, Rooster?"

"I am very good at being a plus one," Oscar put in, catching up to the conversation. "Always one person. Never two. Rarely a fraction."

"I'm wholly impressed."

"*Wooooow*." And yet he was laughing.

Dad stared at us in faint confusion.

"Okay." My pulse jumped again as soon as I said it.

"Okay," Oscar echoed. "It's a plan."

His voice had stalled before the word *plan*—a teensy caesura. He'd meant to say *date*.

We both watched my dad tromp past. We looked at each other. Then Oscar followed him upstairs, a smile blooming on his face.

"Do you hear that?" Oscar stared at an oak branch.

He'd suggested we walk to the museum through the park, which I'd seized on as an excuse not to bother with heels. I listened now, dubious, then heard the *chuk-chuk* of a squirrel, followed by angry scrabbling as it ran farther up the tree.

Oscar started off again. "What instrument would that be?"

"The tree? The squirrel?" I glanced behind us. "A trumpet. But really small so he can hold it."

"Not what I meant." Oscar grinned.

I fake-whispered, "I got that."

"I'm . . . writing this piece." He looked uncharacteristically sheepish. "A symphony. I think it'll be about coming here, experiencing this, whatever happens."

Oscar gazed out at the afternoon light bathing Central Park in orange, like this—walking to the Met—was the first movement of his autobiographical symphony.

I stared with him. "So you're taking that whole 'what is your piece about' thing pretty literally, then."

"Extremely, yeah. I'm playing with that idea of Richard Strauss's, that you can capture experience through sound, each faucet drip, each clink of a fork . . ."

"You're putting *forks* in your symphony?"

"Maybe!" Now he laughed. "If forks become important, they'll go in there. Maybe I'll be eating and somebody chokes at the next table—"

"You're hoping for this."

"Or I taste the most incredible dessert of my life, or I start falling in love . . ."

"What does a fork sound like?"

"Violins," he said, like it was obvious. "Plucked—plink, plink, plink*plink*plink."

I could hear it. Oh my God, he was a terrible singer, but still.

"Depends how fast you're eating. And then the murmur of the restaurant underneath, a steady pulse, that city sound . . . woodwinds."

"You know the 'city sound'?" I grinned. "You've been here less than a week."

"I got it right away. It's different from DC, even." Oscar's eyes met mine drowsily. "Maybe it takes an outsider to hear it."

It didn't. I knew it by heart. I listened with him all the way to Fifth Avenue.

This music didn't bother me. It was my autobiography too.

11.

In the cavernous calm of the Met's Great Hall, closed to all tonight except elite donors and their guests, everyone's well-shod footsteps echoed in a different key. I heard bits of chatter fragmenting, bouncing directionless.

"Extremely intuitive therapist, probably psychic . . ."

"Seven figures. Could have been low eight if they'd timed it better."

"Obviously water's the next big commodity."

"Off the hook. All day. I need a dog as an excuse to leave . . ."

I glanced at Oscar—his eyes were cast upward, staring at the marble multi-domed ceiling, but judging by his perplexed smile, he was eavesdropping too. His eyes dropped to mine and lit up, a shared joke. *What* were we doing here? I bit the corner of my lip to keep from laughing.

An elderly docent motioned the herd around a corner to an exhibition gallery, where a man in blue-framed glasses was speaking into a microphone about the large black-and-white photograph of a Native American woman on the wall behind him.

"Note the use of triangles, the light here and against the facial planes . . ." He pointed, but all I could see were squint lines, resigned shoulders, a woman who didn't want to be stared at. I looked away.

Oscar had drifted idly back into the Great Hall, peering up at the balcony bar above. A few Artemis Circle guests were up there holding cocktails, waiters circulating with canapés.

A string trio was setting up in the near corner. Two violins and a cello.

"Party or art?" I asked Oscar.

"Ah, the eternal question." He smiled. Didn't answer it.

I could start to see myself getting into the art side—lines, form, working to preserve history, culture. *Passion* wasn't the right word, but I could make a philanthropic impact here without it rending my soul apart. Which was, you know, a plus.

Actual mingling, though? Not without Nora.

A noise from above made my head instinctively tilt to watch the string trio tune, plunk, nod, launch into song—Vivaldi . . . no, Corelli.

The music fell around us, a shower, and Oscar and I turned to catch it like we were dying of thirst. The music sang of spring, renewal, young things growing and sparking and daring and flying. Brilliant things. *Genius.*

Pain dug into my throat and spread roots. Love it all I wanted, it wasn't mine.

The people in the gallery were looking at me. Even if they weren't, they were *averting* their eyes, and the music was still playing, and—

"How 'bout neither."

I blinked. Oscar's hands were in his pockets, casual, but there was something careful in his expression.

"Neither?"

He leaned closer. "Do you think we have the run of the place?"

"I don't know," I whispered back, my shoulders loosening slightly as our conversation drowned out Corelli. "Nobody's said we *don't.*"

Oscar's eyes narrowed mischievously. They darted from me to the sign reading *Egyptian Art.*

I grinned.

He offered his arm and I took it, gliding with Oscar in a pas de deux away from the music, away from the party, my body finally releasing the moment we rounded a corner and the sound behind us dropped away.

We broke slowly apart as we strolled the silent aisles of antiquities, stone sarcophagi, glass cases full of tiny ornate tools, textile fragments, reconstructed pottery. Oscar veered from one to the next in a looping dance, walking backward to grin at me, eyes crinkling.

I grinned back. "*Okay,* rebel. Be careful."

"I'm not gonna break the art, Ruby." He let his hand linger centimeters over a stone tablet, as if waiting to see if I'd squeal. "So. Serious."

"You have some impulse control issues, don't you?"

"Believe me." He shot me a sidelong glance. "There are plenty of impulses I'm controlling."

That made me go warm. "You're like some wild creature."

"Wild? Creature?" he scoffed, leading us idly into the great glass sunroom housing the Temple of Dendur. "*I'm* gonna choose to believe that isn't an unconscious racial signifier . . ."

I stopped walking. "Are we seriously talking semiotics right now? That's something that's happening?"

"Oh, it's happening." He strolled backward along the reflecting pond, grinning shamelessly at me. "Nice pivot."

I shook my head, smiling back like a goon. "I solemnly swear it was not a comment on your—"

"I mean, you live in New York, you're way above that, right? You must know two or three black people already. Maybe four."

"I know *a lot* of black people!" *And* all the blood drained from my face at the sound of my voice echoing through the hall. I kept walking, straight into the temple itself, like I could entomb myself here to escape mortification.

Oscar stepped in beside me. "You're listing them, aren't you? In your head. That's how many black friends you have, you can list them in your head."

"Stop!" I fought not to laugh. "Okay, just so you'll shut up— Walter, Bernice, Darian, Maya, Erika, Lenox, Jacie. Seven current black friends."

He considered, nodding. "Not bad. Better than I expected."

I put my face in my hands. "I feel dirty right now."

"As well you should." His voice was soft.

He reached up to gently unfold my hands from my eyes. When I blinked up at him, his face held a wholly new expression. Not teasing. Just open—so himself that it made everything in my body go perfectly quiet.

"I like you, Ruby. More than I probably should."

I suddenly felt terrified to look at him. I let my eyes drift to neatly etched graffiti on the temple wall, *AMATO,* left by some continental tourist centuries before we were born . . .

"I've known you for a weekend, but I like you," he said. "I like how hard you try to be serious and how bad you are at it. I like that you know what *semiotics* means."

I let out a whispery laugh, daring myself to glance up at him. His eyes found mine and locked into place.

"I like that you're the one touching the art right now," he said—and I realized I actually was. I'd been tracing *AMATO* without realizing.

I started to draw my hand back, but he laid his own on top of mine instead. Breath held, I lifted my fingers to let him slip his own in between. I felt every edge where our skin met, heat racing up my arm, along my spine.

That's us, I marveled, staring at our hands as he leaned closer.

I looked up. "I like you t—"

"Excuse me," a middle-aged security guard shouted from the far doorway.

Oscar and I shuffled apart, hands locked tight by our sides as we stepped out of the temple.

"This area's off limits for tonight, folks." The guard's voice was carefully neutral, in case we were major donors.

"Sorry," I mumbled as we made our way past him. The guard grunted.

"Couldn't resist," Oscar said—and that got a chuckle out of him.

We went as fast as we could without running through the Egyptian Wing, taking a wrong turn into Arms and Armor. Oscar eyed a Mongolian display curiously, but I tugged him away, whispering, "Let's not press our luck."

We clip-clopped through the empty Great Hall, burst into the humid dusk air, then trotted down the stone steps in synchronized rhythm. When we got to the bottom, our shadows preceded us, monumental, glowing at the edges, like we'd grown into gods while we were inside.

"We should get dinner." The careful cadence of Oscar's voice told me he was asking for something more.

"Sounds good." I twisted a loose thread on my dress. "What are you in the—?"

"Oscar!"

It took me a few seconds to adjust to the incongruity of Dad's voice coming from a parked Bentley at the curb. I turned to see him leaning out of the back window.

"I've got to steal your date, Rooster," Dad said, winking before turning back to a stunned Oscar. "Johann Wittenstein. Conductor at the phil."

Oscar nodded quickly. "I know, he's one of my—"

"Wants you to shadow tonight."

"Oh my God." Oscar scrunched his hands in his hair.

"I've been trying to reach you." Dad squinted between us.

I winced. "My phone's on silent. I thought it was more ... polite ..."

"Mine too," Oscar said, rubbing his face.

"Never mind, we'll make it." Dad opened the car door and stepped out. "Slide on in. Erich, make some room, would you?"

Oscar turned to me, mouthing, "*Erich Fuller?*"

My dad's weird German friend. Most important minimalist composer in history.

I shrugged wildly and motioned him off. "This is awesome, go!"

"Aren't you—?" Oscar glanced at the car.

I smiled softly, knowing better. "No room for me. I'll catch you later."

Oscar, flummoxed, disappeared into the car, hand extended to introduce himself.

Dad waved to me as he got in with them. "Thanks for being a good sport."

"No worries," I said to the empty sidewalk as they sped away.

Then I made my way back across the park, listening to every tree rustle, every bike click, every heartbeat along the way, wondering what it would sound like in a song.

The music woke me up—slower, sadder, sweeter, higher. It danced around the first one like a firefly.

I grabbed my phone. Two a.m.

"Oscar," I groaned, half laughing as I buried my face in the pillow. "This is unacceptable."

I went to shut my window, but found myself closing my eyes instead. He was playing with the tune—not finding it, trying a deceptive cadence, a more prosaic resolution in a minor key. Then starting over. *Almost right . . . almost . . .*

I threw a cardigan over my camisole and pajama bottoms, slipped into flip-flops, hurried downstairs.

It had started drizzling. I ducked my head and sprinted around the corner to knock on his door.

It opened immediately. Oscar turned back into the apartment like he'd been expecting me.

"Come in, you're getting wet." He laughed, seeing me hesitate. I ducked inside and he reached out to wipe beaded raindrops from my hair. "I want to play you something."

It's too late at night. Just tell him to turn it down.

But my mouth was too busy gaping at the scene in front of me— our studio, transformed. His dorm bed, jutting from one side of the room, was unmade and rumpled. He appeared to be using the desk to hold the entire stacked contents of his luggage, while the roller bags served as nightstands, glasses of water perched precariously on top of each. Against the other wall, a sofa looked like a composition book had exploded onto it. The pages were brimming with music, some markings pristine, others almost violently scribbled out.

"Sorry. Just . . ." Oscar walked to a bare spot on the far wall, near the galley kitchen, then slid sitting and patted the spot beside him on the floor. "I'd clean the couch, but I've got all the pages the way I want them . . ."

I peeked as I passed, too furtive to get any real impression. I sat beside him, half hoping it wasn't as completely out of my league as I suspected it would be.

His AC unit was turned off, the window open above it, which explained both the noise and the fact that it was so insanely warm in here.

I watched as he futzed with his phone. He was wearing an undershirt and the nice gray dress pants he'd had on at the Met. His belt was on the floor. He must have slowly shed his outfit when he got home before getting distracted by the tune in his head.

"Okay, here," he said, and music started to play from small speakers I hadn't noticed, framing the far side of the room. "There's an app for this too!" He grinned, then put a finger to his lips like I was the one who'd been talking.

I primed myself with a polite smile, but the music was . . . not his. It was *Daphnis et Chloé*.

I peered over at him again. He had his eyes closed. This was what he wanted me to listen to? A hundred-year-old ballet?

My shoulders relaxed. Worse ways to spend an evening than listening to some Ravel. Especially this, the best part, the "*Lever du jour*."

It opened with woodwinds percolating—a sylvan glade, alive with birdsong. Strings slid along in the background, a breeze. I smiled in recognition as the bass line crept in, rumbling slowly higher as dawn started to break.

And then more than dawn. Heat, longing. The sense of a body . . . waking up. A tiny tremor rippled through me at the rising sound.

The gentle melody swelled and strained. Beside me, I could hear Oscar let out a slow sigh, his hands falling to rest beside mine on the cool floor. Not touching. An inch away.

Voices joined in, a wordless chorus, and the strings became sweet, pleading, everything swirling into absolute ecstasy. You didn't need to have seen the ballet to recognize the moment of connection—Daphnis and Chloé discovering each other.

I closed my eyes. Oscar's fingers slipped gently onto mine. The music dwindled into a burbling hush, the oboe's refrain pierced by violin. And then it ended, that final note lingering, unresolved . . .

My head lolled on the wall, facing Oscar. He was looking at me. We both laughed, a little breathless.

"There's something in this. Something I'm trying to get at. The way it gets into your bloodstream."

"The park? Is that what you're trying to put into sound? I . . ."

"Not the park." He watched me, fingers still tangled in mine. "Something else."

"Play it for me." And I meant it. I couldn't believe it, but I did. I had to hear his piece.

He swallowed, eyes flicking away, returning. "I hate this keyboard. I need a piano . . . I can play it for you in the—"

I grabbed his hand tighter. "Now."

He frowned. "Your dad . . ."

My mouth grazed his ear. "We can be quiet."

He wasn't breathing now and neither was I. Then, abruptly, he stood, pulling me up with him. We raced for the door, up into the cool rain, up to my stoop, where I fumbled for keys in my cardigan pocket.

He pulled me to the piano bench and physically sat me beside him, like he needed me that close. Then he raised the cover, pressed his fingers to the keyboard, and began to play.

It wasn't quiet. But once it started, I didn't want it to be. It was too gorgeous. The melody came in—I knew it by heart by now—solid as flesh, and then the countermelody, a firefly sweeping over it, inside it, below it . . . and then he stopped.

"That's all I've got so far."

Our knees were touching.

"What do you think?" he whispered, his expression almost pained.

I let one of my hands rise to his shoulder while the other found his fingers on the keyboard. "You know what I think."

My eyelids shut, all systems down. I felt his slow drift, the heat of him—

The light came on.

Dad. Garden of Eden angry. He was going to smite us where we sat.

Oscar jumped up, smashing the keyboard with a clang. "Marty . . . sir, I—"

Dad raised his hand, silencing him. "What were you playing?"

"It . . ." Oscar glanced at me. I froze, just as thrown. "It was what I've been working on. The start of this piece. I've been trying to . . . Ruby's been helping me . . ."

I slunk off the bench, arms crossed tight, wondering when Dad was going to look at me.

But his shock had already cleared. He was shaking his head. Clapping slowly. Crossing the room with his arm extended to draw Oscar in.

"This is *remarkable*. This is . . . This needs to be . . ." Dad ran a hand through his white hair, then his beard, waking himself up the way he did first thing in the morning. Then he snapped his fingers and pointed. "There's a general meeting tomorrow. We'll have donors there, alums, Nora, Bill. I want you to come. Play this for them."

"It's fifty bars . . ."

Dad was leading Oscar to the front door. "It's the start. It's more than a start, you've cracked it, kid. You get some sleep now." He opened the door and eased Oscar out. "You'll need to be your usual charming self tomorrow. Don't worry about anything."

Oscar looked over his shoulder at me, but I couldn't read the expression in his eyes. The door shut behind him.

I waited for Dad to look at me, but he was staring at Mom's piano like she was sitting there. When he turned to me, his eyes were so pained that I took a step back.

"You look like . . ." he started, but swallowed hard, like he was tasting poison.

I dropped my hands, watching.

"I remember when you first sat at that piano." He motioned vaguely, the height of my shoulders. "You were so little. Just . . . tiny."

He turned slowly, sleepwalking back upstairs, lost in his own thoughts again.

And I stayed below, staring at Mom's Steinway, trapped in mine.

12.

Sunshine blasted my eyes when I opened them.

Flat daylight.

I leaped from bed and into running gear.

Jules was sitting on her stoop texting when I got to her house, but her splotchy skin and mussed hair told me she'd already finished her run. She glanced up at me blankly, then snorted. "Two hours late? *Really.*"

"I slept in!"

"I gathered that."

"I can't believe it. I've never needed an alarm clock. I always wake up at six—"

"You don't need to give me the rundown." She stood, pocketing her phone. "Shit happens."

"I was up in the middle of the night with Oscar and I think it threw everything off."

"Oscar? The genius guy? The one you hate?"

"I don't hate him. I . . ." I swallowed. *"Really* don't hate him."

"This is very intriguing," Jules said. "I'm not being sarcastic, I am actually intrigued. But I need to take a shower before I ferment in my own sweat."

I made a face. She curtsied, holding the edges of her running shorts, then skipped to her door.

"We're going out tonight, though," she muttered over her shoulder. "I'll come get you so you don't, like, take a nap and forget to meet me here for *two freaking hours*."

She waved sweetly and disappeared into her house.

I was tempted to creep home in shame rather than venture out alone—but no. I was dressed as a runner. A runner I would be.

I maintained pace all the way to the boathouse this time. My chest felt like a giant had stomped on it, my legs were itchy, and my face felt like it had swollen, making me wonder if I was somehow allergic to exercise, but hey! Progress!

The cool-down was much better. Hypnotized by the light flickering off the pond's surface, I felt my body buzzing. Damp hair curled against the back of my neck and the city's sounds were muted, a song playing in another room.

As I walked, my mind kept snagging on Oscar. His fingers, his warmth, his *I like you,* his music, those freeze-frame moments last night when something delicious and dangerous was about to happen.

I glanced up and I was at the Alice in Wonderland statue, all the way across the park. I'd climbed it some blurry long-time-ago, a woman hovering on one of the toadstools, arms outstretched in case I fell—but had it been Mom or my nanny, Rosie? As much as my mind strained, I couldn't picture her face.

As I walked home, a text came in from Alice. *Where's Dad??*

I stopped to type. *Amberley meeting with Oscar. Everything okay?*

Just weirded out he wasn't picking up his cell

Everything from Uber to pigeons weirded Alice out. So.

Anything I can help with?

Alice wrote back: *Nope!* :)

I appreciated the extra effort of the smiley face, even if I did wonder what was up with her most of the way home.

The Ultra-Super-Duper Awesome Composer Duo came back later than expected. As I walked downstairs, dressed to go out, I could hear their voices filling the house, the force field of their excitement simultaneously drawing me in and repelling me clear across the Hudson. Oscar and Dad, in Oscar and Dad's world.

"So, what do you think?" Oscar danced onto the balls of his feet. "In-house? Workshop performance, or . . . ?"

"*The* performance!" Dad stood behind Oscar, shaking his shoulders. "Whatever you need, the school will provide. They're getting plenty from this too, so never feel bad for asking."

Oscar's eyes clouded. Then he spotted me, blue skies restored. "They liked it!"

"What did you play?" I leaned on the table. "Those fifty bars, or . . . ?"

"He played the first movement," Dad boomed. "You should have seen him."

I hadn't realized that was an option.

"He started out with that motif, described what it conveyed, the bridge, coming into the city, the Romantic theme—"

Dad meant it with a capital *R*. *Romantic*. As in the musical style.

But Oscar's shoulders drew in like Dad had said too much. "Ah. I sort of improvised from there, but . . . you know, it wasn't bad. It sketched out where I want to go with it. Minus the details, of course, and that's where the music really . . . lives . . ."

His eyes rose to meet mine.

"We're staying in to work, Rooster," Dad said, walking into the kitchen. "What do you feel like for dinner?"

I knew Dad well enough to know what that meant: What do you feel like *getting* me for dinner? It had never annoyed me before, but it did now—so the knock that sounded on the door, right on cue, felt extra satisfying.

"I'm heading out, actually."

Oscar glanced at me, shoulders slumping.

Dad popped his head out of the kitchen, quizzical, like he'd heard me wrong.

"I've sort of reconnected with Jules—do you remember Jules?" He looked even blanker. "Julie Russo? Our neighbor?"

"The ten-year-old?"

I laughed. "She's not ten anymore. Neither am I, by the way."

Oscar fought a smile as he headed to the front door. The second he opened it, Jules strode through, holding a sequined top out to me.

"Try this," she said, then glanced over her shoulder at Oscar. "I'm Jules, nice to meet you."

"Oh," he said, "I'm—"

"Hi, Mr. Chertok!" she shouted into the kitchen. "Long time no see."

"You look the same," Dad said, which made Jules and me exchange a delighted giggle, before she pulled me up the stairs like she was the one who lived here. She remembered exactly where my room was.

"Strip," she said, as soon as I shut the door.

I raised my eyebrows. "Are you hitting on me?"

"Don't you wish. We're just in a hurry. Everybody's already there and my phone is going to break from all the pissy texts I'm getting."

I slipped the shirt on over the black dress shorts I was wearing.

"Do you have a vest or something?"

I winced a "huh now?" as she played with my messy braid.

"Never mind, this is fine, he'll like it, let's go."

"He'll . . . *what*?" I flushed, thinking of Joey. Logistically speaking, last time couldn't have been a setup, but what about tonight?

Jules trotted down the steps ahead of me. "Aren't you inviting him?"

I only had enough time to put "him" and "Oscar" together, a thrill shooting through me, before Jules waltzed past the study—its door still open—poked her head in and called out, "You coming tonight or what?"

"Oh. Um." He was sitting at Dad's piano, Dad nowhere in sight. The toilet flushed down the hall. Oscar looked at me. "I didn't know there was a tonight to come to."

"Well, you should. If you want." I turned to Jules. "Same place?"

She shrugged a yes.

I pivoted back to Oscar. "Yeah, so this club . . . it's meh, it's fine, and the music's really bad, but if you want to come, you should?"

"Sounds *amazing*," Oscar said, grinning. He played a lightning-quick arpeggio. *Show-off.* "Gotta work, though."

"Right."

"The symphony's in the performance calendar, no going back, so I've got to . . . yeah." Oscar looked woozy.

"If you change your mind, text Ruby!" Jules linked elbows with me to drag us both down the steps, whispering, "Jesus, *nerd love*, spare me. I can see why you're into him, though. He's intense."

I trailed her out to the sidewalk. "Intense?"

Maybe she meant it in the sense of, like, *intense* sunshine, but the word out of context sounded like a synonym for *tortured*.

Jules stood in the middle of the road, apparently trying to hail a taxi by forcing it not to hit her. "Those *eyes*. He looks at you like he's staring deep into your soul."

I scrunched my nose, wondering frantically whether she meant he looked at *me* that way, or more of a general "you." In which case I'd been misreading him; I'd been acting the way everybody probably acted around Oscar Bell.

I was at the very least determined to distract myself for one night while hanging out with my brand-new social circle in our super-lame-but-didn't-card clubhouse.

"Hey!" Joey said, jumping up from a conversation with Sam to wave at me. "Figured out your future yet?"

"Not yet," I said, flopping down on my own banquette.

It wasn't a lie. The best thing about the Met event had been the part when I was hiding from it. Maybe I wasn't cut out for that particular brand of socialization. Or maybe I just needed more time with Nora . . .

"I'll pick your future!" Sam clapped, pulling herself up from a slouch. "Mmm . . . *zoologist*!"

I laughed. "Okay, I *get* that, but I don't think I could deal with the poop."

Her eyes filled with horror. "Oh God, I never even thought of that."

Tyler appeared from nowhere to hand me some sort of red drink on the rocks with two tiny straws sticking out of it. I thanked him and sipped. It tasted like cough syrup. When nobody was looking, I left it on a bar table as I walked with them to the dance floor.

My phone buzzed with an incoming call. I ducked to the side of the already crowded room and took a peek. Unfamiliar number . . . Maryland area code?

Then a text came in. *Your dad gave me your number so we could meet up.*

Then, a few seconds later: *Or not. Either way.*

Then, as I was trying to type back . . . *This is Oscar. Should have said that first.*

Reading these texts made me feel like a hot-air balloon.

I replied with the cross streets and he wrote back: *On my way.*

My heart started pounding louder than the music. I blinked at Jules over the thumbnail I was biting. She waved for me to come dance but I couldn't do more than pace, glancing compulsively at the door. Then I remembered the bouncer and ran out to wait on the sidewalk.

The street was busy. A taxi stopped down the block and I started toward it, but it was a middle-aged couple with a cat in a carrier. Somebody touched my shoulder and I turned, clutching my chest.

"I couldn't work," Oscar said, smile flickering. "Couldn't concentrate."

The ultimate compliment.

"We go this way," I said.

The doorman was nice enough to make a show of examining a piece of gum stuck to the sidewalk as I took Oscar's hand and led him into the back alley. There was a line tonight. God knew why.

"Are you gonna mug me?" Oscar asked.

"Maybe."

He'd dressed up. Black tee, gray pants, almost enough to make him look like a New Yorker. The gleam in his eye gave him away, though, the way he took in everything—dingy back door, dumpster, fire escape ladder—like he'd just dropped into Oz.

And then his eyes crash-landed on me—and burst into flames. This couldn't possibly be an everyone thing. He reached out to tease one of my curls loose from my braid, letting it bounce against his finger.

My breath got stuck. I stepped back, swept the hair nervously back into place, and opened the "VIP entrance," waving for him to walk through.

The music was deafening as we reached the dance floor. I tried to ask him if he wanted a drink, although I wasn't sure how you procured such a thing, but he was already heading for the center of the crowd.

Jules spotted him and gave him a hug, like they were best friends, then shot me this icy "What the hell is wrong with you" glare. Then, to make it even clearer, she mouthed, *"Come! Dance!"*

I edged my way through the crowd, jostled on all sides, wondering anew what the appeal of this was.

When I reached Oscar, he pressed his hand to the small of my back, as if to balance me, and bent to shout-whisper, "You were right! This music is terrible!"

"Right?"

They were playing some generic song with lyrics that went, *"Grind up, gotta grind up, you know you grind up on meeeeee."* And repeat.

Oscar was barely bobbing to the music, his expression distant but intent, like he was taking the beat seriously. Then he caught me staring, eyes bright, and leaned in to explain. "There's *something*. I don't know. There's something good about this."

"What?"

"I'm still looking for it!"

His arm tightened around my waist as the crowd closed in behind me, some drunk twenty-something girls jumping up and down, scattering the other dancers. My hips hit Oscar's, flush, practically connected. He looked at me as if asking if this was okay. I didn't know how to dance with someone else—or, um, at all—but I let my arms drape over his shoulders.

We were one unit now, protected against the crowd, a bubble all our own. And yet this felt more dangerous than a million drunk jumping girls in spiky stilettos.

"*Grind up on meeeee*" went the music, and then the beat overlaid and shifted, the DJ segueing into another track.

Oscar's warmth fell over me as he started to move us—not a dance so much as a sway with a downbeat. *This* I could understand. The lights hit his face in scattered time, turning him from brown to blue, then fuchsia, then yellow, then himself, as sweaty bodies moved around us in a humming blur.

His fingers shifted along my lower back, traveling up my spine. My pulse went staccato and part of me wanted to run—this was insane. This was inevitable, and that was the craziest part.

I stood on my tiptoes instead, drawing him closer, as we shifted with the music. The beat, drop, beat-beat, the treble horns, closer, closer, the space between us getting smaller and smaller until the gaps between us felt physically painful.

His thumb traced my jawline, drawing my head up. His eyes asked permission. Mine gave it. And his mouth slid down onto mine.

Our lips barely grazed at first, light and warm, but in the next gasping breath, they opened and we gave in.

It didn't feel like a free fall so much as a landing, being caught, exhilaration and relief mixing in one heady rush. He tasted sweet, like cherries laced with something new, salty and intoxicating. Someone bumped us from the side and we broke apart, foreheads touching while we breathed, and then I craned my head up again, thirsty for more. *Finally, finally.*

This kiss was deeper, faster, the taste of him even stranger. I clutched the back of his shirt with one hand, my other grazing his cloud of hair. His mouth, those full lips roved to kiss my jawline, my neck, my collarbone with a low groan that ricocheted through me.

Then he laughed, his exhalation warm on my shoulder. "I can't believe this is happening."

I couldn't either. But something about the way he'd said that, out loud, rattled me a little. I stared at the dance floor lights above us, blinking up at them like it would shake some sense into my brain. Then his hips moved against mine, a one-degree turn, and I was kissing him again. I couldn't stop.

"Hey now," Jules said from behind me. "Having fun?"

I startled alert and turned back, arms still laced around Oscar's neck.

"I'm going to the bathroom." She pulled my shirt so I would follow.

I winced at Oscar as I pulled away. He seemed too dazed to take it in.

The bathroom was packed with girls. Jules leaned against a stall door, fixing her hair in the square inch of mirror her reflection could squeeze into.

"So," she said. "You work fast."

"I did not expect that to happen."

Jules arched her eyebrows, not buying it. Of *course* I'd expected this. From the moment I saw him standing in my living room playing my piano, some part of me was waiting for it—and the other part was still shocked that he would want to. I wasn't *that girl*. I was . . .

"So is this a controlling-the-situation type deal?" Jules asked, sliding into a vacant stall and shutting the door.

"What do you mean?"

"He's this genius, taking all your dad's attention, you know, all the shit you told me the other day, so you're going to get the upper hand by seducing him. That old song and dance."

I stumbled into the dryer. "No! That . . . that's, no. What—do you mean, like, I'm sabotaging him?"

"Ooh, I like that word." She flushed the toilet and came out, squeezing past the line to wash her hands. "If not that, then what?"

"I . . . I have no idea." *I like him, he's everything I'm not and I should resent the very fact of him, but I like him so much.* "I have no idea why I'm doing this." *He's brilliant and hot and vivid and funny and . . .* "It's stupid and reckless and not me at all. I just can't seem to help myself."

The strangers at the sinks turned to look at me. Something like respect bloomed in Jules's expression.

"Makes sense," she said. "Sounds like me and Ty. Lord knows why I even return his calls. 'I can't seem to help myself.' I like it."

Tyler was waiting outside the door. Apparently he couldn't help himself either. She beamed at him, slinking under his outstretched arm, then turned to wink at me.

"Have fun, use protection."

My cheeks prickled. I glanced at my shirt, tugging the neckline up. It was too crowded. Too many older guys staring at me. Too loud, too sticky, too chaotic.

I scanned the dance floor for Oscar from a distance, nervous to jump back in—to everything—but I couldn't find him.

Sam walked up, playing with her purple hair.

"Outside," she shouted past my ear. It took me a second to realize she was talking to me. "You can probably catch him."

I walked out slowly, wondering whether he'd thought better of this and ditched me. Maybe then my stomach would stop this aching swirl, my skin would settle to a normal level of sensitivity, and I could get on with figuring out the rest of my life. But he was waiting by the curb, staring out into the street—and hot relief flooded my veins.

I touched his elbow, carefully, reestablishing all the broken boundaries.

"Hey," he said, turning to me. "Sorry about that."

"About what?"

"It got a little much. That place. Do you . . . do you maybe want to head home? Or you can stay, I'll—"

I tentatively reached for his cheek, cupping it in my palm, then stood on my toes and kissed him again before I had time to make a conscious decision about whether it was a good idea. He wrapped his arms around me, tilting his head to deepen it, and I closed my eyes and melted against him, my leg drifting around his to get closer—then he jerked back.

I opened my eyes to see his arm waving into the street, hailing a cab. It had its light on but kept going.

I laughed. "Didn't want us making out in the back."

Oscar pinched the end of my braid and said, "You try."

I flagged the next one as he stepped back. It pulled up right away.

"See?" I grinned at Oscar and slid inside. "Seventy-first and Central Park West."

As we rumbled uptown in bursts and jerky stops, I tried my best not to fall into that late-night club girl cliché. But Oscar's mouth had found the curve of my neck and started exploring and there was not one cell in my body willing to stop him.

I managed to break out of this hot haze long enough to hear the driver murmur something about near corner or far corner, to answer, "Here's fine," to pay, exit, immediately start making out with Oscar again.

I stood on the corner, incapacitated by rapture, dimly noticing the crosswalk light flash and go solid. I kissed him and my feet didn't know how to move anymore. My eyes didn't know how to blink.

When the light changed again, Oscar pulled me across the street by my fingertips, gliding backward. When we got to the far sidewalk, I tucked myself under his arm and he kissed the top of my head like we'd been dating for three years and this was our routine.

We stopped outside my place—*our* place, Jesus—and I slid my hands over his taut waist, around to his back, tilting my chin for more.

But he drew away, eyes hesitant. "I guess I should have considered this earlier . . ."

My skin went hot. How far did he think we would take this tonight?

"Um. Is your dad gonna be okay with this? You . . . and me . . ." He peered up at the darkened windows of the townhouse.

My mind spun, stopped, spun in the other direction. "Why would he care?"

"His daughter. I mean, you're a *Chertok*, and I'm . . ." Oscar stepped back, out of reach, running his hands over his hair. "Do you know how he might feel about this? The thing is, I *really* don't want to cross a line and mess up what I've got going with him. This mentorship. It's pretty much the best thing that's ever happened to me and—"

"Oh." *Oh. Oh. Oh.* I crossed my arms, my skin blanketing with goose bumps, the sidewalk glazing ice-solid, leaves falling dead from the trees. "Honestly, I don't think it's a problem, certainly not one I've ever butted up against before, ha, but . . ."

What was I *thinking*, hijacking him like this? I should have stuck with the original plan, dust sheets, blinders on. I was not why he was here and he was—

"Wait." Oscar reached out. "Ruby . . ."

I stepped up. Onto my stoop. "No, you're right! We—we shouldn't. This summer's so important. For you, and . . . yeah. Tonight was fun, but it's cool, I completely get it! Have a good night."

I hurried into the house before the careful, casual expression on my face could melt into sludge.

Then I stood with my back against the closed door, heart thudding, brain a stuck dance track, shouting, *What. Did. You. Just. Do.*

13.

Jules looked surprised to find me waiting when she trotted down the front steps of her building in running gear the next morning.

"Thought you'd be *sleeping in*," she said, making it sound filthy. She stooped to pick up an ankle and bend it to her butt.

I tried to copy her, wobbled, gave up. "No, I had a hard time sleeping and—"

"Does he snore?" A grin broke through her poker face.

I whacked her with the back of my hand. "Shut up! I slept alone. Totally alone." My throat went tight. "Anyway, I need a run."

A wild gesture from an oncoming pedestrian drew my attention— Sam, of all people, jogging comically toward us, dressed in a cobbled collection of regular clothes that kind of looked like you could exercise in them, complete with a pair of beat-up Chucks.

The unfair thing was, of the three of us, she looked like the real runner.

"I've been curious!" she chirped. "I wanna try it too."

"Yay!" I clapped.

"Let's do it," Jules said, action-hero serious, then took off down the block the wrong way, Sam following at a slower trot.

"Um."

"Riverside!" Jules shouted back. "Mixing it up!"

It took the crosswalk light for me to catch them, and the effort of launching myself into a sprint nearly did me in. My head throbbed—lack of sleep doing me no favors—and my legs felt rusty and sore, underused and overtaxed at the same time.

My body *hurt*. It was the best distraction I could have asked for.

By the time we passed the Seventy-second Street dog run and continued under the thundering parkway, lights danced at the corners of my vision—but I pushed on. If I stopped, my brain would restart, repeating the events of last night, including how it had ended. Not only that, but if I wasn't running, I'd have to return home, risking an *encounter*. So I outpaced Sam and chased Jules's ponytail up the wide concrete path, dazzled by the light reflecting off the Hudson.

This park always felt like the edge of a snow globe to me, like if I tried to swim out, I would hit a glass wall and have to come back. I'd left the city plenty, of course, traveling with Dad or Mom to events, from Teatro Colón to Royal Albert Hall to the Sydney Opera House, or down south to see the grandfolks, but never by myself. Alone, I felt bound to this island. I tracked the edge of the imagined glass as I ran.

By the time we got to the boat basin, my lungs had started to sting so much, the pain went white and vanished. Was this runner's high? It felt more like runner's anesthesia.

"Hey!"

I glanced back to see Jules stopping beside a bench. How had I gotten ahead of her? The second I slowed, my knees decomposed into jelly. I walked back to her like a drunk person pretending to be sober.

"Look at you," she called out, palms clamped against her legs while she caught her breath. "Don't injure yourself."

"I won't." I fell sitting beside her. "I think . . . I'm done for today."

"Good. I only run like that when I'm pissed off. And then I don't know when to say when." She pulled her hair from its ponytail, mussed it peevishly, put it back in. Then she turned to me. "So?"

"So . . . what?" I winced. My lungs were stinging again.

"What are you pissed about? Did something happen last night, besides what half the city got to witness?"

I wiped my face, annoyed that she was bringing it up—even more annoyed that I'd given her a reason to. "I don't know what that was. I think it's already over."

"You *do* move fast."

"Not because of me. He . . . Oscar's worried it'll mess up the work he's doing with my dad, which is fair enough." I untied and retied my shoe for no reason. "This whole thing started *and* ended because he thinks I'm a Chertok, or whatever, like my family, and I get that, and I'm supposed to be finding a way out of that world, that's what this summer was for, so . . . it was going to fizzle at some point anyway. It's completely fine!"

"*Double* back. *Re*wind." Jules's eyes narrowed. "You really think that's why he's into you? Because of musical ability? Or are you actually just talking about your last name?"

"Both, but not on a conscious level." I motioned vaguely in the air. "More a *pull* kind of thing."

"A star-fucker thing." She winced. "Sorry, that was crass. Potty mouth."

"I am not a star. So."

"You're a classical music princess." She shrugged. "Still twinkly."

The word *princess* felt a million times crasser than what she'd said before. I stared at my lap, but she leaned her head way over so I would see her.

"Maybe he just *likes* you, Ruby. Did you think of that?"

"I . . . have considered the possibility?" I gripped my knees. "It's just, it's not something I've in any way earned. If somebody like Oscar is into me, it needs to be because I've achieved something. Preferably something incredible."

"Cool, cool. Yeah, I take it back, you are *way* too weird to be a princess. So. Freaking. Bizarre!"

I laughed. "I am working hard to spin this conversation as a friendly one."

"Dude, I'm just trying to *follow* it!" She squinted at me. "You don't think you deserve love unless you, like, cure cancer? Or are we still talking about playing an instrument really well, which is . . . I *guess* an achievement?"

I let the jab about music slide. "It's not about deserving. It's about *earning*."

"You literally just gave me a synonym for *deserving*."

I knew I sounded ridiculous, but this felt important. I thought of Oscar—all that brilliance, all that work—and me, everything just *there*, at my feet.

The very first memory I'd replayed this morning was that taxi bypassing Oscar. And me, blithely flagging the next one, painfully clueless.

He deserved more. Better.

Jules was still looking at me, exasperated. She was never going to accept that answer.

"I don't know what I think. I just know . . ." I heaved a cheerful sigh. "That I am not going to figure it out after running that far. My brain is mushy. *Twinkly* mushy."

"Fair enough, mine too." She stood, offering me a hand up. "Listen, back to a conversation I can understand, that Oscar guy seems cool and God knows you two looked into each other, but there are plenty of guys out there who would fall all over themselves to be with you, okay? This is all I'm saying. It is *not* that complicated."

I smiled. "Thank you."

"My guess is that he's holding a boom box up to your window even as we speak, *but* on the off chance he isn't . . . this isn't exactly the best time for you to be in a relationship, right? So maybe keeping it platonic is—"

"What?"

She walked over to lean on the guardrail, peering out to the river. "You just broke up with your first love. You need to rebound before you can move on to something real."

I understood a beat too slowly. She meant the piano, of course. My first love. It wasn't that overblown a metaphor, because when I thought about it—recognized it—my heart started to hurt in a way that had nothing to do with exercising.

Jules was watching me with sympathetic eyes when a tangle of arms and legs flapped its way toward us so gracelessly that it took me a second to realize it was Sam.

"This! Is! Not! Fun!" she screamed. "What is the *matter* with you two?"

"I sort of agree," I said.

"Come on," Jules said, linking arms with both of us. "Let's undo this run with some doughnuts."

I was laughing when the three of us got back to our block, sugar glaze sticky on my lips. Sam was trying to catch us up on five seasons of this show *Triplecross*, playing every role in quick time, oblivious to all the pedestrians glancing back at her as we walked by.

"And then Chase Hernandez came out in real life? And they made his character bi to boost the ratings? And it was *awesome* because it turned out he'd been screwing the douchebag guy the whole time and they were the masterminds behind like everything from season one on. It's a terrible show."

Jules slowed down, pointing at my house, and whispered, "*What* did I tell you."

Oscar was sitting on the stoop. Spotting us, he stood, and I was so paralyzed that it took me a second to see that he was holding a bouquet of multicolored carnations.

"Awwww," Jules cooed under her breath. "How tacky!"

I kicked backward at her. Accidentally got Sam.

Jules patted my butt as they passed me. "We'll leave you to it." Then turned around to mouth, "*I'm psychic.*"

Oscar stepped into the middle of the sidewalk, owning it as always, pedestrians parting instinctively around him.

"I heard a rumor you thought flowers were a nice gesture?" He held the bouquet out.

I took it, examining each petal closely. "Don't let Win find out. He'll mock you forever. *Not* that this is a first date. I . . . yeah."

"No. Right." Oscar stuck his hands in the pockets of his navy-blue shorts. "This is more of an apology bouquet."

"Carnations, yes, the universal symbol for—"

"Acting like an asshole." He grimaced. "I've ruined the flowers."

"No!" I laughed, too loud. "They're great. I'm going to put them in some water."

"Hey, before you do that . . ." He cleared his throat. "Or . . . *after* I guess—there's this thing I have to be back for later, but I have the morning off while your dad's notating the Mahler . . ."

Oh, right, I remembered dimly. *He's guest conducting in London next week.*

"And I was wondering if you'd mind helping me fill it. The morning, not the Mahler, although I'm supposed to work on that at some point too."

I froze on the bottom step. *He means it platonically.* "Sure, great! What do you feel like doing? We could hit the park, go downtown, grab dim sum . . . ?"

"I'd like to talk, actually. If that's okay."

"Of course."

"Could we go someplace, um . . . quiet?"

Instead of an inner debate, I felt a still, calm certainty. Of all people, he would understand why I loved it so much. Even just as friends, I was ready to share it.

I smiled. "I know someplace very quiet."

14.

Oscar didn't ask where we were going. We rounded the corner onto a side street full of antiques shops and low-rise office buildings. Walking by the mid-point at a New York pace, you'd think the buildings were connected via a narrow alley, nothing of note. But if you *really* looked, you'd see mosaic tiles and, a few feet in, a wider space beyond.

I led Oscar into that space.

My courtyard. I had no legal claim on it, but it was mine all the same, sweet and simple, framed by low buildings with overflowing window boxes and one rusting fire escape. The far building housed three apartments by the looks of it, but I'd never seen another soul here, inside or out. That wasn't what made it so special, though.

I watched Oscar's face to see when it would hit him.

When we stepped in, the city buzz hummed around us. The next step, wind swooshed without so much as rustling our hair. Then one more, to the center of the courtyard, and—

"It's silent." Oscar touched his ear. Let it go.

"I can't explain it." I whispered, not wanting to spoil the effect. "I come here when the city gets to be too much. This place and the Ramble are where I go to feel alone."

"Is it . . . public?"

"I doubt it." I glanced up at the empty windows surrounding us.

"But nobody's ever kicked me out." *And I've never brought anyone else here. Just you.*

"How did you find it?" He sat cross-legged on the center of the spiral of courtyard tiles.

"I was lost. Which is probably how most people find things." I sat next to him, silence settling around us like a tent. "I was out with my mom and dad getting lunch. I'm . . . not sure what happened." *They were arguing. They forgot me.* "They were hailing a taxi one minute and the next I was alone."

Oscar let his wrist rest against mine. "When was this?"

"I don't remember. I was eight, maybe?" *Five.* "Anyway, some delivery guy with a cart—he was probably nice, I was just freaked out—he tried to stop me so he could call my parents, and my stranger-danger alarm went off and I started running and ducked in here to hide. And the sound thing . . ."

I beamed slowly, peering up and all around.

"I had this *The Lion, the Witch, and the Wardrobe* pop-up book and . . . I literally thought I'd slipped into another world. I was so *happy*. It made sense, why I felt the way I did in that other world. Out there." I motioned to the street. "Anyway, it started getting dark, and I came out and all the noise hit me again and a cop found me and . . . I guess half the city had been looking. So that was something. And my mom made me hot chocolate and we sang together."

Oscar smiled.

"It was winter," I added. "Forgot to mention that."

His knuckles had been idly dancing against mine. They stopped.

"*How* winter?"

"January winter."

"You could have frozen."

"It was cold. I remember that. But so was Narnia, right?"

Oscar turned and started rubbing my hands.

I laughed. "What are you—?"

"Warming you up." He breathed onto our balled fingers. "You poor Dickensian urchin."

"It's July!" I swatted him away, feeling seven kinds of hot. "And if I were in Dickens, I'd be someone awful. Estella Havisham."

"Wow, now that you mention it." He tucked his hands back into his lap, scrutinizing me with a grin.

I slo-mo punched his shoulder. "Only I can make that joke."

"Exactly what Estella would say. You're not helping your case."

"*So.*" I leaned in and away, a subject change. "Did you want to talk about something specific? I'm the one blathering on—"

"Yes." Oscar's shoulders shrunk in. "I mean, yes, I do, not yes, you've been blathering on. Now *I'm* blathering. This is how blathering, I think, is defined . . ."

I smiled, waiting as his face relaxed.

"Talking." He drew a breath. "Okay. Here goes. I like you. As evidenced by the four hundred times I've told you I like you. Among other things."

Say something funny. But my brain was too stuck on the *other things.*

"But here is where I'm at." He spread his arms wide. "This is . . . mind-blowing. All of this, coming here, studying at Amberley, with *your dad.* It's like some fairy tale. I can't believe my luck. But . . ." He faltered, searching for words. "No, that's it. I can't believe my luck, so I'm concerned about, ah, messing with it. By pushing it."

I recrossed my legs to face him. "How would you be pushing your luck?"

"I didn't expect to meet you this summer." Oscar's eyes met mine.

"I mean, I expected to meet Ruby Chertok, Martin Chertok's daughter. I . . . didn't expect to meet someone like *you*."

Someone like me.

"Well. Likewise."

"Exactly! And you have things to do that I'm distracting you from, right? You have a whole life here."

Half a life. The start of one—a weird blend of exercise and D-list clubs and high-couture high-mindedness—but he wasn't wrong.

"*And,* if I'm being honest, which is the purpose of this exercise . . ." Oscar sighed. "Okay, so back home, I'm this anomaly, right? I make my music, everybody kind of stares at me, 'there goes Oscar again with his composition thing,' and it's this neat trick I do. No big deal. But here, it *matters*. And at the same time, I'm not that unusual, you know? I'm sitting in class with literal geniuses, most of whom worked a hell of a lot harder than I did to get here. But I'm still an anomaly."

I wasn't sure if it was my place to prompt him. He seemed to want me to. "Because you're black."

"Listen, I knew there wouldn't be many black kids at Amberley. I didn't realize there would be *zero*." He made an O with his fingers.

"There are a few in the university programs. But I totally get it."

I totally get it could have gone on our list of Things White People Say. I only understood how he felt on an intellectual level.

He still looked relieved. "Like I said—I am used to being the odd one out. This is just a special kind of odd."

"You don't seem odd to me." I squinted. "You're so . . . confident."

"See, but that's the thing, you get really good at that over a lifetime of 'what's up with that kid.'"

"At school?"

"Not so much school. Everybody's good-weird at my school." He scratched his face. "I mean . . . at home? My dad—super supportive, same as Mom—but he doesn't really *get* composition. He's always teasing me about classics versus classical, like it's some debate we're gonna settle. Classics being Otis Redding, Sam Cooke, Billy Stewart, Etta James . . ."

I smiled. "That's what he listens to?"

"We fight over the car stereo. Mom likes nineties R&B, Bri's all Disney Channel pop, Etta hates music—"

"Hates music."

"She's lying, it's her little rebellion." His smile sank a little as his eyes drifted. "We've got this big family on my dad's side, three aunts, two uncles, I don't even know how many cousins. They all live, like, forty-five minutes away, so we do a lot of Sunday dinners, and . . ." He laughed. "Mom grew up in Carmel, California, and you know her health hang-ups. She always turns up with escarole cranberry salad. Quinoa burgers. One time my cousins called me Carlton."

I grimaced.

"It's all good—like I said, I'm used to it. But *this*? A world-class conservatory program? 'Odd one out' here means . . . it means a whole lot more attention. Higher stakes. Implications that stretch and stretch and . . . yeah. I don't know. This is new."

I wanted to link my arm through his, but I stayed put. His eyes shifted to meet mine and he smiled, slumping a little.

"So here's where I'm concerned. Not concerned, like *worried*, just contemplating. What does it look like . . . out there"—he motioned past the courtyard—"for . . . let's say the *'new kid on the classical music scene'* to immediately hook up with a Chertok?"

I flinched at the sound of my last name.

"It looks deliberate, doesn't it? And it isn't. I promise, this is accidental."

The way he looked at me when he said *accidental* made the air shimmer.

"They . . . ask about you, you know. The Amberley students. They're curious."

I pulled at a snag in my hair. "What do they ask?"

"What you're like." He nudged me. "When you're debuting."

I let out a mirthless laugh. "Right."

"I don't tell them anything."

"It's fine, tell them whatever. But I get what you're saying. I'm, like, this added *thing*. So . . . people would talk." I very nearly rallied with a rousing "*Who cares what they think?*" before stopping myself.

He cared. And whatever his reasons, they mattered.

"So. All that on the one hand. And on the other . . ." Oscar stared at his open palm, then up at me. "You're what I think about."

"When?"

"At all times."

I drew a slow breath.

"I'm done, I promise. Sorry to unload. This is not something I do much of. I don't have anybody I can talk to about this stuff without seeming . . . I don't know. Ungrateful. That's a big thing with my parents, practicing gratitude—"

"You can talk to me about anything. I'm here to listen. Whatever we are." I drew a slow breath to keep from wincing.

Oscar stared at me for a second, then he smiled like he'd made a decision. Instead of telling me what it was, he took my hand and uncurled my fingers, one after another, and pressed his palm to mine. I watched him as our fingers slipped together and folded shut. It was so quiet, I swore I could hear his pulse catching up to mine as we sat together, perfectly still.

This was limbo, but here in the courtyard, I didn't mind it. We'd fall one way or the other, but for now we were both friends holding hands and . . . not. The nicest imaginable version of Schrödinger's cat.

I lost all sense of time until his thumb crept up to nudge the watch on my wrist, Mom's birthday gift to me from two years ago. I wore it every day and never looked at it. But Oscar's eyes were sharpening, his face falling.

"It's *one*? How is it one?"

"Is that . . . late?"

"Um." He straightened, perching to stand. "How long do you think it'll take to get home?"

I got up, looking out to the street. "We can grab a taxi. What do you need to be back for?"

"An interview." He brushed off his shorts as he stood. "It's not till one fifteen, but Ms. Visser said she wanted to prep me." He laughed uneasily. "Whatever that means?"

"For the alumni magazine, or . . . ?"

"I actually have no idea."

I stepped onto the sidewalk, feeling my posture cement as the wall of city noise rose around me like the roar of an oncoming army. I went funny like this every time I left my house, skin hardening into armor. I'd often wondered if every New Yorker felt this way. Oscar sure looked tense as we rode silently in the back of a taxi, but that was probably more to do with this mystery interview.

As we got to the stoop, Oscar's phone started to ring. The Farzone theme song—TJ calling from his gamer chair.

We both smiled, then I reached idly for Oscar's pocket. It wasn't until I'd handed him the phone, watching him press the button to mute it, that I realized how familiar a gesture it was—the kind of thing a girlfriend would do. Not whatever I was.

I peered up at Oscar, testing this teeny-tiny boundary, hoping I hadn't made him uncomfortable. There was surprise shining in his eyes—but warmth drowning it out. He stepped closer.

The front door swung open. I jumped back, surprised to see Nora welcoming us like we'd teleported to her house in Gramercy Park.

She looked thrown too. Her eyes darted between the two of us, widened, sparked, narrowed, all in the space it took me to squeak, "Nora! Hey!"

"*Hello,* my angel," Nora said, stepping onto her tiptoes for an air kiss. "How was the Met?" The question felt teasing, like she knew exactly what that night had led to. She gave my elbow a playful tweak—the universal mom-gesture for *we'll talk later*. Then she let go to reach past me with both arms. "Oscar, our renegade!"

That was her kind way of saying he'd shown up massively late. As she craned her neck into the room behind her, I looked back to see Oscar peering past me with an expression as cheery as hers. No one could possibly tell how frantic he'd been hailing a taxi a few minutes ago.

"He has arrived!" Nora sing-called, steering us both inside.

I latched the door behind us, adjusting blink by blink to the fact that my house was full of people. Dad sat in the dining area, in lively debate with a small middle-aged man I didn't recognize. Bill Rustig perched stiffly on the edge of the velvet armchair that filled the nook facing the stairwell, looking like he really was rusting, and assistants filled all other available corners, leaning on walls, typing on cell phones.

Nora ushered Oscar all the way back to the dining room, hand glued to his back as if he were her son. I bit back a laugh, imagining teensy ginger Nora producing tall, brown, elegant Oscar.

Nora can't have kids, I remembered. Mom told me that.

I looked at my feet, chastened. Only a few days ago, Nora had pressed her hand to my back, guiding me through a party. And it was nice, wasn't it? Comforting.

"This is our wonder boy," she said proudly.

I leaned on the wall, desperately curious, despite all efforts not to be.

"Oscar, this is Simon Wilkerson of the *New York Times*."

My feet slid. *Holy crap.*

"The *New* . . ." Oscar pivoted ninety degrees, instinctively fleeing—but Nora patted his back like she was calming an anxious pony. He extended a hand, recovering his height instantly. "It's a pleasure to meet you, sir."

"The pleasure is all mine," said diminutive Simon Wilkerson of the *New York* Freaking *Times,* his accent hovering between British and American. "Shall we find someplace quiet to chat?"

Oscar looked over his shoulder at me, eyes glowing. I felt a twinge, wishing that we were still there, locked in that ambiguous moment, away from all this.

"There's a great patisserie on Columbus," Nora suggested, blinking around at everyone. "If you've got time for a bite—"

"L'Orangerie?" Oscar asked.

Nora clapped, beaming. "Look how much of a local he is already."

They all rose and exited the house at a glacial pace, like a ceremonial procession in an opera—Mr. *New York Times* already asking Oscar how his love of music began, Nora linking arms with Dad while Bill surged ahead on a tiny invisible Segway. I thought for a second Nora might stop and make good on that pinch, but she didn't even glance over her shoulder at me as she left with the others. Only Oscar did—faint regret shining in his eyes before he turned away again, continuing the conversation.

The door shut, the procession proceeded, the house sank into silence around me, and my brain . . . crescendoed.

Okay, what the hell were we? What had felt nice and unique and balanced in the courtyard was now jangling in its discord. How was I supposed to feel right now?

I cleared up the half-full coffee mugs they'd left on the dining table, determined to distract myself. Whether we were a thing or not, it wasn't as if our individual lives were going to stop. And if anyone had a life, it was Oscar—a rammed schedule, a symphony to write—none of which could be put on hold for . . . whatever. I got it, understood it, wouldn't let it affect me, even if I had shared something with him that felt way more vulnerable than any make-out session.

A courtyard. A couple of childhood memories. Oscar's secret vulnerabilities and feelings for me and—*calm down,* I told myself, *this is fine.*

But it wasn't until I closed the dishwasher and leaned against the counter, task completed, that another source of uneasiness hit me.

Oscar wasn't just some guy I was ambiguously hanging out with. Somehow, along the line, I'd started blanking *who* he was—Dad's protégé, Amberley's most gifted recruit, a bottomless font of brilliant music. Now he was officially someone the *New York Times* wanted to interview, and I was still . . . a blur.

Oscar was right to put the brakes on. This summer was his moment. It was in no way mine.

A knock sounded in the entryway. I thought for a confused second it was Oscar back already, but when I opened the door to the street, Nora stood three inches away, shrugging broadly.

"Am I right?"

Oh God. I couldn't stop my cheeks from flaming. "About . . . ?"

She shot me a playful glare as she walked past me into the house. "I could be wrong, *but* I'm usually right about these things. I have an eye for gossip." She peered at the Steinway for a second as if searching for Mom on the bench, then turned. "So. You? Young Oscar Bell? Is this a *thing*?"

"I . . . duh . . . he . . . um . . ."

"I *am* good!" She walked over to wrap me in a dancing hug while I continued to express myself with startling eloquence. "Listen, you don't have to tell me, but if it's the start of something . . . ? I could not be more pleased."

I felt a spark of surprise, but couldn't pinpoint why. Maybe because of what Oscar had said—or because last week she'd been a tap away from setting me up with somebody named Charlie Weatherby.

"As much as you want to get away from Amberley, my dear, it's in your veins. I *knew* we'd get you back."

Amberley? What?

"It's practically your birthright." She brushed off one of my shoulders. "And I, for one, am glad you're finally claiming it."

As my stomach started a slow descent, her phone rang. She peeked at it.

"Ugh, I have to run, *again,* but . . . lunch soon? Monday? Meet me at my place at one and we can jet from there." She blew a kiss and was lifting her phone and out the door before I could so much as squawk a reply.

It took me the whole walk up to my room to connect the pieces of that disjointed conversation. *Oscar. Amberley. Claiming it.*

I sat on my bed, stinging.

Oscar didn't need to worry about public perception. The board chair herself applauded the idea. Dating a musical genius was my *birthright,* as far as she was concerned. *Proximity to Greatness: The Ruby Chertok Story.*

If anybody needed to worry about looking like an opportunist, it was me.

Tell the truth. If he were a nobody, no talent, no connection to music whatsoever—would I like him better?

The simple answer: *Hell. Yes.*

But then his music started playing in my head, that snippet from the other night, and I felt so overcome that it took lying down and staring at the ceiling to get my own gravity back.

Whatever we were, whatever this was, we'd left simple behind in the courtyard.

15.

the cure for buzzing thoughts was busy hands. The kitchen was done, the study too daunting, so I tackled Dad's room, making the bed, placing columns of bedside books back onto shelves, removing cups and mugs, throwing away an old flower arrangement, cleaning the pile of dry petals beneath it.

I was surveying the now orderly room from the doorway with a slow, calm breath when I noticed that the drawer of one of the night-stands was closed at a funny angle.

Mom used to sleep on that side.

I went very still. Then I crossed the room in a full sprint to wiggle the drawer back into place and push it shut. It was full of random papers—one of them stuck in the back. I tugged it loose, wary of look-ing too closely.

Too late. It was a glossy program from a concert in Vienna, a full nineteen years ago. Mom was the headliner. Grieg's *Piano Concerto in A Minor*. A newspaper clipping was stapled to the back of it—a review from a German newspaper, presumably glowing.

I picked up another scrap of paper from the drawer. And another. These were all hers, interviews, programs, flyers, reviews. The earliest ones were all pasted into a little notebook at the bottom of the pile— her recital at Amberley, her philharmonic debut—but then there was a gap, nine years, ten, and everything since was just tossed in here, sloppily. Almost angrily.

Why had she kept it like this? What was the point? And she hadn't cleared it out before leaving. Neither had Dad. He just kept sleeping next to it, night after night.

I climbed up to my closet, grabbed the shoebox my new sneakers had come in, ran back down, filled the box with paper scraps of Anna Weston-Chertok, shut the lid, closed the drawer, took the box back to my room, and stared at it.

What now? I could mail this to her. I didn't even know where she was.

I put the box in my closet and shut the door.

The sun was going down. I wandered to the kitchen to forage, and a text came in from an unknown number.

I immediately started grinning. I hadn't even put his name in my contacts yet.

I'm conducting till 8:30 but do you want to get together after?

And then . . . *If you're up for it. I can hang out wherever.*

I started typing a reply, then let my finger hover until—another message: *If you're busy tonight I totally get it.*

Then: *Blather on, verb (See above)*

I flopped over the kitchen counter, typing fast. *Are you conducting your piece?*

Nonononononooooooo Then: *Not ready yet. At all. Tonight is THE MAN*

I turned my phone upside down, like that would make his message make sense.

Eine kleine Nachtmusik

Nice! I replied.

They're not killin it but we're getting there, then: *aaa break's over, text you when we're done*

I typed as quickly as I could. *Are you leading the orchestra tonight*

He didn't reply. Either he'd switched his phone to silent or he didn't know how to answer such a pleb question. Of *course* the conductor would lead. But it seemed like he was describing the job of a real conductor, not a student—the musical director. Were they really giving a kid with next to no experience, running on pure instinct and enthusiasm, free rein with the Amberley summer orchestra?

I couldn't picture it, but found myself desperately trying, eyes closed, stomach pressed tight against the counter's edge. For the first time in months, I allowed into my mind the image of Lilly Hall and Lincoln Center—light spilling in interlocking pools, gorgeous crowds clustering around each building's doors, silhouetted figures waiting by the fountain for their dates to arrive while, inside, musicians listened with bated breath for the first chair oboe, tuning their nerves to match its perfect A.

I swiped on mascara, an arbitrary nod at respectability, and headed over. The traffic was synched, letting me walk the entire way without waiting for lights. My hands clenched as I left the common sidewalk, but I could barely feel my feet hit the ground.

The rondo echoed in the Lilly Hall lobby, and only then did my step falter. I knew the music; everybody knew it, right? But there was a new energy underneath—a sense of having fallen through time and stumbled into Mozart conducting his own piece.

It was a work-through, the orchestra's main conductor, Emil Reinhardt, hovering in the wings, arms crossed over his Amberley T-shirt—but there was still a scattered audience here watching in rapt silence. Oscar was dressed in the shorts he'd worn earlier today, the orchestra members similarly casual. Aside from that, this could have been a season opener of the philharmonic.

He was . . . electric. Such an overused word in music criticism, but

I swore there was lightning bursting from his fingers, his baton, his incredible hair. I sat in one of the velvet seats, tucking my knees under my long skirt so I could clutch my legs tight.

I couldn't see his face but I knew what it would look like. Joyous. Rapturous. A man in love. There was *nothing* unformed about Oscar in this moment, nothing of the nervous boy he'd shown me in the courtyard. Up at the podium, he was himself, powerful, unapologetic. He was Mozart and he was Oscar Bell and he was every member of the orchestra and he was the audience, and, right now, he was the entire world, because he was *this music* that was playing, lanterns in a night garden, stolen kisses, laughter.

The final notes resounded. The twenty people scattered through the house burst into applause—and I headed for the lobby. *I can't.*

A man walked out ahead of me, holding the door so I could pass. He looked dazed too, like he'd been kissed by a supermodel. It took me a second to recognize him as the *New York Times* reporter from earlier today. This would go in the piece he was writing. Oscar's brilliance. His promise. His work with the great Martin Chertok and this prestigious school. His incredible future.

As the reporter left the building, I stood in the empty lobby, excitement and despair coursing through me in alternating currents. And something else. Something dizzy.

This was an obvious mistake. Coming here, listening to this . . . I wasn't ready. But at the same time, I'd *needed* it. Everything looked sharper now. The air was charged in my lungs. I'd missed it and I *hated* that I felt this way, but anger still felt better than the awful numbness I'd endured since April. I loved this. I had no right to, but oh God, I did.

My phone buzzed, a text. *Done now, you home? :)*

Oscar must have picked up his phone the instant he put down his baton.

I'm here, actually, I texted back, swiping for the right, charmingly sheepish emoji. *Lobby.*

The door swung open from the hall. I pivoted, but it was a few people from the audience chatting quietly as they left. They looked familiar—friends of Dad's?

The door behind them creaked again and Oscar burst through, holding the top of his head with both hands. "I had no idea you were here."

The audience members turned, curious, and I realized they were Amberley board members. They must have turned out to see Oscar in action and found a bit more gossip than they'd bargained for.

They would talk no matter what we did.

Oscar rubbed his eyes, like he'd sleepwalked here. I could feel energy pulsing off him—macho, wired, *massively* distracted.

"You wanted to hang out?" I lifted my cell phone, entering it into evidence.

"Yeah, I'm done, let's . . ." He pressed his fingertips to his lips.

I knew that expression—the look Dad got when he was listening to something only he could hear. Still, it was jarring, seeing it on Oscar.

I stepped back. "Do you want to grab dinner, or—?"

"I ate earlier." His eyes met mine, fuzzy around the edges. "Could we hang out in my room? Is that . . . would that be okay?"

His room. My pulse quickened, deepening until I could feel it everywhere.

"I just . . ." He scratched his face. "I've got an idea for how to spice up the recapitulation and if I don't get it down quickly, I'm afraid I'll—"

"Oh!" I let out a tight laugh. "Right, yeah. That's fine, let's . . . get back."

He sprinted out of the hall with me, waving vaguely to the board members as we passed them on our way to the sidewalk.

"Sorry to be so frantic," he muttered. "I've never worked on something with this scope before and I usually have my school notebooks with me, you know? Something to jot the idea down on."

"Write on me," I joked, extending my arm as we hurried around the corner. "I've been trying to get a tan, but it hasn't worked, so you might as well take advantage."

"Do you have a pen?" Oscar asked, dead-serious.

"Oh." I stopped walking and fished one out of my bag. "It's purple. Is that weird?"

"Purple is stupendous." He took the pen and twirled it idly between his fingers, squinting to himself as I scanned the road.

A cab pulled up at the taxi stand, dropping off a late operagoer. I raced to snag it.

"Seventy-first and Central Park West," I said, slamming the door behind us. Then I offered my arm to Oscar.

He cradled my wrist, smoothing one finger along the bone, like he was worried about breaking me. Then he bit the cap off my purple pen and started to write. I closed my eyes, enjoying the rocking of the taxi, the tickling, sliding touch of the pen marking me. Oscar's music, covering me.

I felt him sigh, a warm gust, and opened my eyes to see him staring at my face.

He smiled slowly. "Sorry. Just a little . . ."

"You don't have to." I laughed. "It was only an idea."

"*No,* this is great. If you really don't mind." He kept going, quickly now, all the way up to the curve of my biceps.

When he finished, he kissed my palm lightly, a thank-you, and my whole body went fizzy.

As we got out of the cab, Oscar held my arm gently upright, like he thought the notes might tumble onto the sidewalk.

It was dark inside the basement apartment. Oscar fumbled for the light switch, and when the overheads came on, I let out a surprised laugh. The mess of composition pages had spread, carpeting the floor around the sofa, while some sparse neater pages taped to the wall flapped in the AC unit's breeze. How did he live like this?

Oscar wandered to his bed, pulling me with him. He smoothed a corner of his striped duvet for me to sit on, then joined me on the mattress. It felt like a line crossed to sit here, even though Oscar was working, carefully transcribing his music from my arm to his notation paper.

"This okay?" he murmured, scooting closer.

"Yeah." I kept still, feeling the gentle heat of his exhalations—distracting myself by trying to make sense of what he'd written. That note was an E, maybe, if it lined up with the dots he'd drawn on the side? F sharp, after that?

His finger slid up my arm. I refocused on the music. Were those eighth notes, sixteenths . . . would Dad know? Could *Mom* look at this and decipher it?

"What do you think?" Oscar asked, tossing the pen onto the ground. "Oh. Sorry . . . here."

He handed me the sheet of paper where he'd transcribed the notes. In these few minutes, he'd added chords to it, a winding counter-melody along the bass line. I could pick out the main theme now. I hummed it and it started to take form, an echo against stone, lilting but sad . . .

A grin flitted across Oscar's face. "You have a pretty voice."

"Oh. Thank you." I cleared my throat—a harsh sound, ruining it. "My mom always had me sing the melody of a keyboard piece before I started working it. She said I sounded happier singing music than playing it, so I needed to . . ."

I pressed my lips together, not liking the direction this memory was headed.

"So . . ." Oscar nodded to the paper, a question in his eyes.

"Yeah, it sounds . . ." I waited for the surge of memory to ebb. Then I drew a breath. "Why do you care what I think?"

"Why wouldn't I?"

"I don't have an eye for this. Or an ear. Maybe an arm."

He ran his thumb down my wrist again. "Thanks for that."

"I'm not an expert. It sounds . . . lovely to me? But I can't hear all of it in my head the way other people seem to be able to."

"Hum it for me again."

I went warm, but picked up the paper and teased out the melody. When I stopped and looked up again, Oscar's eyes were glowing.

"You do get it." He took the paper from me. "You get it in a different way."

I smiled through my puzzlement. This moment felt so tenuous, like the early-morning haze before the sun breaks over the skyline, everything insubstantial, from the duvet under me to the boy in front of me.

Then he crumpled his composition into a ball.

"What are you doing?" I rose onto my knees, reaching for it.

He pulled it away. "It's cool, this was an idea. You gave me a better one."

"How?"

"Trust me, it's fine!" He tossed it at what looked to be the discard pile beside the sofa. "This will get me there but . . . yeah. Not it."

"Oscar—"

"Especially after the Mozart. Hearing that and then writing this? I don't know. Maybe I need a quiet room for a few days to get Wolfgang out of my head." He reached out, letting my curls pool in his palm. "Maybe I need your courtyard."

"Wolfgang might follow you. I've always heard music more clearly there. That was part of it, the way it could make the music in my head sound so . . . pure."

My ritual—sitting alone in the courtyard, eyes closed, visualizing myself on a stage, playing the most breathtaking piece the world had ever heard. It had felt real there. Possible.

And now even the memory of imagining those things felt like a false one.

"Music in your head?" Oscar looked weirdly excited. "Do you ever write it down?"

"Not that kind of . . . no." I shook my head. "I don't compose. I don't do anything but listen."

"Oh. Well, without listeners, there's no reason to play music."

"Fair point. Count me in among the masses, then."

If there was a hint of venom in my voice, Oscar ignored it. He moved closer. "Did you like what you listened to tonight?"

"Tonight was . . ." I stared at my lap, then back up at him, unable to be anything but honest. "It was like . . . a *miracle*."

I half expected him to jump up and do a victory leap, but he didn't move a muscle. "Do you know what I was thinking about when I was conducting?"

I watched him move closer.

"Nachos?" I whispered.

He closed his eyes and I closed mine and there were his lips, warm and parting, my arms sliding up around his neck to sink deeper into it. Relief surged over me like a warm bath. In the same moment, we both seemed to remember how polite we'd been all day, how very upbeat and chaste, and smiled against each other's lips, then more kissing, more urgent, more greedy.

He pulled back a few inches. "How did you know I was thinking about nachos?"

I laughed.

Oscar peered at me—a question.

"So." I shook my head. "Are we . . . ?"

"I don't think we have a choice." He looked almost exultant.

I beamed, catching the joy on his face. But then he frowned—and the litany of worries he'd recited earlier today ran through my head like a news-ticker.

His mouth dipped to my neck, and I blurted, "Nora thinks it's great. You and me."

He looked up. "Ms. Visser?"

"Yeah!" *Why why* why *would you bring her up right now?* "In case you were worried about how, um, Amberley people would react." Sweat prickled my armpits. "She guessed this morning and she gave me a big . . . thumbs-up?" I demonstrated, scrambling to wind this conversation back to the point before I'd derailed it. "I didn't tell her anything. Obviously. I didn't know if there was anything *to* tell."

"Wow." He leaned away, thoughtful. "That's good to hear, actually. I shouldn't care, but . . . huh."

My face burned. Oscar lapsed into silence and I suspected if I tried to fill it, I might say something even more wrong-headed.

There were dirty dishes piled up on the counter of his galley kitchen. I gave his shoulder a soft tap, and went to fill the sink.

"You know, we switched the piece tonight. They were supposed to be rehearsing *L'Apres-Midi* with Reinhardt, but I mentioned Mozart in the interview, so everything got shifted. They'd done *Night Music* already, last Thursday." He kicked his legs up with a cocky grin. "But not like that."

I looked back down at the soapy basin, the dishes I was scrubbing, my wet arm, all the purple notes running together.

"Ah. Ruby." Oscar jumped up, crossing the room in three long strides. "You don't need to do that."

"I don't mind." I stacked clean plates to the side. "What did you say about Mozart? In the interview . . ."

Oscar grabbed a dishrag and started to dry. "That he's my north star, basically. That I admire everybody, but Mozart's the one who nails what love sounds like."

"Mozart." The brazenness of that statement forced a laugh out of me. "Not, I don't know . . . the *Romantics*?"

"Okay," Oscar said, hopping up on the counter. "How about, Mozart nails what I *want* falling in love to feel like." He let his legs swing out, back in. "If I could choose, I'd much rather have that purity, that peace, that *grace* to come home to than any drama, however gorgeous and sweeping and complex and . . . you get it."

I peered up at him, elbow grazing his knee, feeling a lot of things, none of them pure. "Most people would disagree with you. Everybody seems to want to get destroyed."

"My brain is messy enough." He slid back down. "I need a Mozart kind of love."

I felt him move behind me, warm and steady, his hands falling to rest on either side of me against the counter. I washed one more cup— his breath on the nape of my neck, his hips drawing closer to mine . . .

But he reached for my wrists, stilling them. "You don't need to take care of people so much, Ruby. You can take a break."

My hand closed around the drain plug, shoulders locked tight. "It's the only thing—"

He peered around me, intent. "What?"

I pulled the plug and dried myself off. "I really don't mind!"

He watched me cross the room. "I noticed you the other day, going into Marty's study. Like, sneaking. And then when we went in to work, it was immaculate—"

"Dad can't concentrate when it's messy and he's a naturally messy person, so . . . I don't know." I picked at my thumbnail, flustered. "I sort the mail, get his music in the right order. I vacuum. It's not like I'm curing cancer."

Good lord, if Jules heard me say that . . .

"You're helpful," Oscar said, stepping closer. "Kind." Another step. "Beautiful."

I smiled, speechless.

"So," he said.

"So . . ."

He leaned against the wall. "There's this Amberley thing I have to go to this weekend, while your dad's away. This young donors' cocktail reception something-something?"

"Wing Club?"

"Yes! You know about it?"

"Nora mentioned it to me." *Practically your birthright.*

"Oh, of course." His fingers nervously tapped the wall. "Well, are you going? Do you want to be my date? Sunday night. It would make it a *lot* more fun."

There was an edge to his cheerfulness, like he was daring himself to say all this. Was this his way of getting past all the things he was worried about?

"I wasn't actually planning to go," I said. "But Wing Club *is* really nice. And you're really nice to ask me."

Not an answer, but all I could conjure amid all the *Alert, Alert, Alert*s clanging in my brain. I pinched the buttonhole of his polo shirt to distract myself, my thumb grazing warm skin as his arm looped around me, pulling me closer.

"Thank you for this morning," he whispered. "And tonight. And everything."

Before I could say "You're welcome," he kissed me again, and I forgot what day it was, let alone what happened this morning.

16.

"You'll *think* about it." Jules paused from painting her toenails silver to gawk at me. "You seriously said that? It's not like he was asking you to bear his children. Although that's obviously next."

I pulled another pillow behind me at the top of her bed, craning my neck to avoid her nail polish fumes. "'I'll think about it.' Yes. As in . . . what you say when you don't want to do something."

"I don't get it," Jules said. "You don't want to go to a party at Wing Club."

"*No.*"

"With cocktails and champagne . . ."

"I'm seventeen. They won't let me—"

"And tiny adorable food circulating and music playing . . ." She turned her attention back to her toenails. "Yeah, I don't get it."

Then her head darted up.

"This is a wardrobe issue! You have nothing to wear!"

"What? No." I sat straighter. "I've been going to Lincoln Center events my entire life." *If you don't count the past two years.* "Half my wardrobe is black-tie." *Well. Black.* "And I bought a couple new things . . ." *Workout clothes.*

"What would you wear, then? Hypothetically."

I pictured my bleak closet and made something up. "I have a silver dress, thank you very much, with a Peter Pan collar."

"Cap sleeves?" Jules sat up, smirking. "Hem to here?" She pointed to the bottom of her kneecap.

I squinted. How *dare* she mock my imaginary dress. "And?"

"And that's what a twelve-year-old would wear, tagging along with her parents to a grown-up party. You said it yourself. You're seventeen—"

"I said it in the context of not being allowed to drink."

"I'm taking you shopping for something age appropriate. *And* you are going to this goddamned black-tie cocktail reception if it kills both of us."

"It's not as simple as . . ." I clamped my lips shut.

Jules hit me with a hard stare. "As?"

How could I explain this to her? That if music was my recently broken-up-with ex, this was the equivalent of being a guest at its wedding? That people there would either know and pity me or, worse, not know and ask me when they could expect my big triumphant debut? That Oscar and I would be subjected to the glare of the classical music scene before there was even an *us* to glare at?

That this whole thing felt weirdly like a trap?

I chose the easiest complaint. "There will be photographers there who might see this as, like, my introduction to the . . . scene. Or whatever."

"The *scene*?"

Wrong direction. She leaned forward.

"Are we talking, like, high society here, or . . . ?" At my expression, she slapped the bed. "Oh my God, we *are*. And this would be . . . what? Your debut? Holy shit, this is *so* happening!"

In fact, Jules was clearly so determined to ensure that this was happening that she skipped the second coat of paint on her left foot and immediately shimmied into gladiator sandals, dragging me behind her down the hall to her living room.

"I haven't decided about this!" I laughed, stumbling in my worn-out penny loafers. "I don't want to buy a dress for no reason."

"The reason is so I can live vicariously through you, do *not* deny me, hi, Grams!"

Jules's grandmother stepped out of the kitchen, holding a pile of mail. Her face lifted at the sight of me.

"Oh my *God,* is that Ruby Chertok? I've seen you go by, down on the street, but you're so *tall.*"

"Yeah, she's an Amazon, minus battle skills," Jules chirped. "We're friends again! All is right with the world!"

I snorted, but she wasn't wrong. Nearly everything did feel right, including, improbably enough, the prospect of going dress shopping.

Out on the sidewalk, I turned to her. "What did you mean by 'living vicariously'? You're the one who's out every night—"

"Not every night. Never anywhere nice."

She walked faster, avoiding the conversation. I took the hint.

The truth was, pieces of Jules's life that had felt to me like fun facts as a kid carried more weight now. Where my house was crammed with instruments, dusty books, and moldering antiques, Jules's "trendy" mid-century furniture was chipped and faded from decades of actual use. She lived with her awesome bohemian grandma because her parents were addicts who couldn't take care of her. Her mom had been born in that Central Park–adjacent house, grown up there, gone off the rails there, left her child behind there, and the rent had remained largely unchanged.

Our street was the same. Our lives were different. I needed to stop whining about party invitations.

"Where are you taking me?" I asked, the hiss of a stopping bus rattling me back to the here and now.

"Cravat." She pointed up Columbus. "It's a boutique on Seventy-fifth. Everything is, like, the tiny side of sample sizes, so . . . perfect for you."

When we stepped inside the cheery, spare shop, a girl in the back perked up. "Hey, girl! Love those shoes."

Jules kicked one foot behind her, posing like a pin-up. "You know where I got them."

"Do you shop here a lot?" I asked.

Jules looked at me like I was crazy. "I work here."

"Oh! Wow." I turned to a rack of all-black tops and started blindly sifting through. Everything seemed to be organized by color. "I didn't realize you had a job."

"You wouldn't, would you?"

I tensed, but her voice was wistful.

She nodded toward a curtained area in the back. "Dressing room. I'll bring you stuff."

I hesitated, watching her pick a neon-green dress with no neckline beyond a bit of gauze.

She glared. "I know what I'm doing."

I put up my hands in silent surrender.

I'd just managed to close the curtain and shimmy my shirt off when three dresses rocketed over from the other side. Neon green, dark green, fire-engine red.

"Um . . ." I held the red one with the tips of my fingers.

"Put them on!"

I did. All three. And Jules was right—she knew what she was doing.

I tried the bright green dress last, examining my reflection in the mirror from every angle. A sleek, modern, put-together adult-type person peered back at me. Not quite me. But maybe that was a good thing.

I couldn't help but imagine the dress floor-length, unfussy, comfortable, my hair in an elegant up-do, heels just the right height for working the pedals. My imaginary concert dress. Even my face looked different than I'd always thought it would.

Jules poked her head in. "That one. Definitely."

"Yeah, it'll work."

"*It'll work?*" She scoffed. "That's it? That's all you're giving me here?"

"It suits the occasion, it's . . . attractive," I tried, spinning so the skirt swished. "I don't know! It's *clothes,* it's not . . ."

Her eyes turned into knife blades. "It's not *what?*"

I smiled sweetly. "Curing cancer?"

She throttled the air in front of her. "The word is *aesthetics,* not clothes, asshole. As in, a key part of human civilization . . ."

I groaned, waving off the oncoming lecture. "*Okay.*"

"Think of this dress as a suit of armor—"

"It's *spectacular,* Jules, oh my God, I'm going to faint from the fashion!"

"I hate you."

"Kisses!" I yanked the curtain closed again and pulled the dress gently off my head.

"I'm giving you the commission," the shop girl said to Jules as I fumbled for my credit card.

"Don't you dare," Jules said from behind me. "I am one hundred percent off-the-clock."

I turned to see her scanning the racks with a closed-off look in her eye. "Why don't you try something on?"

She looked away. "I get stuff here sometimes, but only when they're being pulled from stock or returned for a minuscule hole or whatever. They give us a really deep discount."

"Let me buy you something. As a thank-you."

"Yeah, thanks but no."

She said the word *no* like she was etching it into a stone tablet. I knew not to press the issue.

"Maybe you could get me ready," I said instead as we stepped from the shop into a wall of hot air. "You might have guessed that I'm not such a makeup expert, and how do I even do my hair with this thing . . . ?"

I rattled the garment bag.

She grabbed it, holding it still. "Of *course* I'm doing your hair, that was the plan all along." I could tell by the bounce in her step that she was glad I'd asked first. "We poor motherless children must help each other however we can."

I stiffened—I wasn't motherless. But neither was she. Our mothers just lived in different places from us. And hardly ever got in touch.

I forced my attention onto my garment bag, spinning it gently as I walked. "I do like this dress."

"You'd better, at that price." Jules's eyes glowed even as she covered them with sunglasses.

"It makes me look like a real person."

She stopped mid-stride, fingers pressed to her temples. "*Just* when I think you're getting less weird, you pop out with something like that. A '*real person*'?"

"You know what I mean." I shrugged. "Someone who can make an impact."

She started walking again, watching me out of the corner of her eye. "You keep bringing this up, this impact thing. I don't get it."

"What's not to get?"

"Why do you have to do anything? *Be* anything?" She rifled through her purse. "Please do not construe this as me talking you out of becoming a socialite—"

"Philanthropist."

"But can't you, hypothetically, be a person living your life like everybody else?"

She passed me a mint.

I popped it into my mouth, scowling around it. "You make me sound like some egomaniac."

"You're not *enough* of an egomaniac," she said softly. Then she hit me. "You're so down on yourself! That's what I don't get."

"It's not about ego either way." I stepped briskly aside while a dog-walker passed with a million terriers. "It's just . . . what am I putting into the world? That's part of why I feel weird about this party. I'm either going as a plus one to the guest of honor or as a Chertok, and . . . that can't be *it*, you know? Looking good and showing up can't be all I have to offer."

"This family of yours . . ." Jules started, darkly.

"They have a *purpose*." I skidded to a stop as an electrician's van barreled through the crosswalk. "They were born to play music."

Jules looked like she was straining not to roll her eyes.

I nudged her. "No, stop. You were right, what you said about aesthetics—culture *is* important. It—it elevates everyday life. So in that way, their existence makes perfect sense, whereas I'm just . . . taking up space."

"So take up space! You have every right to it."

"I know that. Logically." I frowned at my loafers. "But I don't feel it."

The light changed and we crossed.

"How much of this has to do with Mr. Guest of Honor?" Jules asked, her voice eggshell careful.

"Oscar? *None,*" I backtracked, weirdly protective. "Zero percent."

She looked dubious. I glanced away so I wouldn't wilt under her glare and confess every worry I had swirling around in my head.

"I shouldn't have even mentioned him. One hundred percent of this is coming from the fact that I quit piano in April and I've been waiting for something to take its place, fill the vacuum, and—"

"In three months?" She laughed. "Tight window for finding the *grand purpose for your very existence* . . ." She put her hand out, Shakespearian.

I laughed. "Forget *purpose.* That's pretentious, I give you that. But I need a job—"

"Do you, though?" She blinked slowly at me as we rounded our block. "*Do you.*"

"Yes. I do." A scowl crept into my voice. "I'm not some heiress. And I'm one of four kids, so it's not like I have a huge fortune waiting for me."

"But you do have a trust."

"Yes, I have a trust." *Which I've come into, as of my seventeenth birthday, and done nothing with except hidden the monthly account statements that come in the mail* . . . "Given to me by my father with specific instructions not to blow it on living expenses. I am expected to have a career."

"Well, you're in the best possible position to look for one. It's not like you have to apply for a job at Cluck-Cluck Chicken Shack this weekend." She nodded behind her. "Or Cravat."

"I realize that. I do. I just wish there were a clear path forward."

"You're going to have to live here in the murk with the rest of us." She winked over her sunglasses at me. "Come on in, the water's blah."

We'd reached her building.

She leaned against the iron railing of the stoop. "I mean, who the hell knows what I'm going to do. Work retail through college and then get some marketing job to pay off student debt and dream of a better career until it's time to start dreaming of retirement."

"Marketing?" I held up my garment bag. "Not fashion?"

" 'Fashion'?" She made air quotes.

"This is the place to do it, right?"

She snorted. "Yeah, if you're rich. I could intern at *Vogue* and earn next to nothing. I'd lose twenty pounds, what with the whole no-money-left-for-food thing."

I nodded up at her building. "You have free housing, at least."

"No, I don't." Her voice sharpened. "I pay as much as I can. Just because our rent is cheap doesn't mean it's free and . . ." She heaved a sigh. "I'm sorry, I'm on my period and I don't feel like talking about my financial future." She kicked my loafer. "Much more fun to talk about yours!"

I laughed weakly, my stomach twisting. Why even bring up money? I had no idea what I was talking about. Again.

But Jules seemed perkier as she faced me, playing with my hair. "Some people are born to be socialites and some to be shop girls, and contentment lies in accepting which one you are. You're a celebutante-in-training for Christ's sake. *You* should go work for *Vogue*. I'll be your PA."

"You would definitely have to dress me."

"Already do." She reached out a finger to twirl my dress.

I grinned a good-bye as she raced up the steps to her house. And in my head, I crossed "fashion" off my list of possible paths to glory.

That future belonged to Jules.

17.

I texted Nora before Oscar, since she'd been the first to invite me. She wrote back, *Brilliant, Ruby, BRILLIANT!* which did make me feel brilliant for all of six minutes.

I was making too much of this. It was a party. In a world I knew. A chance to try out the other side, get dressed up, eat tiny food, report back on it to Jules.

Nobody would whisper behind their hands about my non-debut or my Amberley audition. Or my mom. Or my date.

It would be fine.

I'd planned to tell Oscar I was up for the party in person, but our paths didn't cross all day. On Saturday morning, after Dad left for the airport, I texted: *Hey do you still want me to come to that donor event? I bought a dress.*

I hit send before I could double-guess it. Then I read it back—and buried my head under a pillow. *I bought a dress?*

My phone beeped with a reply. But it was Alice.

Free for brunch?

I should have expected the text. Alice always invited me for one-on-one time when Dad traveled so she could reassure herself that I was alive and well. In the past year, it had become a revolving date.

Dad jetted off at least once a month for quick engagements—but this trip was longer than usual, and I'd forgotten to ask him why. It was a long flight. Maybe he wanted some time to decompress on either side of his gig at Royal Albert Hall. He was getting older, after all.

We met downtown, because that's where Alice insisted on living now, even though the philharmonic was up by us. I liked visiting her in SoHo. It felt like a different city from the Upper West Side, and transformed Alice into a more contemporary person, which meant I was cooler by proxy.

The sidewalk café she chose was a Brazilian place with unlimited weekend mimosas, which everybody but us was taking advantage of. Alice wasn't a drinker. She did, however, eat a basket of cheese bread within the first five minutes of sitting down.

"What's going on in your world?" she asked between buttered bites. "I have to admit, I'm kind of fascinated by you right now."

"Only now?" I shot her a mysterious look.

"You've gone civvy. What do you do with your free time?"

"Good question." I searched for answers in the zigzag pattern of my T-shirt. "So far, I'm experimenting."

"Oh yeah? Do any of these experiments involve our young genius?"

"What young genius, I don't know any young . . ." I yawned broadly. "Oh, do you mean *Oscar*?"

She raised an eyebrow.

I squeezed lime into my water. "I don't like calling him a genius. It's othering."

"Look at you, little miss not-even-an-undergrad."

"And . . . maybe."

"*Maybe?* I knew it!"

Before I could hide my grin by sliding all the way under the table, her phone beeped—and her neck went red.

She blinked up at me. "Tell me more. When did this start?"

I took a massive bite of papaya French toast, forcing her to wait while I chewed. "You first."

She stared, expressionless.

I stared back.

"*Fine*. His name is Daniel. He's a public school teacher." A smile started to spread across her face. "He bought his grandmother a season pass and he takes her to all the Meet the Orchestra events. It's their thing. And he chats with me afterward. I mean, it's been years of this. And . . ." She leaned way back in her chair. "I always wondered if there was more to it—didn't want to be presumptuous. But last month, he asked me out. He was so shy about it."

She slumped, as if she'd run out of breath thinking about him.

"And?"

"I freaked out. I said I had a busy rehearsal schedule before the season starts again, which is true, but . . . ugh, I don't know."

"Why? Because he's a teacher?" I grinned, teasing her. "Too nerdy for you?"

I had a flash image of Mrs. Swenson's piano studio—a Carnegie Hall program from her concert pianist days proudly displayed over a framed cross-stitch of a bear playing a baby grand—and felt my heart clench.

"Not at *all*." Alice leaned over the table. "I love that he's a teacher. It's . . . noble. And the way he talks about the kids . . ."

She was going to explode like a party popper if we kept talking.

I stirred my water with the lime. "So why didn't you say yes?"

"Because I'm crazy and weird, like the rest of this ridiculous family. Win's a wrecking ball, Leo's talking to burning bushes, Dad's out to lunch, Mom's unmentionable . . ." She leaned on the table. "Can you please turn out to be a normal person, Ruby? For the sake of the rest of us?"

"That's the working plan," I said drily.

"Good," Alice said, perky as she put her phone away. "Full disclosure, I saw him again and asked him out, and it's now a verified *thing* and it's lovely and that's all I'm going to say for now."

I smiled around my straw. She seemed happy. Flustered, but in a good way—waking up to a racing heart every morning, wondering what was around the corner, when she'd see him again . . .

"I've been thinking about you, you know," she said. "What it would be like to make the same call."

The sunlight shifted. I shaded my eyes. "What call?"

"You know." She ran her fingers through her chin-length curls and gazed across the narrow street like her future was beckoning from the Williamsburg Bridge. "Walking away. Choosing normal."

Choosing normal? Why would anyone *choose* normal?

"You're first chair viola at the New York Philharmonic."

"I know. It's amazing. And all-consuming. And it's making me kind of deranged, I think? I keep daydreaming about taking a break. What if I went away for a few weeks, somewhere tropical?" She lifted her mango iced tea as if to demonstrate what she would drink on vacation. "We have a recess coming up, I could do it. But would I bring my viola? *Could* I take a couple days off from practicing or would I lose my edge and my chair and my *will* to do it in the first place? Is there even a way for me to do something else, or is this it? Am I just—trapped?"

Her voice got louder and louder, like now that she'd told me one thing going on in her personal life, everything else was fighting to come out.

"I didn't know you felt that way," I said. "I always thought your life was . . ."

"What?" She leaned in.

"Perfect."

"Fair enough," she sighed. "But let me say, it's easy for a life to be perfect when there's hardly anything in it. Anyway, I don't know how I feel yet." She cut her omelet into triangles. "So tell me. Are you happier now?"

I considered the question, then took a bite of my brunch, closing my eyes as the papaya topping burst against my tongue. "I feel more awake. More like a real person."

Jules might not have understood what that meant—but Alice did. She watched me for a moment, quietly nodding, then changed the subject. "Any wild plans for the weekend?"

Perfectly on cue, my phone pinged, and I picked it up to see a reply from Oscar to this morning's awkward text: *THANK! GOD!*

I grinned. "I'm going to a young donors' event at the Wing Club."

Alice put down her fork. "For Amberley?"

"Yeah, with Oscar."

"Huh. Well, have fun but, whatever you do, don't give that woman any money."

I laughed at the very suggestion, then squinted. "*That woman?* You mean *Nora?*"

Her mouth was set in a tight line. "I'm serious. I know she's your godmother, and Dad said you've been spending a lot of time together—"

"Not that much time . . ." I frowned at my lap, marveling at how quickly Alice had managed to put me on the back foot.

"Listen, just be careful. Those two are wearing Dad out as it is. Sometimes I wish he weren't so attached to that school."

"*You* went there."

"Like I had any choice!" She nodded as if I'd proven her point. "All I'm saying is . . . I know Nora's all cotton candy and bunnies in a meadow—"

"Ha-ha, *what*?"

"But she's a lot smarter than she lets on. And don't forget how close she and Mom were for all those years. There's a reason those two got along so well."

I winced, thinking of the word she'd used for Mom. *Unmentionable*.

I didn't want to ask. Needed to know. "Are you still not talking to her?"

Her eyes shot to mine. "Are *you*?"

My mouth opened. "I . . ."

"When she calls you, I'll call her," Alice said, shut-down mode. "Until then, *somebody* needs to hold her accountable."

I wanted to talk Alice back from the brink like the last hundred times we'd had this conversation, tell her it was no big deal, it didn't bother me, she didn't need to be my champion, Mom was not toxic, she just had emotional baggage to struggle with, dead-mother-young-age etc., etc., but I couldn't gather the energy this time. And something else was gnawing at me, her "wearing Dad out" comment—but before I could rewind far enough to ask about it, my phone pinged, another text from Oscar.

I bought a new suit! Well, my dad bought me one. Got it UPS—it's sharp!

My mood went from slate gray to midday sunshine, picturing Oscar's dad picking something out for his son to wear to a swanky Manhattan fundraiser, packaging it to be delivered . . .

"Look at you," Alice said quietly. "You *like* him."

I started curling back into a ball.

"It's okay to be happy, Ruby. It's sort of the point."

I watched her push her omelet around her plate, her mind swooping up and away. She was thinking about her public school teacher, but I wasn't going to tease her about it.

Not when she'd finally cracked the vault and allowed me a glimpse inside.

"Stop moving!" Jules growled, her curling iron dangerously close to my ear. "Is this what you do at whatever one-percenters salon you go to? I hope you tip well."

I scowled. "I haven't even gotten a haircut since last year."

"So that's the problem." She set down the curling iron and shimmied to the side, bobby pins sticking out of her mouth.

I sat staring at Jules's cracked cabinet doors to keep from squirming, and a memory sprang to mind. Mom, getting me ready for my eighth-grade dance. She'd built it up in her mind for some reason, insisting on staying behind while Dad traveled to a conducting clinic in Japan, going to four shops with me to pick out just the right dress, doing my hair and age-appropriate makeup, taking pictures of me and my date, Wally Lew. We were firmly Just Friends—he would come out to me and Farrah a few months later—but Mom had acted like we were getting married, hands clasped to her heart. It was too much. She was trying so hard that I'd felt a weird kind of vicarious exhaustion that I couldn't shake the whole night. I didn't go to any dances after that. I think she was secretly relieved.

If she were home now, would she be ready with her camera?

I never even saw the photos she took of me and Wally. She'd probably deleted them.

The realization hit me like a slap, forcing a blink—so I didn't notice Jules's scissors heading for my face until they were already snipping, hair cascading in black spirals to the floor.

"What are you—?"

"Shhhhh," Jules whispered, snipping the other side. "This is all we're doing."

She gathered my hair high, set it into some odd position with the pins, and once her mouth was empty, picked me up by the armpits, pivoting me like a puppet until the mirror loomed—and there I was.

My hair hung in loose ringlets, not frizzy-curly tangles. My face was fresh and rosy, eyes huge and smoky. I didn't look anything like that little girl playing the piccolo or the one going to the eighth-grade dance. Maybe, just maybe, nobody would recognize me. I could just be Oscar's plus one.

Before I left, I added one last touch—a silver pendant in the shape of an oak tree, a gift from Nora when I was ten. After the Lincoln Center photo shoot with the piccolo, etcetera, all the usual Amberley suspects had come here for drinks. Later, while Mom performed, Nora drew me into the kitchen and handed me a blue box, whispering, "This reminded me of you. All the incredible ways you're growing up. Wonderful shoot today, sweetie—I am really, really proud."

It was a tiny moment, no more than a minute, but it had saved me that night. I wondered if she knew how much.

Oscar was sitting on my stoop when I made it down the street from Jules's. He stood, seeing me, and dawn broke over his face.

I glanced at my electric-green dress and new high heels. "Do you like it?"

He stood still, hands calm at his sides. "You're perfect."

I let out a white-hot breath of a laugh.

Tonight was a good idea. Being brave, showing up—it was the right call.

I turned, searching the street for a taxi, but Oscar pointed to a familiar black Bentley heading our way.

"Oh my gosh, that is so—" I started to say, as Oscar explained:

"Ms. Visser's loaned it to me while your dad's gone. I have this frenetic schedule right now, so the driver stays on top of where I need to go."

"Oh, that's helpful." I nodded, thrown for no good reason. Of course he had a rapport with Nora—even if he did still call her Ms. Visser.

Oscar held the door for me, then slid in with a "Hey, Jerry!" to the driver. They chitchatted the whole way, Oscar feigning interest in local sports teams while stealing glances over his shoulder that betrayed how clueless he was. I tried not to laugh.

And then I saw it ahead—Corinthian columns up-lit in blue.

18.

The Wing Club used to be a stuffy place. I remembered exploring all the empty rooms at functions I went to as a kid, cringing at the musty smell that pervaded the place, a mix of mildew and quinine and elderly folks. But apparently, after a renovation last year, it was the hot place to be seen if you were young and moneyed in Manhattan. And wherever there was money, there were fundraisers.

A guy in a suit and a jaunty cap opened our car door for us as we pulled up outside the blue-lit building. Oscar motioned for me to go in ahead of him, all courtesy—but glancing back, I wondered if there was more to it. He looked knotted up, walking like his shoes were too tight.

My shoes were tight too, but I plastered on my event face and made it up the stairs past the empty dining room, hearing a peal of laughter and low music issuing from a golden-lit room down the dark-oak hall.

It's just a party.

"Ready?" My voice shook.

"See, that's an interesting question." His smile looked locked in place. "It implies prep, and now I'm wondering if there was a workshop I missed. Intro to Schmoozing?"

I glanced behind us at a few tempting doorways. "Want to explore?"

I was referencing the Egyptian Wing, but he grinned like I'd made an innuendo.

"I've been here before," I whispered, taking his hand. "When I was peak cuteness, they would bring me along and sit me at the piano with my mom, and the donors would go crazy."

"You're peak cuteness now," he whispered back.

I traced the edge of a framed photograph, a black-and-white shot of lounging partygoers from the 1920s. "I always felt like I was behind glass. There was me and my family and the musicians and . . . everybody else."

"Yes." Oscar stopped walking and turned to me, hollowed by the glow from the wall sconces. "That's exactly what . . ." He shook his head, a line between his brows. "Did you know there was a human exhibit at the Bronx Zoo?"

I laughed, shocked. "What?"

"Way back. They kept a man in an enclosure. An African, a Pygmy."

"Oh my God. That's . . ." I couldn't think of the right word.

But Oscar's expression cleared, as if by force. "Hey. Come here, you."

We ducked into the next empty room we came across. Oscar turned toward me, his fingers grazing my back, our hips touching first.

I heard a noise in the darkness—shuffling feet—and spun with a gasp.

Nora Visser and Bill Rustig stood at the far end of the room, veering away from each other like they'd just finished saying hello in passing. Nora walked briskly toward us, drawing herself up to her full, tiny height, while Bill stood in place, powered down.

My own body went pins and needles. I'd seen nothing. I knew I wasn't supposed to have seen it.

"Oscar and Ruby!" Nora chirped. "We were *looking* for you two."

In a random room. With the lights off.

Bill reanimated enough to amble over, hand extended. "Thanks for coming out tonight."

"Absolutely," Oscar said, his own back straightening as he shook Bill's hand. "It's my pleasure, thank you for the invitation."

Nora motioned out. "Shall we?"

She glanced fleetingly in my direction as she linked arms with Oscar, then did a double take. "Oh my goodness, Ruby." She pressed her hand to her heart—because of the necklace? "You hired a stylist."

I beamed. Jules would die if she could hear this conversation.

"Promise you'll give me her name," Nora called over her shoulder.

"I will. But you look perfect already!" I motioned to her sequined dress, then smiled at my feet, following the others into the glass-walled events room.

The reception was in at least half swing, sleek twenty- and thirty-somethings clustered around high-rise tables, drinking champagne and cocktails from an open bar as a string quartet performed in the corner.

I snuck a peek at the musicians, confirming that, yep, despite how polished they sounded, they were nearly as young as I was. Amberley. I wondered if they felt like there was glass separating us.

A waiter stood near the door with a plate full of mini tarts, so teensy that only one fruit fit atop each. Oscar turned to it, eyes wide, but Nora steered him to a cluster of young partygoers in business suits. She was as grabby with him as Dad and Win—no glance to see whether Oscar might, in fact, *like* to stop for a fruit tart. She acted like he was hers.

Something urged me to walk up and extract him, but as Nora

launched into introductions, I stopped myself. He *had* to shake hands. That was why he was here.

"Oscar, this is Scott Tambliss, he is a *real* up-and-comer on Wall Street, but before that, would you believe he played the trombone?"

Oscar shook, greeted, all polish. I was being silly, he was made for this. Nora graced me with a cheerful glare, the kind you give a puppy for *come*, but I let my eyes drift, clinging to my current status: Oscar Bell's anonymous date.

"Champagne?" A waitress in an all-black uniform offered me a glass.

"Um."

Her tray wavered. She looked tired already and the party had just begun. Part of me wanted to help her hand these out.

"Thank you." I took the flute carefully, like the stem might notice I was underage and snap in protest.

The last time I'd come to a party at this club was four years ago—a Diamond Tier reception following a performance of *Rigoletto* at the Met. Thirteen-year-old me had ordered a ginger ale in a champagne glass and felt transgressive, waiting for someone to cry out in shock. Nobody looked at me the whole night—Mom, Dad, any of the guests. I could have just as easily been drinking the real stuff.

Well, I was drinking the real stuff tonight! It fizzed and burned and swirled as it went down. And this time people were looking at me.

Men were looking, in every corner of the room. My instinct was to slump, cross arms, duck into shadows, but I didn't. I pulled back my shoulders. I sipped my illicit champagne, steadied my ankles in my heels, smiled vaguely back at groups of strangers while Oscar worked the room.

Standing beside the window with what looked like a married couple, a guy—too old for me by a measure of decades—raised his glass in a tiny toast. I sipped from my own in reply.

Maybe Jules was right. Maybe aesthetics could be a kind of armor. Standing here with strangers' eyes roving my body, I felt more invisible than when I was a kid, hiding behind the roll-up bar, stealing cherries while the grown-ups talked. This dress, this hair, this makeup, was more of a costume than anything I'd worn yet. Skimpy as it was, it covered me completely.

And yet I could feel it taking over. To all these people, I was the green dress girl. I could do nothing but stand here and they would think they knew something about me.

I scanned the room, spotting a brunette in a brocaded cocktail dress laughing at something the man with her had said before turning away, her face sinking with boredom for a telltale blink. Could I guess what *her* life was like? Did she have a job, a passion to pursue, a singular impact, or did she flit from event to event, patron of the arts and sciences and social service organizations and children's hospitals . . .

"Oh, would you *please*?" Nora's voice rose above the string quartet like she was trying to accompany it in a light lyric soprano.

I turned to see her dinging her champagne flute with a knife she'd produced from God knew where. At the sound of it, the musicians stopped playing and the room's conversation settled into a curious hum. Beside her, Oscar rocked back onto his heels, waiting.

"I've spoken to many of you tonight about our newest prize pupil here at Amberley," Nora sang out. "Well, I'm pleased to tell you that he has just agreed to honor us with a *performance*."

"*Ooooh*," went the crowd in unison as Oscar shot them his spotlight grin and strode to the piano. His step was so assured that I had to assume he'd been prepped on this "impromptu" in advance. Then his eyes flitted to mine—briefly, imploringly—and the world stopped.

He'd been put on the spot.

But, without hesitation, he started to play, calling out a casual "Here's a little something I came up with on my ride from the airport."

The whole party laughed appreciatively, and there it was, the fugue—the first "Bell" tune I'd ever heard—and I wondered why I'd bothered to worry. This was where he lived. This was where he made sense.

As he was reaching the end of the exposition, he glanced around the room and said, almost flirtatiously, "Requests?"

"The song from YouTube!" a young blonde called back, her fuchsia-lipped friend giggling beside her.

Everyone in the room shouted agreement. Had they *all* seen the video? Oscar wasn't embarrassed in the slightest. He launched into it.

"An abbreviated version of the *Kudzu Variations*. Let's call it the *YouTube Suite*."

"A world *premiere*, ladies and gentlemen!" Nora said, sweeping across the room to whisper in another woman's ear before arcing back in my direction.

I took another swig of champagne and ditched it on a side table before she could reach me, feeling unbalanced as I glanced around. Oscar was playing, layering, ornamenting. The music—you could taste it, fizzy, tart—why were these people *chitchatting* over it?

Nora played with the clasp of my necklace as she stood on her tiptoes to whisper, "You're doing so well. I'll introduce you around in a second."

I mouthed a quick thank-you, but didn't know what she meant by doing well and didn't care. My world was this "premiere," the birth and life of Oscar's song. I didn't want to matter. I wanted to listen.

Oscar's grin dropped as he concentrated, composing as he went. He was trying to block the party din out, but it only grew. I heard the music shift to an inverted seventh and into the first strains of a Mozart homage—then he shook his head, sketched an arpeggio and closed it out, the music dropping off a cliff so quickly that I gasped. Oscar frowned at the silent keys.

The crowd whistled, applauded. His smile returned. "Thank you for indulging me. I'm no pianist. Not like Miss Chertok here, who was kind enough to accompany me tonight."

No. What. No, no.

Everyone was looking at me now, their expressions shifting as their assumptions about me made a 180. Still wrong. Completely wrong. I noticed some familiar faces among them, shapes popping out of a wallpaper pattern—donors to the opera, a couple of teachers. Arnold Rombauer, by the bar, watching me with strained pity.

"Perhaps *Ruby* could play for us," Nora called out. Her hand was on *my* back now—nudging me in the direction of the piano.

I stared in horror, body locked in place. Nora *knew* me. She'd been there seven years ago, the last time I'd played for a gathering of this stature. She'd given me this necklace, eased the shame of that night. She knew that what happened in April was the final straw, that I was done—that it wounded me to even talk about it.

But Nora was wearing her fundraiser mask. Was this how she got people to give money? By telling them they were going to, in front of witnesses? Was I still a child to her? A photo-op?

"I'm not . . . I can't play anything." My voice hardly came out.

The crowd was clapping halfheartedly, curious about my name more than anything. I turned to Oscar in desperate appeal, but he was shifting down the bench, making space.

"We could duet," he murmured, his innocence cutting. "Just something easy . . . a Chopin waltz? And I'll do an embellishment. Sound good?"

Heat raced up my body like I was tied to a burning stake. Everyone turned to watch as tears sprang to my eyes, sweat stung my forehead, my curls stuck and melted flat.

"*I can't play.*" The room fell strangely silent, everyone sensing drama unfolding.

Oscar cocked his head, *still* not understanding.

A clock chimed down the long hall and I nearly let out a hysterical laugh.

Instead, I took my cue, cutting a line through the crowd, clip-clopping faster, down the stairs, out the door, into the muggy night, past a drunk couple, straight to the curb, desperate for a lit taxi to swoop me safely home.

19.

"Ruby!"

As I clomped into the street, Oscar burst out of the building behind me.

"What . . ." He stumbled to a stop, hesitating on the sidewalk. "Are you . . . okay? What *was* that up there?"

I turned, anger boiling in my throat. "I don't. Play. The piano. I've been telling you that over and over but you don't seem to want to listen to me."

"I'm sorry." He ran his hands over his cheeks. "Oh God, Ruby, I really am. I don't know why I put you on the spot like that. I guess I panicked and figured you were *used* to it, being—"

"I'm not. And you know what? I don't *have* to get used to it. But you do."

He shuffled backward. "I guess so. I mean, you're right."

A taxi dropped somebody off on the near corner. I raised my hand for it.

"Where are you going?" Oscar asked, a note of panic in his voice.

"Home."

"I'll come with you."

"No." I leaned on the car door. "No. Oscar. That's sweet, but . . . you need to go up there and shake more hands."

"But—"

"They're giving you this platform. You have to help them fund-raise." I squeezed the bridge of my nose. "That's what Dad's always done, that's what Win does, even Leo and Alice, when they're asked to. It's part of the job. You were doing great, keep it up."

He glanced over his shoulder at the lit-up windows and let out a little laugh. "I feel so . . . on parade."

"Yeah, well."

"No, I mean . . ." His jaw clenched through his smile, like he wanted to confide something.

I waited, holding the cab door open. Oscar leaned in, exhausted, letting his forehead fall against mine. I closed my eyes.

"Hey, kids!" The voice behind Oscar was older, male, but as I leaned out to identify the source of it, a light flashed in my face. A camera? It turned off before I stopped blinking, but the photographer seemed satisfied—a short, bald guy, I saw now. He waved, shouted "Thanks!" and vanished toward the Wing Club entrance.

Oscar squinched his eyes shut. "What the actual—"

"These things attract photographers," I said quickly, hoping he couldn't see how shaken I was. "It's fine." I squeezed his wrist. "You'll be fine."

He straightened. "Okay. You're right. See you back at the ranch, then."

The photographer snapped another shot of him as he strode back into the club, bouncing more with every step.

Rattling home in the taxi, I caught a glimpse of my reflection in the darkened window, eerie and pale. This version of myself was easiest to look at. All that fuss over my outfit and hair, and for what? Half a champagne glass, *zero* tiny food items, and a graceless exit with the glitterati watching.

I don't want to do this.

This life isn't for me.

The realization came as a shock of relief, like taking off a scratchy sweater and letting the air hit my bare skin.

Not this. Try again.

I could breathe.

The house felt crypt quiet when I shut the door behind me. But as my ears adjusted to the thick silence, the world grew gradually noisier.

I could hear the hall clock ticking. I could hear the AC growling. I could hear the city outside and the neighbors arguing and . . .

I could feel my piano waiting.

I sat. Lifted the keyboard cover. Tried the pedals, one, two, three.

I thought for a second. And then, tentatively, quietly, I played it.

My Amberley audition.

Schubert's *Piano Sonata in A Major;* Bach's *Fugue No. 24 in B Minor;* Debussy's *Arabesque No. 1*—one tiny rebellion. They'd wanted something virtuosic for the third selection. I'd picked something I liked instead.

The piano still felt cold beneath my fingers, but I kept playing, buffeted by the memories I'd been blocking out for the past three months—the sweet orange oil smell of the audition room, the stage lights flooding the blind screen in opaque yellow, the three vague shadows beyond, the bench still warm from the last auditioner. I remembered exactly how I'd rushed that glissando, flubbed this B-flat, how there had been a voice in my head whispering, "*Is this good enough? Is this good enough?*" like every time I played. I remembered a real voice, Arnold Rombauer, saying "Thank you," in dismissal. Flat. Bored. Faintly irritated.

And I felt once again what I'd felt then, hearing that verdict—*relief.*

It was an ax coming down. It was an answer.

Tonight, here, now, I muddled through to the Debussy. I missed a few notes. And then more. And more, and more, and *more,* my fingers falling over themselves, begging me to stop.

I did. I gave in, slumping.

A floorboard creaked behind me. Oscar stood leaning against the doorframe, listening, his expression deeply peaceful. He straightened as I turned, clearing his throat.

"Back already." My voice sounded empty.

"I was worried about you."

I looked down. "You heard me play?"

"The last piece."

He sounded thoughtful more than friendly. Slowly, he strode over to stand beside the piano. I waited for him to lie: "You play beautifully." Or "I can see potential." Or "There's plenty of work out there for a good accompanist!"

But he stayed silent, watching like he finally understood.

I felt my shoulders relax. This, his silence, was as much a gift as Arnold Rombauer's dismissal had been back in April—an acknowledgment of what I already knew, of what Mom had always known.

Oscar walked behind me, lightly touching my fingers. "Your hands are small."

He didn't say it like he was trying to make excuses for me. More as a simple observation. Almost an endearment. Or maybe a reason to touch my hand, turn it over, run his fingers along each of mine.

My heart beat faster. "Mom's are small too. They say it's part of why she's such a brilliant musician. She had to work harder—change the traditional fingering in difficult pieces to suit her own hands, which makes it sound fresh, I guess. Unexpected." I drew a shaky breath. "I always thought that was what it took. Working as hard as *she* did, practicing the same number of hours, in the same schedule, the exact same . . ."

I touched the keys but didn't press them.

"The thing is . . ." I started to go on, but my voice clenched.

Oscar sat on the bench next to me.

"I love music. I love *experiencing* music. But the second I start to play, something sort of shuts off inside me. The joy evaporates—I feel like a machine. But I mean, a machine would at least be technically adept, right? I miss notes and lose my place and scramble to get back, no matter how many times I practice. Mom and Alice and everybody else, that doesn't happen to them. Which makes me wonder what's different about me? What's *missing*?"

My hand rested against my throat, as if to soothe the raw knot rising in it.

"And if it's not hard work and dedication," I went on, gritty, "then, I mean, maybe it's my soul. Maybe I don't have the soul for it?"

I'd never admitted it before, out loud or otherwise, but there it was. Giving up piano hadn't felt like a redirection or even a failure. It had felt like an admission—that I was lesser. That I was empty.

I caught a distorted glimpse of myself in the fallboard and forced my eyes away.

Oscar stared at the entryway. "Do you know what I thought, the first time I saw you? My very first impression? I thought you were a ghost."

I let out a surprised laugh. "I *knew* it. I looked—"

"You looked *beautiful*. You looked otherworldly." He turned to me.

"And I keep seeing it. You try so hard to be what other people need you to be, but then there are these moments where you're just . . . no bullshit. It's like your body's not there, and you're pure emotion, whatever the emotion is. Embarrassment or sadness or . . ." He frowned as if heartbroken himself. "I think it's why I can't stay away from you."

He stood, and I wanted to pull him back to me but stopped myself, my hands falling weakly into my lap.

Then I felt him walk behind me again. His body grazed my back and lowered—settling behind me on the bench. I slid forward to make room as his legs swung over, framing mine.

"I keep thinking about . . ." Oscar's warm breath swept my neck, shooting shivers along my skin. "How much I'd like to see you like that, pure emotion—but *happy*. I . . ."

His arms crept forward, around me.

"I want to be the one to make you feel that."

I waited for his fingers to move onto the keys, to compose something for me, the *Happy Ruby Suite*. But his hands landed on my knees, covering the green fabric of my dress and then slipping under, cool against my bare skin.

"Can I try, Ruby? I . . . I really want to try."

"Okay," I said, my own whisper shaking hot, as his fingers tingled up my thighs and higher. Then he kissed my neck and I couldn't say anything at all.

Higher still. And even more under.

My nerves skittered and settled.

This is new. It should be scary. After all, my prior experience consisted of a few underwhelming kisses from a Wildwood boy or two. But the scariest thing right now was how relaxed I felt. It was like I was alone in my room thinking about Oscar. But better. And better.

I let my eyes fall shut, my mind quieting to a sweet hum as I leaned against him and let his mouth find mine—maybe not pure emotion, not completely, but closer with every touch.

20.

The sky was ferociously blue, a brisk breeze softening the sun's blaze. It looked and smelled like France here.

"I feel like a bad influence." I glanced behind us, seeing only a docent and an elderly woman meditating on a bench. "Encouraging truancy."

"I told you, it's a sick day." Oscar spun. "Cough-cough."

"I just hope you don't get caught."

"What, here? In the year of our Lord eight hundred and seventy-eight?" Oscar kneeled to read a placard poking out of the monastic herb garden: *Pimpinella anisum*.

I stepped back, scanning the low-arched pink colonnade, tiled rooftops, square stone tower, cheerful little fruit trees, remembering the last time I was at the Cloisters—Mom, Nora, a swirl of adults, starlit, bleary. Visitors were sparse today, so I could do what I used to do as a little kid—imagine something parallel, better.

Me and Oscar in a world apart.

The thought started to unravel in a dangerous direction. I remembered last night—how far we'd gone before pulling back with effort, our chaste good-night, returning to our separate rooms, neither of us sleeping at all. How he'd waited on the stoop this morning to tell me he was playing hooky today, there was no way he'd get anything productive done. And now, here we were, free to do . . . whatever we wanted.

Oscar was watching me. I reached for him. His hand slipped into mine so easily now, like we'd been meant to fit together all along.

"I love it here," I said. "There are a handful of places in New York where you feel like you're somewhere else completely."

"Your courtyard," Oscar said.

"Yeah, that's one."

"It sounds like you're desperate to get out of the city."

"Not exactly." We glided through the walkways, footsteps echoing. "New York is magic. These places where the wall between worlds seems thin is part of it. It's probably the same in Paris or London or . . . anywhere with actual history, but still. I like it here."

"I do too." I wasn't sure whether Oscar meant New York or the Cloisters or right here with me, but the glint in his eye told me he meant it as a compliment. He nudged my shoulder. "New York's got history."

"I mean, yeah, for *America*—"

He motioned grandly. "The great Ruby Anna Chertok was born here."

"Hmmm, a common fallacy. The correct answer is Charleston, South Carolina."

He stopped mid-skip. "Wait, really?"

"Yeah, my grandparents live there—well, *near* there, on Wadmalaw Island. My mom was visiting and . . . whoops! Six weeks early. I spent the first four months of my life there. Mom stayed a while so her step-mom could help take care of me." I felt a wave of sadness chased with guilt, missing Grandma Jean way more than Mom. "Win teases me about it. Calls me a Southern belle."

"I'm a pseudo-Southerner too," Oscar said. "No wonder I like you so much."

He curled a finger around one of the belt loops of my shorts and gave a tug.

Would it be acceptable to make out in the middle of a model monastery?

"They have the unicorn tapestries here." I motioned to the stairs with a smile. "If you want to see them."

"I want to see them." Oscar laced his fingers into mine.

As we walked up the stairs, a tourist with a tight red perm started down, her broad husband trudging behind her. Her eyes flew right to Oscar and me and widened. She opened her mouth as if to say something, then shut it.

I turned my head casually away. But then she veered to us—impact in three, two . . .

"I'm sorry, but I have to say it," she launched in, staring daggers at Oscar—at our hands, locked together.

I held my breath. This couldn't be happening. Not in New York.

"That getup is *too*! *Much!* It is *so* nice to see young people dressing up for the museum."

Oscar grinned, stepping back to give her a better look at his suspenders. "I dress like this all the time!"

"*Good* for you," she said, then patted him approvingly on the back and continued along her way, glancing back at my outfit in apparent disappointment.

"Jesus," I muttered as we started to climb again. "I thought . . ."

"What?" Oscar eyed me.

"Nothing." That tourist wasn't racist, but now it felt like maybe I was. "You're so *charming* all the time. With total strangers. It's like you're setting out to dazzle them."

I'd said it to cut the tension, but Oscar's frown deepened. "I am. I have to."

We got to the top of the steps. I watched him, confused.

He sighed, turning our hands over to look at them together. "I need to give people a quick impression of who I am, what I'm about."

Before I could ask *why,* the answer hit me like ice water—

Because he was a seventeen-year-old black man. In America.

I didn't say anything, just squeezed his hand.

He squeezed back, silent a beat. Then: "I live in a, let's say . . . *affluent* neighborhood. My parents get pulled over every other week, I get tailed taking our beagle for a walk, so . . . I have to short-circuit whatever people's assumptions are going to be. It doesn't even always work."

"Don't you ever run out of energy?"

"No." He looked startled. "I can't, it's the only safe way to operate in spaces like this." He nodded upward, but I knew he didn't just mean the Cloisters. I thought about how his accent changed slightly when he spoke to my dad. Did he change it for me too?

I opened my mouth, not even sure what to say besides, "God, I'm sorry," but his eyes had already darted to the side, distracted. His hand slipped gently from mine, holding on at the fingertips, his body propelled around the corner, as if under some spell. He was taking us the wrong way.

"Hey," I started, but then I heard what had drawn his attention—singing. "Oh! There must be a concert."

We followed the sound to the chapel, where five voices filled the eaves with rapturous music. There were no seats in here, a sprinkling of visitors standing frozen as museum displays while they listened. The singers wore casual clothes. We'd stumbled into a rehearsal.

Oscar stood behind me and wrapped his arms around my waist. I leaned against him, letting the sound cocoon us. I couldn't see his face, but I sensed his eyes were closed. One note rose above the rest, plaintive, and we squeezed each other tighter at the sound.

As the singers finished, the chapel echoed with their final notes, then fell into the usual humdrum footsteps, coughs, conversation.

Oscar didn't say a word until we'd walked back outside. Then he drew a lusty breath, like the air smelled cleaner now that he'd heard that.

"What's this neighborhood?" he asked as we walked back to the subway.

"Washington Heights."

"Should we explore?"

"If you want to. We've pretty much seen what there is to see here."

"That was my first thought too." Oscar was looking at a mother and two kids on the opposite corner. "But people live here."

"Yeah. A lot of people. This being the city and all." I pulled out my phone. "Why don't I see what else there is around—?"

"No, it's cool." His eyes were troubled. "Another time."

"There's actually a lot," I said, holding up the map on my phone. "Morris-Jumel Mansion? Apparently haunted?"

I glanced up but he was already walking into the subway tunnel, MetroCard ready. Before I ran down, I scanned the street, desperate to see what had caught his attention—the half-scrubbed club posters clinging to a brick wall, the smell of chicken on a spit, music trickling out a second-floor window, its bass notes shaking the panes . . .

The downtown A train was pulling up when we made it through the stiles. As we settled into our plastic seats and rumbled south, one of the vocal lines of the song from the Cloisters got stuck in my head. I hummed it to get it out.

"That voice of yours." Oscar stretched his arm behind my neck. "You sing to yourself a lot."

"It's because I'm alone a lot. It's annoying, isn't it?"

"I love it." His hand draped lazily over my shoulder.

I nestled in. "Mom used to tell me I had a singer's musicality. But I think it was her way of discouraging me from playing the piano."

"I don't know, she might have a point. Did you pick out the tenor voice just from listening back there? Or can you remember all of them?"

"Um . . . no? I can't pick out . . ." I leaned away, laughing. "I've heard that piece a million times."

Oscar looked delightfully blank.

"It's di Lasso. One of his polyphonic masses?"

"Do you have a recording at home?"

"I can't believe it—*finally* something you don't know!"

Oscar gave a tight shrug, smiling even bigger. "There's a ton I don't know."

The train car stopped, letting people off and on. Oscar scooted closer to make room for a woman with a toddler in a stroller. I glanced down to see his foot tapping a frenetic beat against the floor.

I touched his leg and it stopped. My hand stayed there, on his thigh, and I watched, gratified, as the tension in his eyes softened into something warmer.

He was anxious. Trying to hide it.

"Are you thinking about your piece?"

"I should be." Oscar laughed. "No, I'm thinking about how I'm seventeen and I've got old men calling me 'maestro.' It's . . . a trip."

"You know how many people would kill to be called 'maestro'?" I shot him a playful glare. "Old men. Women, any age. *And* people in their thirties, forties . . ."

"I do know. This is the *dream,* right? Sometimes I think it might be better if I were in my thirties. This all feels weird to me." His voice sounded upbeat—but his arm was taut against my back. "Like, overblown. Do you know what I mean?"

I thought about the *New York Times* interview. The splashy premiere for a symphony that hadn't even been written yet.

"I saw your YouTube video," I said.

"When? Before . . ."

"No. Right after we met." I turned to him. His thumb idly stroked my shoulder as he waited for me to go on. "You're really good."

He leaned his head against the dark window. "Really good. See . . . I like 'really good.' *Really good* feels sturdy. Every time I hear the word *genius,* it feels like I'm in a prank video. I start looking for the hidden camera."

He mimed paranoia, shielding his face, and I laughed, debating what to say. Should I tell him how much that word got thrown around at this level of the classical music world, so often that you became completely immune to it? How, despite that, I used to fantasize about overhearing someone use it about me? *"Ruby's take on the Nancarrow is stunning, Anna. You've got another genius on your hands . . ."*

Oscar snuck a tickling kiss on the curve of my neck, returning me to the real world in one happy gasp.

"Do you think those guys were monks?" he whispered into my shoulder.

"Who?" I laughed. "The singers?

"Do they live at the Cloisters?"

I fell against him as I giggled. "It's a museum! A replica."

"There could have been a place to sleep. We didn't tour everything."

"They weren't monks. They were wearing, like, shorts . . ." He started to argue, but I grinned, talking over him. "And one of them was a *woman*."

Another stop. A pregnant lady stepped in, holding on to the bar. Oscar jumped up to give her his seat.

"Can't women be monks?" He stood over me, our legs interspersed like a backgammon board. "This is the twenty-first century."

"No, they still can't be monks." I pinched the knee of his trousers, wishing I could drag him down. "They can be *anchorites*."

He nodded. "Good word."

"I used to be sort of obsessed with the idea of becoming an anchorite."

"Normal."

"I thought it was a good threat whenever I got in trouble. 'I'm moving to the woods and becoming an anchorite and you'll never find me!' It sounded fun. Hole up someplace pretty, some, like, forest idyll that's quiet and private. And you have an *order* or whatever that checks in from a distance and makes sure you're not deathly ill and in the meantime, you can do whatever you want with your life. Dance or plant flowers or play your instrument or talk to the animals, with nobody around to witness it."

The train began to slow. He rocked against me, legs touching, left, right.

"You don't want to do that anymore, though, do you?" Oscar's eyes were warm on mine. "Leave the world behind. All the people in it."

"No." I peered up at him. "I don't."

My pulse felt steadier, saying that out loud.

Oscar glanced over his shoulder. "Is this—?"

"Oh crap, this is us."

We zoomed out like toy cars as the doors were sliding shut.

"Where to now?" I asked Oscar.

"Home," he said, a dangerous edge to his smile. "Let's be anchorites."

21.

We maintained a G-rated distance from each other even after we ducked into the basement apartment and shut the door. Oscar's couch, walls, floor were carpeted with composition paper. But the bed was clear.

He sat on the end of the mattress. "Come here."

I walked over slowly, then stood in front of him the way he'd hovered over me on the subway. He lifted my shirt, gently, like it might disintegrate under his fingertips, and kissed my stomach.

I closed my eyes and my knees softened, the rest of me folding down, Oscar guiding my back to the side until I was lying on the bed and he was above me. Something told me this wasn't something anchorites did much of.

He kissed me, slow and deep, his chest grazing my own, hips falling onto mine. I pulled him closer, thirsty to my bones. The more familiar his kiss became, the more it seemed to affect me.

His right hand cupped my shoulder and his left slid under my shirt, tracing the lace of my bra. His touch was so soft it felt respectful—reverent. He drew away to look at me, brown eyes wide, almost pained.

"Ruby," he said. "Ruby Ruby Ruby . . ."

"*Oscar Oscar Oscar,*" I teased—but my mind was whirring back to life.

His voice had made my name sound apologetic. Like there was a caveat hanging over his head. Then I looked over his shoulder and saw it, pinned to the wall, strewn everywhere. Oscar's "sick day" could only last so long. He hadn't come to New York to make out with me, after all.

And there was one thing I was good at—I'd been doing it my whole life.

"Hey." I cleared my throat and pulled myself sitting. "I'm distracting you."

Oscar propped himself up on one arm. "What?"

"You've got serious work cut out for you here. And I'm—"

"I'm not worried about the symphony."

"You are worried about something." I pulled my shirt down and crossed my arms over it. "Do you want to talk about it? Or . . . ?"

"I'm good. You don't need to . . ." He grinned, letting out a breathy laugh. "I'm fine!"

It was convincing. But his hand was clenching and unclenching next to him. I wondered if he even knew he was doing it.

"Okay. Well." I slid off the bed. "I've lived with a composer my entire life, so I seriously do know the drill. You need space to be inspired. If you don't get enough of it, stress builds up and . . ."

You get short-tempered. You throw things and trash your study and barely say two words to your entire family for weeks.

I blinked, hard. "Get some work done, that's all I'm saying. And then find me when you're ready to take a break. You know where I live."

I nodded upstairs, like he needed the visual aid.

"When does your dad get back?" Oscar blurted.

My mind ping-ponged between the many different reasons he could have asked that question. "Friday morning."

"I'm supposed to have a second movement to show him by then."

"Ah."

"You're right, I should probably make some headway."

He peered up at me, waiting for a counterargument to my own argument. I felt a tugging in my chest, like I'd been hooked and he was reeling me closer.

"Or . . ." I said, my knees sinking onto the mattress.

He grinned. "*Or . . .*"

My phone beeped—a text, a nagging memory rising with it.

I stood up again, grabbing my phone.

Nora. *Still on for lunch?* :)

"It's Monday. *Crap.* I was supposed to—I am so late!" I turned around, pointlessly. "Ugh. I'm gonna cancel."

Oscar stood. "No, if you've got something to—"

"It's not . . ." I clicked my phone off. "In any way important."

"No no no, you've got your life," he said, holding my arms, steadying me. "I get it! And, you're right . . . I should . . . yeah . . ."

I opened my mouth to protest, but his eyes had already drifted to the sheets hanging on the walls—lost in music in the space of a blink.

Nora's house was cool and dry. It smelled like lilies and wood polish. As a woman in a housekeeping uniform shut the huge mahogany door behind me, I took a step farther into the grand entryway, and the sound of it echoed up three curved flights of stairs, making me crane my head as if I could follow its flight.

Nora poked her head over the banister. "Come up, sweetness! I'm just sending an email."

I walked up the stairs slowly, glancing back to make sure I wasn't tracking anything onto her plush blue runners, passing another maid, arms laden with linens, a door ajar to a gold-lit room with wall-to-wall bookshelves, two white dogs running away from yet another house-keeper, and then the highest level, where Nora was coming out of what looked like a bedroom, slipping her phone into her purse with a decisive, "Done! Ah, you're so pretty, I can't *stand* it."

"I'm so sorry I'm late," I sputtered. "I—"

Nora shushed me, eyes twinkling as if she knew exactly what I'd been busy doing. She started down the stairs at a trot and I kept pace behind her, wondering how somebody as clumsy as she was managed not to trip.

At the golden room, she slowed to call out, "Stephen! Just popping out for lunch with Ruby Chertok."

An older gentleman appeared in the doorway in shirtsleeves, a copy of the *Financial Times* stuck under his arm. I knew this was Nora's husband—I'd even met him a few times—but it still took me a second to connect this face with his name. He peered over his glasses at me, having the same trouble.

"The littlest Chertok? Christ, look at you."

Nora laughed, pulling me with her as she shouted back up. "Dinner with the Hewetts, don't forget!"

He'd already disappeared back into the study.

"I'm glad you came," Nora said, her heels clicking cheerfully on the wood of the foyer. "I wasn't sure if you were going to forgive me for last night."

She turned quickly to face me, so I couldn't quite land the unruf-fled reaction I'd been aiming for.

"The last thing in the world I'd ever want to do is embarrass you. Or make you feel small. I hope you know that."

"Of course." I did know that. I remembered. But it didn't connect with what happened last night. And was that even an apology or a weird kind of denial? "It was fine!"

The first housekeeper I'd seen held the door for us. Nora smiled at her as we stepped out onto the porch, met with sour humidity and the blast of a car honk—buffeted by the real world in an instant.

Nora started toward Gramercy Park and I followed, stomach rumbling in anticipation.

"So." Nora glanced back at me. "Can we talk about Oscar?"

"I . . . sure?"

"A tiny request from your loving godmother . . ." She linked arms with me and squeezed. "Watch out for him."

I blinked, reeling. Had Nora changed her mind about us?

"He's so special, and confident when it matters, but . . ." Nora sighed. "This is a lot for somebody so young. I don't want the stress to wear on him."

I let out a silent, relieved laugh. "I get that. I've been basically telling him the same thing."

Nora turned to me. "Is he having trouble?"

"N-no!" I sputtered, pinned. "Not at all. You know Oscar, he's got, like, super-human confidence."

"As he *should*." She pressed her lips together. "But keep an eye on him, Ruby. If he looks like he needs a lifeline—come to me first."

Um. Instead of Dad? Was that what she . . . ?

Before I could answer, she patted my hand and kept us walking. I skipped to catch up—she had a fast stride for someone so short. We hit the fenced edge of the park and I glanced inside. The gate was usually locked, available only to those residents lucky enough to have keys, but it was flung wide today, a group of teenagers sitting on the

194

pathway with sketchpads while a teacher motioned to the trees, tracing lines in the air with his fingers.

"Oh." Nora stopped walking. "They're not supposed to be in there." She turned to me, eyes huge. "Do you think I should call someone?"

She looked like a child, asking permission.

"No," I blurted, surprised. "That's not—"

"You're right, they're harmless." Nora glanced at her phone for the time, slid it back into her bag. "I'm so sorry, I can't believe this, but I'm going to have to table our lunch."

Table, meaning eat at a table, or . . . ?

"Something's popped up. It's urgent, obviously, or I wouldn't dream of canceling on you . . ."

Canceling. You have got to be kidding me.

"But are we good? I really do feel terrible for putting you on the spot like that."

She peered up at me with big eyes and I finally understood Alice's "bunnies in a meadow" comment.

"Don't feel terrible," I said. "We're good."

Nora stepped to the curb and waved for a taxi. As the cab rolled away, I wondered why she wasn't taking her town car—and why she'd just told Stephen she'd be having lunch with me.

It's none of my business, I told myself.

And Oscar is none of hers.

He was Jules's business, apparently.

"You prissy little Puritan, I want some goddamned details!" she snapped, jogging beside me along the mossy edge of the Turtle Pond. "Give me a base."

"*What* grade are we in?" I laughed—and then marveled at the fact that I now had enough stamina to *laugh* two miles into the morning jog. "Third."

"You or him?"

"Sort of both?"

"Nice!"

We veered right, through the trees toward Belvedere Castle.

"So why are you in such a huff? Or is it a tizzy?" She narrowed her eyes. "I'm leaning toward huff."

"Because . . ." I sighed. It did, in fact, sound like a huff. "That was Sunday night. We hung out Monday too, and got, um, interrupted, and I'd at least expected him to text me later. I'd laid it out there for him. But it's Wednesday—"

"Thursday."

"Really? Ugh. This is what happens when your life has no schedule. *Any*way, I haven't heard from him since then. Or seen him. Nothing."

"Have you texted him?"

"Yeah, twice. Once asking him if he wanted to grab dinner, another one that was, like, a confused-face emoji."

"Wow. How do you manage to ghost somebody who lives upstairs from you? I'd be impressed if I weren't so indignant."

My pace flagged. Jules jogged a few steps ahead, then turned. I powered on.

"So what is your deal, anyway?" Jules looked at me. "Are you two exclusive? Is he dating other people? Do musicians even manage to hook up or are they too busy rehearsing all the time—?"

"No, they hook up." My mouth felt dry. "Especially in summer programs, it's like this weird teenaged bacchanal. With less booze. Not that I've ever . . . yeah."

"Is *that* where you used to go every summer? Music programs?"

"Yeah. Wildwood. Adirondacks."

"Not Amberley?"

"I'm not good enough for Amberley."

"How do you know that?"

"Because I auditioned."

Jules slowed, hunching, and motioned us to a bench—and for one split second, my angst was replaced with a surge of pride that I'd managed to outlast her for the first time. Then the angst surged back, full force. Maybe Oscar decided there were too many points against us being together. Maybe he was caught up in his composition and forgot I existed. Maybe—

"You should show up," Jules said, hands pressed to her thighs.

I squinted.

"At his, like, Rachmaninoff Baroque quartet rehearsal or whatever."

A snort burst out of me. "Sorry . . . you called Rachmaninoff *Baroque*."

"Whatever," she groaned. "Go to Lincoln Center, sneak in, observe unseen. Take a look at what's going on when you're not around."

"You don't mean confront him, you mean *stalk* him." For some reason, that came as a relief.

"Potato, potahto." She nodded to the path and we started to jog again, more slowly this time.

I thought about her suggestion. The idea started to swirl and gather, a perfect storm of compulsions.

"Hey, so," Jules said, her tone approaching awkward. "Kudzu Giants are coming to Amsterdam Ballroom in August and we got you a ticket."

"We?"

"You know, the 'gang.'" She rolled her eyes. "Well, I'm the one who bought the ticket, but everybody's hoping you'll come."

"That sounds awesome. Wow." I smiled, touched. "I mean, I don't listen to a ton of hip-hop, so I probably won't know the songs . . ."

Jules turned with a snort to match my own. "You called Kudzu Giants hip-hop."

"Are they not?"

She slung an arm over my shoulder. "We have so much to teach each other."

We passed a block lined with white trailers for a film shoot. Jules grumbled at having to detour, but I still caught her glancing back to see what they were shooting.

I grinned at her. She ignored me.

When we reached the house, I stooped to peek into the basement window. It was dark inside, Oscar already gone.

"Listen," Jules said. "I think you should definitely go spy on genius boy, but . . ." She scuffed the sidewalk with her sneaker. "Maybe use it as an opportunity to clear your head? To see that he has this whole Amberley *whatever* life . . ."

She drew a circle in the air.

"And you have your whole amazing *awesome* life and . . ."

She swatted at her nose. I was guessing that wasn't part of the illustration.

"You're a perfectly complete person with or without him. And—if you want to be 'beckoned,' like you said, if that's what you're into, then great. Just . . ."

I waited, watching her flail for the right words.

Then she looked me right in the eye, as serious as I'd ever seen her. "You do what *you* want to do, Ruby. Take what you want out of . . .

this." She gestured upward into the air. "It's our chance to stop living for other people. This summer. Right now."

"I'm . . ." I winced. "Not sure what you mean? Oscar's someone in my life, but I wouldn't say I'm living *for* him."

Her face fell. Then she smiled. "Okay. Well. That's ideal. Text me after your stalking session!"

She blew me a kiss and trotted down the block and up the steps to her apartment, and I stood on the sidewalk, mulling.

No, I decided. *This is* ridiculous. *I'm going to give him space. And myself. Why rush to define the relationship? If it even is a relationship—we're hanging out, seeing where it goes, right?*

I texted Jules at 4:02. *What's the right outfit to stalk somebody?*

The reply came instantly: *Earth tones or grays, classic lines, soft soled flats, ponytail.*

"Okay then," I said out loud. "I guess I'm doing this."

22.

*b*ad idea. I hit West Sixty-sixth Street. *So many levels.* Sixty-fifth.

When I stepped onto the plaza, I expected to feel the same controlled panic as last time—an astronaut bracing for reentry—but the place seemed to have lost some of its turbulence.

Maybe because I had a singular purpose this time. It wasn't stalking—it was *truth-seeking.* Totally honorable.

I seemed to remember Amberley's rehearsal schedule being fairly regular. Mornings for class, afternoons for sectionals, evenings for full orchestra rehearsals. I "seemed to remember" it because I used to sit in the back of Lilly Hall and watch them, sure I'd be among their ranks one day. It was easy to be sure when you were nine.

I stepped into the ice-cold lobby—empty, good start—and listened. There was no sound in the auditorium except someone talking, too far to hear. I stepped forward, tentative, and then—

The orchestra erupted.

It was familiar, stone and color and wind. I squinted, listening, trying to identify the composer . . .

"Oh my God," I mouthed. "*Oh* my *God!*"

Soundlessly screaming, I opened the door to the auditorium, sliding inside to crouch in the last row. All the house lights were up, but there were a lot of lookie-loos, and not one head turned to see who had popped in. They were all staring forward.

Watching Oscar Bell conduct *his own symphony*.

It was the theme he'd played me, but hearing it on my piano had been like watching that single light shoot up in the sky before the fireworks go off. Now they had exploded, unexpected colors, a million new directions, and I was stunned. I didn't know where this chair, this floor, this hall ended and I began.

I only knew, with absolutely certainty, how I felt about the composer.

The second theme came in. The Romantic theme, Dad had called it. I held my breath, listening to it tease and hide and caress the first theme, heal it like balm on a livid burn. It felt like a whispered message meant only for me.

But then, from my hiding spot behind a row of seats, I saw who was playing it. First violin. She was standing up, watching Oscar as she drew out the notes with her bow, piercing in their beauty and longing. It was gorgeous enough to make you believe *she* was feeling it. That he was too.

The orchestra swelled with a syncopated march beat that I picked out as the sound of the subway, the swoosh and stop and sway and stop. But my eyes kept darting between Oscar, his broad back, hair bobbing, arms flying, and that violinist, playing so beautifully. She was astonishing.

She was impaling my heart with every note.

The strings rose for a bar, then Oscar waved his hands and dropped them and everybody stopped.

"That's what I'm talking about!" Oscar shouted. "That was great, but if you can get to that fire, that"—he made a loose fist—"*oomph* by bar twenty, it'll make that pizzicato more jarring. Does that make sense?"

The string section laughed and nodded. A man—Reinhardt, the regular orchestra director—tapped his watch from the side of the stage with an indulgent smile, and Oscar straightened as if startled.

"Ah crap, that's it! That's all we have time for tonight, thank you guys so much, this has been amazing. *Will* be amazing."

He put down his baton and the orchestra settled, starting to chat. I shrunk into a seat, wondering whether to escape now or continue my recon. The violinist beelined for Oscar as he stepped away from the podium and that made the decision for me.

I froze, watching. She touched his arm to whisper in his ear. He threw his head back to laugh, exposing the elegant length of his neck like he was inviting her to kiss it. She curved her body into that telltale S shape that meant "I'm into you." And then he leaned forward . . . and whispered back.

See, this—*this* made sense! So much more sense than me and Oscar, whatever we were. They could have *such* a future together. Midnight music sessions, a joint concert tour, a dozen brilliant prodigy children, who was I to stand in the way? And I'd find someone else. A Joey. Joey was great! Nice, friendly, above-average at math, an easy keel through a normal life . . . it was lovely, inevitable. I would get used to the feeling of my heart hemorrhaging with every beat. *Totally* fine.

I slid from the aisle the exact moment Oscar turned.

He saw me. And he did not smile. He looked stricken.

He had something to hide. He cared enough to *want* it hidden.

I started away, but Oscar raced up the aisle, hand outstretched to intercept me.

"You heard."

"I did." My voice shook even on those two little words.

"It's not anywhere close to ready, but they want me to start working it with the orchestra so that I can move on to the second movement . . ."

I had to sit against the stiff back of a velvet seat, I was so thrown. Was he *not* hooking up with that girl?

"If I'd known you'd be listening, I don't think I could have gone through with it."

"The rehearsal? I . . . why?"

He took my hand and ran his rough thumb over it. "Because I want you to think I'm brilliant."

"You *are* brilliant." *That's the problem. That's the whole stupid problem.* "This . . . symphony is . . . it's true, you know? It has breath in it. A soul. I . . ."

My eyes welled up. I was such a lunatic.

Oscar's eyes were glistening too. "You *like* it?"

I could only nod—overcome with relief, with wild affection, with recognition of how much I'd *missed* this.

"It wasn't—?" he started.

"It was *incredible*, Oscar." I finally let myself smile. "It's going to be—"

He stopped me with a kiss so fervent, the ground, the chandeliers, the entire hall disappeared around us until all of existence consisted of our two bodies, floating in space. When he pulled away, smoothing my hair, Lilly Hall crept back in, detail by detail, blurry with unreality.

I glanced back at the orchestra and saw the violinist's head darting quickly away, like she'd been watching. She did have a crush. I no longer blamed her.

"Do you need to get back?" I nodded to the stage.

"No, I'm done. They're rehearsing Ralph Vaughan Williams next. He couldn't make it out tonight to conduct."

"Being dead and all?"

"Unprofessional, but what can you do?" He pulled a frown and I laughed. "Shall we?"

We stepped into the plaza, our shadows stretching endlessly along the flagstones.

"So I haven't—" I said, as he blurted, "I'm sorry I haven't—" He chuckled, uneasy. "Go on."

"I was going to say something along the lines of *long time no see*."

"And I was going to say something along the lines of *sorry I'm such a hermit asshole stereotype of a musician*."

"Oh, *that* old expression." I nudged him with my shoulder while I listened hard for the real answer.

"I've been in a fever, all this music coming out since we went to the Cloisters. Since we . . ." He drew a breath and seemed to hold it. I held mine too, remembering a few nights ago. "I needed to orchestrate the first movement and all the pieces seemed to come together."

"You did all the orchestrations in the past two days? How—?"

"I haven't really been sleeping?"

Now that I was looking more closely, Oscar seemed thin. His hands were trembling. He caught me looking and shoved them in the pockets of his pants.

Thunder rolled somewhere to the east, the light shifting orange.

"So have you been home this whole time?" I asked. "I would have helped you, you know. I could have brought you food or—"

"I didn't want to bother you. You've got your own life."

His words were an echo of what he'd said before I went to Nora's. An echo of Jules's words too. They heartened and worried me.

We stopped at a crosswalk. A drop of rain hit my head. Oscar looked up as if he could identify the source.

I turned to him, blood pumping. "Okay, so, I really don't want to be 'that girl' and I know we've only known each other for a few weeks, so this might sound like it's coming out of left field, but what—?"

"Do you want to be my girlfriend?"

I blinked. "Do I . . . ?"

"I feel like I'm eight. Check one for yes, two for no." He bit his bottom lip, eyes alight.

"You had girlfriends when you were *eight*?"

"Elisa Meyers, lasted three days, what's your answer."

"Yes." My voice sounded like *I* was eight. "Yes, option two, I will be your girlfriend."

Oscar hugged me tight, his mouth pressed to my forehead, rocking me back and forth. Then he murmured into my ear, "Girlfriend was option one."

I poked him in the ribs. He laughed and dodged away. The rain started coming down hard. We ran across the street, holding hands, but were already drenched by the time we hit the opposite curb.

"Ack!" I let out a mock-scream, head ducked to avoid the deluge.

Oscar pulled me to a corner store, and I thought for a second he was leading me inside, but then he stopped us outside the flowers, under the awning where the scent was thickest, and kissed my wet face. My forehead, my cheeks, my chin.

He glanced up at the flimsy awning. "Can't have my girlfriend getting wet."

"How gallant." I could barely think, I was smiling so much. "There's this expression, 'Don't like the weather in New York? Wait five minutes.' Hardy-har-har."

How was I still talking with his mouth tracing the curve of my neck?

He straightened, staring into my eyes. "Every city has that expression."

"Not Phoenix." I nodded, just as serious. "It's sunny all the time."

"We should go there," Oscar said, edging us back into the rain. "We should go everywhere."

I pulled him faster. "Let's start with home."

23.

my clothes were saturated, cool and clinging. I felt every inch of my own skin and I wanted it bare. I wanted to feel him peeling these stalker earth tones off me.

Oscar's pockets were so sodden, it took both of us to tug his keys out. I had my own, but I liked the feeling that this was his place, not mine, that I was being invited in.

He danced me inside and the door swung shut, pushing a damper pedal on the rest of the world. His white button-down shirt was practically translucent. I started to unbutton it, neck to waist, airing one inch of beautiful brown skin at a time, and his breathing went funny. His head dipped low, watching me, then he ripped the shirt off like it was hurting him and reached for me.

I kissed him like this was the only chance we'd ever get—it might have been, with Dad coming back in a matter of hours—but he touched me, languid and slow, making me move even faster.

I started to tug my shirt up. Oscar hesitated—just a beat—then bunched the wet fabric in his own fingers and pulled it up over my head. I laughed, stumbling. This looked so much more graceful in the movies. But then his mouth was on my neck and his fingers were dipping gently below the line of my bra and I was all nerves, all want.

Before it could overwhelm me, I pulled him to the bed. He lowered himself over me, eyes hazy and eager. But as I arched my back, lifting my mouth to his, he blinked hard, waking himself up from a spell.

"Ruby . . ." He brushed my wet hair from my face. "We should slow down."

"Why?" I ran my fingers along his smooth back, thrilling at the shiver he responded with. I didn't want to slow down. I wanted to charge ahead, know what I was missing. I reached for the button of his pants.

He drew a sharp breath, then pulled my hand away.

I felt my body freeze in a rolling tide from my toes to my face. He didn't want to. I was his girlfriend as of tonight and we'd run through the city in the rain and we were all alone and it wasn't going to get more romantic than this, so what could be . . .

I sat up. "Do we need to get protection?"

I wobbled on the word *protection*. I'd never said it in this context in my life.

"Ah . . . I do have some condoms. After the other night . . ." Oscar motioned upward, indicating the spot where my piano bench sat. "I guess I was feeling optimistic."

He was smiling, but he was also shifting as far across the dorm bed as he could get.

"Well, great. So . . ." I felt really naked now. And wet and cold, with Oscar's window-unit AC aimed straight at me.

"Oh, crap, let me get you a towel," Oscar said, hopping off the bed. As he walked away, my skin went goose-bumpy. I crossed my arms over myself, weirdly ashamed, like I'd thrown myself at him instead of reciprocating.

He draped a striped beach towel over my shoulders like a queen's mantle. "I think this is a little fast. I mean, I'm gonna sound like you now, but it feels like we just met. Do we know each other well enough for . . . this?"

My mind raced back to the museum, his rebuttal. "I know you better than you think."

"Really?" His eyes lit, playful.

"I know your favorite composer, whether you'll admit it or not."

"Who?"

I whapped him. "Come on. 'The man'?"

He almost smiled. "What else?"

"Um." I bit my knuckle. "The way you write, the way your fingers move when you're composing in your head . . ."

I demonstrated, a tiny spell.

A grin flashed over his face. "Fair enough. But . . . there are key things we haven't even . . ."

"Oh." I waited for him to admit it—the cause of the tension I could still see whirring underneath his smile. Was it what he'd started telling me that night at Wing Club, the feeling he had of being on parade?

But he shrugged. "Your non-summer life. My life back home. My friends, my school, your friends, your school. Whether I have pets. I realize this sounds stupid—"

"You have a beagle." I tucked my knees under the towel, the fever of a few minutes ago feeling more like an illness now. "Sorry, go ahead."

Oscar let out a frustrated groan. "I don't want to be some fling for you."

I closed my eyes, reliving that shock of emotion I'd felt tonight listening to his symphony. Not *fling*. *Catapult*.

"Anybody else, not you. I don't want to wind up some story you tell your friends, about that time you were seventeen and . . ." He cleared his throat, nervous. "This feels more important than that. To me."

I started to reply, turning the word *fling* over in my head one more time, but then he blurted, "I haven't done this before, is the thing. I've done . . . other things. There are girls I've gone out with, but I haven't had sex." He watched for my reaction. "So that's why I'm, ah, jittery?"

"I haven't had sex either. I . . . haven't done anything? I haven't been with anyone at all, I've kissed two guys before you, one at a middle school party and another at Wildwood, but neither of them were anything like this. So."

Silence filled the room. I hoisted up the beach towel and tried to bury myself under it.

He tugged it below my face so he could cup my cheeks.

"This is *good*. This is what I want to know. I think I . . . I had the wrong take on you. I've been catching myself trying to, like, woo you with my musical prowess—"

I almost cackled. "*What?*"

"I know. I'm gonna dial it back, I promise."

"There's nothing to dial back. Wait, what was your *take* on me?"

"Ahhhh." He nestled next to me, playing with my hair. "I think your friend Jules threw me. All the, like, society stuff you do with Ms. Visser. And the way your family joked about you never having a serious boyfriend. I figured you were, you know, on the scene, different guy every week . . ."

"If by guy you mean Ben and Jerry's flavor, then maybe." I blinked hard, rebooting. "Yeah, no. That girl, out at the club, it was a life I was trying on. A different one from my own. And . . . ditto the philanthropy stuff. Society. Whatever."

"So what is your own life?" His voice was quiet.

The only things that sprang to mind were choices I could eliminate: musician, socialite, *Vogue* editor, normal teenager. "I don't know yet."

The corners of his eyes crinkled up. "Best possible answer."

"Really?" I relaxed into the pillow, turning to face him, our noses nearly touching. "It feels scary."

"Life should feel scary. It means you're living it. I don't know what my life is going to look like in ten years. I have no fucking clue."

"Oh good grief." I grinned. "You're going to be a star, Oscar."

"A star *what*?"

"Composer, conductor, international ambassador to the classical music world. The toast of the cultural scene wherever you go. And whatever else you want to be."

"That's what I thought before I got here. I was sure of it." He closed his eyes and rubbed them with his knuckles. "I think ahead now and it's . . . static. Totally blank."

"You're just in the thick of it." I touched his temples, his smooth jaw. His eyes stayed closed but seemed to relax under my fingers. "You shouldn't be thinking ahead anyway, like you said. Try to enjoy what's happening."

"I'm enjoying parts of it." His eyes opened, laser-locked on mine.

I wanted to kiss him, to roll him over me, break down every physical barrier between us—but I pulled my hand back and pinned it safely beneath me. Not yet.

"What school do you go to?"

He draped his arm over my waist, smiling softly. "Farnwell Prep."

"Why does that sound familiar? Did you already tell me—?"

"I might have. But no, it's sort of famous. It's where the president's son went, lots of politicians' kids. Fancy-fancy."

"Do you like it?"

"I do!" His eyes wandered to the ceiling, like he could see a model of his campus hovering there. "It's funny, I wasn't sure at first. It's very, ah . . . Anglo. But it isn't that prep stereotype, either. Everybody's nerdy, so everybody's chill."

"TJ?" I smiled.

"*He* might be more nerdy than most. All my core people have, like, obsessive interests, though, not just orchestra. TJ plays trumpet but he wants to design games. Seamus paints these amazing murals . . . It's a good school."

"Are all your friends orchestra people?"

He scratched his head. "That's kind of the way it goes. How about you? Your . . . seven black friends?" Oscar smiled, teasing, but there was a current of intensity under it. "Are they orchestra geeks?"

"No," I said, and he nodded like he'd expected that answer. I wasn't ready to admit that none of those school friends were my "core people," as he'd put it, so I said, "They've got pretty eclectic interests too. My friend Farrah is first chair in our school orchestra, but she's not, like, going pro. She wants to be a medical researcher." Curing cancer. Ha, I hadn't thought of that. Go Farrah. "Honestly, Exton is a pretty standard private school—"

"That's another nice thing about Farnwell." Oscar propped himself up. "They let me veer off from my class schedule if I have a day that needs to be all music. Which is more than I can say for my parents."

I frowned, surprised. "Are they not supportive?"

"They're the most supportive parents in the world. But it's all college all the time. My mom monitors our GPAs on, like, a week-to-week basis. She's terrified that I'm not 'well-rounded.'" He sighed. "She means well. She wants us to be safe in the world."

I marked his choice of words. Not *successful,* not *happy—safe.*

"What about you?" Oscar asked gently. "The piano . . . was that something they pushed?"

I wished I could say yes. That it had been foisted upon me against my wishes. Giving it up would have been that much more cathartic.

Mom's voice echoed in my head. *Put her on mute.*

"No." I swallowed. "They never pushed anything on me."

We were getting close to something I didn't want to touch.

Oscar's fingers traced my spine. "When did your mom leave?"

Something detonated in my chest, shrapnel scattering. There it was. "She's on tour."

He went still, waiting for an answer. Something true.

"July. *Last* July." My eyes started to well. "Almost a year ago . . ." A tear fell, my nose stinging. I swiped it, heaving a jerky breath. "Ugh, I don't know what's *wrong* with me."

He held my face gently and wiped the tear with his thumb. "You miss her?"

"No, I don't want to." I sniffed, forcing my eyes dry. "That other piano in our sitting room is hers. Nobody ever dared touch it. She rehearsed on it every day—it was her *home,* do you know what I mean? It bugs me that she never came to get it. I think it's what bugs me the most, but maybe that's part of touring, soloing, if you're successful. You need to adapt. And she's busy, I know she's busy." I filled my lungs until they stung. "Anyway. We'll make up for lost time when she gets a break."

"And you've got your dad."

"I texted her that I quit the piano. Back in April, after my Amberley audition."

"You auditioned—?" Oscar's eyes widened. "Sorry, no, go on."

"She didn't . . ." I pressed my lips together. "She probably didn't know what to say. I don't know, she didn't write back."

Oscar perched on his elbow. "She didn't write back about that? Or . . ."

"No, I haven't . . ." I exhaled the rest of my sadness away. "I haven't heard from her since March, I guess? Anyway. No big deal. Tell me about these girls you went out with but did not have sex with."

Even Oscar's teeth seemed to blush.

"What?" I smiled. "It's my turn, right?"

"Yeah, fair enough. They were orchestra girls. One played the . . . I guess they all played the violin."

"Oh God." I pulled the towel up, laughing. "You have a type and it's not me."

"It's you," he murmured. "It's only you."

I dropped the towel.

He cleared his throat, lips pressed together to stifle a smile. "My turn. Favorite piece of classical music. I've got a hunch you actually have an answer to this one."

"You're going to make fun of me."

"'Rock Me Amadeus' is not classical."

I laughed, pushing his shoulder. "How do you even know that song? How do *I*?"

"The answer is always YouTube. But for real, what's your favorite? I won't laugh."

I bit my pinkie. "'Clair de Lune.'"

"'Clair de Lune' is incredible! Why would I make fun of that?"

"I feel like it got ruined. Have you seen—?"

"Oh riiiiight. Mr. Romantic Vampire, playing the piano. There's a reason they picked that song, though. It's lush."

"Right? It feels powerful, you know? Like you're swimming in the ocean, and you can't stand anymore and the water . . . takes your weight."

I lifted my hands, palms up, demonstrating.

Oscar's eyes went twinkly. He brushed my hair from my forehead, silently mouthing my name.

I could still hear the music in my head. "It's so beautiful."

"It's love." Oscar peered at the ceiling again. "Most classical music is. Not all, but most. You know . . ." He rolled over to face me. "I can appreciate all kinds of music, I really can. I think there's something there. But hip-hop, pop, it speaks to *front,* you know? It's the face you show the world, what you want to project. Classical speaks right to what you're feeling. What you hide. What you long for."

"What do you long for?"

I thought he might say something cheesy or grab me and kiss me, but his face went even more serious.

"To be seen."

It took me a second to speak. "Me too."

His eyes fell on mine. He saw me. And then, yeah—he kissed me. And in a strange way, that felt like being seen too.

We did not have sex.

We talked.

We ordered burritos and ate them.

I changed into dry PJs upstairs and raced back to him as fast as my sandaled feet could carry me.

We kissed, rolled, explored, did not have sex, talked about having sex, talked about talking about having sex, talked about when we were little and bigger and whatever size we were now, we talked . . . we slept.

And we woke to Dad pounding on the apartment door.

24.

"**P**arty's over," Dad bellowed. "I'm back!"

"*Yooooooooo,*" Oscar murmured, eyes instantly wide. My hair clung to his face as he sat up.

"Come up when you're ready," Dad shouted, to the street as much as the apartment. "I'll have Ruby make us coffee."

I whispered, "He doesn't know I'm in here," holding Oscar in place. His heart raced against my arm. "No?"

"Ogre voice. Messing with you." I reluctantly extricated my limbs from his.

He bounded out of bed like a superhero sensing danger, threw on a black T-shirt and corduroys, and disappeared into the bathroom.

"We'll go separately. I'll say I went out running, or . . ." I yawned and got up.

"Ruby." He poked his head around, a toothbrush sticking out of the corner of his mouth. "Your outfit."

Ah yes. My camisole and pajama pants. "Well. It'll be a short walk of shame."

I leaned blearily against the bathroom door. Oscar was tidying his hair in the mirror. He stopped and looked at me.

"You don't—you're not actually feeling ashamed or anything, are you?"

"Are you kidding?" I joined him at the sink, pulling my hair back into my best approximation of an I've-been-awake-for-hours ponytail. "Not at all. And anyway, we didn't . . ."

Oscar peered at me through the mirror. "We were saints."

"Maybe not saints," I said, remembering some key details.

"He's going to know."

"I'll tell him I popped down to bring you a coffee and we started talking and time got—"

"He's your dad, Ruby. He'll know."

Not this dad. He wouldn't notice if I flew around the living room sprinkling pixie dust into all the vases.

"Maybe we should tell him." Oscar scratched his cheek. "Get it out there."

He was agitated—and no wonder. This was the culmination of everything he'd confided to me. *My famous, establishment dad. My solidly liberal but still extremely white dad. His mentor.*

I stopped smiling and reached for him. "We can tell him if you want. I honestly don't think it matters to him either way, but if that's what you want to do . . ."

"I don't know." Oscar sighed. "No time like the present, though."

I led the way outside, up, and back in. Dad's voice filtered down the stairwell from his study. And someone else's . . .

"Oh," I said, my step slowing. What was she doing here? Nora popped by semi-regularly, but having her here now, this morning, felt seriously intrusive.

Oscar's hand dropped from mine. "Ms. Visser's here."

"I'm sure you can call her Nora."

"I prefer Ms. Visser."

"Oscar, that you?" Dad bellowed down the stairs—then, in the other direction, muffled, "Ruby, you wouldn't run to Zabar's and grab some breakfast?"

I rolled my eyes and mouthed "*See?*" Oscar managed a smile but it died abruptly, like his fuse had been tripped. He needed me to be the brave soldier marching into the vanguard—so I did, straight up to the study.

"Promise you'll be objective here," Nora was murmuring. "This could be *gold*, take a look."

Yes, both of you, take a look at anything but the hallway.

I reached the study, seeing Dad's head craned over Nora's phone while she murmured, "Can't buy that kind of placement . . ."

I got out, "Hey-Dad-Hey-Nora-I'm-actually-heading-out-for-a-run . . ." And was *past* the door before they saw my PJs. Oscar hesitated outside the study.

Dad's voice flew into the hallway like a lasso. "Ruby. Oscar. Both of you in here right now."

I backed into the hallway, caught my flip-flop on the runner rug, had to hold the wall to keep from falling.

It's fine, I mouthed to Oscar, then ducked in after him.

Dad was now seated at his composition desk, head slumped, holding Nora's phone.

Nora smiled up at me. She was wearing workout clothes but her bob was immaculate, so I wondered if she'd popped by on the way to her trainer or if the outfit was for show.

"You're in the news, my darlings," she chirped, staring at the phone. "Gossip pages. But still!"

I turned to Oscar with an encouraging smile, then caught the plural. Did she mean Dad and Oscar or—?

"*Wait, what?*" I hurried to peek over Dad's shoulder, spotting a clickbait post on a New York tabloid's gossip page:

"*You'll NEVER GUESS Who's Hooking Up at Lincoln Center.*"

There was a photo underneath—me and Oscar standing beside a yellow cab, my arm on his shoulder, his forehead touching mine. This must have been the shot that guy took at Wing Club. Dad scrolled, almost accusingly, and there we were, another photo—at the Met in tight formation. We hadn't even been a couple then, but we sure looked like one.

My eyes flitted up to meet Nora's, and I remembered suddenly what Alice had said: *Smarter than she lets on.* Nora's placid smile told me she hadn't been all that surprised. Her eyes—diamond-sharp and dancing—made me suspect something more.

Had she been the one to place it? Did she tip off the photographers or hire them herself? How far had she gone with this?

Dad read the rest in a bored drone. "*Rumors have been flying about Martin Chertok's hot young protégé since he was whisked from the mean streets of DC to the upper echelons of UWS society, but viral sensation Oscar Bell has found his footing quickly—with the help of Marty's sexy daughter, Ruby . . .*"

"*Sexy?*" I recoiled, crossing my arms over my chest. "Oh my God."

Oscar was blinking rapidly into his own phone. "'*Viral sensation.*' I, uh, wow. I don't know how I feel about—" His eyes went wide. "Wait, mean streets of *what* now?"

Nora slid her arm around him, muttering something about her sister, of all things, but I wasn't listening anymore. I had to read to the end of this thing.

"*. . . seen cavorting in Manhattan clubs, the classical music princess's* *appearance at rehearsals for Oscar's debut symphony has only spurred more romance rumors . . ."*

I felt all the blood drain from my face as I stepped away. "'*Cavorting*'? I have no idea who wrote this, but that is—"

"*Cavorting* means *frolicking. Prancing,*" Dad said drily. "Maybe you're thinking of *canoodling.*"

"I'd be even *happier* with *canoodling,*" Nora said perkily, "but this is fantastic enough as it is. Marty, why didn't you *tell* me?"

Dad shot me a dangerous smile. "Tell you what, exactly?"

Oscar and I turned to stare at each other, like a hook would tug us off the stage if we answered wrong.

"Oh. Well." Nora glanced around the room, a sparrow looking for crumbs. She'd planned to come in today and pretend not to know about me and Oscar, to be officially brought into the fold. She didn't expect that I wouldn't have told Dad in the first place.

Or maybe she was amping up the awkwardness on purpose.

Get a grip, Ruby, I ordered myself. *You're becoming as paranoid as Alice.*

Nora grinned, breaking the détente. "Anyway, Nancy's going to be *thrilled.* This kind of gossip is exactly the buzz we need to build our audience."

"Audience?" Oscar shook his head.

"For your debut!"

"Who is *Nancy*?" I cut in.

"My sister." As if remembering something she'd forgotten to do, Nora snatched her phone back from Dad, and started typing. "She's got a PR firm in DC—high-level political spin stuff, but Oscar, I believe you know her daughter, Tessa?"

I glanced at him. His face was blank.

Then he jolted. "Cello! Yeah, she's a freshman, she's not bad."

"Well, Nancy was *at* that YouTube concert and texted me from the audience. *You've got to snap this kid up. Real deal.* And when the video was posted, her firm boosted it."

"Her firm *what*?" Oscar backed up a step, holding his head.

"She's extremely influential," Nora said proudly. "She wants to help you. And the school. Lucky us!"

"Farnwell?" Oscar leaned against a desk chair, looking as lost as I'd ever seen him.

"*Amberley*." Nora swatted him, like he'd made a joke. "She's coming Thursday through Saturday, that's all she can manage, but she's got a big surprise lined up for you. You're going to be interviewed . . . for the ATV News . . . by *Shawna Wells herself*."

Oscar glanced at me as if for help. "I'm not sure . . . we don't watch a lot of news."

"Top news anchor in the country." Nora's smile ticked down a few notches. "She's black!"

I cringed so hard, my eyes closed. *Why are we like this.*

"Oh!" Oscar lifted his eyebrows, the closest approximation of excitement he could muster.

"That's all the news I've got for today . . ." Nora chuckled to herself, so apparently that was a Shawna Wells impression.

Dad stood. "All right, thanks a bunch, Nora. If that's it, I think Oscar and I had better get to work."

"Perfect. Lunch again soon, Ruby?"

Again? We'd never had lunch the first time.

I smiled noncommittally and waved good-bye, relieved to hear her sneakers squeaking down the wooden steps, through the living room and away. Then I turned to see Dad staring at me, finally taking in my

PJs, my mussed ponytail. His eyes met mine, a shuttered look obscuring whatever his real reaction was.

"Welcome back, Dad." I crossed the room to give his cheek a kiss, then started away.

"Sir? I . . ." Oscar's voice was loud. I froze in the doorway. "I'd actually like to ask for your blessing. For—"

Dad coughed, glancing in my general direction. "You proposing marriage? Seems a little rushed."

I pinched the doorframe, stung by the acid in his voice.

"No." Oscar tried to smile. "I'd just like to *date* your daughter."

"I see." Dad sat again, like he was too tired to stand.

He seemed older today, his actual age catching up with him. I wondered how draining that UK trip had been, despite the extended stay. Or maybe it was this conversation making him look like a series of small objects was falling onto his head.

"I don't think you'll have much time for dating this summer, son." He squinted up at Oscar. "Your premiere is in *five weeks* and you've got—"

"We didn't plan for this to happen," I interrupted, while Oscar blurted, "She's helping me. She's a *huge* help, kind of a muse—"

"All right!" Dad lifted a hand, not looking at either of us. "You don't need to ask my blessing. Just don't let it affect your work."

Oscar spun toward me, exultant, and I smiled back. But as I drifted into the hall, I felt more spectral than ever.

He was relieved—of *course* he was—because my father gave the okay. I knew Dad would, in the end. I'd even known the words he would use. They didn't mean Dad approved, they meant he didn't care enough about the subject to argue.

"Show me what you've got so far." Dad closed the door to the study.

Even with my own door shut, I could hear Oscar playing on Dad's upright. I sat on the edge of my bed and listened, bracing for my heart to sink into the trench I'd dug between music and me—but it didn't. It bloomed, slowly unfurling.

That music was Oscar's. And Oscar was mine.

25.

"**M**use." Jules held the door to the pizzeria with her foot. "He used that word."

"It's sort of corny, but . . ."

"It's sort of insulting."

"He was scrambling. My dad can be intimidating."

"But not, 'Your daughter is amazing, I love hanging out with her.' He says he needs you as a *prop* to make his *music* happen, basically? It's so pretentious."

I watched her, comprehension dawning, as I walked to the counter. "You don't like him."

"I don't know him! I just . . . worry for you." Jules glared at the slices on display. "And I think you're a hell of a lot more than some dude's 'muse.'"

"Thank you," I mumbled. "That's nice."

"It's true."

"While we're saying true things, I think you're better than this 'born to be a shop girl' dramarama." I kicked her ankle. "There's nothing wrong with shop girls *what*soever. But you've got talent, Jules—"

She side-eyed me hard. "You are changing the subject."

"I'm . . . talking about potential! Yours, mine."

"Which brings us back to what *I* was saying." Jules paid for her slice and followed me to a table in the back. "This *purpose* thing you have. I might not know what you're going to devote your life to, but I know it's going to be incredible and I hope like hell it's not, like, facilitating some dude's personal journey. Because . . ."

She made a barfing noise.

"It's not like that," I assured her. "We are facilitating each other."

"Dirty!" She folded her slice. "Speaking of which . . . ?" She smirked.

"We haven't. Not that." I took a bite and chewed, smiling. "We're getting to know each other first."

"You are such a goner."

"I know." I rested my forehead on the table. "Ugh, I know."

"Sorry for the muse thing," Oscar said the instant I set foot in his apartment that evening. "So pretentious. I couldn't think of a better word!"

"They were powerful creatures, right? I can't remember my Greek mythology."

"Goddesses." He sat on the edge of his kitchen counter, legs dangling. "The living embodiment of each of their disciplines."

"Oh, *that*." I snorted. "Well, then I'm definitely not a muse! Dad should have seen right through it."

Oscar cocked his head. "You totally embody classical music to me."

"You heard me play."

"And I've heard you sing. And hum. And I've seen you listen and analyze and walk and . . . you *are* music."

Shame flash-flooded me. Had he seen my Lincoln Center poster? Was he teasing me? The bold print caption *"I AM MUSIC"* had been cropped out of the photo hanging in the hall.

Even then, they must have known how laughable it was.

But Oscar's eyes were warm. Those words were a coincidence.

"Sometimes when I'm working and I need to concentrate, the instruments drop out, and I hear you humming the melody."

"*Really?*"

He shrugged one shoulder, smiling. "Plus I am picturing you in a tiny toga right now, and I have to say, it's working for you."

I walked over and shoved him, mostly as an excuse to bridge the distance, to invite him to pull me between his dangling legs and "apologize," kissing my earlobe, my neck as he slid down standing.

He pulled away before I wanted him to—but his whole body looked like it was smiling. "Wanna help me work?"

"Is that a euphemism?" I half hoped it was, but he laughed, striding into the morass of strewn papers to grab some blank sheets and his keyboard.

"I've got threads in my head for how to develop the second movement—it's about dichotomies, the arts, the street, those hidden portals we talked about . . ."

I nodded as if I had any idea what he was talking about.

He sat on the edge of his bed with the keyboard seesawing on his lap.

I put it to the side. "Come play on my piano."

"Is *that* a euphemism?"

"No!" I laughed, then forced myself serious, thinking about how Dad was out to dinner with Nora and Bill tonight, wouldn't be back for hours and . . . no. *Serious.* "You cannot compose on that *thing* anymore. Pianos only from here on out."

"Sir, yes, sir."

I dragged an armchair from the sitting area to avoid using Mom's piano bench. Then I leaned against my knees and listened while Oscar worked through a new motif in fits and pauses and bursts. His mind was a remote satellite. I couldn't begin to understand how these thoughts were forming, these notes coming to life. But as the piece took form, his gibberish about dichotomies started to make sense— and so did what I'd noticed up in Washington Heights.

This new section was a nod to the mass we'd heard sung at the Cloisters, pure and sacred, interlaced with a higher, more contemporary melody. It took me a second to identify the syncopation as a *bachata* swing—Dominican-flavored, that music I'd heard pumping out of an apartment building. I watched Oscar, wondering whether he'd wandered back without me during those lost days, listening for the sound of the neighborhood. He must have. And here it was, dancing with something ancient—before drowning it out with an almost triumphant cadence at the end.

Almost. My muscles felt antsy, like I was kicking rocks off the edge of a cliff.

"It peters out there, doesn't it?" I heard myself murmuring. "You resolve it so quickly, it doesn't feel like there's anywhere for it to go and you're . . . how many bars in?"

"Forty." He scratched his hair. "I'm not sure *where* I want it to go."

I tried to think like Dad. "What are you trying to say?"

He leaned against the piano, head slumped. "Something . . . about high art vs. quote-unquote *low* art, music, pop culture, culture in general. *This* life, real life. You have the Cloisters, this oasis, but is it an *oasis*? Is it better than everything surrounding it? Who decides that? So I start out . . ."

He played the contrapuntal section, an analog to early music.

"And then it starts to get heckled . . ." The Latin melody came in.

"But in the end, the bachata . . . it's joyous, right? It's *now*, it's the *pulse* of that neighborhood, it should win."

"What about other pop forms? To keep developing it. Hip-hop!"

His eyes went wide—and my own scrunched tightly shut.

When I opened them, he was shaking his head slowly with a disappointed smile. "Ruby Chertok . . ."

My cheeks were flaming. "I know you don't listen to hip-hop. I don't listen to it either. I don't know why I—"

"You don't know why."

"I . . . am shutting up now."

He grinned. "No, I'm gonna let you sit in this a minute longer."

"EDM maybe? Klezmer? Polka? I am an idiot."

He reached for me and I walked to stand by him, his arm looping around my waist. "Definitely polka. I'm a polka fiend."

I leaned against his shoulder, still cringing inside. "Okay, so, back to the music at hand . . ."

The thing was, he identified with the bachata on some level—and with the plainsong. He wasn't just writing about a trip to the Cloisters here. Multiple cultures—he lived in them and they lived in him, variations on the theme of Oscar, and he switched them up when he felt he needed to.

He'd joked that he was a perfect plus one, never two, but he was more than two. He was as many people as he needed to be. It had to wear on him.

"So think about how it relates to the first movement," I said, smoothing a bent corner of his composition page. "Is this a layering, is it a debate . . . a dance-off? Is one going to win, or . . . do they need to find a way to . . . ?"

Oscar peered up at me. "Cohabit. The thing is, I don't have an answer."

"I continue to have no idea what I'm talking about."

"No." Oscar squinted at the keys. "No, this . . . it's something. It's a *question* and that's . . . yeah. I think you might actually be a muse."

As cheesy as the word *muse* might have been, it didn't feel insulting. It was a job, a purpose, a definition. And I was enjoying it.

He played and I listened. I frowned when it wasn't quite there and clapped when it was and somehow my thinking walked the same lines as his. He strung it together, went back to add, jot, cross out—a quick harmonic sketch, the full orchestrations would come later—and then he played the whole thing.

And we looked at each other.

"Second movement."

"I think so."

We high-fived over our heads.

It was dark outside. We'd been at this for hours.

"Hungry?" I asked.

He stood, closing the fallboard, then reached for me. "Ravenous."

"Fast-food restaurant."

"This one." I nodded up at the Burger Barn menu. "Fried potato product?"

"Seasoned, curly. You?"

"Shoestring." I smiled at the cashier. "Small shoestring fry, classic double, please."

"Same for me, no pickles on the burger," Oscar said.

I looked at him. "No pickles?"

"No pickles."

"I'll take his pickle."

Oscar stifled a laugh. The cashier rolled her eyes.

As soon as we found a seat, Oscar's shirt pocket started ringing Dvořák.

"'Songs My Mother Taught Me'?"

"And I'll give you one guess who's calling . . ." But he silenced his phone and put it to the side.

"You can answer! It is your mom, right? Am I—?"

His hand froze like this was a life or death decision. Then he stood. "Moms! Hey! Yeah, sorry it's been so . . ." And he strolled out to the sidewalk.

I wondered how many days it had been since their last call. Did they have shared jokes? Would she ask him if he needed anything? Make sure he was eating well? What did mothers do when they were away from their kids?

I unwrapped my burger, watching him through the plate glass windows—pacing, smiling, frowning . . . walking away. "Um."

A minute passed before he came barreling through the Burger Barn door, clutching today's copy of the *Times* instead of his phone.

When he reached the table, he set the paper down and started flipping page after page. I pulled his burger out from underneath.

"My mom says hi," he mumbled, turning to the next section.

"She knows about me?"

"Last week she asked if I'd made any friends and I said I had a girlfriend."

"I wasn't your girlfriend last week."

He glanced up. "To me, you were."

My smile was no longer stifleable. "Well, hi back to your *mom*." I sipped my soda. "Sounds like a dis, totally wasn't."

"My article came out. The . . . interview thing."

"Oh my God, awesome!" I reached over to see how far he'd gotten. "It's the weekend paper, so it'll be in the Magazine or the Arts—"

"Mom said Arts section. She was . . ." His hands stilled, pressing the pages as he breathed. "Weird about it? Excited but . . . I don't know, I need to see it. I told her not to worry . . ."

I scooted my chair around so I could sit closer, then pulled the paper gently from him and pointed. "Top right."

He startled, seeing his name. "It's short!"

"It's *good*, though, Oscar. It's In the Wings."

"What does that mean?"

"It's all people they think are going to be important one day. Win was in there after he got his first conducting spot. Lin-Manuel Miranda, Virginia Cheng—"

"Who?"

"She's a painter. This is across all arts. It's really cool!" I scooted my seat back, swiping a fry.

"Ah, this is . . . exciting." He kept scanning it, a frown etched into his forehead even as he kept grinning. "I can't believe that interview took like two hours and there are only five questions on here. Oh. The intro. That must be . . . huh."

I read it again, upside down.

Oscar Bell, 17

Hometown: DC

Discipline: Classical composition

I blinked at him. "Is it the composition thing? Do you not feel like you've—?"

"The DC. I'm from Bethesda."

A smile wavered on my lips. "Isn't that fairly close to DC?"

"It's not the same place. But, yeah, I mean . . . that's not a big deal, right?"

That gossip piece about the two of us sprang to mind. "Is it that 'mean streets' thing you're worried about? I doubt *Times* readers overlap much with the *Post*."

"I'm not worried."

His finger landed later in the write-up.

" '*His mother played him Mozart as a child, hoping to foster a better future for him.*' " He stared blankly at the page. "My mother runs the biggest private hospital system in DC. You can't get much 'better' than that."

I picked at my burger, appetite fading. "Do you think she was upset?"

"She'll be fine." Oscar sniffed. "She's excited for me. This is cool! Either way, it's . . . yeah."

I glanced at the article one more time, the details he mentioned standing out like they were written in bold. "Why don't you get in touch with the reporter? I'm sure my dad knows him. You can ask him to print a clarification—"

"*No*, I'm not gonna rock the boat here. I mean, there will be other interviews, right?"

"Shawna Wells."

"Oh shit. Right. And that's *soon*." He was leaning so hard on the table his chair started to slide away. "See, it's all good. This is amazing."

When we got up to leave, he bussed the newspaper to the trash along with our wrappers.

"Hey," I said, prying it away. "What are you—?"

"Oh, right!" He laughed, watching as I carefully folded it and put it in my bag. "Good catch."

He held the door for me with an elaborate bow. I slid out, smiling through my worry.

I'd caught the newspaper. But how much else had I missed?

26.

the piped-out smell of deliciousness dissipated as we walked away from Burger Barn.

"Huge progress today." I bumped Oscar with my hip, nearly sending both of us careening into a construction pylon. He grabbed me tighter, steadying us.

"It's still missing something." To my relief, his voice was the right kind of fuzzy—thinking hard instead of covering up. "It's pretty, I think, and it's starting to say something, but it's missing that key piece, that *God* piece, you know what I'm saying?"

"You want it to sound like God wrote it? That's lofty, even for you."

"Not that he wrote it *himself,* I'm not even sure that would be something anybody would be ready to listen to. But maybe he left a fingerprint, here and there."

"You're serious!"

As if on cue, light spilled out of a dingy Irish pub, giving him a saintly glow. "Well, yeah. Maybe it's a composer thing. The act of creation, the need for a higher source of inspiration, for humility. I'm sure your dad gets it."

I winced. "Hate to break it to you, but Dad's an atheist."

Oscar leaned away. "Really?"

"Since he was ten. He went to a yeshiva in Brooklyn. One day, he woke up and announced he was never going back and he wouldn't set foot inside their synagogue either. It was like a Biblical revelation, except, you know, the exact opposite."

Oscar looked weirdly troubled. I squeezed him as we walked.

"That's why he got into music. Have you not heard this? My grandparents were looking for some way to keep him engaged in the community, so he started working for a music shop owner down the street, a friend of the family from back in Belarus. You can't play instruments during Shabbat, so Dad studied music instead, pretending it was for fun. Traditional music at first, then poof . . . everything."

"But . . . his music has such *heart.*"

I laughed. "And?"

"I'm not saying atheists can't write great music, but a lot of the modernist and post-modern stuff leaves me cold. I like it, I appreciate it, the deconstruction is sort of . . . unnerving. Your dad's stuff isn't like that. Even his *Jersey Suite* is so humane. It's wry, it's a commentary, but you can hear grace in it."

I knew what he meant. "Dad has a word for it. You must have heard it, working with him . . ."

"The 'ineffable'?"

"That's it." I smiled.

"He's mentioned it once or twice . . ."

" . . . an hour."

Oscar laughed. "Not sure I have a grasp on it yet. It being *ineffable* and all."

"He gave a conductor talk once that finally made it make sense for me," I said, turning the corner. "He definitely believes in that invisible piece, but he sees it as . . . the composer, basically. Every life experience you've ever had, every thought, memory—everything you bring to the piece before you sit down to write it, distilled into one magical element. It's not God . . . it's you. I started thinking about what that would sound like for me. If I could write music. Which I can't, so . . . meh. It would sound like *oh well.*"

Oscar fell silent, working the ineffable out as we walked.

I watched him for a moment. "So you're religious."

"In my own way. My granddad's a reverend, so . . .'"

"*What?* How have we not talked about this?"

"Yeah, we're Baptist. Grandpa's seventy-two, so he's pretty much retired now."

Same age as Dad.

"He gets a guest pulpit from time to time, but he doesn't have his own flock anymore. I think he likes staying above the fray. Church politics get pretty wild. Anyway, his faith and my faith are two different things. Mine's more centered on music. Every song I write is a song of praise in its own way."

"Wow," I said. We'd reached the house.

"Are you an atheist?"

"I wouldn't go that far? I think that I would *prefer* to believe in God, but . . . only if he likes me. Which isn't exactly the tagline for Judaism."

Oscar laughed. "Have you been to services?"

"Ah, no. I went to a Passover Seder at Leo's place once. It was intense and ended with him screaming at Dad across the table and Mom storming out and Alice chasing her and Win cracking up the whole time. Leo turned conservative after he met his wife and since then, he hardly talks to the rest of us. We're goyim now, I guess. Mom was raised Methodist, so technically *he is too,* but nobody ever points that out. It's sad, though, he's got a little boy and girl and they're so cute. I'm an aunt—I think I told you that? But yeah. I mean, it's nice that he has that faith! I'm happy for him. I do wonder what it would be like to be that . . . sure."

Oscar was staring at me with a mix of sympathy and admiration.

"Your family is . . ." His voice drifted out.

"Live studio audience."

"Hopefully you'll like mine."

"You think I'll meet them?"

"I hope so." HIs fingers laced into mine. "If only so my mom will admit I'm not making you up."

"So . . . you wanna work some more?" I nodded upstairs. "Find the God piece? That sounds . . . wow."

He grinned. "No, it'll come." He reached for his keys and started down to his apartment. "I'm gonna keep . . ."

His hand hovered an inch from the keyhole.

I waited a beat. Two. Three.

He whirled around, mad-scientist electrified. "I need voices."

"Oh-*kay*?"

"This . . . this needs voices." He hit his chest, like that was the cabinet where the music was being filed. "A choral symphony."

"*Jesus,* Oscar . . ." I couldn't help but laugh.

"Amberley's got a singing program." He grabbed my hands. "No, listen, this is good. The third piece, the ineffable. I don't even have to write the lyrics—it can be wordless, like *Daphnis et Chloé,* I can trust the music to speak to what this piece is saying."

"What *is* this piece saying? Have you figured that out over burgers, or . . . ?"

Instead of answering, he pulled me into a kiss and staggered with me inside and I'd already forgotten my question by the time the door shut behind us.

He was distracted, though. I wasn't totally surprised when his mouth drew back, eyes drifting, and he said, "Let me get a few things down."

I sat on his bed, twirling my ankles while he lay on his stomach, scribbling, humming, scribbling some more. Then he handed me the sheet.

"Can you sight read?"

I scoffed. "Of course. I'm not *that* bad, Oscar."

"Sight-*sing*, I mean."

"Oh. Right now?"

I held the sheet out. Of *course* I could—that had always been my starting point with every keyboard piece, hearing the music, humming it in the shower. But I felt self-conscious, like this was some sort of audition.

I started, tentative, on a *la,* then stopped. "Is there a better vowel, or—?"

His eyes were closed. "That's great, keep going."

Knowing he was in the clouds while I stayed down here made this easier. I curled my legs under me and sang with more confidence, letting my voice fill the room, hesitating a few times on notes that at first felt peculiar and then, upon hearing them, perfectly conceived—flowers bursting from branches.

It paralleled the Cloisters theme. That through-line wasn't written out here, but I had a hunch this vocal piece would work in tandem, choir and the orchestra dancing around each other before the Latin notes even came in. It wasn't a debate anymore. It was a braid.

Oscar took the paper from me and scribbled something out, then

238

rewrote a few notes differently, the tune climbing upward before dipping again to end on a low D. "Can you try it this way?"

I couldn't understand why he'd changed the notes, what made this better, how he'd come up with it so effortlessly. But I pictured myself in a short toga and garland crown, holding a lyre, crooning into some dumbstruck Grecian's ear.

"Of course," I said, and sang.

Jules's invitation came in a series of rapid-fire texts.

Double-date Wednesday, El Pueblo, 8pm, no outs because:

1–If you're thinking of doing that thing where you get a boyfriend and vanish, NOT ON MY WATCH

2–I would prefer to dislike your boyfriend on his own merits and for that I have to hang out with him

3–Music brings everybody together lalalalala

I wasn't sure what El Pueblo had to do with music until we got to the restaurant and found a sign on the door reading *Wednesday Night Karaoke!* I would have made a U-turn if there hadn't been so many people walking in behind us.

Jules was already sitting at a corner table for four, scrolling through a black book with laminated pages.

She looked up at me. "I picked you out a song!"

"Holy no," I muttered.

"I love karaoke!" Oscar waved. "Jules! So great to finally hang out."

"I *know,* right?" Jules narrowed her eyes at me while slapping Oscar's hand.

"I'm not singing," I said.

Jules flipped another page. "And I ordered us nachos."

I glanced around while Oscar scooted my chair in for me. "Where's Tyler?"

"Mars. Antarctica. Stuck on the 1, impossible to tell."

"Sorry," I murmured.

"I'm used to it. So. *Oscar*." She leaned forward. "What level of genius would you say you are?"

"*Jules*." Every ounce of energy I had went into my glare.

"Like Isaac Newton genius or dolphins-are-actually-really-smart genius?"

But Oscar was stroking his chin thoughtfully. "I would say that I am . . . Marvel villain-level genius."

Jules nodded. "Interesting. Go on."

"Yeah, so I can concoct a plan, it's big, it's impressive, but in the end, I'm still going to get my ass beat."

"Self-awareness." Jules pointed at him. "I like that."

I laughed, but watched him, hoping he didn't really believe that.

Applause rang out from the next table as a girl finished singing some song I didn't recognize. I clapped along.

"Ruby Chertok, you're up!" said the man with the mic.

"What. I. No." Everyone was looking at me.

"Yay!" Jules stood and clapped. "You can do it!"

"You are such an asshole," I growled.

She curtsied.

"Ruby Chertok?" they called again.

Oscar's smile dropped. He leaned in. "You don't have to. They'll go on to the next person and we'll eat some nachos. Let's eat some nachos!"

He was thinking about Wing Club—I wanted to jump into his lap and kiss him. I wanted to curl into a ball from the memory. Instead I wobbled upright.

Jules waved for me to sit back down. "It was a dumb joke, you don't have to actually—"

"I'll do it." I shrugged, with effort. "It's singing, it's fine."

Jules let out a surprised whoop and Oscar started clapping along. I wandered to the mic. "I don't even know the song."

The guy with the mic winked. "Everybody knows this song."

And *crap,* the music had already started and I was holding the mic. In the middle of a Mexican restaurant with big windows open to Amsterdam. But I needed to do this. This was silly, pointless, the lowest of low culture, and dear God above, I had to see *something* through.

The words *Tommy used to work on the docks* appeared onscreen.

I opened my mouth, silent.

"Come on!" Jules shouted. The music kept playing.

I shrugged wildly. "I don't know it!"

Some frat boys at the bar started to boo, as well they should. I couldn't even make it through a karaoke song. I buried my face in my elbow, the mic making a long scratching sound on my hair, when a terrible voice rang out through the speakers.

"She brings home her pay for love . . . for looooove!"

I opened my eyes to see Oscar standing next to me with his own mic, taking up the reins of whatever song this . . . wait, I *did* think I knew it! And here came Jules too, sprinting across the restaurant to lean into the mic and sing along.

By the time we got to the chorus, I had it and I was singing too, all three of us together, cacophonous, laughing.

I didn't even notice when they dropped out. I just knew I'd finished "Livin' on a Prayer" by myself and didn't die and even got a standing toast from those drunk guys.

"*Damn* you've got a good voice," Jules said, pulling me happily back to our table.

"Doesn't she?" Oscar beamed proudly and I couldn't help but beam back.

I'd survived. I'd stood up and embarrassed myself in front of an audience and emerged unscathed. My heart continued to beat. My stomach continued to rumble. I was me, a bit braver.

"Bravo," said Tyler, appearing from nowhere to plop down at our table, stealing a bite of the nachos we didn't even know had arrived. "Sorry I'm late."

Jules ignored him as she sat, her eyes locked on mine, waiting until the boys were locked in conversation to give me a barely perceptible thumbs-up, marking her approval of Oscar.

I waited for my chance to return the favor with Ty. It never quite came.

27.

"So?" Oscar turned, arms outstretched.

After hours of debate, this was the chosen look—hair supernaturally natural, dark skin shining, smile stupefying, a soft button-down with faint blue stripes, pale gray pants, lace-up brown boots, a bow tie in deep green that I couldn't believe wasn't a clip-on until I saw him retie it with my own eyes. He looked like he should be riding a unicycle on his way to the polo grounds.

"Perfection," I said, kissing his cheek and breathing in minty aftershave. "Let's taxi it so you don't melt."

His expression wavered between a giddy grin and a deep frown the entire ride to Lincoln Center, his hand clenching mine with every turn.

"You're going to do great," I said as we walked across the plaza to Amberley. "Just be yourself."

"I wish you were interviewing me."

"Oh yeah, all my incisive questions . . . 'Tell me Oscar, what do you feel like for lunch?' 'Who would win in a keyboard battle, Bach or Liszt?'"

"Bach. Next question."

"Maybe I'll become a TV journalist," I joked.

Oscar pointed to me. "Maybe."

"I'll keep it on the list."

"On the Liszt?" Oscar said, nudging me, then his shoulders slumped. "God, I'm nervous. Don't let me pun in front of Shawna."

"I'm sure you'll *conduct* yourself just fine." I pushed him. "*Get it, get it?*"

He covered his face.

"You'll end the interview on a *high note*—I'm stopping, sorry."

The antiseptic smell of the Amberley administrative offices hit us like a wall as soon as we stepped inside the marble lobby, like we'd entered some sort of sealed-off lab. There weren't any students milling around today—just news people waiting with clipboards and microphone gear.

A blonde with a tight braid perked up at the sight of us. "Oscar Bell?"

"Yes!" He extended a hand.

She lifted a finger, hoisting her phone to her ear.

"He's here. Second floor? On our way." Then she finally shook back, swiveling on her heels to push the elevator button. "I'm Libby, Ms. Oneida's assistant."

Ms. Oneida? The producer, maybe?

"Everyone's waiting in Mr. Chertok's office."

"Oh." Oscar held his arm through the elevator door until I stepped through. "Is, ah, Mr. Chertok there as well?"

"He is!" She beamed like she was an elf taking Oscar to see Santa, then stepped through the opening elevator door and pointed to the hall. "All the way on the right."

I tried my best not to smirk. I knew the way to my dad's office, thank you very much, but since this woman hadn't so much as glanced at me, I didn't feel the need to volunteer that information.

My eyes darted to Oscar's, but he was looking away, adjusting his bow tie like it was strangling him.

I heard a funny chattering halfway down the hall—the Mystery Spot, I'd named it as a kid—the two square feet where on one particularly bored day, I'd discovered a trick of the ventilation system that let you eavesdrop straight into Dad's office. Dad talked to himself a lot, so I'd found it an endless source of ridiculousness over the years.

Out of habit, I slowed my step, veered right toward the overhead grate, and heard an unfamiliar voice saying, "Don't let *your* moment get swallowed up by his mome . . ."

Oscar glanced back, reaching for my hand. I grabbed on, my skin going cold.

As we reached Dad's thick oak door, it started to open, pulled by a red-haired woman, her face so identical to Nora's that I nearly went in for the requisite cheek kiss before realizing that this cheek was a foot higher than it should have been.

"The wonder boy, eeeeee!" she squealed to the room, simultaneously shaking Oscar's hand and tugging him inside. "I'm Nancy Oneida, Nora's sister. Tessa's mom. You've probably seen me lurking around Farnwell at school functions." She winked. "But it is *such* a pleasure to officially meet you."

"You too!" Oscar said, way too loud. He *was* nervous.

"And don't you look *dapper*." She started to shut the door before I could walk in. I pushed it and her eyes looked through me. "Oscar . . ." She turned. "Would your friend mind waiting downstairs? This is a small room and we need to start getting focused—"

Nora swooshed into the doorway. "*Nancy*. This is Marty's *daughter!* Ruby sweetie, ignore her, come on in."

Nancy gasped. "You're Ruby Chertok. Oh my God, I am *mortified!*"

"It's fine." I smiled. "Don't feel bad."

She reached over to hug me, and I stiffened until she let go and I could turn to Nora for an air-kiss.

Dad waved from his desk, his shoulders jittering with silent laughter. "You're '*Oscar's friend*' now, Rooster. How do you like *that* for a title?"

I ducked into the dimmest corner of the room to hide my sinking expression. He hadn't meant to be mean. He couldn't have known how that would cut.

My favorite spot in Dad's office was an Empire-style chair beside two built-in cabinets. I lowered myself into it now, careful not to jostle the sixteenth-century lute perched precariously on the second shelf. Sitting in my usual place, I felt like another piece of antique furniture. Not in a bad way. In an "I belong here" way.

"So, *are* you an item?" Nancy asked, her shrewd eyes dancing merrily between us. "I wasn't sure if this was creative drama on Nora's part, but you two certainly look cozy."

Oscar smiled sheepishly at me. "Ah . . ."

I beamed back in confirmation.

But Nancy wasn't looking. "We can chitchat later. Let's get you changed first. Shawna's people are going to be ready in about ten."

"Changed?" Oscar glanced at himself. "Like . . . clothes, or—?"

"*Yes.*" Nancy pressed her fingertips to her lips, looking at Oscar's outfit. "See, I *love* this, but I think if you wear something more . . . teenaged?" She glanced at Nora. Nora nodded. "Yeah, we've got something that I think will have more impact. This is your big spotlight moment!"

She grabbed Oscar's hands and shook them. He laughed.

"Until your symphony premieres, that is. You'll wear a tux for that, yes?"

She turned to Dad. He shrugged, smiling like an impassive god, his feet kicked up on the corner of his desk.

"But for this . . ." She crouched to dig into a Louis Vuitton duffel bag on the floor, her voice trailing off.

As I leaned forward, curious, Nora reached for me. "We probably *should* give them some breathing room, actually. Do you mind?"

Her arm was linked in mine and pulling me out of the room before I could even process what was happening. I glanced back at Oscar, but his eyes were locked on the bag like it was Pandora's Box.

Nora sighed musically once the door shut behind us.

"*There.* Thanks. I get a little funny in tight spaces." She paced the hall, smiling brightly and rubbing her hands like we were waiting to go into a party. "I think I'm more nervous about this interview than he is!"

"Why?"

Her eyelashes fluttered for a second before she answered. "This is just such a big moment for him. And I *care.* You know how I am, I just . . . internalize things."

I glanced back at the closed door, then whispered, "Why is she asking Oscar to change? He tried on like ten different outfits this morning, trying to get the right mix. He's . . . good."

"*That* is adorable. Oh my God." Nora pressed her hand to her lips. "He's got a great sense of style, doesn't he? This is just . . . interviews are a special beast. That's why we're lucky to have Nancy. Oh! Speaking of which—would *you* be up for an interview?"

"I . . . what? What would I have to say? About anything?"

"We could give you talking points."

"And I would . . . recite them?" I goggled at her.

"Hmmm . . ." Her eyes drifted. "Maybe one of the outdoor shots—"

The door opened and we both spun around, but only Nancy walked through, a vague smile planted on her face. "He needs a minute."

Nora's smile went very tight. "What about Ruby? Helpful?"

Nancy shook her head, not looking at me. "It's great overall, but I think it undermines this particular appeal."

I stared between them with creeping embarrassment. "No interview?"

Nora glanced at Nancy. Nancy didn't react.

"You're off the hook," Nora said. "So thoughtful of you to offer, though." I hadn't offered. "I love the way you've been doing your hair lately, you know. So chic." It was in a ponytail.

I let her squeeze my hand, once, tightly. Her fingers were clammy.

We stood leaning against the gray fleur-de-lis wallpaper until the door opened, and a strange parallel-universe version of Oscar walked through.

No jacket. No bow tie. Black jeans, a blue hoodie, a white T-shirt, a sleeveless Washington Wizards jersey. He looked like a basketball fan. From DC.

I felt my brain flipping through scenarios, none of them even remotely adequate. What were they *thinking*?

"Perfect." Nancy patted him on the back and started to lead him to the elevators.

Under Nancy's touch, Oscar's shoulders drew in, almost imperceptibly.

"I am . . . confused," I said.

"Don't be!" Oscar shot me a smile as he walked by, but his eyes didn't make it to mine. It was like he didn't want me to look at him. "It's cool, Ruby, I'm fine."

I started to follow, but Nora held up her hand.

"Like I said, sweetheart, we've got it covered, but *thank* you! There's food in the lounge, if you're hungry. Strudel!"

I was too thrown to argue or force myself into the elevator with them, so I turned back to the office. Dad was sitting in the same spot, moving a glass paperweight from one side of his desk to the other.

"What the *hell*, Dad." I shut the door behind me. "He doesn't look anything like himself."

Dad grunted. "He will at the concert. This is just one of those things."

"Why would he even go along with this?" I turned, dizzy. "Because this Nancy person said so, and that's it? Fall in line?"

Then I looked at Dad, realizing. They'd been alone for a good ten minutes.

"What did you say to him?"

Dad flipped through loose pages on his desk, chopping them into a neat stack. "I told him it was all a pile of shit, but part of the job is shoveling it. I said the PR people want a Cinderella story and that's what we've got to deliver. He asked me if I'd do the same thing and I said *absofuckinglutely*."

Hearing Dad curse, I flinched, as unnerved as if he'd started speaking in tongues. He sounded so angry. And yet he'd apparently been the one to talk Oscar into going on television in someone else's clothes.

"You wouldn't be *asked* to do the same thing, though, would you?" I pressed him, my uneasiness growing by the second. "What, would the board make you wear a yarmulke and grow payote? It isn't the same—"

"They would if it meant increasing the endowment," Dad snapped, his eyes landing hard on mine. "This is a school, a nonprofit, but it's a business too. Without money, all of this goes away. And I mean forever."

"And how does dressing Oscar in a costume bring in money?"

"You're being glib, Ruby."

"No, I'm seriously asking. And why do they need money anyway? Look at this place!" I motioned to his oak-paneled office, the hall beyond with its Persian runners and glass-boxed original scores. "They get tuition money, they get NEA funding, right? And all those black-tie donor events . . ."

Nora, making the river flow. Nora, sweating down to her fingers.

"We're located in the *center* of Manhattan, with incredible competition for dollars, people are getting their pockets emptied by shady hedge fund managers left and right, and the margins are . . ." Dad growled, pushing himself standing. "Listen, I need to get down there to support Oscar. When you want to have a grown-up conversation about this, I'll be happy to fill you in."

I stiffened into a statue as he breezed past me.

Out in the hall, he glanced up at the descending numbers, held the elevator door while I jogged to join him, then stepped inside and jabbed the lobby button. "Honey, why don't you wait in the lounge? You don't need to get wrapped up in this."

I'm his girlfriend.

But I still got out at the lobby and watched the numbers go up again as the elevator went to the fourth floor without me. They must have been filming in Nora's office suite. I glanced behind me, seeing another ATV crew setting up what looked like an exterior shot of the school.

My phone beeped. A text from Jules. *I'm bored. Come be weird around me.*

I could keep vigil in the lounge for however many hours. Eat. Worry for my boyfriend, even if he *was* smiling, agreeing, cooperating. I could wait to see if Nora talked her sister into giving me a photo op. *Oscar's friend . . . how do you like that for a job title?*

There was no place for me here that made any sense at all.

I texted back to Jules. *On my way.*

Oscar came home at four, wearing his other outfit, the real one—shirt untucked, sleeves rolled, bow tie shoved into his pocket. I hurried to meet him on the sidewalk.

"How was it?" I asked, breathless. "Are you okay?"

He nodded, looking tired. "It was good. Yeah. Shawna was nice. I wish you'd been there."

"They wouldn't *let* me. Dad said—"

"I figured. It's cool."

I should have fought. I should have insisted on being there. I should have picked at a strudel in the lounge.

"You know," Oscar blurted, his voice more gravelly than usual. "I don't have a problem with that outfit. I don't feel any kind of . . . *judgment* toward it or anything like that. If brothers want to dress that way, they should dress that way. But it's not how *I* dress. And I'm not trying to shut myself off, pretend that I'm not part of a bigger conversation—I'm just not sure that this *is* the conversation."

"Okay." I reached for him, then dropped my hand.

"And yeah, of course I want black kids to be able to see someone who looks *just* like them. On TV. Being interviewed by Shawna Wells. Conducting an orchestra." He sounded like he was reciting someone else's words. "It's *all* I want. I didn't need to be told that."

"Oh God, was that Nancy's pitch?"

"It doesn't matter," he said, which meant *yes*. "I don't want to . . . I don't know what people's intentions are, you know? I just met her."

"Yeah." I wasn't sure what to say, except that he was being too nice.

"*Ughhhh*." He lifted his fists to the sky and let them fall. "I can't even explain this. My thinking is . . . muddled right now."

He shook his head, like he was disappointed in himself. Did he wish he'd pushed back more?

I should have spoken out. Right there in the hallway when he stepped into it.

But, "I'm sorry," I said. "I'm here if you want to talk it through."

"I'm fine." I took his hand. He squeezed back and let go. "It's all good, right? *Shawna Wells!* I'm gonna have to start watching the news."

"You hungry?" I asked.

"Not yet." He glanced at his door, jangling his keys. "I'll text you in a bit and we can work or . . . whatever."

I grinned at the *whatever,* but all humor flitted away when I saw his expression—the smile sloughing off, the raw exhaustion underneath.

"Okay," I said. "You know where to find me."

The sun set, he didn't text, call, knock. I got into bed and listened for him.

But I couldn't hear his music all night long.

28.

Oscar wasn't himself up there.

His movements were forceful, jerky, a tiny bit sluggish. The orchestra looked out of sorts and the newly anointed symphony choir like they'd been dropped into a war zone. Their sixteen voices didn't float over the woodwinds like echoes from the past. They were performing a completely different song.

Oscar lowered his baton, slumping. "Have you guys . . . rehearsed this?"

The choir mistress, Liz, a contralto who used to run the children's chorus at the Met, stood from the front row.

"We have," she said, polite, tightly coiled. "What you've *given* us. There are twenty new bars we're working through tonight—"

"I'm writing as *fast as I can*," Oscar yelled, and everybody stopped breathing.

Oscar never snapped. Oscar laughed, teased, encouraged. This voice was a new one. It seemed to shock even him. He stood at the podium, muscles locked tight.

"Right," he said quietly. "Right. I apologize."

But he didn't budge. Didn't lift his baton. Stared at his score while the orchestra shifted and coughed.

I started to rise from my seat as Dad shot from the wings. I hadn't realized he was here tonight.

Dad placed a hand on Oscar's back and murmured in his ear. Oscar nodded, motioning feebly for Dad to take the baton.

A ripple ran through the musicians. Martin Chertok—*the* Martin Chertok, the Once and Future Maestro—was taking the podium once again, lifting his hands like feathers, drifting, settling, until everyone's instrument was at the ready.

Oscar walked down the aisle, then stopped to turn back, listening.

They'd begun at the start of the *andante con fuoco*. The choir was better this time—the tenors too loud, but that was easily adjusted. At least their voices made sense in the context of the piece. They were approaching something ineffably lovely, dawn rising slowly over a cityscape . . .

Oscar turned from the stage and started away.

I jumped from my seat, my arms a roadblock.

"Hey," I whispered. "Hey!"

It took a second for his eyes to land on mine. "It's so off. I need to toss it out, start something—"

"It's not off," I whispered urgently, willing his voice quieter too. "I promise, it's not. This is the first time they're rehearsing it."

"It's not what I have in my head. What we have when we're working."

He reached out to run his finger over my cheek, pulling away a stray eyelash.

"Well, then, I shall sing tonight." I raised my chin like a prima donna.

"You always sing."

"No, here." I nudged him. "I'll sit in. I can be a ringer."

Me, a ringer, helping all these pre-professional opera students achieve a better performance. Hil*ar*ious.

But Oscar had turned toward the stage, taking my wrist, leading me straight to the choir seats.

"Wait wait wait, no no no." I dug in my heels to stop. "I was one million percent joking! I forgot to say 'get it,' but I'm saying it now! Oscar!"

"Do you mind?" He turned to lock eyes with me. "It's a good idea."

"*I mean.*" My heart ratcheted to express-train speed. But, oh God, would this really help him . . . ?

Dad had finished rehearsing that section—concluding a few bars after the brass section picked up the Latin theme—and as he waved for everyone to pause, the orchestra broke into applause. I glanced between Oscar and Dad, not sure which they were cheering, but Oscar was whispering in Liz's ear, motioning to me. She looked perplexed, obviously, but waved for me to join them.

The choir scrambled for another chair.

I waved them off. "Floor is absolutely fine!"

I sat cross-legged next to the sopranos. The girl next to me scooted her ankles away. *Yeppers.* I closed my eyes. This would be over soon.

Oscar mounted the steps, patted Dad on the shoulder, and took the baton back. Dad clapped for Oscar, the orchestra following suit— less rapturously this time.

But then Oscar raised his hands, murmured, "From the beginning," scanned the orchestra, found me on the floor, and smiled with such gratitude that his eyes crinkled.

Then he struck the downbeat and the orchestra began to play. Four bars till the choir and . . .

It was fine. Not as scary as I'd expected. I knew the soprano line, when to come in. And I reveled in the feeling of the orchestration—everything we'd imagined taking form now, bursting joyfully into the real world. Sitting up here, physically immersed in the music, sound swirled around me the way it had that day in the Cloisters. It seemed to reverberate inside my body, my nerve endings, down to the molecular level. Was this the God thing Oscar was talking about? Dad's "ineffable"? If not this, then what?

He continued past the point where the chorus ran out, but his eyes kept dancing back to me every few bars, life returning note by note.

As we finished up, I scanned the house and noticed fewer onlookers tonight, thank goodness. But I did see a flash of red hair as Nora Visser slid out the back door, glancing back one more time. Right at me.

"That was helpful," Oscar said as we waved good-bye to the musicians and made our way through the night-lit plaza. "Having you up there . . . yeah. Thank you."

"It really helped?"

"It did," he said, with a sideways grin. "You're my cannon blast."

Our arms swung together in counter-time to our steps.

Across the plaza, a camera flashed. I pulled Oscar so his back was turned. Was Nora seriously going to keep siccing paparazzi on us? Oscar looked behind him, and only then did I realize it was a group of tourists taking a selfie by the fountain.

I linked arms with him, pretending that I was being playful, that I was not, in fact, the most conceited person in the world.

"I know this is important." Oscar motioned behind him as we left Lincoln Center. "This is part of why I'm here, but I wish I could get this piece *finished* first. You know? Every second I'm working with the orchestra, I feel like I'm wasting time."

"Why don't you ask Dad? I'm sure—"

"He said this is a good introduction to the way things work in the professional world with commissioned pieces. So." Oscar pulled at his face. "Yeah, I have to make it work."

I felt my own frustration rising. "But this isn't commissioned. It's yours."

"*Is* it?"

I wasn't sure what that meant, but I grabbed his arm. "Of course it is. And you're a student, you're seventeen, this is—"

"I have to do what they ask me to do. It's cool." He swiped his face, like he was trying to get rid of the last remnants of whatever had come over him back at Lilly Hall. "Will you sit with me tonight? While I work?"

"Of course."

I sat on his bed. He wrote on the floor, filled a page, tossed it, started again, murmuring to himself. He didn't ask my opinion, and I couldn't give one. This wasn't the moment for it. So I kept vigil. And at some point I fell asleep.

When I woke up, the room was dark, one corner illuminated by a roving beam. It took my eyes a second to adjust before I saw Oscar holding a tiny flashlight in his mouth, scribbling so fast, his fingers blurred. He would stop—head tilted like he was hearing a ghost—then nod in recognition and compose.

I grabbed my phone to check the time. *11:36 p.m.* The sudden glow made him startle, dropping his flashlight. He laughed, holding his chest.

I sat up. "Why are the lights off?"

"I didn't want to wake you. You looked so sweet."

I smiled, rousing myself to pop on the lights for him again. But it nagged at me now, not hearing what he was hearing. Not understanding what compelled him to stay up and get something down—how someone could come *up* with that something in the first place.

He was someone who heard music singing to him in the night, who stayed up, who answered its call.

I was someone who fell asleep watching.

When I got back from the next morning's run and waved good-bye to Jules, Nora was waiting on my stoop playing with her cell phone, a giant Birkin bag dangling off one arm. She gasped when she saw me, like I'd vaporized from nowhere.

"Hi." I pulled my keys from my pouch, still winded, but managed an elbow wave.

"You're a runner!" She stood surveying me. "Hidden depths! Are you doing the marathon?"

"No." I laughed. "I'm new to this. And it's just for fun."

"Fun! Ha! I do it because I pay someone a *lot* of money to scream at me until it's finished. And because . . ." She motioned to herself. "This does not want to stay like this. But you're a sylph, my God. Anyway, good for you."

I started to unlock the door, discomfort creeping back. "Dad's up at campus already, I think."

"I know." She stepped into the house behind me.

"Oh." I turned.

"I was hoping to catch up with you." Nora trotted in her heels to the kitchen, opened the cabinet, and popped a coffee pod into the Keurig.

"Want one?" she asked. "Ooh, *Arabica,* I love that word . . ."

I smiled at her rolled *r.* "I'm good."

Leaning against the wall, I frantically rehearsed a resignation letter. *Thank you so much for all you've done for me, but after careful consideration, I've decided to take a semi-permanent hiatus from social engagements, no matter how important the cause . . .*

"So I *had* to tell you," Nora started as the coffee poured. "I was at Oscar's rehearsal the other day."

"I saw you," I admitted, stiffening even more. Was she here to dig for dirt on Oscar's stress management? If so, what could I tell her? Should I bring up the "wardrobe change" or was it not my place?

Nothing. I would say nothing.

She retrieved her cup and sat peering at me, chin resting on her fist. "Ruby, I was *stunned* by your singing."

I blinked, thrown. "Oh. I—whoa."

"I had no idea you were a singer. All this time, this talent you've got and you've hidden it away! Is it something you're planning to pursue?"

"Um . . ." I drew a dizzy breath. "I don't know. I haven't given it a lot of consideration."

"Well, you should." She squeezed my hand, smiling with pride. Like I was her child. "You Chertoks never cease to amaze me."

Emotion swelled in me, so strong, I could hardly speak, cathedral chimes in my chest. *You Chertoks.*

"I know that you've been trying to keep away from Amberley, to create a life that's yours . . ." She leaned in conspiratorially. "*And* I know we haven't made it easy for you, at *any* point. We put you on a poster, for Christ's sake! '*I Am Music*'! No pressure at all, right?"

I smiled. I couldn't help it. *She gets it, she does.*

"But a gift is a gift, Ruby. It would be a sin to ignore it. I'm sure you've started this process with your dad, but in case you haven't . . ." She picked up her bag with a guilty smile. "I hope you will forgive your dear godmother for overstepping a little here?"

Her tiny hand disappeared into the Birkin bag and emerged with a huge stack of brochures. She dropped them on the oak table with a *thunk,* stood, and started riffling through. Dizzy, I took in the names on the covers: *Bucknell, Manhattan School of Music, Peabody Institute, San Francisco Conservatory* . . .

"Okay, so these are all excellent vocal programs," she murmured, passing them to me for inspection. "This one is really coming up. Their showcase last year was astonishing . . ."

I sat next to her, flipping through them, some part of me still not understanding.

"Auditions are mainly in February, so you've got some time to prepare," she said, flipping through the Peabody brochure. "Take lessons, get a repertoire together. And would you be interested in joining Oscar's symphony as a member of the choir?"

It took me a second to respond. "I'm . . . not an Amberley student."

"Well, it *would* just be for Oscar's piece, but you'd still get to put it on your college applications, which I think would be helpful."

She got to the last brochure in the pile and passed it to me, almost shyly. *Amberley.*

"Couldn't resist. I hope you'll at least consider us?"

She reached out for my hand.

"I . . ." There were no words. All gone, *poof.*

She squeezed and let go. "So I hope you don't mind too much, but I've already spoken with Liz about the choir bit. You remember Liz Trombly?"

I nodded.

"She thinks it's a *fantastic* idea." Nora crouched to pull out an embossed memo pad and a mini ballpoint pen. She scribbled a room number and the words *Wed/Fri 10–11:45* onto one page, turned it over, and slid it across the table like a job offer.

"I've got to scoot, and I'm so sorry for bombarding you like this, but I couldn't in good conscience let this pass." She flopped to one side. "It's kind of what I do. So why don't you start by trying a rehearsal or two and . . . see if you like it?" She rose, tapping her fingers cheerfully on the table. "Could be the start of something."

I waved, mute, as she left the house, too stunned to do much more than stare at the pile of college brochures she'd collected for me.

The start. Of *something*.

29.

i found the rehearsal room fifteen minutes early and walked the Amberley halls to kill time, listening to music spilling out of other classrooms, a trombone player doing scales, an oboist working a difficult passage over and over, a drummer and his teacher laughing at a mistake, trying to duplicate it as a joke.

I laughed silently along, feeling carried away for a good five seconds, like maybe I knew their secret password after all.

I walked into the choir room at ten o'clock sharp, but everyone was already seated in sections, music propped on stands in front of them, Liz in the front.

"We try to *start* at ten, Ruby, so if you don't mind coming earlier."

I flushed lobster red. "I'm so sorry. I was here . . ."

She motioned to an empty chair at the edge of the soprano section. "No need to sit on the floor today."

Everybody laughed, but it was a friendly sound. A tenor waved hello and other singers smiled as I walked past. They were my age, of course—summer students. I wondered how much they'd trained to get here. Voice students tended to start studying later than other musicians, because their voices took time to mature. If I had a gift for this—*an enormous "if"*—I could start now and not miss a single beat.

The girl next to me scooted her stand closer to me and flipped to the last photocopied page, this one written in Oscar's careful hand.

"The beginning of the third movement," she whispered. Then she smiled shyly. "What am I saying, you probably have it memorized already."

"I haven't heard this yet!" I squinted, trying to pick out the notes, while Liz stood.

"Okay, from one eighty-seven." She turned to my section. "Sopranos, since our ranks are bolstered, let's keep the volume more moderato?"

She gestured for us to begin. I drew a hasty breath and sang. The girl next to me had a voice like a mountain brook, crystalline ice water. Liz walked closer, her head cocked, listening. Then she waved and everyone stopped.

"Ruby, could you sing the first few bars?"

I shrank into my seat, knees clenching against the plastic edge. Here it was. The test. If I was going to even entertain the idea of becoming a singer, I would need to get over my nerves. I closed my eyes, quickly, calming myself, and sang.

She stooped to touch my stomach.

I glanced down, confused.

She nodded. "From the diaphragm."

I breathed more deeply and sang it again.

She looked pleased. "You sing out, Ruby. That's lovely. Don't worry about volume. All right, once more?"

We sang again, working through the piece, my confidence growing with every note. She'd asked me to sing out. That was more encouragement than I'd gotten in an entire lifetime of playing the piano.

I felt a stab of guilt, like my piano teacher was listening to my thoughts. Lovely Mrs. Swenson had encouraged me twice weekly, for thirteen years. She'd been paid to do it, but still. She used to give me jelly beans from a jar she kept across the room when I got my scales right. She *also* snuck me jelly beans when I messed up, saying, "Chin up, Ruby. Try again." I got far more jelly beans that way.

Chin up, Ruby, I thought now, leaving rehearsal, my steps keeping time to an imagined waltz. *Try again.*

I popped by Dad's office on the way out, but he wasn't in. There was a doctor's business card resting on top of the messy pile of paperwork on his desk, so he must have popped out for a checkup. He never answered his cell phone and I didn't want to wait for him to get back, so I skipped out to the street and called Win.

He picked up right away. "Ruby Rooster! To what do I owe the—?"

Some guy giggled in the background and his voice went muffled. He wasn't alone.

I started to blush. "Um, quick question. Do you remember Dad talking about that opera singer friend of his who teaches now?"

"Friend . . . who . . ."

"She's super famous, why can't I remember her name . . . ?" Maybe because my heart was thudding louder than the jack-hammer across the street. "She's a mezzo, she was in *The House Guest*, gah . . ."

"Odile—?"

"Odile Michaud! Thank you *so* much, talk again soon!"

I hung up before Win could dig for why I was asking. I would tell him—I'd tell everybody—but only if it turned out to be real.

I googled Odile's webpage, remembering the year-long wait list Dad had said she accumulated the second she announced she was teaching. Somehow, I knew she'd find a way to squeeze in Martin Chertok's daughter. As I picked up my phone, a burst of hot adrenaline shot through me—almost enough to wash away the gray in my stomach, that same murky shame that sloshed in whenever I thought about Amberley.

But this was different. This was real.

I gritted my teeth and dialed.

I got my own folding chair at the full-orchestra rehearsal and a friendly wave from the other choir members. We sang the same section as Monday and it gelled now—Oscar barely paid us any attention except to search for me every twenty bars or so, lock eyes like he was recharging a battery, carry on.

When we finished just after nine, Oscar led a round of applause for ourselves, the usual routine, then we broke into collegial chatter. I tried to relax into it—the trumpeter teasing the French horn about how long it took her to put away her instrument, three oboists chatting cross-legged on the edge of the stage comparing reeds, a clutch of brass players debating a tricky rhythm so passionately, they drew a small crowd. This reminded me so much of Wildwood, school orchestra, all these things I'd missed—but inside, even my new soprano friend's "See you Friday!" gave me a physical thrill as I left with Oscar. I was one of them, in a completely unexpected way.

I figured we'd grab post-rehearsal dinner and then get back to his apartment for another composition session, so I'd thrown on a comfy black dress, but when he met me on the sidewalk to head out again, he was dressed to the nines.

"I have a surprise for tonight," he sang.

"Another section?" I grabbed his shoulders and jumped up and down. "Please please please?"

"No." His dimple flashed. "*Yes*, but it can wait till tomorrow."

"Such a tease!"

"No, no, it's rough. And we need a night off." His eyes lit with mischief. "A night *out*."

The taxi pulled up outside a low-lit building with no sign marking it. The line to get in stretched all the way down the block.

"Um." I eyed the burly doorman, then looked at Oscar. "Is there a VIP entrance?"

"Yep." He smiled wickedly. "This way."

Taking my hand, he led us directly to the front of the line. My dress suddenly felt a million times clingier.

"Hey." Oscar gave the bouncer an up-nod. "Yeah, I'm Oscar Bell."

The huge dude up-nodded back, waved the line a step away, and opened the door for us to go in. I glanced behind us, totally bewildered, just as a flash went off—this one aimed at us.

"Whoa," I whispered as we hurried past the vacant coat check. "Are *you* a celebrity?"

"I think I might be!" He shot me a double thumbs-up, the Mr. Cool act from seconds ago thankfully discarded. "You'll have to give me pointers."

There was too much there for me to unpack, so I just asked, "Where *are* we?"

Before he could answer, I heard music from the next room. Not awful Top 40. *Jazz*. "Is this Speakeasy?"

"You got it." He wrapped his shirt-sleeved arm around my shoulders. "A bunch of the philharmonic guys have been moonlighting here. They said I could jam with them, so I've come a couple times, sitting in on the piano. Once on the clarinet."

I stared at him, my mouth open. "When did you—?"

"Middle of the night!" He shrugged. "I popped in last Tuesday after you went up to bed. I told you I don't sleep much."

"You play the *clarinet.*" Of course he played the clarinet.

"Eh, it didn't go that well. They didn't make fun of me too much, though."

Oscar waved to the trumpet player on the stage, finishing a solo. He raised his instrument in greeting.

I couldn't stop staring. "Who *are* you?"

"Your boyfriend! Come on, we're audience members tonight."

He found us a tiny table toward the back and drew a chair for me to sit. As I settled in, I scanned the snappy crowd, wonderstruck.

Then I stood again so fast, I nearly knocked the table over.

Oscar was staring too. "Is that . . . Alice?"

"It can't be. She never goes out. She never does anything!"

"I'm surprised the line didn't make her turn around and give up." His eyes were laughing. So he *had* clocked her ridiculousness when he met her.

I nearly laughed too, but couldn't get over the fact that my sister was *right there,* dolled up in a silver 1920s-style dress, her lips cherry-red, laughing at a joke some guy sitting millimeters from her was telling. He was around her age, dark-haired, good-looking, wearing a well-tailored, inexpensive suit.

"It's the *teacher.*" I grabbed Oscar's shoulder. "It has to be. We need to crash their date, this is too good, I might never get another chance again."

Alice looked just as stunned by the sight of me. She rose to kiss my cheek, hissing, "*You are seventeen,*" through her smile.

"Don't tell Dad!" I whispered back.

"Ruby, this is my friend Daniel Ruiz," she said, perfectly gracious as she turned to the table. "Danny, this is my sister, Ruby. And Oscar—"

"Oscar's my boyfriend," I interrupted, grinning giddily.

She hit the table. "I *knew it!* I am taking full credit for this."

"Great to meet you both," Daniel said, recovering from our sudden entrance. "Ruby, I've heard so much about you, I feel like I've known you for years."

"You've been talking about me behind my back," I deadpanned to Alice.

She ruffled my hair. "I'm *obsessed* with you."

Daniel pulled chairs over so we could join them. I didn't dare drink with Alice around—her discretion had its limits—but this was too uncanny an event to miss witnessing, a solar eclipse, Halley's comet, a volcanic eruption.

Alice! Personal life! On display!

"Oscar is a budding composer," she said to Daniel. "He's studying with my dad."

"Is that right?" Danny nodded to him like he was conferring a knighthood. "That's incredible."

"Thanks! Yeah, it's . . ." Oscar glanced up at the stage, half listening to the drummer riffing. "I'm composing a lot less this summer than I do back home, at school, but . . . I think I'm growing a lot, so. It's been good."

Daniel laughed. "Jeez, I'm trying to think what I was doing when I was in high school. My baseball team went to regionals, that's about all I can brag about."

"You have a lot to brag about," Alice said, eyes glowing, and they held hands across the table and oh my God, they'd *totally* had sex already, hadn't they?

"I played baseball for a hot two minutes." Oscar grinned. "We did not go to regionals."

I stared at him. "You played *baseball*?"

"Outfield." He glanced back and forth from the stage. "My dad really wanted me to be on a team, any team, so I picked baseball because it looked like it gave you a lot of downtime."

"Especially in outfield." Daniel pointed at him.

Oscar leaned over the table. "I got hit in the head a couple times. Still didn't catch the ball."

"I am . . . agog," I said, picturing him wearing a baseball mitt.

"You ever done a sport?" Oscar nudged me. "Apart from running?"

Alice let out a snort on my behalf. "Running? *What?*"

Right on cue, the music on the stage amped up several notches, making conversation nearly impossible.

Oscar lit up, his feet keeping time under the table.

"You like jazz?" I yell-whispered.

"It's pretty physical," Oscar answered. "I'm more . . ." He gestured to his heart. "But I like it."

I nodded. "Jazz probably makes more sense if you've been drinking!"

Alice slid her glass away from me.

Daniel turned to Oscar. "You ever think about doing a school visit? Mine's an experimental charter, so we run through the summer."

"He never gets a break," Alice said, making it sound like a compliment.

Daniel held her hand as he went on. "I gotta tell you, the kids are fantastic and music is a big focus for them. I think they'd love to hear from somebody who—you know, looks like them, who's on his way up . . ."

I glanced at Oscar, worried at that echo of Nancy's words, but his expression was thoughtful. Open. Maybe because this offer was coming from Danny, a teacher, last name Ruiz—not some clueless white guy.

"Things are hectic right this second," Oscar said. "But that'd be amazing. Yeah. What dates are you thinking?"

They started talking details.

I turned to whisper into Alice's ear. "So you're out and about."

"Yes? And?" Her face remained placid, locked on the stage.

"Did you bring your viola? So you could practice in the ladies' room?"

She whapped me. "No, I did not. In fact . . ." She glanced around like there were spies everywhere, then leaned in to whisper. "I'm considering a break."

"A tropical vacation?"

"No." She paused, then sipped her bourbon—Alice was drinking bourbon!—and said, "Longer."

The piano took the solo line and my mind drifted with it, reeling.

Alice. Planning a break from music. Drinking bourbon. Dating teachers. Looking happier than I'd ever seen her.

Oscar. Tapping the table along with the music. Crackling and alive. Back to himself.

The world was wild and chaotic and bursting with possibility, for Alice and for Oscar, and maybe even for me?

The musicians on stage pulsed on, playing notes that sounded like *yes, yes, yes.*

30.

Odile Michaud lived across the park in an Upper East Side luxury apartment building, as befit a legendary opera doyenne in repose. I'd met her a few times over the years, but checking in with her doorman and riding the mirror-paneled elevator up to her suite made my skin go prickly.

As I hesitated in the hall, I reached for my cell phone to turn it off. Then, my nerves already firing at level ten, I quickly clicked to Mom's number and shot off a text. My first attempt at contact in months.

I'm about to have a voice lesson with Odile Michaud!

Then I turned my phone off, pocketed it gingerly like a live grenade, and knocked on the door.

Odile took a long time to answer, but as soon as the door swung open, she leaned in to kiss my cheeks.

"My goodness, you are a woman now." She walked away, motioning me to follow.

I peeked at doorways we passed, a small kitchen, a dusty sitting room piled with books, until we reached a dim living room with a piano filling half the space, a faded velvet sofa taking up most of the rest. A white Persian cat was asleep, purring loudly. He opened his eyes when I walked past, then shut them again as if unimpressed.

The whole place smelled like potpourri. Nobody else seemed to live here. I wondered what her life must be like.

She sat on the piano bench, her thick pearl necklace clattering against her silk blouse. "I did not know you were a singer, Ruby."

"Well, I *hope* I am."

She pointed a bent finger at me. "That is a good answer. Let's find out."

I'd prepared a simple aria from *Don Giovanni* that I'd heard a gazillion times, watching from my child-of-the-conductor seat in the pit. But Odile started me on scales and warmups.

"Hmmm," she hummed, between each one. Then, after a series of arpeggios, she stood. "How long have you been singing, darling?"

"Forever, on my own. This is the first time I've—*oh*."

She was touching my stomach, the way Liz had. "Let's work on your breathing."

We sang through some exercises together, her fingers pushing my abdomen, her own voice ringing out through the parlor with astonishing power.

Then she walked away. "Yes. Right."

Her eyes crinkled as she looked at me.

"I brought a song," I said, to fill the sudden silence. "Um . . . 'Vedrai Carino'?"

"*Non*. Deceptive, that piece, although the range is certainly . . . hmm. I think this is a good start. I'll give you exercises to work on at home and we'll take it from there."

"So . . ." I clenched my toes, gathering courage as she led me to the door. "Am I a singer?"

Her mouth fell open, then she smiled. "You are a *Chertok*. You have that drive to succeed, I can see that in you. Tell your papa we've made a good start."

"Thank you!" I grinned, then blurted, "*Merci,*" like a goon, and she gave a grandmotherly wave as she slid the door shut, the *click-click* of locks following after.

On the elevator ride down, I turned my phone back on.

Mom had written back. *That's fantastic, sweetheart, let me know how it goes!*

I reread her text three times on the bus ride home. And I pictured myself on the stage of the Met, singing Pamina, Susanna, Mimi to rapturous applause. I wouldn't be making the river flow, I would be the water itself, story and song swirling into one.

It was better than any daydream I'd ever had before.

When I got back, Oscar was up at my house, eating cereal at the dining room table at four p.m. I glanced around to see if we were alone, then bent to kiss him. He pecked back, chewing, eyes locked on the bowl.

"You okay?" I asked, my mood starting to fizzle.

He nodded upstairs. "I had an argument with your dad. He's gone now . . ."

"*What?*" I sat. This was a first. "Why?"

"Well, it started because the BBC included the *Summer Symphony* in a round-up of pieces debuting this season . . ."

The BBC. Good lord. They knew about him in England.

"A quick mention, which is great, it's amazing, but . . ." Oscar rubbed the bridge of his nose. "They called it *jazz-infused.* 'Rising prodigy Oscar Bell's jazz-infused *Summer Symphony,* Amberley's Lilly Hall', etcetera. I . . ." He exhaled loudly, shoving the spoon so it sloshed the leftover milk. "I'm getting pretty fucking sick of this."

I touched the band of his wristwatch carefully. "Sick of what?"

"You don't see it."

"Well . . ." I scratched my forehead. "Your piece is *not* jazz-infused."

"*Thank* you!" He stood and paced in a circle. "Marty was trying to tell me it was."

"What?" That surprised me. "The second movement."

"Yes." He leaned against the back of a chair, watching me.

"That's bachata. I wouldn't say that's the same thing at all . . ."

"Yeah, but here's the clincher." He sat on the edge of the table. "The BBC hasn't heard a *note* of this symphony. Nobody has! Either they were guessing or that's the language from the press release Amberley sent out."

"But why *jazz*? That's so . . ." My body went stiff with the realization.

"And your dad . . . I love your dad, I do, but he started going on about Ravel and Copland, Gershwin, Bernstein—all these white guys who *were* influenced by jazz, like that's supposed to negate this. I just . . ."

"Ugh. I'm sorry."

"You seem happy." His mouth smiled but his eyes didn't. He looked tired. "I don't want to spoil it."

I pulled myself up to foist a kiss on him. "No, you should talk about this stuff with me. I always want to know what's going on with you."

"I . . . yeah. Thank you." He took my outstretched hand and ran his fingers along it. "So where you been?"

"At a voice lesson." My body jolted with the thrill of announcing it. "My first one ever."

Oscar jolted too, a malfunction blink that his eyes took a second to open from. "As in . . . singing?"

"Yeah!" I walked into the kitchen, searching for a snack. "I'm finally getting the message that the universe is sending me. Took me long enough, right?"

I dug into a bag of wasabi trail mix.

"I mean, Mom *always* said I was a singer, and now Nora and you—maybe this is what I've been looking for. It's August, right? Just in time to apply to conservatories! I don't know . . ." I pulled myself onto the counter. "I think this might be my career."

I popped a spicy pea into my mouth and turned to see Oscar staring at me with thick confusion pooling in his eyes. He *was* tired.

"Career?" he asked. "Like . . . opera?"

"No. Pop. I'm gonna be the next Taylor Swift."

"Oh!" He brightened.

I threw a pea at him. "I'm kidding! Of *course* classical. This is home for me. Always will be."

I breathed the townhouse in, dust and books and music.

The front door jangled open and Dad strode through.

I stood quickly, hoping to defuse whatever tension lingered between them with my own good news. "Hey Dad, guess who I just saw."

He blinked between us. "The Dalai Lama."

I laughed. "No. Odile Michaud."

"Oh! You ran into her?"

"I had a lesson!"

"A singing lesson?" Dad grinned, squinting at me. "What for?"

My own smile faltered. "Um."

"For Oscar's piece? Ah, right, Nora told me she'd roped you in. Listen, sweetie, don't worry about that. Nobody's gonna hear you up there, you've got real singers drowning you out and your pitch is fine.

Just show up and have a good time!" He bustled up the stairs to his office, shouting, "Give me fifteen minutes, Oscar, and I'll be ready to hear the new stuff!"

"Yep," Oscar called, his eyes locked on mine, melting with . . . *no*. With sympathy. With not knowing what to say.

My hands started to shake.

I put down the bag of trail mix. "Tell me. The truth."

"I'm one person, Ruby . . ."

"Tell me."

He sat and hung his head.

I started to disintegrate. "You said my voice was the one you heard."

"It is." He gripped his knees, peering up at me. "It always will be."

"But—"

"It's a sweet voice, Ruby. Your dad's right, you have good pitch, but in terms of professional—"

"Holy shit." I couldn't listen anymore. I hurried up the stairs, Oscar bolting after me.

"Ruby, listen!" He grabbed my arm. "I just don't want you to get your hopes—"

"Nope, no big deal, I don't *have* any hopes to get up!" I wiggled away and kept climbing without looking at him. "I already *knew*, I already . . ." I swallowed down something sharp. "I'm not Florence Foster Jenkins, okay? I just daydreamed. For two seconds and I shouldn't have and—I'll be fine."

"You're not fine."

Somehow, him saying it made it true—made every dark thought I'd been shelving for later perusal tumble around me, papers flying, ground giving way.

"I . . ." I spun around, laughing wildly. *"I don't know what you see in me*. We are *not* equals. I am at a serious disadvantage in terms of what I offer to the universe. And I'm counting down the hours until you figure out how pointless I am and move on. But it's *fine*—when that happens, I'll be fine!"

"*What?*" He reached out for me. "Ruby, you're being crazy."

"Oh, now I'm crazy too! Ha-ha, *awesome*, yay."

I took the last flight two steps at a time and shut my bedroom door and sat at the foot of my bed and took a few breaths—from the diaphragm, whoopee—and here it came. Tears. I'd cried in the lead-up to my Amberley audition, little jags of stress and worry and frustration—but not afterward. Not once I knew. I'd thought I was strong, but I must have been storing the tears up for months, because now they were spilling down my cheeks in great, hot gushes. They left me drained, like I was bleeding out. It was too much, too all at once.

Stop crying. Stop!

"Ruby?" Oscar murmured from the other side of the door. "You can be an opera singer if that's what you want to be. I'll support you one hundred percent. You can do anything you . . ."

Boyfriend-talk. He sounded like he was reading out something he'd found on the Internet. It didn't mean anything. I knew now, I *knew*. I just didn't know how I could have been so stupid. So *recklessly* hopeful.

I'd been doing it all my life, though, hadn't I? When I'd asked Mom if she thought I was good and she'd said that *good* was an unhelpful term and I hadn't pressed her further. When I'd asked Dad why he didn't want me to enter competitions yet, and he'd said I should wait until I was older so I could make a big splash, never mind that Alice had been competing internationally since she was eight. When Mrs.

Swenson said how much she enjoyed our lessons and I'd thought she meant it as a reflection on my playing rather than my company. I was brilliant. Or I was going to be, any day now.

I'd never wanted to know.

I bit the heel of my hand so Oscar couldn't hear me crying. So I couldn't either. After a minute, my dad's voice shouted from his study and I heard Oscar trudging away and the door downstairs creaking shut behind him. And then the music. His goddamned taunting music.

Even through the blanket I shoved over my head, I could tell Oscar was off today. And still a million times better than I would ever be.

They'd ended early. I peeked out my window to see him walking around the stoop to his apartment, rubbing the back of his neck. He looked up to my window.

I ducked away. Sat on the bed.

Then a giant's thudding steps sounded on the stairwell, followed by three great knocks on my door.

"Ruby," Dad said. "It's time we had a talk."

31.

dad sat on the corner of my bed while I crawled up to make a nest of pillows, wondering how long it had been since he'd been in this room. Years, maybe.

Besides me and our old housekeeper, the last person to set foot inside was Mom. She'd sat next to me right here, languid and soft and warm, playing with my hair, comparing toes, before getting into it. We'd already had the "this is an amicable divorce, nothing needs to change" chat with Dad in the kitchen the week prior, and this had been the follow-up—the "I want to talk you through my tour dates" conversation. I'd been stoic even as she flipped to a new month, and another, and another. I'd told her how exciting it was.

Now, wiping my eyes dry only to have them fill back up again, I wondered what might have happened if I'd cried then like I wanted to. Would it have changed anything? Would she have cared enough to stay?

"Honey." Dad rubbed his beard. "I try my very best not to dictate what you do with your life. If you *want* it, my job is to give it to you, period. But this isn't a good idea. And I think you know it."

"Yeah." My voice came out like a kid's. I pressed my lips together to keep from tipping into sobbing. "I'm not a singer, I was being stupid. I don't know."

Dad's brow creased. "Not the . . . if you want to sing, you should sing. Christ, Odile's not cheap, but I'm happy to pay for lessons if that's what you want to do. No. Ruby. I'm talking about Oscar."

My arms went cold. I reached out to flip off the AC and picked up a pillow to hug. "What about him?"

Dad cleared his throat. "I want you to give him a wide berth."

"You're . . ." I clutched the pillow. "Wait, is . . . ?"

My mind swam between visions of Nora and her sister debating my usefulness and Dad's face, closing off, when Oscar asked for his blessing. The way he'd been avoiding looking at me all summer.

Dad raised a hand. "Maybe in another life, another time, the two of you would make sense, but this is—"

"Another *time*? This is the twenty-first century, Dad. And we're us! Progressives, *smart*." I stood from the bed, pressing the glass of the window. "I cannot believe you're saying this!"

"You're not listening, Ruby." He groaned, pinching the bridge of his nose. "I'm not such a wordsmith, as you know, so I'm going to be a blunt instrument here. I don't think you're what he needs right now."

"What he needs." I could only dully repeat his words as they fluttered around in my head. *Oh.*

Oh.

"This is his shot, Ruby. This summer, this school—everything is conspiring to give him a launch pad into an incredible career. I believe in Oscar like I've never believed in a student before. He's the real deal, but this"—Dad motioned to me with both hands, sketching the general shape of a girl—"isn't helping."

"I'm not *distracting* him," I croaked.

"You say that."

"I'm not. I'm not pulling focus, I'm not doing *anything* but supporting him."

A chill shot through me, like I'd confessed something deeply incriminating.

Dad gestured to my face. "And look how happy you are about it."

Another goddamned tear slipped out.

Dad scooted over to wipe it off, but I flinched. Undeterred, he leaned forward and wrapped me in a hug. I was angry, I wanted to wiggle loose, but it had been so long since he'd held me like this, a real squeeze. I'd missed it—his scratchy beard, his musty vest, the way the world seemed like a diorama that just belonged to the both of us: *Marty Chertok and Daughter at Home.*

"Listen, I'm not asking you to make a hard-and-fast decision," he murmured, patting my hair smooth. "But I have a suggestion."

I leaned away to look at him.

He smiled, eyes sad, then pointed to my digital picture frame. "Why don't you head down and spend some time with your grandparents? Couple of weeks, fish off the dock, clear your head."

"I never fish off that dock."

"Dangle your feet." Dad nudged my shoulder.

I was thinking about it. The coastal island where they lived. Grandma Jean's cooking. Gramps's jokes. Their vegetable garden. The endless dock where seabirds landed. Cicadas and crickets and marsh frogs. At night, fireflies came out, flashing and swirling. They had a porch swing where I used to watch the stars, feeling like I was on another planet entirely. A world of my own. An anchorite.

I'd wanted space this summer. I'd found other things—but I hadn't found that. And if it was only for a couple weeks . . . ? I could survive it, the distance.

An ache tore through me at the prospect of missing Oscar. And that scared me more than anything. *Could* I be on my own? On top of everything else, was I now incapable of even that?

A whisper shuddered out of me. "Is this an offer or a demand?"

Dad stayed silent, and that was his answer.

I stayed silent too. And that was mine.

"I'll book it," Dad finally said. "They'll be glad to spend some time with you."

He stood slowly, hunching to fit through the open doorway. "You're a good one, Ruby."

A good what?

I bludgeoned myself with the question as he plodded downstairs.

But soon I would be somewhere that rendered it moot. No instruments. No debuts. No *busy busy*, no self-importance, real or false, no champagne teas, no photographers, no casual lies, no manipulation, no confusion.

No music. No Oscar. My breath left me again at the thought of it. It hurt. Too much.

I dragged a roller bag out of the pile in Win's bedroom.

"Two *weeks*?" Oscar paced the sidewalk, pulling his collar. "That's . . . you'll be getting back right before the concert."

"They haven't seen me for years, so I owe them a long visit. And honestly, Oscar, this will be good for you. A chance to focus and get the rest of it finished. I'm distracting you from writing—"

"You're not distracting me from writing the symphony, Ruby, you *are* the symphony."

He stopped pacing and stood staring at me from five feet away. A clutch of commuters passed, swerving in both directions.

I felt like I was being crushed by the air between us. I took a step forward and it got worse.

"The third movement could be about us missing each other."

"The capitulation should be hopeful," he said. "Not . . ."

His eyes had drifted. He was considering it.

"I have to be honest, Oscar, I need to get away."

He gave a surprised blink before his expression closed off.

"*Not* from you!" I reached for him. "From the city, my usual life. I'd thought I could figure some stuff out this summer from home, but it hasn't happened, so maybe I'll get some perspective while I'm there. I'm trying *really* hard not to say 'find myself' because oh my God would that ever go on the list of things white people say."

Oscar smiled back absently. "Yeah, that's . . . that'll be good. You should do this, it's important. It's pretty sudden, but—yeah, it's all good."

Dad had booked me out on the first flight tomorrow morning. Something told me if there had been an evening flight to Charleston, I'd already have been on it. And secretly, I welcomed the rush. It gave me less time to talk myself out of going.

"I mean, you're right." Oscar stepped closer. "It'll give me a chance to focus."

It was true. It was what I wanted. But it hurt to hear him come around to it.

Oscar reached out to run his hands through my hair, gathering curls between his fingers and watching them fall.

"We do have tonight, though." His lips grazed my forehead.

"Tonight." I let the word cascade over me. "Whatever should we do with it?"

"You kids hungry?"

Dad shouted from the top of the stoop. I hadn't even heard him come outside. He was grinning but his eyes were scalpel sharp, taking in the shifting energy between us. Oscar stepped away, straightening his collar again.

"In the mood for French food?" Dad asked.

"Always!" Oscar said.

"Liar," I whispered, nudging him. He nudged me back, a little green.

"My treat." Dad's voice brooked no argument. "Come on."

I glanced at my shorts and layered tanks. "You can't mean Roland, Dad, look at me."

"Of course I mean Roland, and . . ." He shrugged. "You're a Chertok, wear what you want."

I turned away so I could silently scream.

"What about me?" Oscar asked.

I laughed, taking in his button-down, skinny tie, pale green khakis. "You're always dressed for Roland, Oscar. Come on, time to get over your aversion."

We started down the block, failing to keep pace with Dad.

Oscar whispered, "Is there a kids' menu?"

I snorted.

"I'm serious!"

"Get the steak frites. It's amazing."

"I'll trust you."

We rounded the corner to the park just as a dozen joggers in matching pink T-shirts were crossing the street ahead of us.

"Hey now!" Oscar called, pointing. "Is this your competition in the marathon? Should I heckle them? Is that a thing?"

I laughed, grabbing his arm.

Dad turned, confused. "Are you running in the marathon?"

The same ridiculous question Nora had asked me. For some reason, it made me laugh louder. "No!"

"If you do, I'm coming." Oscar reached out for my hand. "I'll wave a banner at the finish line."

"An entire banner."

"I have long arms."

We swung our hands as we walked, even as a weight of sadness fell over us. Oscar would have to travel from DC to be at the finish line. And I wouldn't even be running, so no visit.

And I was leaving tomorrow.

We tightened our grip, fighting reality as long as we could.

32.

dad's table was waiting when we got into the tastefully dimmed restaurant, the maître d' ushering us straight to it with hushed greetings.

Dad waited for us to order. Oscar asked for steak frites with perfect composure and an even better accent, then Dad smiled at the waiter and said, "You know what I like."

Oscar's eyes went wide. Dad always did enjoy a touch of spectacle. No doubt he would have come here alone tonight if it were any other Saturday, but I knew in my gut what this meal was—a chance to show Oscar a glimpse into his future.

Sure enough, Dad turned right to him. "You speak French, don't you, Oscar?"

"High school level," Oscar said quickly. "But I've studied some German and Italian too, out of curiosity."

"Good." Dad swirled his giant glass of Bordeaux. "That'll be helpful."

I'd just nestled into my chair, peering at all the poorly lit oil paintings decorating the walls, tuning out, when Dad said, "What do you say, kiddo?" and I realized he was talking to me.

"It's their centenary, a one-night deal," he went on. "But my schedule isn't set yet. I could clear some space. We could see Leo and the kids, visit some colleges around Boston. Or hop on a plane, check out another city. What's on your list so far?"

This was the first time we'd ever—*ever*—talked about college. I thought of Nora sitting at my kitchen table and my mouth went sour.

"Nothing yet."

"You're gonna be a senior, Rooster," Dad chuckled. "We'd better start brainstorming."

"I totally agree. It's high time." I smiled across the candlelit table at him, hoping that Oscar was right about me being an open book. Sure enough, Dad cleared his throat, eyes darting away.

"I should start narrowing it down too." Oscar glanced between us. "Boston's definitely on my list. Berklee, I mean."

That was one of the brochures Nora had brought me. Why had she done it? I still couldn't understand. Couldn't even face it. The thought made anger and hurt and confusion bubble toxic in my veins.

I breathed deep. Tonight, tonight, and nothing but tonight.

Dad put down his wineglass. "I certainly hope Amberley's made this list."

"Oh!" Oscar forced a laugh. "Of course. But if I don't get in."

"Ah, well, congratulations." Dad winked. "You're in! Consider this your acceptance letter."

"Wow." Oscar grinned broadly while his eyes flitted to mine.

"I'd like to look at BU," I blurted, throwing out college names at random. "And Emerson."

"Not Harvard?" Dad asked.

I choked on a sip of water. "My grades aren't good enough for Harvard, Dad."

He opened his mouth like he was going to say something—*offer* something—but then he put his hands up in surrender and said, as if it took great effort, "I'd be happy to visit any of those schools with you, sweetheart."

"My sister applied to Harvard," Oscar said, buttering a steaming roll. "She didn't get in, wah-*wah*. It was a stretch, but she still cried when she found out. She goes to Duke now and loves it, so I don't feel too bad for her."

"Is Duke the school with the creepy mascot?"

Oscar squinted at me. "You *might* be thinking of Wake—"

"When your folks come up, we'll be sure to get them a full campus tour," Dad said.

We stared at him.

Oscar nodded. "That'd be great."

"I'm assuming they're coming for the concert?" Dad sipped his wine, arm resting on the back of the banquette.

"Yes! I . . ." Oscar took a quick sip of water and leaned forward. "I wanted to ask you about that. Do they need to buy tickets or is it free admission, or—?"

"*Free?* Not by a long shot."

"Oh." Oscar's fingers slid anxiously along the edge of the table. "It doesn't look like the tickets are for sale yet on the school's site . . ."

"They're planning to pop that up right after your ATV interview airs. It's a fundraiser, so they're charging top dollar. But don't worry about any of this. I've got a block of seats reserved under my name for special guests."

"They can pay . . ." Oscar started.

"Please." Dad lifted his glass like a stop sign.

"Thank you," Oscar said, watching the food arrive with a dazed look on his face.

I felt befuddled myself. End-of-year performances typically *were* free admission, reserved for friends and family members of students. Why were they using Oscar's premiere as a fundraiser? And why was the timing of this interview so important?

After we started eating, Dad steered the conversation to French cuisine, then gossip about Leo pissing people off everywhere he soloed with his elaborate greenroom requirements. There was enough rich material under that subheading to get us through the meal and most of the way home.

"I try to talk to him," Dad said, "but do you think he listens? You're the only one who hears a word I say, Rooster."

He rustled my hair.

I smoothed it back. "That's not true. Win—"

"He doesn't even listen to himself! He jumps from whim to whim, but it seems to be working for him, so who am I to judge? And Alice . . ." He sighed heavily, shaking his head. "Did you know she's thinking of applying for a sabbatical from the orchestra? Not medical leave, not maternity—that I *know* of—just a breather? Whatever that means?"

It meant carving out a corner of her life that had nothing to do with music. But Dad couldn't even conceive of such a thing. Music was his snow globe.

"She might have mentioned it to me," I said to the sidewalk.

"And *you* might mention that she shouldn't expect to waltz right back into first chair when she's returned from finding herself."

"Maybe she won't want first chair. Maybe she won't want anything."

"I just want her to be happy," Dad said quietly. "That's all I want for any of you."

His eyes crinkled as they landed on mine, as if he were asking forgiveness. Before I could decide if I wanted to give it, verbally or otherwise, we reached the house, and he drifted over to lay a hand on Oscar's shoulder.

"All right, let's call it," he said, extending his other hand. "Ruby's got an early flight."

Dad shook with Oscar like he was finalizing a deal, then strode straight to me, physically shepherding me up the stairs.

"I'm taking her to the airport," Oscar called out. "To see her off."

Dad turned to see my reaction. I nodded.

"Ah." Dad sniffed. "Well. That's nice. Take the car. I'll make sure it's here with plenty of time to get you out before rush hour hits. Night!"

He held the door open, watching me step through, then latched it shut behind us.

While I packed, Dad sat in his study with the door open, listening to a recording of Prokofiev's *Romeo and Juliet Suite,* as if trying to send a subliminal message about the dangers of young love.

I put on my pajamas, then popped my head into Dad's study to say good night. He had a million scattered folders open on his desk. The top page was a row of numbers. Financial records.

Dad jammed the papers together at the sight of me, his face going pale. "You scared me."

"I have that effect on people."

He didn't even try to smile.

I sat in his armchair. "Amberley stuff?"

"It is. It's nothing to . . . It doesn't . . ." He leaned his mouth against the knuckles of one hand, then straightened. "Yep. It's all gonna be fine."

The room seemed to wobble. "This doesn't have anything to do with *our* finances . . ."

"If it did, we wouldn't have gone out to Roland tonight, I'll tell you that." Before I could inquire further, he stood. "Get some rest, sweet-heart. I'll be up in the morning to see you—ah, see you and *Oscar* off."

I turned my cheek so he could kiss it.

As I was walking out, he said, as if musing to himself, "He's pretty invested in you, kiddo. I hadn't seen it until tonight. Still not sure it's a good thing. You know what he is, don't you?"

The question sounded so sad, so raw, that I had to turn and let him finish the thought.

"A lightning strike."

Dazzling, incredible, beautiful, keep your distance.

"Not an easy road," he said, slumping against his desk. "Being with somebody like that."

His voice trailed away, and I took the opportunity to flee, wonder-ing at the pain in his eyes. Was he talking about Mom . . . or himself?

As I slid away, the record reached Act Three, the lento, the lark singing. Juliet and Romeo waking up together after their wedding night.

I paused on the steps outside my bedroom, listening. The music stopped mid-phrase, Dad pulling the needle up cleanly and turning off the deck. The light turned off in the study, in the hall below. He tromped to his bedroom and shut the door.

I sat perched on my windowsill, staring at the wash of light from Oscar's apartment. Then I stepped into my quietest flats and slid downstairs, soundless, a ghost.

Oscar met me at the door before I even knocked. He pulled me inside by the tips of my fingers, spun me to kiss me and we both backed up to shut the door. I pressed him against the frame and let my hands go where they wanted—up his chest, around his neck—my body stretching along the length of him. Then I felt the ground give out.

"Ack!"

Oscar caught me by the arm, keeping me from falling.

I laughed, finally looking at what I'd slipped on—the entire floor was carpeted with composition paper.

"I'm so sorry." Oscar reached for the offending page. "This place is a minefield."

I turned and took in more of the mess—loose pages now drifting all the way to the galley kitchen and, more crucially, covering parts of Oscar's bed. "I was going to say the perp's house in a serial killer movie, but . . ."

"*Ouch.*"

At that smile of his, half-devilish, half-innocent, a fresh wave of nerves swept over me. We had tonight, but tomorrow I'd be leaving, and he'd be alone, and this would get worse.

"Let me help you organize," I said.

"Ruby," he groaned. "*Now?*"

"It won't take long." I waved for him to sit on the bed. "You direct me."

"Okay."

I picked a sheet at random off the bed and showed it to him. "Keep?"

He recoiled at the sight of it, like it was an embarrassing memory. "Anything on the floor, I'm not using."

"Great." I started to crumple it.

He touched my wrist to stop me. "But I don't . . . I can't throw it away."

"We'll make a pile, then." I narrowed my eyes playfully. "An *organized* pile."

He laughed. I turned away, gathering paper off the floor, hoping this focused work would slow my racing heart, quell the dread I felt at the prospect of leaving him.

A bead of sweat trickled from my forehead down my cheek, my neck, over my chest, down my shirt. I stooped and picked up another composition sheet, this one nearly torn in two.

I added it to the pile—and as I stood, I felt him walk quietly up behind me.

"The ones on the wall. What do you want to do . . . with . . . ?"

My voice evaporated. His lips were touching my shoulder. His kiss drew a soft line up my throat and then down again, while his hands found their way under my shirt and around my waist, urging me gently back against him.

I started to reach for one of the neatly written composition pages pinned on the wall, like we were going to keep working—then I gave up and pressed my hand to the rough stucco wall, bracing myself against Oscar as my eyes shut.

"Do you know how much I'm going to miss you?" His voice was so low it made me shiver.

"I know," I whispered back. "I . . ."

My thoughts gave out. I slid slowly around so I could kiss him, letting my limbs loosen while he held me up, slippery skin and all. I felt his heart beating through his shirt, multitudes upon multitudes shimmering beneath the surface. I pressed my hand there, splaying my fingers, then balling them all into a fist. He drew a sharp breath, leaning back to look at me as if he were about to burst into laughter.

"I love you, Ruby, you know that, right? I'm just . . . gone."

He wavered, delirious, and I felt dizzy too, from the heat, from hearing those words, from all of this, my skin, my veins, everything crackling inside of me so quickly I felt sure I might fly apart.

Say it, Ruby. Just say it!

"Me too," I said. *Coward.*

I stood on my tiptoes to pull him even closer and he glanced at the bed.

"Are you . . . ?" I asked, nervous.

"I am," he answered. "Ready. *So* ready. If you are, I'm—"

"Yes."

A smile flickered over his face, quick as a spark. "Yes?"

"Yes," I said again, beaming as he gathered me up and walked me to the bed.

Two sweeps of his arm and the pages littering his duvet went flying like frightened pigeons. I took the space they vacated but still felt them fluttering until beautiful Oscar, *my* Oscar, was above me and everything was us.

And then our world was kissing and hands roving and undressing and sharp need, then reaching for protection and scrambling to open it and awkward giggles, then kissing again while the taste of him changed, undressing more and seeing how we fit, the strangeness of it, the pain, then breathing together, moving together, this way, a different way, ridiculous and serious and better and not quite and perfect and *us.*

Everything was us and us and us.

33.

The silence here was the loudest thing I'd ever heard—frogs, crickets, palm fronds, dragonflies, a South Carolina audio sampler. Six days in and my mind had gone drowsy, blurred at the borders, body warm to my bones and browner on the outside.

Nothing much was going on, and that was the point. Nothing to grapple with, agonize over, decide about. A break from drama . . . and it was surprisingly stressful.

Peace and quiet had a funny way of putting me on edge, waiting for an explosion to shatter it.

For now, Gramps's classic country station played faintly from the porch as I watched the tidal river flow past the edge of the long dock. As Dad had suggested, I was out here dangling my feet. I was also checking my phone every twenty-five seconds to see whether any new texts had come in.

One bar turned to *no service*. Again.

I shoved my phone behind me, replacing it with *Something Sweet*, the latest in the pile of paperbacks I'd foraged from Grandma Jean's shelves. After a few days of reading, I'd found myself confusing my actual setting with the fictional ones I was immersed in, wondering whether I was Ruby Chertok or this mom in her mid-thirties reeling from a divorce while trying to get her bakery off the ground.

Was this how real people lived? In small towns and beachfront villages, cities in decline, sprawling suburbs, in jobs that you never thought about until that job was yours. I'd patronized L'Orangerie nearly every week for the past five years, and never had it occurred to me in any active way that "baker" was a job that I could train for and get. There were *thousands* of things I could do—and it wouldn't even need to define me. I could show up, get paid, fall in love, have a family . . .

My heart started thudding in answer to that thought, then aching, then bursting apart, dawn-of-the-universe hot. I let the book fall shut in my lap.

Oscar had seen me to the security cut-off.

"Keep your phone on you," he'd said. "I'm going to be stream-of-consciousness texting."

"Okay."

"And I'll be here the day you get back."

I showed the TSA agent my ticket and she waved me into the line.

"With balloons!" Oscar shouted, side-skipping to follow me down the line. "And a marching band!"

My grin had gone manic with the realization that he might actually do this. Then I saw his face through the moving passengers. He wasn't smiling anymore.

"Ruby," he called out.

I paused, waiting. The businessman behind me looked annoyed, but I didn't care. My eyes locked on Oscar's.

Oscar opened his mouth, closed it, blurted, "I'll see you soon," then walked away slumping, shaking his head like he was furious with himself.

"I'll see you soon too."

I hadn't realized even then how endlessly distant that *soon* would feel. How raw and starving my body would feel this far away from him. How *horrible* the phone reception would be just fifteen miles outside Charleston.

And despite all that, how good it would feel to be out of the snow globe.

So now, day six, vacation. Summer heat, thicker and hazier than New York's by a factor of ten. Tomatoes from the garden, fish from the river, Gramps trying to "fatten me up." We talked about college sports more than music, and it was obviously what I needed—except for this *pain*, the one I was feeling right now. I would breathe, it would go away. I would think of Oscar and it would get worse and better at the same time, like the relief I felt as a little kid, pushing a loose tooth back into the ache.

Our calls were making it worse. We talked on the landline every night, after my grandparents went to bed, and there was no discernable longing in his voice. New York was great, the symphony was shaping up, rehearsals were amazing, he didn't say *I miss you,* didn't attempt *I love you,* I had to maintain rapid-fire subject changes to keep him from rushing me off the phone, and—

Eight more days. I gazed at the light on the river, shifting endlessly. *Peace. Space. Dad pacified, Oscar's symphony complete, and I'll be . . . I'll . . . I'll just be.*

I nodded. Then I headed back to the house, feeling either completely enlightened or about to faint from heat stroke.

"Your dad's on TV!" Grandma Jean called down to me as I was rounding the pool. "You're probably used to it, but come up if you want to see!"

I squinted up at the porch. Dad didn't have a premiere to promote. He used to host these *Welcome to the Symphony* network specials, but those stopped airing before I was born.

Then it hit me.

I sprinted into the living room and grinned at the non-Dad close-up on the mounted screen. Oscar. My Oscar. He looked close enough to touch.

"It's a dream come true," he was saying, his voice strangely rote.

Grandma Jean pointed past me. "Is that the boy who's been staying with y'all?"

"Oscar Bell, yeah," I answered, excitement tugging me onto my tiptoes. "Can you rewind it? Or—"

"I think so. Let me . . ." She stared at the remote.

By the sound of it, Dad had only referred to him in oblique terms—not surprising, given that he'd sent me here to protect Oscar and his delicate creative process from the perils of my feminine allure.

But I wasn't sure why I hadn't confessed what he was to me. Maybe because thinking about him hurt enough. *Talking* about him might have ripped me apart entirely.

"There!" Grandma Jean sat as a commercial ended and the clip began.

It was ATV's morning news program, a panel of perky hosts sitting around a coffee table with Shawna Wells, who looked like she'd descended from Olympus and didn't want to stay long.

"I recently had the opportunity to meet a *remarkable* young man who could very well revolutionize the classical music world," Shawna started. "He's the highlight of Lincoln Center's summer programming and—get this—he's only *seventeen*."

The anchors glanced at each other with a chorus of murmurs, and I let out a squeal, gripping the edge of the sofa to keep from floating off the ground.

The story began with shots of Lincoln Center, then Dad—*hi Dad!*—strolling to the Amberley side, waving to passersby, while Shawna talked about how white and Asian the classical music world had remained in the past century. A crash of music and . . .

Oscar! In rehearsal! Not his music, a Chevalier de Saint-Georges concerto, which was so perfect and . . .

I slumped into a crouch beside the sofa. Even at the podium, he was wearing that interview outfit—the hoodie and jeans and basketball shoes. He wasn't conducting with the same gusto as I was used to seeing. But he was magnificent.

Then the interview.

Shawna, smiling indulgently, with more than a glint of *let's be real* in her eyes: "How did a kid like you get into classical music?"

My smile fell away as I watched Oscar fighting to hold on to his.

"I always loved it," he said. "From birth, pretty much . . ."

Then his voice was drowned out by a well-known rap track, face replaced by a POV shot of a car driving through an urban downtown area, Shawna talking about how he'd grown up in DC and his mother had saved up to send him to an elite private school for a chance at—there it was again—*a better life.*

His father wasn't mentioned. Etta at Duke, Bri, who wrote fan-fic. Anyone watching would think he was raised by a low-income single mother in the middle of the projects. It made for a wonderful story.

"This isn't . . . *true,*" I sputtered. "None of this is true."

"What's not true, honey?" Grandma asked.

I bit my thumbnail, waiting for another shot of Oscar. It came in the form of that YouTube video, with a graphic of the views counter going up and up, framed by a blurry Beyoncé video and a baby trying to juggle Cheerios.

Then back to Oscar, thank God. He was smiling for real now.

"This music," he said, leaning on his knees. "It's at the heart of humanity. It burns, it tells the truth. I wish more people had the opportunity to hear it the way I do."

"And the venerated Amberley School of Music is helping to make that wish come true," went Shawna's voiceover, cutting to a shot of Nora and Bill sitting with Oscar in Nora's pastel office.

"Diversity is a *huge* push for us here at Amberley." Bill's usual android expression was replaced with a politician's thoughtful squint. "We want our student body to reflect our community. And we want the music of the future to breathe the air of this generation—what they experience out there on the streets."

On the streets? What was he even talking about?

"Our mission moving forward is singular—a *diverse student body*," Nora chimed in, patting Oscar's hand. I knew that gesture well. "But I want to tell you . . . Oscar is not just the vanguard of that, he is a star in his own right."

I stood again to turn in a slow, stunned circle, too angry to speak. *Of* course *Oscar Fucking Bell is a star in his own right. Nobody would have thought otherwise if you hadn't said that!* What was the *matter* with her?

I remembered suddenly that little snippet of conversation I'd overheard through the vents, her sister—*Don't let your moment get swallowed up by his moment.*

They cut to the most awkward campus tour imaginable—Dad and

Bill poking their heads into, *one*: a rehearsal room where what might have been the summer program's sole Latina student was practicing the French horn, *two*: a voice class led by a famous black coloratura I seriously doubted had time to teach, and *three*: a quartet comprised of two South Asians and two white kids with olive complexions performing a piece that I knew for a fact they'd swapped the wrong instruments in for, just to throw these people together for the photo op.

The piece ended with a too-quick shot of Oscar conducting again, then a link to the school's fundraising page. I stood, numb, watching the morning news anchors transition to a segment about India-inspired cocktails.

"I'm going to donate," Grandma Jean said, rewinding to the screen with the fundraising info. "I think it's wonderful what they're doing there."

I watched her, reeling, as she jogged past me to her computer. "What do you think they're doing?"

"Helping those kids. Getting them off the streets and into a better life."

I bit back a scream. "You *really* don't need to donate, Grandma."

"I'd like to!" She was already typing.

And the dots connected themselves. The costume Oscar had had to wear. The push to make his premiere a fundraiser. The "new agenda" for the school. This was about making the river flow.

The world went white as if from the burst of a flashbulb. Even that visit from Nora, that stack of college brochures, getting me into the symphony choir—it was all designed to keep Oscar on track, wasn't it? He was their cash cow. And now he knew.

I tried Oscar on the kitchen landline, but it only rang once before going to voicemail. I put the cordless phone on the counter. Then

I picked it up and dialed again, heading out to the porch, as if that might improve my luck.

It did. He picked up this time. "Hey gorgeous, how's it going? Are you tan yet?"

"Hi, um, sort of. You'll see. Listen—I just caught your interview. Have you seen it?" I bit my lip, heart pounding, waiting for his reaction.

"I have."

He fell silent. I gripped the porch swing chain.

"Sorry, crossing the street. Yeah, it was pretty dope! Good exposure, right?"

I let out a relieved sigh. He sounded happy. But the slant of that interview, the way they'd packaged him—was it my place to even bring it up?

"Listen, I'm heading into rehearsal . . ." His voice got muffled. "Yo Sammy . . . mfff . . ." He laughed, so he must have been making a joke with someone he was passing. "I might not be able to talk tonight, so could we pick this up tomorrow? Hope you're having a great time."

"I miss you," I said, my voice raw.

"Yeah." I could hear him drawing a long breath. "You too. I'll see you."

And click.

He was fine. It should have been a relief. I should have been celebrating with a lemonade already, instead of clinging to the back of the swing, my eyes shifting between Gramps weeding in the garden and the gray crosshatch mesh of the porch screen penning me in.

That boy in the interview wasn't Oscar. Neither was the boy on the phone.

One more week.

34.

Poolside. Home stretch. Three days left. I could do this. I was on paperback number five, our environmentalist heroine *finally* having sex with the developer she'd sparred with for most of the book—but my mind kept drifting to another bedroom, my mouth on Oscar's shoulder, his hands in my hair . . .

Holy hell, it was hot out here. Even a splash in the pool didn't help. I wrapped a towel under my armpits and started up to the porch to see if there was sweet tea in the fridge.

He's busy. I've left him two voicemails, that's plenty. He'll call me back. He will.

Peace. Quiet. Find your Zen, dammit.

Grandma Jean was in the sitting room, talking to someone in a clipped tone. I sprinted for the kitchen before I could be spotted half-dressed. Halfway into the fridge, reaching for the plastic pitcher, I heard the visitor answer—and the sound of her voice, plummy, low, sent me staggering into the kitchen island.

Oh my God, how—?

I ran so fast, my towel dropped, tangling around my ankles, discarded entirely by the time I reached the sitting room.

Mom rose from the sofa with a delighted laugh. "Look at *you*! You're a *Sports Illustrated* cover!"

I stood mannequin-still as she reached out to cradle my damp hair in her palms. Then she drew me in for a hug and I grinned so wide it hurt. She was wearing that jasmine perfume she liked. She was soft and warm—the exact temperature of a mother.

"*Surprise*," she laughed.

I'd missed her. Oh *God*, I'd missed her.

I inched back. "I don't want to get you wet."

"I'm *sweltering*, cool me off." She pulled away, glanced at her outfit, then back at me, sighing happily. "You are a sight for sore eyes."

"The two of you standing next to each other," Grandma Jean said, shaking her head. "It's uncanny."

Mom smiled softly. "She's more grown-up than I was at that age."

I felt a swell of pride, but Grandma Jean looked strangely pained. "I don't know about—"

The front door opened and I turned to see a man coming through, lugging bags. He was unfamiliar but recognizable, like I'd seen him in pictures before. I spotted a cello case already sitting beside the umbrella stand.

Is that . . . ? I thought as Mom said, "Ruby, this is Victor Durant, the cellist."

"Wow. Hi." I extended a hand to shake, then laughed as Grandma wrapped my towel back around me, tucking it in at the edge and pulling it flat.

"Pleasure to finally meet you, Ruby," Victor said, his voice lightly accented.

Finally?

Mom swiveled to wrap an arm around his waist. My body went very still, numb with understanding.

She patted his butt, pointed him up the stairs. "We're on the left."

Before I could ask any questions, Mom turned and started twirling my hair, tucking it behind one ear. "I swear, you've grown an inch since I last saw you."

"Half an inch," I admitted, leaving the rest out. Half an inch in a year. A *year.*

"And your *voice* must have changed too, to get in with Odile . . . !"

All possible responses fled my head.

"You'll probably keep growing into college. I did. Oh, speaking of which . . ." She touched my shoulder. "Where are you *going?*"

I stammered another non-reply, my mind buckling under the weight of everything wrong with that question—but was saved from answering by Victor trundling down the stairs in loose linen trousers and a matching jacket.

"I'm not changing," Mom called past me, shrugging, her resort sundress flouncing with the gesture. "We're running downtown for a quick drink."

Downtown Charleston was half an hour away. She made it sound like it was down the block. And it was the afternoon—shouldn't she be practicing?

She started toward the door and panic blurred my vision. Mom was back. Mom was leaving.

As if sensing my reaction, she stopped with a smile. "We'll be home in time for dinner. I'm *so* excited to catch up, Rooster."

You don't call me that, I thought. *Dad and Win and Alice call me that. You always call me Ruby.* It was as if parenting me had been a play, and now that she'd been off the stage this long, she'd started to forget her lines.

The door shut.

Grandma Jean brightened forcibly and said, *"Your mother,"* like I should know what that meant. "She was so excited to hear you'd be coming. Swore me to secrecy."

That was something. I sat at the kitchen island sipping sweet tea, toes tapping restlessly against my stool—whether from sugar overload or the thought of my mom finally detouring to see me, I couldn't tell.

Seven thirty. They still weren't back. Gramps wouldn't let us hold up the meal.

"I'm hungry!" he shouted, his affable grouch routine. *"Ruby's* hungry!"

"I'm not that hungry."

He shot me an I-don't-believe-you glare, his bald spot gleaming under the kitchen lights, and I let out a snort.

Grandma Jean set five places at the table as slowly as she could while I dealt out the silverware. I'd clicked back into usefulness here, helping wash up, peel veggies, like all of us did every time we'd visited as children, even Win. It was hard to think of Mom doing that, growing up here. Maybe compulsively practicing the piano had been her way of getting out of doing chores. Maybe "a quick drink downtown" was her way of getting out of it now.

We'd nearly finished eating our pot roast when they paraded through the front door, laughing like they'd just stepped out of a comedy club.

"Sorry!" Mom called, slipping in her low heels. I hoped she hadn't driven. "Ugh, the bridge traffic was *insane*! I swear, it gets worse every year."

That led Gramps into a rant about overdevelopment and infrastructure as they filled their plates and sat, Grandma Jean drumming up cheerful side-conversation with Victor. She seemed to know him already.

I ate the rest of my dinner, drained my water, couldn't take it anymore.

"How long are you staying?" I asked.

She must not have known this was the end of my trip. Maybe I could change my ticket, stay longer? *Except . . . Oscar.*

Mom sipped her pinot noir, then swallowed, wincing, and said, "Two nights. I wish it were longer."

"Oh." So she did know. At least she'd carved *some* time out, even if it wasn't a ton.

"We're at the Gaillard Center tomorrow night, then we have to jet all the way to Tucson, which is three flights, if you can believe it."

Gaillard . . .

"Wait." My hands trembled against my lap. I clenched them around my paper napkin. "You're . . . performing?"

She froze, carefully placid. "That's why we're here."

"I thought you were here to see me."

I'd said it without thinking. For once, I didn't wish it back. It was the truth.

"Well, it's a nice little bit of serendipity, isn't it?"

She beamed, stretching her hand across the table as if I would take it right now. As if I would let her anywhere near me.

"Is that what you said when you got pregnant with me?" I didn't recognize the voice coming out of me, but I let it talk. " '*What a nice little bit of serendipity*'? Or did you even notice I'd shown up?"

"I noticed." Her cheeks twitched. "Believe me, I noticed, I was sick for months—what are you trying to say here, Ruby? You're starting to sound like your sister."

Rage pulled me from the table. "Who are you? Who the fuck *are* you?"

Grandma Jean went pale. I raised my hand.

"Sorry Grandma, I don't mean to curse, I just . . . I want my *mom* back. I had one once, I swear I did."

My face contorted but the tears didn't come, scorched dry by my anger.

"You left me and—look at you, you don't even care. 'A nice little bit of serendipity'? Who *are* you? Who says that about their child? What am I, a dollar you found on the sidewalk?"

Mom had her face buried in her hands, Victor's hand on her back, hiding from me even now.

I backed away, grinning wildly. "And Victor, you seem like a great guy and you look super awesome in your pantsuit, but *who the fuck are you?*"

Mom shot up from the table. "Ruby, say what you want to me, but—"

"Introduce him, then, Mom. *Introduce* him. Not, this is a famous cellist. Say 'This is the man I've been sleeping with this whole time.' Or is he new?"

Victor chugged his wine.

"He's . . . not new."

"Did you leave Dad for him?"

"*No.*" Mom's jaw twitched. "I left your dad for *me.*"

There was such ferocity in her voice that I forgot to breathe for a second.

She pointed to herself. "So I could live. So I could work. Out of his shadow."

"Do you—?" My mouth clamped shut. I couldn't say it. I was marathon winded, vision spotting.

Grandma Jean stood, rubbing my shoulders like she was trying to make me smaller. "Why don't we cool down, honey? Get some air outside."

"Or we could see this through," Gramps cut in—the retired judge issuing his verdict. "Anna, you're my only child, I love you dearly, but you have a hell of a lot to answer for."

Mom let out a shocked laugh. "For what? Giving my teenaged daughter freedom for once in her life? Most girls would kill for that chance. And if what I'm hearing from Winston is right, she's taking full advantage. It's even been in the New York gossip pages, didn't she tell you?"

The sparkle had returned to her eye. It was a shield she was waving, lightness, breeziness, not a care in the world.

"Is he as brilliant as everybody's saying?" She winked, she *actually* winked. "The next—?"

"Do you ever miss me?"

The room fell silent at my question. Around me, everyone held their breath—while I exhaled for what felt like the first time in a year.

"I do." Mom stared at a knot in the floorboards. "But it hurts. So I think of other things."

I let out a sharp laugh. "*Oh* my *God.*"

She glanced up, her eyes flaring right back. "It was a hard call. A brutal one. You or my career . . . *one* last chance at the life I'd always thought I would have. It ripped me apart."

Victor, silent as ever, reached out to take her hand, running his thumb along it like she was the child here, vulnerable and wounded.

"You poor thing," I said, unflinching. "That must have been so tough for you."

"Okay." Her eyes stayed on mine—but something behind them shut off like a switch. "You want honesty, Ruby? Here's honesty. If you're asking me if I would make that call again, the answer is yes."

With that kill shot, Mom swiped her face dry and motioned to the stairwell with a nod. Victor stood, bowing politely to my grandparents as if this had been a totally normal meal.

"We need our rest," Mom murmured behind her. "I'm playing *Rach Three*."

And she walked up the stairs, away, away, away.

"Ruby." Grandma Jean started crumpling in on herself.

I walked out the back door, still not crying—skirting the pool, tip-toeing down the long dock until I reached the end and stood staring at the moonlight contorting on the water, my bare toes inching off the edge.

I felt curiously empty. My whole life, I'd struggled to understand her, make allowances for her, reshape myself to fit her mold, no matter how many times she told me it was impossible. Now the final burden was gone. The last thing that I'd always believed made me *me*.

I didn't care who I became, so long as it was anyone but her.

"She was always a contrary one." A gravelly voice rose up behind me. I turned to see Gramps kicking shells off the dock into the sea grass. "We'd say it's time to go, she'd run straight back to the beach. After her mother passed, I was just outmatched. I'd tell her to study for her math test, she'd stay up all night playing the piano. I'd tell her to apply to a liberal arts program, she'd only apply to conservatories. I'd tell her 'That man, however famous, is much too old for you. He'll overpower you, your life will become his life.' And she married him."

I sat, letting my legs dangle. Gramps sat beside me, chucking bits of shell even farther. I looked over at him, his bald head, sunspots, wrinkles, and realized he was probably a few years younger than Dad. It had never occurred to me before.

"I'm glad she married Marty. For obvious reasons." Gramps patted my hand. "And I like him! Still do. We email." He shrugged. "But I'm not surprised your mom did what she did. I'm just shocked it took her so long."

Something about the way he frowned after he said it made me feel like there was another thought he was holding back. So I went ahead and quietly voiced the suspicion I'd held for a very long time.

"Was she planning to leave Dad when she got pregnant with me?"

Gramps clicked his tongue. "She never said so. She did say she was thinking about touring more."

We both knew what that meant.

"She doesn't love me." I rubbed my knees. "I'd always thought she did. She acted like she did."

Even now, scenes were replaying in my head like a remake of a familiar movie. Me filling every page of a coloring book while she practiced the piano. The day she forgot to pick me up from school and my first-grade teacher had to take me to Lincoln Center in search of my dad. The day I found the courtyard. The party after the photo shoot, my disastrous attempt at a performance. All the hours I practiced from then on, timing them so they didn't conflict with her hours but still overlapped, so she'd walk in and hear me and maybe even spark to me this time if I worked hard enough. The way she'd strained herself before that eighth-grade dance, visibly twisting herself into the shape of what she thought a normal mother should be. How much it had hurt to see her fake it.

Not to mention all those fuzzy memories—climbing on the Alice statue, someone there to catch me. Was it Mom? Did it even matter if all she'd wanted in that moment was to be free from me?

"She did love you. She does. Of course she does." Gramps stared out at the night sky. "Just not as much as she loves herself."

Hearing that knocked the wind from me. But my next breath felt easier. And the next, even better, deeper, my shoulders relaxing, toes uncurling.

If I'd been gifted, a piano virtuoso, the next Mozart, she would have left all the same.

"I worry for Victor," Gramps said, and I turned to see the corner of his lips twitching. "Poor Victor."

"*Poor* Victor."

"We've got tickets to the show, you know," he said, rolling his eyes dramatically, like he was pretending to be a teenager. "If you want to go."

"I do."

He quirked an eyebrow.

I tucked my legs in. "I haven't heard her play in a long time."

"Yeah." He stood, offering me a hand up. "Neither have we."

You couldn't hear a single sigh, cough, shift of weight in the audience while Mom performed. I closed my eyes, transported back home to my living room, sunlight streaming like pixie dust—but it was Oscar I saw, standing at my piano, glancing at me for the very first time as if he'd been expecting me to turn up for years.

I dug my fingernails into my palms, fighting the ache in my chest, clinging to it.

It hurt to think about Oscar. It felt much worse to think about the person playing this concerto.

We waited for Mom out on the gas-lamp-lit sidewalk after the show. She came out holding flowers from some unknown fan, fevered from greeting well-wishers, her expression shuttering at the sight of us.

I leaned in quickly for a hug and said, "You're amazing, Mom."

She pressed a hand to her heart, eyes brimming. "That means *so much*—"

I walked away to the parking garage before she could finish.

I'd now said every single thing I needed to say.

35.

As soon as I'd hugged my grandparents good-bye and made it through the security checkpoint in Charleston, I pulled out my cell and listened again to the last voicemail Oscar left me.

It must have been windy there—half his words were cutting out.

"Um . . . it's done! I feel . . . I mean, sort of good . . . empty. I think I'm done too. I can't . . . really need you. Hope you're finding . . . or whatever you needed. I'm not being sarcastic, I really . . . lost track of the point. Anyway, sorry for all this, only needed to . . . when you get back. Bye."

I'd only discovered it last night when we drove into Charleston for Mom's concert, back into cell reception range. There were a lot of worrying things about it—but the thing that troubled me most was that he'd left it *four days* ago, on my cell phone. It was too spotty for me to even begin to figure out why there hadn't been any calls since. Why, for the past four days, he'd skipped our nightly check-ins, letting my calls go straight to voicemail. Why he hadn't picked up when I tried him again late last night, or this morning.

For all I knew, that message was a breakup.

A new text popped up, from Jules: *When are you back? STOP IGNORING ME.*

I sat on the edge of one of the seats by my gate, crossing my ankles to keep them from jittering as I dialed him.

Straight to voicemail. Again. I put my phone away and started to board. *He's busy getting the marching band together.*

When the plane took off, my body went still and calm, recapturing the feeling I got sitting on the dock—light on water. I peered out at the vista below, the marshes, the ocean, the endless expanse, the whole world one big curved horizon.

I didn't need a clear path forward. I just needed to remember this view.

No band on arrival, no balloons, no Oscar at all. I scanned the waiting crowd as I walked out of the terminal, past security, into the baggage claim area, but then succumbed to reality. He hadn't shown.

I stepped to the side of the escalator, scanning now for a man in a suit holding a sign with my name on it. Dad would have sent a car if Oscar wasn't picking me up. But I didn't see that either.

Which was fine! *This is all fine.*

I pulled my bag off the conveyer belt, fighting growing disorientation, like I was in an old *Twilight Zone* episode—I'd stepped off an airplane and into a world in which I'd never been born.

I tried Dad on the taxi ride into Manhattan. His phone rang but he didn't answer. I pressed my knees together as the cab lurched its way to my neighborhood, dread spreading from my stomach until every breath I took seemed infused with it.

As I passed Oscar's low window, I peeked inside. The room was dark, AC unit off. He wasn't there, so I let myself into the house, hauling my roller bag behind me.

"Hello?"

Upstairs, Dad's clock ticked.

I sat at the kitchen table, waiting for somebody to walk in. Something to happen.

They were probably at Amberley, hard at work. I could unpack, get changed, unwind. Give them space. Extend my vacation from music that much longer.

I bolted out the door.

It felt like the current was with me. I made every light all the way to campus. My watch said 4:16. Just a few days until the premiere, so they'd be rehearsing the full program daily.

Halfway across the plaza, I looked up at Lilly Hall—and nearly fell over. Oscar was on a banner, a monumental version of him, conducting at the podium in silhouette, his natural hair amplified by a graphic designer's curlicued illustrations.

They'd made him an icon. I wondered if they'd asked him first.

Quick movement drew my attention—Liz Trombly heading toward Lilly Hall—and I teetered under a wash of guilt. *Oh no.* I'd never told her I was quitting the choir.

I peered up at the sky, remembering that feeling of expansion I had in the airplane only hours ago. I'd apologize, check it off my list, feel that much freer. One less tie to the ridiculousness of my old life.

I jogged to Liz. She glanced over and her face closed off like I was a panhandler.

"Liz, hi," I started. "I am *so* sorry I vanished on you. Some life things came up, but I should have called and let you know and—"

"I wasn't surprised."

"Oh." I had no response to that. "Well . . . again, I apologize. I hope it wasn't too big an inconvenience." I smiled, hoping to convey what we both knew—that I'd added precisely nothing to the work she was doing.

Liz didn't react.

I coughed, waving toward Lilly Hall. "Has rehearsal started? I just landed, but—"

"Ruby." Liz crossed her arms over her chest, like she might explode if she didn't physically hold herself together. "My God. You are not a member of this choir anymore. You missed two weeks of rehearsals—"

"Oh. No!" She hadn't understood. I let out a nervous laugh. "I'm not trying to—"

"I know this is a lark for you, Ruby, and you're used to getting what you want, but this *matters* to us. Do you understand that? It's in our blood. These kids"—she pointed at the Amberley dorms—"get up and practice until they're exhausted and then do it all over again. They've devoted their entire lives to this."

"I . . ." I tried to speak, say, *I know, I know, I know,* but I let it dry up in my mouth.

I could tell Liz that I'd bled for this too. I'd spent four hours a day practicing the piano for the past seven years, back aching, wrists screaming, fingertips dulled, the rest of what passed for a life falling by the wayside, that it was the great unrequited love of my life, but she'd think I was lying. And what difference did it make in the end, anyway?

She wasn't wrong. I wasn't like them.

What Liz saw when she looked at me was a dilettante. Nora Visser in miniature—and I'd done nothing to dispel it, had I? I'd dressed up pretty, gone to parties, posed for pictures. Pretended to be someone I wasn't.

"You don't understand and that's fine." She sighed as if exhausted, backing away toward Lilly Hall. "That is more than fine. But why don't you enjoy *your* life and leave the music to the musicians?"

Without waiting for a reaction, she swooped inside the glass foyer, nodded to the guards, and took her place in the auditorium.

Lincoln Center loomed like an Escher painting now, knife-blade edges, blinding glass, monstrous shadows, stairways leading up and down and nowhere at all.

I staggered to the fountain and sat on its edge while tourists milled around me.

You're a tourist too. I smothered that thought while it kicked and flailed. *Leave the music to the fucking musicians.*

I looked up at his banner again, Oscar's illustrated hair blurring into a meaningless swirl. Did he want me here? I had no idea anymore.

I swiped my eyes angrily dry—sick to death of crying—and Liz stood in front of me. Again. Her arms were still crossed but her face was open in entreaty.

"I need you to come with me." She waved me up. "Please."

Panic bled through that *please.* I caught it myself, heart pounding, and followed her across the plaza, almost running. Something was wrong.

When I walked into Lilly Hall, I saw the orchestra gathered, instruments ready, the choir in their usual seats, Emil Reinhardt pacing in front of them, scratching and scratching his chin.

Nora Visser popped up from the front row like a jack-in-the-box and Liz continued past her.

"Here." Liz motioned to me. "Maybe she can get through to him."

"I have sympathy," Reinhardt called out from the stage. "I do. But—"

"*Five* minutes, everybody!" Nora shouted, walking over to clasp my arm. "If we're not back, use this time on the Mozart."

"Where is he?" I asked Nora, too flustered to whisper.

"His *greenroom,*" Liz answered, sarcasm tightly coiled.

Even Nora looked confused.

Reinhardt's eyes were softer than Liz's as they met mine from the stage. "Rehearsal Room B. Second floor. Marty set up a quiet space for Oscar to work . . . but sometimes he won't come out."

"*What?*" I stumbled forward a step. "Why?"

"*You* should conduct it," Liz muttered to Reinhardt.

He rubbed his head. "That's not my call to make . . ."

The orchestra started to whisper.

"Let's deal with this situation," Nora sang out, walking briskly up the aisle. "And then we can discuss."

I'd heard enough to follow Nora into the lobby, nearly outpacing her for once. What was happening here? This wasn't the Oscar I knew, the one on the phone, the one in the interview. That Oscar had told me that everything was great. That rehearsals were amazing and productive. Had he lied? To *me*? Maybe two weeks had been too long. Maybe I was the very last person who'd be able to get through to him now. My step faltered on the marble floors. I scanned for the stairwell linking Lilly Hall to the rehearsal rooms.

"Where's Dad?" I asked Nora, glancing back like he might be trailing us.

"He should be back from his appointment any minute." Nora trotted up the steps ahead of me. "But he's not what we need right now."

"This way?"

She pointed. I kept going.

"So glad you're back, by the way! You'll have to fill me in on your big trip after all this is . . ." Nora sighed, flustered. "Yep."

I didn't want to chitchat, or face her, confront her about why she'd lied to me so blatantly, turned my hopes into a stampede and then steered them straight off a cliff. I wanted to find . . .

Rehearsal Room B.

Nora stepped back. And back again.

I knocked. "Oscar? You in there?"

My hand shook as I lowered it. A muffled sound came from inside the room—a scrape—a chair being kicked.

I tried the door. It was locked from the inside. *Right. Okay.*

Gathering up all my energy and dubious acting abilities, I knocked again, this time louder. The noises inside the room stopped.

"Oscar, I'm back! Plane landed, um, two hours ago. Let me in, I want to see you!"

There was a long pause—and then the door cracked open and Oscar said, *"Ruby?"* like he'd thought I was dead.

I glanced quickly back at Nora. She slid soundlessly around the corner. I wished she would go all the way downstairs. Or home. *Go home.*

The door swung wider, so I could finally see him. Oscar looked exhausted, wired, wrong. No swagger. No grin. No front. I swore he was thinner than when I left. Older somehow, too. But this was still the face that had filled my mind every second I spent in South Carolina trying desperately to clear it.

"Hi." He let out a feeble laugh, as if his greeting had been sarcastic.

I touched his face, his shoulders, and pulled myself up into a hug. He clung on and stepped backward, leading me into the rehearsal room.

I'd successfully snipped the first red cord. I hadn't defused the bomb.

"So . . . things have gotten a little stressful while I've been away, I take it?" I smiled, holding his hand. "I had no idea."

He let go. "Did they send you?"

"They . . ." I glanced at the door. "Told me where you were. I came here looking for you. Like I said, my flight—"

"I'm sorry, ugh, I shouldn't have . . . I'm not . . ." He sat in one of the plastic rehearsal chairs. "I missed you."

Now there was longing in his voice.

I sat next to him. "I missed you too."

A blizzard of thoughts swarmed me at once, apologies for leaving, confusion over the conversations we'd had, descriptions of the peace I'd found in tiny pockets, my mom showing up and all that that entailed, but none of them made their way past my lips—because all I wanted was to kiss him. So I did.

In the middle of the rehearsal room, both of us nearly careening off our plastic chairs, hands in each other's hair, we kissed like the room was filling with water and we were each other's only source of oxygen, and I kept thinking, *Finally, finally, finally I'm home.*

But time was running out.

"I want to hear your piece." I kissed his forehead. "Can you play it for me?"

Oscar knew what I was really asking. He knew damn well I'd been put up to it.

Even so, he took my hand, stood up, and walked out with me, passing Nora without a glance, fingers gripping tight all the way to the stage of Lilly Hall.

The orchestra didn't applaud his appearance this time. But they snapped to attention when he drew himself up and took the baton.

And then they played.

I watched from the wings with Nora flanking me, the great enormous world constricting into one narrow lane, two endless glass walls on either side.

The orchestra. Oscar. Nora. Me in the middle, fighting to breathe.

36.

It took me half the walk home to ask him. We stopped at a busy crosswalk, the city din around us amplifying our own silence, and I tapped his sneaker with my toe.

"When we talked . . ." Emphasis on the *when*. "I thought you were doing well."

"You were on vacation. I didn't want to ruin it."

Unsatisfactory answer. "So what's been going on with you? The truth."

He glanced up, as if startled by the question. "It's been happening for a while. Today was bad."

"Would you say you're having anxiety attacks?"

"I mean, yes?" He swallowed. "I've seen the school psychologist a few times. We talked about referrals, prescriptions, but . . . I don't know. I worry about side effects, given everything I need to get done. Maybe after. But maybe I won't need it anymore when this is over. I don't *know*, I don't know."

"Is this something you've dealt with at home?"

"There have been bad days. Bad weeks. I always got through them. This is . . . worse."

I let my hand curl around his arm as we crossed the street. "What is it, three more days until the concert?"

"Three more days." He said it like it was a death sentence. "And I'm on dangerous ground now, you know? I have to keep it sunny, easy, charming. It's the price of admission here. Not angry. Not stressed. Just—"

"Where is *here*? Amberl—"

"Anywhere! It's a fucking tight rope."

I didn't know what to say, except, "I understand."

"No!" He broke away. "You *don't* understand, Ruby. You can't."

I watched him. A woman's bag hit me as she passed. "I . . ."

Dammit, I was going to say it again. *I understand.* Like I understood any of this.

He straightened. Reached for my hand. I let him take it and held on tight.

"I'm sorry," he said.

"No." I shook my head. "Don't. It's . . ."

"I'll be better now," he said, not confident but trying. "You're back. It'll all be fine."

Why? Why should anything hinge on me when you won't let me in, when I don't understand, when you didn't even tell me in the first place?

But I was his girlfriend—it *should* be my job to make him feel better, however I could. I squeezed him closer as he kissed my temple, ease returning with every block. Two people walking through the city. A happy couple. Normal.

Then we got to his apartment.

The walls were a museum installation, a complete symphony, beginning to end in gently waving rows. The rest was an abomination. Every horizontal surface was awash in a sea of discarded composition pages, refuse swimming in its depths. Oscar walked ahead of me, stepping over an empty takeout carton, a greasy paper plate, a trailing pile of dirty laundry, a half-full glass of orange juice, crumpled, matted napkins . . .

"You can't live like this," I said, frozen in the door. "*I* can't live like this."

Oscar turned back with a sheepish smile. "I'll clean it, I promise, let's just get some dinner first."

But I'd already started—I had to—frantic, first with the obvious garbage, not bothering to sort things out for recycling, as much as my arms could carry.

"Do you have trash bags?"

"Ruby, stop," Oscar said. "We'll go someplace else."

"It's no wonder you feel the way you do, you can't . . ." I dug for a bag in his kitchen drawer, tried to shake it open, dropped the whole pile. "This is . . ."

I had a sudden memory from a decade ago, Mom in the upstairs hallway, holding composition paper, recoiling as Dad screamed from the study, "*Put them down exactly where you found them.*"

"How did you let it *get* like this?" I leaned over to pick up the rest, tears dropping from my eyes onto the floor, circles of gray on white paper, everywhere paper.

"Whoa, *Ruby,* no." Oscar crouched to stop me. "You are not my housekeeper."

"You can't have it both ways! I can't be the answer to everything, your entire symphony, and not even know who you *are*. Not, you know, do stuff like this to *actually* help!"

"Why don't you relax," he said, rubbing my back. "Go sit on the bed. I'll do this."

I stared at him for one heartbeat. Two. Three. Tears pooling, breath still.

"Do you remember that day you called me an object?"

Oscar frowned. Waiting.

"You were so embarrassed, but it didn't bother me. At all. Honestly." My hand started shaking again. I opened and shut it, tight. "Do you know why? Because I fucking *am* one."

I stood. He stayed crouched, watching me with wide eyes.

I picked up a composition page and waved it at him. "This is all I have to offer. Tidying up. Do you *get* that? Let me be your Roomba."

He stood up slowly, looking like he wanted to laugh but didn't dare. "You can clean if you want to clean, Ruby . . ."

"I *don't* want to *clean*!"

Now I was the one laughing, hot tears streaming past my chin.

"I don't want to be your housekeeper, your plus one, your muse, Oscar, I don't want to sit on the bed and relax anymore. I want *this*." I clenched the composition page tighter, staring at all the notes he'd scribbled out. "I know it's selfish, but yeah. I want to write symphonies. Sing beautifully, play brilliantly, I want to matter! I want to matter to *you*, enough for you to . . . *trust* me. On a basic level. For anyone to."

I let the paper drop onto the floor again.

"Or, failing that . . ." *And I am failing that.* "I just—I want *out*. Out out out, forever out."

Oscar shook his head. "What do you mean?"

Of course he's confused. He will never have to understand this.

I sputtered wordlessly into the ceiling—then shouted, "*I want to be a small-town baker!*"

He burst out laughing. "*What?!*"

"I want to get amnesia and start over," I said, my words barely audible through my sobs. "Away from here. A new name, everything. I can't..."

I started for the door, room spinning.

Oscar reached for me but didn't grab hold. "Ruby . . . I'm sorry I didn't tell you. I thought I was protecting us. Obviously it was a mistake."

I turned on him.

"No, see, here's the thing, Oscar. You aren't protecting us—you're protecting *me*. From seeing what you're going through, from discomfort, guilt, from looking hard at myself . . . I don't even know what. You're protecting me from *reacting*. I think deep down you want somebody you can keep *over here*, who's got their shit together, who can be your back-up life raft, who can sit nicely and listen . . ."

"That is *not*—"

" . . . *wait* to listen when you're ready to talk, and I don't know if it's me. I don't know if I can give you Mozart love, I'm, like, a baby banging on the keys!"

"I didn't ask for this either, you know," Oscar snapped. "This isn't why I came to New York! I didn't want to meet a girl. I wanted to learn, stretch, that was the goal, but I'm just . . . *penned in*."

"By me? By this?"

"By . . . no." He had his eyes closed.

"I'm distracting you." Admitting that made me shrink back. "I'm the problem, Dad was right."

Oscar's eyes flew open. "*What* about your dad?"

I opened the door. "I'm going. I don't know what to do, so I'm going."

The door shut behind me more quickly than I'd expected, way too much finality to its slam. I walked shakily up the steps to the side-walk, hands pressed to my cheeks, wanting to scream again.

I knew I had no right to break down, not when Oscar was going through a real crisis with no one supporting him. I had no right to do anything, and the shame of it made my eyes dry up. I sniffed hard, pulling my spine straight.

"Oh, so you're home now?" Jules stood outside her building, hands tapping hips. "This is how I talk to you now—bumping into you on the street? Feels *familiar*."

I pressed a finger to my temple, spots gathering.

"I sent you eight texts while you were gone. *If* you were even gone. Is this why?" She pointed to Oscar's door, grinning. "No time for your so-called friends now that—"

Her face dropped. She reached for me.

"Holy shit, Ruby, you're crying, why are you crying?"

"I'm not crying anymore. I'm fine, I'm *normal*, everything's fine!"

"Oh-*key* . . ." She glanced behind her, then gathered me under one warm arm. "Let's go inside. Get you some hot cocoa."

I laugh-sobbed, plodding along with her. "It's July!"

"It's August. We'll crank the AC."

She led the way to her apartment, through the living room and onto the edge of her pink bed, then crouched to stare at me, eye to eye.

"Do you want to talk about it? Forget about it?"

I wiped my eyes. "Maybe start with forgetting?"

"How about a sleepover? It's been a while."

"Sounds perfect."

"I'll grab some delivery menus, then." She started into the hall, then doubled back, poking her head into the doorway. "Hey, so did I tell you I signed up for a 5K? It's called the Squirrel Run, no idea why, but it's in the fall and . . . do you maybe want to run it with me?"

The image of my squirrel friend in jogging gear got a smile out of me. "Send me the link. Sounds great."

Me. A 5K. Not a marathon, but still—this was hilarious.

Oscar would want to be there. Pre-debut Oscar. Not giant face on a banner Oscar or locked in a room Oscar or whoever he'd be when all of this shook out.

Jules looked heart-piercingly relieved. "Grams is going to be at the finish line if she can get out of work, but . . . yeah. It'll be good to have a friend there too."

She's lonely, I realized with a lurch. *I think Jules has been lonely her entire life.*

I crossed the room in two strides to give her a hug. She laughed, shoving me away, but as she ducked into the hall, I saw her face soften back into a six-year-old at one of our first slumber parties, whispering princess dreams to me in the glow from her night-light.

I turned my phone over in my hand, thoughts swirling uselessly, then typed a text to Oscar—*Hey*

I need a minute Ruby, he wrote back.

"Okay," I said, but didn't type it.

Two movies down, neither a romance. I'd texted Dad to let him know where I'd be spending the night, triple-checked I hadn't missed a reply from Oscar, then put my phone out of sight.

"You think you're special, Max," the villain snarled on the screen. *"Nobody's special."*

I picked at my shrimp fried rice with my chopsticks, eating one grain at a time. I looked up to see Jules's eyes darting away, then back.

"So . . ." Her mouth bunched up, debating her words. "Is this a breakup?"

"What? *No.*" I gripped my chopsticks tight. "It's a . . . freak-out."

She nodded.

"A selfish one. Oscar's the one dealing with real issues. I'm just a spoiled—"

"You're not even remotely oppressed, no, but you're still allowed to feel what you're feeling."

I stared at my food, less than convinced.

"So how *do* you feel?" she asked gently. "Obviously not hungry."

My chopsticks slid out of my hand and into the carton, giving up the ghost.

"Okay, fun therapy game." Jules clapped. "I'm going to throw words out and you tell me if any of them are right. Um . . . angry."

I shrugged.

"Restless."

Not really.

"Irritated."

Getting there.

"Phlegmatic."

I laughed.

"Making sure you're paying attention. Jealous."

I drew in a breath.

Jules frowned at me for a second. "I spend, like, ninety percent of my day feeling jealous, Ruby. It's okay as long as you don't let it get out of control. It's just something you navigate until you can find your way out of it."

"What if there is no out of it?" I flopped backward on the bed to stare at the ceiling. "You know where I didn't feel it? On the edge of a tidal island, with no phone reception. I started to think maybe it was okay to get up in the morning and sustain myself and go to bed at night. But the second I come back *here* . . ."

"Well, it's plain old senior year in a couple of weeks, right? You won't have to keep thinking about *Amberley.*" Jules made spooky fingers. "How he got in, you didn't. That's got to be a kick in the teeth, for starters—"

"I did get into Amberley."

Admitting it felt like a hatchet hitting the emergency box.

Jules looked as lost as me now.

I pulled myself upright. "I tried out for the summer program in April. It was a blind audition, there was—it's a screen." I mimed pulling a screen down. "An audition screen—between me and the judges, and I was . . ." I let out a hysterical laugh. "I was *so* terrible. It was a disaster. And I still got in. Got my letter in the mail."

Jules watched me, understanding now. "But you turned it down."

"I mean, of course, right?" I pulled a pillow into my lap. "And they begged me to reconsider—my dad, my godmother. Even the piano chair wrote me a fucking email. I'm sure they'd made him do it. *'Think about what it'll mean for Amberley to have another Chertok in our ranks.'*"

Jules smiled wryly. "They want to put you in another ad campaign."

"I wouldn't be surprised. God, the whole thing is so embarrassing and I was hoping to get clear of it and that has obviously not happened this summer. At all."

Laying it all out like this, finally voicing it in actual words, made it lose some of its power. It was something that happened to me. Not everything.

"Okay, confession time?" Jules said, scooting closer on crossed legs. "You're the one I've mainly been jealous of."

"There are *so* many people in this city . . ."

"And I covet most of their lives too." Jules glared out the window in demonstration. "I think it probably started with that photo shoot, a million years ago. I remember tagging along to Lincoln Center and watching you and all the other kid models get styled, and I totally fell in love with it. But it seems like it was a few weeks later that we kind of . . . drifted. And I always pictured you in that world and me stuck in mine and—"

"You're not stuck *anywhere*." I grabbed her hand, but my mind was spinning.

It *was* after that that we'd drifted, wasn't it? It was the next day that I'd decided to become a serious ten-year-old, take up Mom's practice schedule, give up anything that wasn't music. Even my best friend.

"That's exactly what I'm saying," Jules went on. "Don't get me wrong, you've got it permanently easy in all sorts of mind-blowing ways. But I don't think I'm jealous of you anymore."

I burst out laughing. "*Thanks!*"

"I'm dead serious. I thought *my* life was a trap? Good Lord—your family. This world of yours."

"Of theirs."

"You can't get out of it, can you? Except, hey now . . ." Jules pointed at me until she was booping my nose. "You *did*."

"Going down south? I . . ."

"When you said no. When you said fuck this letter, I'm not going to your bullshit school as a publicity stunt, hell to the no."

Now I couldn't stop laughing.

"It must have felt kind of good, right? Making a decision like that."

"It was hard. It hurt, but . . . yeah. It was satisfying."

"So maybe it's not so much about jealousy. Maybe you just need to keep standing up and saying hell no. I mean—that's an *impact*, right? Knowing what you want? Acting on it?"

Her expression clouded. I wondered if she was thinking about her own career goals. I was just about to say so when she jerked her thumb westward.

"Which brings me to *this* guy."

Oscar. My brain blurred again with the thought of him.

"I like Oscar, actually. And that is relatively rare. But . . ." Jules winced. "And bear with me here . . . do you feel like your life is becoming a sublevel of his life? Like you're *his* basement apartment?"

"I mean, yes? But again, I don't know if it's his fault."

"If you took up birdwatching, what would he do?"

I blinked.

Jules whapped me. "Stop, I think about this a lot—what would he do? How would he react?"

"He would . . ." I smiled slowly, remembering him picking a favorite tree. "Honestly, even if he thought it was ludicrous, he'd get his own set of binoculars and go out into the wilderness with me. And then he'd write a symphony about it."

My mind jumped to my family. Apart from Alice, would any of them be able to take their blinders off long enough to root for me in another field?

But there was something wistful about Jules's nod. I had to ask.

"What about Ty?"

"He would resent birds for the rest of his life," she said simply. "He would mock them wherever he went. Like, 'Look at that stupid blue jay, think you're so special.'"

I had to admit, that was a pretty good imitation of Tyler.

"Like I said," she sighed. "I've thought about this a lot."

"You should break up with him."

She covered her face with a pillow, then threw it on the floor. "Yep. I know. He'll be there tomorrow night. *Ugh*. And he's got all our tickets."

"Tickets?" I frowned.

"Kudzu Giants!" She reached for her bedside lamp. "Did you forget?"

I had. Completely.

"No biggie." Jules shot me a wry grin before she turned out the light. "It's only *music*."

Best possible words to fall asleep to.

37.

The sidewalk outside Amsterdam Ballroom was packed when I got out of my taxi. I pulled out my phone to text Jules, who'd gotten here ahead of me . . . and stared at the screen. I'd missed a call. *His* call. How, how—?

I dialed into voicemail. This message was crystal clear.

Okay. Minute over and . . . I miss you. I missed you while you were away, but I think I miss you even more today. The thing is, I would have run screaming too. I'm sorry that you came home to all this. I, um, I did clean my place up. I know that's not what you were upset about, but . . . just know that I'm here now. *I'm not gonna hide. And I think you're exceptional in every way that actually matters. You're not a cleaner, you are not a complication, you're Ruby. And . . . I love you. So there's that.*

My tension unraveled, emotion flooding in its wake, an ocean rising from my toes to my eyes, filling them up.

Someone touched my shoulder and I jumped, tears flash-drying.

"Whoa!" Jules grinned, hands in the air. "You're so skittish, it's hilarious. Don't worry, I know this isn't your scene, but it'll be fun. Joey!"

She called into the crowd, waving him over.

I crossed my arms, trying my best to convey friendly but unavailable. But when Joey emerged, his arm was looped around Sam's waist. She stooped to kiss his neck as they staggered over like a three-legged race.

"*Oh,*" I said. "Oh my God! Hi!"

Relief shot through me, chased by a strong dose of embarrassment.

"Did I not tell you about this?" Jules murmured. "He's had a crush on her since the sixth grade, but she was icing him until that first night you hung out and he was acting all into you. You did a good deed!"

"I didn't even know it."

"You still get the commission."

"Where's Ty?" I asked Jules, preparing myself for the broverload.

"He left." Her expression barely changed, but I could tell how much effort was going into appearing blasé. "I dumped him! For real. He nearly took off without giving me the tickets, the bastard, but . . ."

She held them up, fanned out, and each of us stepped up to take one.

"How do you feel?" I asked, watching her.

She smiled. "Like a *real person*."

Then she motioned us toward the crowd sifting itself into the ball-room's entryway.

It smelled like alcohol in here, of which we could not partake, due to our underage hand stamps. The noise was raucous, the decor straight-up dive. Nothing like a symphony space. But I got a thrill when we found our spots at the front of the balcony and looked down at the empty, set-up stage, holding its breath for the music to start.

Then it did, everybody roaring as the warmup band took the stage. The crowd knew two of the songs well enough to sing along, then ignored the other ones, chatting while the band kept playing. It seemed as rude to me here as it had at the Wing Club, so I stayed quiet and listened, letting Jules carry the conversation.

"I'm so liberated! Is this how you felt after giving Amberley the shaft? I'm sure it just hasn't hit me yet. I'll miss him, I'll second-guess, but right now I'm, like, flying over the Grand Canyon, letting out my *eagle* cry."

She actually did an eagle cry. I shot her a laughing thumbs-up.

Oscar was probably mid-rehearsal at Lilly Hall right now—the last work-through. Tomorrow would be the dress, two full run-throughs without stopping, and then . . . the big night.

I would be terrified—and I'd grown up in that world. As much as I'd always chafed at it, I was somebody who could hide in the wings there, slide into the shadows, but not Oscar. They'd never given him the chance. From day one, Nora and Bill had segregated him right there at the top. *Oscar Bell. African American YouTube sensation, playing live tonight at Wing Club. Step right up and see the eighth wonder of the world.*

Even I hadn't been immune to it. My very first impression of Oscar was that I'd hallucinated him. I hadn't been able to reconcile him in that moment with the music he was playing. How long had it taken me to really *see* him? How long would it take everybody else?

No wonder he'd been having anxiety attacks. No wonder he'd shut himself in rehearsal rooms and stopped sleeping until the symphony was complete. And now it was time to present it to the world. The grandest exhibition of all.

All the sound got sucked out of the ballroom, truth hitting me in hard blasts.

Oscar needed me. Right now. And I was at a rock concert.

Before guilt could overwhelm me, the mezzanine lights went dark, and everybody screamed their heads off. Kudzu Giants were coming on.

I'd googled them this morning and listened to some of their stuff, but I didn't know the song they were opening with. Others seemed to, a ripple of excitement pulsing through the crowd. It was weird—some sea shanty, filtered through an indie rock lens. I tried to relax, sipped my ginger ale, listened with an open mind.

What if Oscar hadn't even made it to rehearsal? What if he couldn't face it? He'd sounded better in that last voicemail, but—

I clenched my fists.

Kudzu Giants were deep into the song now—catchy, I had to admit, the guitars making this susurration with their strumming that seemed to imitate the movement of the ocean. I wondered if they could imitate forks.

"Stop freaking out," Jules whispered, turning my head to face her. "This is fun. You deserve to have fun!"

I bobbed along with the music to show I was trying.

"Yes!" she said, shoving me. I wondered if she'd managed to sneak past the stamp restrictions at the bar. "This is what I mean. It's not *just* saying hell no, you know? You need to seize life, Ruby. Plunder it. Don't think about other people—you do that too much. Take it. Like a goddamn pirate."

Did I think about other people too much? Was there such a *thing* as too much? Didn't we all owe each other something by virtue of being alive at the same time? And when you loved someone, it was a contract. You could walk, break it, fight against the pain, but you'd wind up like Mom. Or feeling the way I felt right now. Fragmented.

Without a pause, the band transitioned into a new song—one that sounded eerily familiar, like I'd heard it a long time ago, played by a different band.

Was it a cover, classical, something that they'd adapted? Or . . . no.

It was "Sparkler," a Kudzu Giants original, but to me it was Oscar's, forever and always, the song he'd turned into the *Kudzu Variations*. I remembered him now as he was in that handheld YouTube video—not a lightning strike—just a bright spark, playful. Free.

I gripped the railing while Jules's advice replayed in my head. "*Take what you want.*"

My whole life had been spent collecting definitions, one after another, piling up, cluttering my brain. The music washed over me, and I let go of them, one by one, watching them drop over the edge onto the crowd beneath us.

Musician.

Socialite.

Daughter.

Muse.

Anchorite.

All gone. I was Ruby. This was my life. So—what did I *want*? More than anything else in the whole, real, world? Right this second, now, now, now?

I answered the question before I'd even finished posing it, engines firing.

To hear Oscar's symphony.

I turned to Jules.

"A for effort." She kissed me on the forehead. "Tell him I say hi."

And with that, I was off, through the crowd, out the door. I flagged a lit-up cab—seconds before it was taken. Then I ran to Madison, waving wildly just in case, towers of lights cheering me on in every direction. Thunder grumbled above, louder than the city drone, and the skies opened up.

The streets snarled instantly, I'd missed a crosstown bus . . . I eyed the way west, running calculations. And I started to jog.

A brisk half block, dodging wet pedestrians, before I hit the park—familiar territory. Jules and I had run it yesterday.

Unfortunately, this route was far easier in Nikes. The darkness rendered everything unfamiliar, the path winding me in the wrong direction, so I pointed myself west, left the pavement, hurdled over a low wire fence, and zipped through soggy grass, clumps of dirt flying in my wake. There went the zoo, the giant boulder, the carnival at Wollman Rink, its jangling music hushed beneath the splatter of rain, up and over and around.

Darting between trees, I felt the ground gave way—the decline slick with mud from the downpour. My shoes skidded from beneath me, sending my butt sledding, my back, elbows, hair coated with loamy soil. I laughed, screamed, got up, *ran*.

I could do this. I was good at this!

Out of the park, onto the sidewalk, into Midtown gridlock, the crosswalk signs interminable, dodging umbrellas, wiping water from my eyes so I could see, this flimsy dress clinging to curves I was sure were now completely exposed, but I didn't care—because I saw the Lincoln Center fountain gleaming tall ahead of me, a mystical vision, the end of a quest.

Two steps into the Lilly Hall lobby and I heard the answer to my last question. The second movement was playing. Oscar was here.

His shoulders were stiff up at that podium, but he was concentrating hard, fighting to stay on that tight rope. The violinist was standing, playing her solo more beautifully than ever. I stepped into the auditorium, and saw her eyes drift toward me.

Her instrument screeched.

Oscar let the next two bars play out, then motioned them to stop.

"Sorry! Sorry," she said. "I . . ."

Everyone was staring now and it finally occurred to me to glance at myself—sodden legs, broken heels, muddy wreck of a dress. I nearly started laughing. My transformation into a low-budget horror ghost was now complete.

But Oscar didn't seem to notice the mud at all. A grin broke over his face.

"Take five," he said, and the orchestra relaxed, watching with bald curiosity as he hopped off the stage and jogged wordlessly to me.

We stepped into the empty lobby and turned to each other so quickly I couldn't even get a breath in before we were kissing, fighting over who deserved to say "I'm sorry," kissing again, arms clenched tight around each other's shoulders.

We were each other's life rafts, finding balance while the river beat on around us.

"It's gonna be okay," Oscar said.

"Yeah," I whispered. "It is."

38.

I woke up steaming, the sun sinking hot through the high window onto my skin, bare to the world apart from the sheets tangled around my ankles. Oscar's arm curved over my waist and I adjusted myself slowly so I could gawk at him without waking him up—marvel afresh at how very naked we were.

The mussed bed contrasted with the rest of his newly cleaned apartment, the wood floor cleared of detritus and shining around us like the frame of a painting. We were the messiest things in here. And the most spectacular.

My heart thudded with sudden panic. I hadn't told Dad where I was staying last night. Maybe he'd assumed I was with Jules. Maybe he knew I was with Oscar. Maybe he didn't care either way, now that Oscar had finished his symphony. But the thought of him coming down and knocking on the door was a bit much for me.

I slipped out of bed and into underwear. Oscar opened one eye, then the other.

"Morning," I whispered.

"Noooooo," he said, burying his face in the mattress. "I'm not ready."

I crawled onto the bed to kiss the back of his neck. "You are, though. Completely. And *it's* ready too."

He rolled to peer up at me. "Really?"

"Really really."

"Well, then, what do they need me for?" He swooped me up and pulled me under him while I laughed. "I'll skip the dress rehearsal and stay here with you, instead."

"*I'm* going to the dress rehearsal. And the performance. And I will be a very angry customer if the main attraction doesn't turn up."

"I'm your main attraction?" He grinned wolfishly.

"*Wildly* attractive attraction," I said, kissing him. "But come on. Don't be late on my account. I'm already persona non grata, let's not add to the list."

"Not true," he said, but got out of bed anyway.

I was past caring about the opinion of anybody at Amberley—whether they thought I was my mom in miniature, or Nora Junior, or a deranged mud-covered stalker. That talk with Jules had done its work. I felt a new sense of pride in what had happened in April. They'd tried to pull me back in. I'd refused. And as stupid as I'd been in not identifying Nora's brochures as one big stack of ulterior motives, my eyes were open now.

I would keep refusing. My presence at Amberley for the next two days would be for Oscar alone. I wouldn't engage with anyone I didn't expressly need to—not even Dad. I would witness the *Summer Symphony*'s premiere on my own terms.

Oscar had paused halfway through getting dressed, staring at himself in the bathroom mirror as if confused by his reflection.

"You're going to be great." I hugged his waist. "Seriously, there's nothing to worry about."

"I know," he said, snapping back to life. "I'll crack a joke, get back into it, like yesterday. It'll be fine. I just need to tune out the bullshit, focus on the music."

"Is there more bullshit?" I asked, wondering what else he hadn't told me.

He leaned against the wall to button his shirt. "Things are kind of weird with my parents."

I wavered, surprised, but didn't say anything.

"While you were away, I couldn't get a straight answer from anybody on tickets for them to come up for tomorrow night. It went from 'Yeah, we'll handle it, we'll fly them out and put them up at the W' to 'We'll make sure they've got seats for the performance' to 'We can talk about that later' and—"

"Who?" I stepped closer. "Who was saying all this?"

"Your dad, mostly." Oscar sighed. "He got distracted while you were gone. He's been . . . I don't know, pressured."

I glared at the ceiling.

"And it wasn't just that. I got the sense—and again, I might be totally paranoid here—but I feel like Ms. Visser doesn't want them there. Like she's been going around telling donors I'm an orphan."

Nora wouldn't—I blinked. *Yeah. She probably would.*

"Anyway, picture me explaining all this to my folks, trying to make it clear that I'm not disrespecting them, I really *do* want them to come, but I don't want to step on anybody's toes." He groaned. "I keep getting texts from my boys at Farnwell too, saying they want to come up, where can they get tickets—"

"Your *parents* are coming, though, right?" I leaned in to button his last button. "Please tell me they're coming."

Oscar's arms dropped. "I don't think so. My mom got her back up about it, sent me an email saying she respects my space and is looking forward to listening to a recording of it. Smiley face, exclamation point." He faked a grin to demonstrate. "Sometimes there's no reasoning with her. And this is after the first argument we had . . ."

He slumped against the wall. I shook my head.

"Ah. Right. I didn't tell you about that one either. In my own defense, I *was* working pretty hard to impress you at that point." He smiled. "Didn't want you to think I was an idiot."

I laughed, stealing his comb to sift through my curls. "Why would I think that?"

"I signed something when I got here." His face went abruptly grave. "I wanted to do it myself instead of running it by my mom like some little kid, so I read it, it seemed fine, I signed it."

"What was it?"

"The rights to my symphony."

My skin went cold, a rolling tide. "You hadn't written it."

"The publishing rights to anything I composed in the program. Which obviously includes—"

"The *Summer Symphony*." No. Nonononono. "When? I . . ."

"Right before classes started. They said it was a barter agreement. In lieu of tuition, they'd accept my music as payment." He groaned, sliding down the wall until he was sitting. "Like I said, it seemed fine, like a scholarship. I mean—who turns down a scholarship? So I signed, but then I told my mom and she was livid. I've kind of avoided talking to her since then."

"Since the beginning of the program?" I remembered the way he'd rushed me off the phone while I was gone, how confused it had made me. Then my brain hit rewind. "Wait, you keep saying 'they.' Who was there when this happened?"

"Nora Visser, Bill Rustig, Sally Chen, the bursar . . ."

I braced myself.

"Marty."

A headache bloomed behind one eye, flashed, died. "Yeah."

Of all people, Dad would have known what this meant.

Oscar leaned forward, trying to gauge my reaction. "It was a bad deal, wasn't it?"

These people were beyond despicable. Oscar spent weeks upon weeks pouring his blood and soul into this music, and he'd never see a dime from it for the rest of his life.

This wasn't just a bad deal. It was a Faustian one.

But there was something flickering under Oscar's watchful expression—a desperate kind of hope. He needed every ounce of confidence he could gather to make it to that podium tomorrow night. He *had* to show up. If he didn't, it would destroy him creatively—not to mention obliterate all the momentum he'd made in building a name for himself this summer.

"Don't even think about it." I kept my voice light. "You own it creatively, and who gives a shit about the rest, right? This is just the beginning of your career. But from now on, yes, you should probably have somebody else look at your contracts. And you should call your mom!"

"I will." He breathed hard, neck tensing. "As soon as the concert's done and my head is clear and . . ."

I picked his cell phone up from the stacked-luggage nightstand. "Why not now? Call her on the way to campus. I'll be—"

"I can't."

I dropped the phone onto his bed. "Okay."

I wasn't going to push him. Not now. He had to navigate this, and I had to find ways to help him that wouldn't send him back into a locked rehearsal room.

For today, linked arms and a stand-up routine consisting entirely of Popsicle stick jokes was enough to get him out the door and all the way to Lilly Hall, where I bid him good-bye with a kiss on the cheek and a cheerful wave.

Then I turned, smile gone, spine straightening into a blade. Oscar needed to stay in the light, to focus on the music. I didn't need a damn thing.

I checked my phone—Find My Friends—watching grimly as Dad's little circle popped up only a few meters away. He was in his office right now.

I turned and headed there, nodding to the guard at the front desk. All the elevator readings were on the top floor, so I jogged up the steps, the burning in my legs nothing compared to how the rest of me felt.

Halfway down the gilded hallway, I heard the echoes of familiar voices, speaking in such an unfamiliar tone that my feet locked in place. I backed up, one step, two, watching for the vent in the ceiling. Just the right spot to hear—

"Since when are you a detective? I mean, come on."

"Bill, stop, he deserves an explanation." *Nora.* Her voice was a purr.

"Damn right I deserve an explanation. And so does every board member you've lied to." Dad, quiet, frothing mad.

All in his office.

"Where did that money go?" Dad growled. "Close to a million missing from the endowment—how are you going to explain that?"

The financial documents. Amberley in trouble. These were the papers Dad had been poring over.

I pressed myself to the wall and listened, watching the hallway for passersby. It was empty. Everybody was at Oscar's dress rehearsal.

"It was . . . a personal loan," Bill said, his voice a shade more conciliatory. "It was all meant to be paid back in January. I had my own investments. But then . . ."

"Jesus," Dad breathed. "You don't mean to tell me you got swindled too?"

What was happening here? I stared into the vacant hall, listening hard.

Bill put the school's money in a fund that went bust? What did he mean by "personal loan"?

"A lot of good investors fell for it," Nora cut in, her voice barely audible. "Some very savvy people."

"A lot of our donors, you mean." Dad exhaled with a hiss. He must have been right under the vent. "But why in hell would you take out that much money? What possible reason—?"

"I'm leaving Stephen," Nora said quietly. "We needed a nest egg."

"So *unnest* it," Dad said.

We? Who is the we? And then, in a flash, I remembered. Nora and Bill-Is-Rusting in that empty room at the Wing Club, the way they'd darted away from each other like repelling magnets. The way she'd looked that day last month when I caught her leaving a taxi with someone else inside—frantic, a cornered deer. The cancelled lunch. The casual lie to her husband.

The way Dad had talked about them for years. *Nora and Bill are coming for dinner. Nora and Bill have big plans for the fall semester.*

Nora and Bill are ripping off the school.

"The money's gone," Bill said bluntly. "We invested it in an offshore account and the firm got raided."

His shoes made a squeak, like he was moving forward. I slunk back an inch.

"Listen, our names weren't anywhere near it. We're not stupid."

"You're not *stupid*?" Dad let out a thunderclap of a laugh. "You're gonna stand here and tell me you're not stupid?"

"Come on, Marty," Nora said, laughing sweetly. "We have a sold-out fundraiser in a matter of days, an unrestricted diversity campaign. We will recover and *then some!* And I'll come up with—"

"Nope. No. I'm not playing nice anymore. It was one thing to cover for you two because I care about you and I care about this school and—guess what? I care about Stephen too. He's a good guy who doesn't deserve this. But you're not just cheaters now. You're *burglars*. You've stolen from this school and I'm not going to stand here and watch you get away with it. You go to the board or I do. It's your choice."

"It won't survive the scandal." Even through the vent, I could hear the spit coming out of Bill's mouth as he whispered. "It'll be the end of this place."

I'd never registered so much emotion in Bill Rustig's voice before. It was jarring—like he'd been possessed.

"It'll be just fine," Dad said, his own voice flat. "Better after you tender your resignations."

Bill snorted. "It'll tick along, maybe. Maybe you'll even be able to keep this campus. But it won't be a school full of Oscars. It'll be *Rubys*."

My hand flew to my mouth.

"Is that what you *really*—hey!"

A scuffle, a grunt, Nora shrieking. My body jolted back to life, and instinctively, I flew down the hall, grappled for the door handle, and burst inside.

Dad's hands were locked around Bill's shoulders, Bill shoving him off, but Dad didn't look like he was attacking. He looked like he was struggling for air.

Nora's eyes flashed in my direction, and in the space of less than a second, I saw every version of her I'd ever known—caring, caught, calculating, vulnerable, terrified.

"Ah," Dad said, staggering like he'd been pepper-sprayed.

"Dad?" I ran to him. He barely seemed to see me.

He pressed his hand to his chest and scrunched his eyes shut. "Ah!"

Nora's lips went white. She scrabbled in her pockets, then waved, frantic.

Her eyes locked on mine and this time there was only one emotion in them—panic. "Ruby. Phone. 911."

39.

I pulled my cell from my bag and Nora snatched it away to dial while I tried to hoist my father up. It was a losing battle—he crumpled quickly, slumping into the too-small Empire-style chair, the closest place for me to aim him.

"Yes, we're at 15 Lincoln Center Plaza, the Amberley School, Room 501, Administrative Building. I'm with Martin Chertok and he's having a heart attack. I'll stay on the line."

"N-no," I sputtered. "That can't be—"

"I've seen it," Nora said. "My husband . . ."

He died, I remembered now. *Her first husband died.*

"I'll flag them from the lobby." Bill rushed off in a rapid glide.

"Dad, hang on," I whispered, cupping his scruffy face in my hands. He was cold, clammy—conscious.

"Ruby?" He blinked, winced. "*Ah.* God."

I glanced up after who knew how many matching breaths, seeing an avalanche of EMTs rushing at us, then I backed out of the room to give them access. I looked for Nora, to thank her for her quick thinking, but I couldn't find her anywhere—only my cell phone propped up against the fleur-de-lis wallpaper, waiting for me to discover it.

She'd run off.

My gratitude burned to ashes as I bent to pick my phone up off the floor. She was my godmother. She was cotton candy and meadow bunnies. She'd dialed 911. She'd cheated on her husband. Stolen from the school. Manipulated Oscar. Manipulated *me*. Disappeared while my dad lay curled up on the floor, fighting for his life. She was probably locked downstairs in her office suite, calling her lawyer even now.

They stretchered Dad down the service elevator and out to the ambulance. A small crowd had already gathered outside, including a clutch of students. Some of them were crying. I felt like screaming at them, telling them they had no right—but they had every right, didn't they? They spent as much time with him as I did.

The EMTs started to slam the ambulance doors, when I let out a wordless cry.

"Only family," the female EMT said curtly.

"I'm his daughter."

"Come on then, quick."

I sat in front with the driver, peering through the grill to stare at Dad's hair instead of all the gear covering him, the needle they were injecting into his arm, the defibrillator they were charging and pressing to his chest.

"Clear," the EMT said, and a scream lodged itself in my throat, watching his chest judder upward.

We were at the hospital before I had a chance to orient myself, and before I could even find the name of the hospital they'd taken us to, Dad was rolling away through doors I wasn't allowed to enter, a nurse pulling me to a harshly lit waiting room, crouching in front of me and telling me they'd give me updates and was there someone she could call for me?

"Your mom, honey?"

I let out a frantic laugh, then clapped my hand over my mouth. She pressed her lips together.

"I'm sorry," I said. "I'm just really scared?"

She rubbed my arms. "It's okay. He's awake now, he's with the best doctors here and we're going to do everything we can for him. Now . . . how old are you?"

"Seventeen."

Her shoulders relaxed. "Well, there's coffee that way if you need it. I'll be back with updates as soon as I can."

I thanked her and settled in for a long wait, watching local news on the wall-mounted TV for God knew how long. Deaths, political scandals, protesters.

I closed my eyes, wanting the drone of it gone.

Bliss to anger to confusion to terror today, and it was only just after noon. A wave of longing washed over me, wishing Oscar were here holding my hand, but the bigger part of me hoped he hadn't heard. That he had his music blinders on, nothing to distract him from his symphony.

I opened my eyes to see a flash of scrubs, a doctor. He kept passing, and I relaxed—but then the front desk receptionist pointed in my direction and he turned with a squint.

"Ruby Chertok?" he asked, mispronouncing my last name.

I nodded, tucking my legs tight under the chair.

The doctor crouched in front of me with a blandly cheerful expression. "I'm Dr. Singh." He offered his hand for a quick shake. "So your father has suffered what we call a coronary spasm . . ."

"Oh," I muttered, relieved. "I'm sorry, I thought he'd had a heart attack."

"In this case, it did lead to a heart attack," he said, almost apologetically.

"Okay." I swallowed.

"He's conscious, resting, responding well to treatment. But because this is a relapse occurrence and the medication he's been taking isn't affecting his arrhythmia as much as I would like, I'm recommending we install a pacemaker. It's a simple procedure . . ."

Dr. Singh pulled a laminated info graphic sheet out of nowhere to show me where the pacemaker would go, what the risks were, how long the recovery would be, but it was too much to absorb. My mind was busy pinballing wildly between key words he'd said—*medication, arrhythmia, relapse.*

How long had my father had heart problems?

The doctor had stopped talking. He was watching me.

"Um." My throat felt too tight to force words out. "When will he go into surgery?"

"We have an opening at four. Could be sooner, depending on how the day goes. He'll be prepped by three."

"Okay," I got out. "Thank you."

The doctor walked briskly through the sliding doors and I exhaled. Then I put my head in my hands and tried to rub sense into it.

"Rooster." Alice's voice drew me upward.

She was wearing a white T-shirt and shorts, practically a tourist. But her face was hollowed with worry.

I stood and hugged her with a gasp. "Oh my God, I'm *so* sorry, I didn't call you, I should have called you right away . . . what was I thinking?"

"It's okay," she said into my hair. "I'm his In Case of Emergency, so it got to me."

"You just missed the doctor."

"And?" She bit the corner of her thumbnail, then stuck her hand in her pocket.

"Heart attack, basically. He's getting a pacemaker put in at four."

"That's smart." Alice rubbed her temple. "Okay."

I stared, tiny memories taking the shape of puzzle pieces—the doctor's card on Dad's desk, the extra-long trip to the UK with time built in to rest, that "appointment" Nora had referenced, that frantic text about Dad not picking up his phone.

Alice, standing here, disappointed. Not shocked.

"You knew," I said.

"Knew what?"

"That he was sick."

"It's not sick, exactly, it's . . ." She sighed, then pressed a hand gently to my arm. "We didn't want to worry you. You've got enough going on and it didn't . . ." She peered unblinking at the doors to the ICU. "It didn't seem like it would lead to anything serious."

"You need to *tell* me things." My face started to sting. "I am so sick of being shut out, you have no idea—!"

"Okay," she said, sounding exasperated.

"I'm not the family pet. I'm your *sister*."

"Okay." Her voice was softer now, her eyes on mine. "I understand that, Roo. I'm sorry. I am. Okay?"

I nodded.

"Can we go see him?" She pointed to the doors.

I put my hands in my hair. "I forgot to ask. I . . . panicked. I don't know."

She strode to the front desk, uncowed by the stern woman manning it. A few seconds later, she pointed to me, got a nod from the desk lady, and walked back to me.

"We can have a quick visit."

I braced myself as we walked into Dad's cubicle in the ICU,

thinking he'd look like he had on the paramedics' gurney, oxygen mask, lines everywhere. But he was sitting up, shirtless, circular nodules connected to his chest, one IV line going into his hand.

He looked tired, otherwise okay.

Before we could say hi, the nurse bustled in to check vitals. Alice and I backed into the hall to give her room.

"You don't have to hang out long, Roo. I've got this."

I started to argue. "I want—"

"He'll stay overnight after the surgery," she cut me off quietly. "Whenever he's allowed to get back, we'll need the house ready for him. Do you think you could tidy a little, stock up on healthy food, that kind of thing?"

Tidy. It stung more than she could have known.

Still, there was a good reason my family always slotted me into that role. I wasn't Alice, striding boldly up to the nurses' desk to ask the obvious question. If I wanted them to see me differently, I was going to have to *be* different.

But this wasn't the moment.

"Of course," I said. "Don't you have rehearsal tomorrow? I can come back, sub in for the night so you can rest . . ."

"I don't have rehearsal." Alice glanced behind her.

"You took a sabbatical?" I wasn't sure whether to congratulate her.

"Actually, no." Her voice had fallen even lower, but she was smiling. "Danny talked me out of it, and I think he's right. It doesn't have to be so all or nothing. I'm not Mom, you know? I can find a balance. I called Sherman on the way here, said I needed a few personal days. I had a whole speech prepared, but he didn't push back. At all."

She sounded incredulous.

"I'm glad you're doing it this way," I said quietly. "You should have it all."

Alice's eyes glowed before she rolled them. "Okay, enough about me—go say hi but remember, the important thing is for Dad to be . . ." She drew a horizon with her hands. "Calm, unstressed, you get it."

"I do," I said, mouthing *thank you* to the nurse as she hurried out. Then I turned back to Alice. "Wait—are you thinking I'll stress him out if I stay here?"

"I mean, it isn't your fault. He worries about you. If you stayed all night, he'd worry about you not sleeping."

"He *worries* about me."

"You're his favorite!" She said it like it was obvious. "I know you don't believe me, but he agonizes. A few weeks ago, you were out late and he wouldn't stop texting me—*what should I do, should I call the cops?* I talked him down, you're welcome. And the years of agita over you studying piano. *I just want her to be happy, Al, how can we make sure she's happy?*" She groaned. "Dad is a mess where you're concerned. He just doesn't want any of what he's dealing with to blow back on you. So he dumps it on the rest of us."

"Because I'm the youngest?"

"It's more than that," she murmured. "You're the only one of us he sees as a human instead of an instrument. He said once that you were the best thing he ever made. *To me!* His *other* daughter! That's how much of a stand-in I am to him, he didn't even think I would care."

I should probably have said something about how much Dad whined about her to me, but all I could get out was "Wow."

She swatted my shoulder. "Don't let it go to your head."

Dad shot me a tired smile as I tiptoed over and kissed him on his bearded cheek. He looked smaller, lying there. Mortal.

"Everything's gonna be okay, sweetheart," he said, gusto leached from his voice. "This is routine."

"I know," I said, remembering what the doctor had told me.

He seemed to consider his next words carefully. Then he looked past me at Alice. "Could you give me and Rooster a minute, Al?"

Her face betrayed surprise. Then she nodded and stepped out, shutting the divider curtain behind her.

40.

dad patted the hospital bed. I sat on the edge and it reacted with an angry creak. We both laughed warily. I pulled up one of the visitor chairs instead.

"We've barely said two words to each other since you got back from your grandparents'." He managed a wry smile. "I've had the sneaking suspicion you might be avoiding me."

I didn't know how to answer. He wasn't *not* right. But I didn't want to agitate him by admitting it now.

Dad's heart monitor kept a steady beat. "I assume you've been spending time with our young friend."

He meant Oscar. I nodded.

"How is he?"

"He . . ." I scooted back, but the question didn't seem loaded, like when Nora asked. "He's definitely got some anxiety issues."

"You don't know the half of it. It's not his fault, it's . . ."

I did know the half of it. Maybe even two-thirds. But he didn't realize that.

There was one thing I had to risk saying. "Listen, Dad, Oscar and I are together. I'm his girlfriend, and I know you're his mentor, but ultimately we're the only two people who should be making decisions about our relationship. So I hope you can find a way to be supportive."

Dad's eyes fixed on mine with strange intensity. I expected an argument, a capitulation, a sigh, but what he said was, "Don't clean our house."

I blinked.

"I heard Alice asking you." He winced, adjusting himself against the bed back. "You know, it took you being away for me to finally figure out what's been wrong. Second day you were gone, I yelled downstairs for you to bring me a coffee. The only person to answer was myself! And do you know what I said?"

I waited, smiling.

"I said, 'Marty? You're an asshole.'"

I started to laugh, but he leaned forward, intent.

"You don't have to be useful, Ruby. You don't have to be anything but happy. Your *job* is to get good grades, do what you damn well please. Within reason."

"Dad . . ." I glanced at his heart monitor. "We can talk about this stuff later."

"I want to get it out now. This *is* routine, I'm not worried, but . . . there are things I need to say."

I settled into my chair again, trying to stay calm so that he would too.

"I'm sorry if I ever made you feel like . . ." Dad squinted strangely, like he'd figured out the right word but disliked the way it tasted. "Like you're less *important* than the rest of us."

My body went pinprick numb. He'd never admitted that before.

"You're my child, Ruby," he said, reaching for my hand. "You're why I'm *here*. In the world, not the ER."

I laughed, wiping my streaming eyes with my free arm.

"See, look at that," he said, sniffing his tears back. "It shouldn't take surgery for me to say these things. I should have said them all along. I should have let you run free and explore the wide world instead of slotting you into our little corner of it. Assuming that if it was right for us, it'd be right for you. It was lazy and it was wrong. And while we're at it, I've gotta tell you something else—I was wrong about Oscar."

He let go of my hand with a pat, retreating.

"He's better with you around, work-wise. Less wound up, more focused. When you're not here, the music becomes everything. And *everything*? It's too much." Dad sighed. "Hard to believe, but I was like him once . . . not this washed-up wreck."

He grinned at his hefty stomach.

"Nobody in the entire universe thinks you're washed up, Dad. You premiered a new opera *two years* ago."

"It was flat, everybody knew it. My best years are behind me, and that's all right. I'm looking toward the future now."

I thought he meant Oscar but his eyes were warm on mine.

"Does Oscar make you better? Happier?"

"I . . ." I frowned, unsure how to answer. "I'm *happy* when I'm with him. But he doesn't make me better. *I* make me better. And . . . he makes me feel like it's possible."

Dad nodded, but there was something endlessly sad in his smile. His gaze drifted upward, remembering something.

"Your mom is a brilliant pianist. Just astonishing."

My throat clenched. His eyes had drifted, the way they had that night he spoke to me at the piano. He was seeing her right now.

"Living with me, my last name, my music in the headlines, my work dominating everything—it suffocated her."

"Do you miss her?" I glanced at the curtain to see if Alice had come back. "You've seemed fine this whole time, so I didn't—"

"God, do I miss her?" He started to press a hand to his chest, then, not wanting to alarm me, let it drop. "I'm going to get healthy, Roo. But that?" He pointed to his heart. "That'll never heal."

He seemed proud of it. My face started to crumple, the pain as fresh as the day I'd watched her taxi drive away.

Dad leaned forward to stop me. "But Ruby, I am *glad* she left. She had to go. She *had* to. She survived here as long as she could."

Mom was selfish. She was unmentionable. But he held no rancor. Just loss.

"She shouldn't have left *me*."

"No," he said gently. "She shouldn't have. And I should have brought you into the fold, instead of resorting to business as usual, like we were . . . I don't know, roommates. I didn't want you to worry about me. I thought it would help you, but—I should have told you more."

"About your health?"

"That, yes."

I squirmed, frustration rising now. "I heard you arguing with Nora and Bill at Amberley. Before . . ."

I motioned to his chest and my anger retreated.

"Right. Well, I *couldn't* have told you about that one. Not until I knew for sure."

I opened my mouth to ask a question, but he cleared his throat the way he always did before a *Meet the Conductor* talk, so I tucked my legs under me.

"I'd been . . . vaguely suspicious for a while," Dad started, eyes fixed on a blank spot on the far wall. "Everything in the open?" He spread his hands like a book. I nodded, yes—*open, open, open.*

"Those two were my lifeline when your mother left. They got me through. They and Amberley gave me purpose. They are also . . . in the midst of a long-term affair." He sighed. "I'd thought that's all it was, that nagging feeling I got in the back of my mind—the way it feels when somebody's out of tune. But then I saw the way they latched on to Oscar. And what they were doing with his premiere—major donors, thousand-dollar seats, making him sign away publishing . . ."

"You were there," I said, a flat accusation.

His heart rate picked up. The monitor beeped and quickly resettled.

"I didn't stop them," Dad said, his voice cracking. "I encouraged him to sign the damn thing. I had no idea what he was capable of, that what he would turn out would be *this.* I thought it would be a minor work, practice, some juvenilia we could frame in the library—not something so . . . monumental. Amberley doesn't deserve the *Summer Symphony.* We don't deserve students like Oscar Bell."

Bill's words sprang to mind . . . *would you rather have Oscars or Rubys?* My stomach twisted with resentment.

"I felt guilty after that, I'm not gonna lie," he went on. "I've been distracted, and I got carried away by Oscar's promise, but I should have protected him. So I got smart. Suspicious. I didn't like the way Nora pulled *you* in, either. It bugged me from the start, and I couldn't pinpoint why. She's your godmother, why shouldn't she take an interest? But there was something about it I couldn't shake. So I faced it, I started digging into the school's financials—and there's money missing. A lot of money."

"How much?"

"Amberley operates on a paper-thin margin."

I leaned forward. "*How much?*"

"Enough to shutter the school."

"And you're sure they stole it?"

"I wasn't at first. I thought they'd mismanaged it. But they gave themselves away practically the second I asked the question." A vein pumped in his neck. "The money's gone. Stolen *and* mismanaged. They'd been hoping to patch the budget gap with donations from Oscar's performance and this new diversity fund—which doesn't even exist! It was a way to throw donations into the general account so they could fudge the numbers before presenting them to the board. It's a damn mess."

"So that's why Oscar is suddenly the face of Amberley."

"It's too much pressure for a seventeen-year-old kid." He let out a disgusted huff. "It's too much for anybody." His eyes slowly rose to meet mine. "You knew it too. The day of Oscar's interview. All those questions you asked about the school, its finances—but I didn't want you to take it on. I . . ." He winced. "No. I just didn't want you to know. I was an asshole. I should have been *proud* of you, but it was self-preservation and I—"

"What now?" I interrupted gently, wary of how tense Dad had gotten over the course of this explanation. "Are you going to tell anyone? Besides me, I mean."

"That's the million-dollar question. Or should I say the *eight-hundred-thousand-dollar* question."

"That's how much . . . wow."

Dad squirmed to get comfortable. I adjusted his pillow behind his head.

"On the one hand, I've got these people, who I'd thought were my friends, who pulled me out of one of the roughest years of my life. On the other, I've got my school . . . the victim of this. I've got the *slight* chance they can pull this off and cover the shortfall, get away scot free, my own legacy . . ." He squeezed my hand. "*Our* legacy intact. Your name, untarnished."

I don't care about my name, I thought, but stopped short of saying it. It wouldn't be a comfort to him. Just a slap.

"And on the other hand," I murmured instead. "You have your conscience."

He gazed silently at the divider wall. This was where I usually waited, silent, preserving the maestro's train of thought.

Not today.

"When I was little and people used to talk about you, your talent, your place in culture, I always thought they were talking about somebody else. Because you weren't that to me. You were my dad, you know? I looked at you and I saw a good man. The *best.*"

Dad was crying now. He reached out and I hugged him like he was little now and I was big.

"That's who you are. Not Amberley. Not your symphonies or operas. You're a good person."

"I'm not," he murmured, his eyes blinking dry. "No. You have no idea how much I appreciate you saying that, Ruby, but I'm not the person I thought I was. I saw myself as a mensch—I did—a mentor, a dad. I've been patting myself on the back for years, but I've got a hell of a lot of work to do. And I can! I'm old—not *that* old."

"You're not old at all." I wasn't sure if the lie was more for him or me.

"What I did to that kid . . . I'll never forgive myself. But I've got to try to make amends." He drew a great shuddering breath, clapped his hands, and said, "So could you do me a favor? Just one, I swear, and then you go be a teenager and Alice can fight the nurses over who gets to fuss over me . . ."

I smiled, nodding. "What do you need?"

"A number." He waved at the windowsill, where a few random objects were sitting—a ballpoint pen, a wallet, an iPhone.

I grabbed the phone and clicked on contacts.

"Simon Wilkerson," he said.

"The *New York Times* reporter?" I glanced at him, finger hovering.

"That's the one." Dad looked exhausted but resolute. "Bring me the phone and I'll call him real quick. Then tell Alice to come in and say hi. And Ruby? In terms of Oscar and everything else?"

I handed him the phone, wondering where his verdict would fall after all we'd hashed out.

"There's a loophole in his contract."

He waited while I switched gears. I nodded and he nodded back.

"Look for the words *in lieu of tuition*. The summer term isn't over until the concert ends. He can—"

"Oh my God." I nodded, quickly now. "Okay, yeah. *Thank y—*"

"Don't thank me. I'm the one who caused this mess in the first place. Just do me a favor and help me fix it." He smiled ruefully. "Since, you know, I'm a little laid up at the moment."

I started out. Then I turned, the reality of his surgery hitting me like a gut punch. I was still angry with him, confused, muddled, but I had to say it.

"Love you, Dad."

He looked surprised, even after all this, and that just about broke my heart. "I love you too, Rooster. You go on now."

Through the crack in the curtain, I could see him squinting at his phone, beginning to search his contacts.

He was doing the scary thing. *Finally* doing the right thing.

Now it was my turn.

41.

Operation La-la-la was about to take effect. Dress rehearsal successfully out of the way, tonight's plan was dinner with friends, non-musical conversation, zero stress. One night for Oscar to actually experience life as a standard American seventeen-year-old.

Before we met up with Jules, Oscar took a quick shower and emerged clean and calm. He still had to sneak a few deep breaths before picking up his phone.

"I'm glad you're doing this." I lingered by the door. "Do you want privacy?"

"No." His eyes darted up to mine. "Just . . ."

"Silent moral support?"

"That. Yes."

I mimed buttoning my lips. He dialed.

The room was silent for a good three seconds, then, "Hey! Moms. Hi. Ha-ha. All done, yep. I don't know about *lit*, but . . ."

His knee was juddering up and down. I sat next to him, hips touching.

"Um, yeah so, as you know, I . . . have a little bit of a situation here." Oscar glanced at me and his leg relaxed. "There might be a way to fix it."

Jules held the door for Oscar to walk into El Pueblo ahead of us so she could hang back and tease me, squealing in an undertone, "Oh my *God*, was that Oscar *Bell*?! Do you think he'd sign an *autograph*?"

Still, she looked surprised as I pulled her arm, drawing her farther away.

"I need you to do me a favor tomorrow night."

She nodded.

"Two favors, actually. First—will you dress me for Oscar's premiere?"

Her eyes went saucer wide.

"Yes! I mean . . . obviously, duh." She couldn't hide her delight. "What do you want? Society princess or—?"

"Evil queen."

"*Nice*." She looked up at the skyline, brainstorming. "Second favor?"

"I need a plus one."

Now her mouth dropped open.

I shot her a wicked smile as I strode into the restaurant and took my place by Oscar's side.

I may not have had talent. But I had incredible friends, more courage than sense, a name that people recognized, and over fifty thousand dollars in a never-touched trust fund.

The pieces were falling into place.

Maybe it was the modern cut of the dress, the half-pinned curls in my hair, the soft evening light streaming through the window, or the fact that I never wore white—but I looked like someone else.

Not a random someone. A specific one. Everybody was right. It was uncanny.

Dad kept her picture in his office at Amberley, as if nothing had changed. Mom, early twenties, right after they met, sundrenched in a cotton dress, black hair spilling around her shoulders. Relaxed, self-possessed, forever halfway out the door.

I blinked at myself and Mom blinked back, beautiful and aloof.

This still wasn't who I was. It would serve me well tonight.

Behind me, Jules was squinting through the mirror like she couldn't decipher my reaction.

"I know it's not the *typical* color you'd think of for an evil queen—but I wanted something striking. Different enough to be intimidating. Snow queen, I guess. Anyway . . ." She let out a nervous breath. "Do you like it?"

She tugged down the dress's layered skirt. I managed a smile, but her eyes stayed locked on the outfit.

"It was an aspirational purchase," she admitted, fussing with it. "Sale at Cravat, me deciding to lose fifteen pounds, which . . ." She glanced at herself, shrugging. "If it didn't happen after running five miles a day for seven weeks, it's not in the cards. I've made my peace with it. But last night I thought of you, your coloring—"

"I love it, Jules." I turned to hug her. "It's exactly what I wanted."

She grinned, adjusting her own gorgeous blue sheath. "I'm getting into this stylist thing. You're my first socialite client!"

"I'd have to socialize to become a socialite. This is a one-night engagement."

"Can't you reconsider? It would be for a good cause."

I laughed as she batted her lashes. "You're going to be wildly successful with or without me."

She shrank. "You know I'm pretty much kidding—"

I grabbed her shoulders. "Enough of this *I am fated to work retail* bullshit. You're *talented*!"

Her eyes slid from mine.

I grabbed her tighter. "Nope. Say it."

She sighed. Squirmed. "I'm talented." She looked at me. "I'm *talented*. Dammit, I am! I'm good at this."

"There, you're a stylist now. Own it or, so help me God, I will own it for you."

Jules grumbled. But she also tugged my dress once more, as if for luck.

As we passed Dad's room, I saw him sitting up in bed, propped by pillows, surrounded by a moat of flowers. He'd cheerfully bullied his way out of the recovery ward this morning, mere hours after surgery. What the maestro wanted, the maestro got.

Alice hovered over him, poking at an iPad.

"Feeling okay?" I called out.

Dad stared at the screen. "Just trying to get the boys on the, ah, video chat."

The doorbell rang and, with a quick hi to Jules, Alice trotted downstairs to answer.

Dad's Skype ringer started to bloop. He adjusted himself in bed, stifling a groan.

I hurried to offer a hand, but Alice called up the stairs, "Don't bother, he wants to suffer. Otherwise he'd *still be at the hospital*!"

"I'm not suffering!" He swished his hand. "I'm better than ever."

Jules motioned to his chest. "You're bionic now."

"Call me Metal Man."

Ordinarily we might have laughed at the pop culture gaffe, but his smile seemed to be withering at the corners.

He'll heal, I promised myself. *He'll be different, but he'll be okay.*

And we'd heal too. We'd never be that perfect diorama again—*Martin*

Chertok and Daughter—but reality brought with it a new kind of bond. It hurt more. It meant more too.

"I hope you're feeling super soon, Mr. Chertok," Jules said, then backed down the hall, pointing over her shoulders. "I'm gonna change my earrings. These are . . . so wrong. Meet you outside!"

"You look amazing, are you kidding?" I laughed, realizing I'd never seen her so wound up before—then *my* nerves kicked in, tonight stretching before me like a dark mountain pass. Was I really going to do this?

Alice climbed back up, hoisting a giant bouquet of daffodils. "From our lovely mother!"

I peeked at the generic note—*Get well soon. ~ Anna Weston-Chertok*—and rolled my eyes so hard, it hurt.

"Still not speaking to her." Alice dumped the flowers on the far end of the room.

Dad's ringer cut out, replaced by a duet of "Hey!" from two familiar voices. Leo and Win must have picked up at the exact same time.

Alice and I tiptoed through the flowers to pop our heads around each of Dad's shoulders, getting an iPad view of not only Win, tux-edoed, joining from what looked like a greenroom, and Leo, sporting a beard to rival Dad's—but Leo's two kids, already in their jammies for the night.

"That's not Ruby!" Leo said, leaning way in so all we could see was his nostril. "There's no way."

"Hi!" I waved. "It's been a while."

"Jesus. You're a grown-up!"

"Isn't it terrifying?" Win shouted.

"Not a grown-up yet," Dad said in his grizzly bear voice. "One more year, and even then, I might not let her leave."

"*Yes,* you will," Alice groaned.

"Nice dress, kiddo," Dad said to me, more quietly. His eyes were sad, and for a second I regretted this getup, looking so much like her.

"Are you going to a party?" Matilda asked shyly from the screen.

"Hey, Tilly!" I leaned into frame. "Yes! Well, sort of. A concert."

"Ruby's headed to Oscar Bell's debut," Dad said. "Everybody who's everybody is there."

"That must be why our audience is half-full tonight," Win piped up, adjusting his collar. "*Tosca* cannot compete."

"You could still go, Dad," Alice said. "We could get you a wheelchair, seat you in the wings. Nobody would even need to know you were there."

"Doc said cut out stress," Dad said with a sanguine smile. "Vicarious nerves would be bad enough, watching the kid up there. And the politics of that place—I don't need it."

There was something behind that smile, a muffled sadness in his eyes—maybe even shame.

Dad didn't think he deserved to be there tonight. And I wasn't sure I disagreed.

He turned to me with a complicit wink. "You and Oscar knock 'em dead."

Alice turned to me, eyebrows raised, my inclusion in that note of encouragement not lost on her. She really would have made a great spy in another life.

Before anybody could ask about it, I waved to the screen. "Speaking of which, gotta jet. *In boca al lupo*, Win! So good to see you, Leo! Good night, Aaron, good night, Tilly!"

A scattered chorus of "Auntie Ruby"s chased me out the door. I hoped Dad would make good on that promise of a Boston visit soon—but school visits and family reunions would have to wait.

Get through tonight, and the rest of my life could finally begin. My real life.

As I passed through the living room, my eyes tethered themselves to Mom's Steinway. It looked so lonely in the day's last light—expectant, almost—so I walked closer and touched it.

Its fallboard was warm. Friendly.

I sat on the bench, careful not to muss my dress, and pressed my fingers to the keys, remembering the last time I'd sat here, when this was the only piano and the room was filled with people, famous friends, musicians, Arnie and Bill and Nora, both my brothers home, Alice—and Mom, frustrated, urging, "Well? Go on sweetie."

I'd been petrified, even with Win cheering me from the steps. It was the first time I'd played for an audience of any size. It had felt like a test, and it was.

I'd played the piece I'd been working on with Mrs. Swenson—Schumann, "Of Foreign Lands and People." Such a gorgeous song. I got muddled in the middle and Leo made this comical grimace, so I decided to start over, the way I did in my lessons.

But Mom grabbed my hands before I could, wresting them from her piano with a strained laugh.

"*Anyway.*" I'd felt her mortification hitting me, like waves of heat from an oven. "She looks the part, doesn't she? All you have to do is put her on mute."

Who was it who'd shushed her then? Not Alice, a man . . . Arnold Rombauer, of all people?

"*What?*" She'd smoothed my hair then, dotingly. "It's a compliment! Not everybody can get by on mute."

It wasn't until she'd swept me off the bench so she could play herself, erasing my performance with a brisk polonaise, that tears started to storm behind my eyes. Leo stayed in the corner, incapacitated by awkwardness. Win started casually toward me, then got diverted, joining in Dad's conversation. Alice went upstairs in a huff.

But Nora swooped straight in, took me aside, gave me a gift. She made me feel so special, strong enough to run back through the party, get to my room, and write down a plan—four hours practice every day.

Time to get serious . . .

I opened my eyes. Here again. There was my piano, and here was Mom's, and here I was, not ten, seventeen, everything different.

Everything, despite it all, okay.

I closed my eyes, wondering if I would remember the Schumann. It was still in me. It was slow, clunky. There were a few missed notes. I played until the piece was done. And then I heard another voice—Mrs. Swenson's.

"*That's lovely, Ruby. Just lovely.*"

It was. It was absolutely lovely.

"Okay." I stood with a smile. "Time to go."

Dad's never-used car from the Metropolitan Opera sat waiting at the curb, empty in the back, having safely delivered the main attraction to Lincoln Center hours ago. I'd suggested we all get ready together, but Oscar wanted to dress there. To be surrounded by music while he prepared.

I understood. But even with Jules sitting next to me, asking a million classical music questions to mask her event jitters, I missed him the whole drive over.

As I thanked Dad's driver and stepped onto the plaza, I willed my spine straight, smile untouchable, like I'd practiced in the mirror. Jules nodded with approval and drew her own shoulders back, effortlessly cool in an instant.

Avery Fisher Hall and the opera house glittered bright as usual tonight, but there was an eerie quality to the light haloing Lilly Hall. It took rounding the corner of the Met to recognize it.

Press lights. Cameras. The park outside the Lilly Hall entrance had become a red carpet, complete with paparazzi and society reporters.

My high-heeled clip slid into an awestruck glide. Was Oscar's symphony this big a deal? I hadn't seen a press turnout like this since *Troilus in Aleppo*'s opening night.

"Sweet Jesus." Jules let out a delighted laugh. "Lincoln Center. Who knew?"

My eyes alit on the banner obscuring the tall front windows of the entryway—Oscar's hair in silhouette, baton raised. Pure *want* clenched my chest and propelled me straight into the press line.

"Go on, Maleficent," Jules whispered. "You've got this."

I knew what she meant—this would only work if I played the role perfectly. If I got their attention and kept it. We'd run a few drills this afternoon.

I stepped out on my own and turned toward the cameras, waiting for the photographers to clock me. Then I turned away, continuing toward the glass-walled entrance, until—

"One picture, please!" "Ruby, quick shot!" "Here to support Oscar?" "Gorgeous dress, Ruby, who styled you?"

I smiled blankly, three-quarters posed, answered loudly, "My stylist is Jules Russo," and watched, exultant, as reporters scrambled to type her name into their phones. "She's here with me tonight!"

Jules sputtered a series of silent obscenities, then pivoted confidently and joined me in front of the cameras for a few poses, tossing her hair every time we shifted.

Jules had just started giggling silently, making me catch it too, when another woman arrived, jewel-encrusted and chic—a middle-aged Manhattan heiress I recognized from nearly every music event I'd ever gone to. Before the tide of interest could shift to her, Jules walked us away from the photo line, neither of us turning back while the photographers shouted after us for one more.

An usher held the glass door open. We swept inside and I turned to Jules, allowing myself a giddy breath. One hurdle down.

A crowd stood clustered in the lobby. Gorgeous, cheery, well-rested—one bright red bob in the center, holding court.

The next hurdle.

I headed straight for her.

42.

nora's face went still when she saw me cut through the crowd, bewilderment lingering in her eyes like she'd been drugged. It wasn't until a man in a light gray suit turned to me with a jovial, "Anna! It's been *ages,*" that I understood why.

Nora laughed, recovering with visible effort. "That's not *Anna,* Stephen, it's her daughter. Christ, you need your vision checked."

He wasn't the only one. For the second time, I'd failed to recognize him as Nora's husband—not that he would be her husband for long. She'd brought him tonight, though. And her smile was brazen.

Nora leaned up for a double air-kiss, which I supplied, beaming along.

She touched my shoulder, face falling. "How is your father?"

I remembered his words. "Better than ever."

"Oh thank *God,* we were all so worried!" She touched her chest. "Ruby, I should have realized. I feel *sick* about it. He hadn't been himself for weeks, he was beyond anxious, kept throwing out these wild accusations. I should have told someone—warned you about it. Do you forgive me? *Please* say you forgive me."

She didn't know what I'd heard. Or if she had any suspicions, she'd locked them all up in a mental vault. Probably the same place she stored her guilt.

"What sorts of accusations?" I cocked my head, turning toward Stephen to include him in the conversation.

"Oh." Nora's chest went red against her blue dress. She laughed. "Everything you can think of, short of alien invasions."

"That doesn't sound like Dad." I watched, silent, as she squirmed.

"I'm . . . so glad you made it tonight. I'm sure Oscar is *thrilled*. Can I get you a glass of wine?"

Stephen snorted. "Jesus, Nora, she's seventeen. What's gotten into you tonight?"

I drifted politely away, working my way back through the crowd. That was enough of that.

Jules stood at the edge of the lobby, picking hors d'oeuvres off a captive waiter's tray. She turned, delighted, a mini-quiche in one hand and a caviar cone in the other.

I nodded behind us. "Want to come backstage?"

"Depends. Is there delightfully tiny food there?" She took a bite of quiche. "I am sneaking a champagne, by the way."

I stuck a ticket in her leather clutch with a wink. "See you inside."

The back stairwell to the rehearsal rooms was empty. I hurried past the rooms where Amberley kids were gathered and drank in the sounds of normal teenagers, instruments set aside for the moment, cracking jokes to dilute their stage fright—then I continued to Oscar's space, a new one, smaller, unblemished by the panic of the past few weeks.

I opened the door, seeing a line of lights over a broad mirror, two bouquets—one I knew Alice and Danny had sent, the other probably from his parents—and then Oscar.

He'd just finished tying his bow tie. He was dark, bright, princely, perfect.

He saw me through the mirror and gawked. "Wow."

"Weird, right?" I twirled so my tea-length skirt became a whip.

"That wasn't the word I was thinking." He turned to catch me mid-spin and touched my dress with the tips of his fingers.

I glanced in the mirror at the two of us, together—tuxedo and white dress—and nearly burst out laughing.

"I really want to kiss you," Oscar murmured. "But I don't want to mess up your lipstick."

It was blood red, perfectly applied. He had a point. Jules would kill me.

"We'll kiss when this is done. Like . . . *so* much kissing."

Oscar's forehead pinched. "How's your dad?"

"Fine." I smoothed Oscar's sleeve. "Resting."

"It's weird not having him here."

"I know . . . but this is your night. He's rooting for you from home." I looked back at the clock. Twenty to eight. "Do you feel ready?"

He drew a long breath. "I do."

"Good."

"How about you?"

I nodded with more confidence than I felt. "I've got this."

"This is your symphony too, you know. We should share—"

"Oh blah." I put my finger to his lips.

"Seriously, Ruby. What would the music have been about if I'd never met you?"

"Trees. Forks. The poor guy who choked to death at the next table while you made musical notations about it, you bastard."

Oscar laughed so hard he started coughing.

"Sorry! Don't *you* choke! I'm going." I stepped back toward the door. He really did need to concentrate.

And I just needed to say one more thing. "I love you, Oscar Bell."

He closed his eyes in reply, absorbing the words like they were a magical incantation. In a way, they were.

I slid the door shut behind me, eyeing those two bouquets. Dad's greenroom before premieres always looked like his bedroom right now, a flower shop on load-in day. Had Oscar gotten even one bouquet from Amberley? Did Nora forget?

Something about that simple misstep struck me hard. She'd always prided herself on cultivating musicians, managing the talent, boosting, pacifying—but with Oscar, she hadn't even thought that far, too busy scrambling to get out, to pull this off, to escape.

She should have left before tonight.

In the corridor, the end of a long line of young musicians headed off to the Lilly Hall stage, instruments in hand. In my head, I wished them luck with the same elaborate handshake routine we used to practice at Wildwood. Then I slipped down a different stairwell, passed through the cacophonous lobby and into the empty house, presenting my ticket to be checked.

Dad's section of seats was as close to the stage as you could get without crawling on. Alice always joked that Dad would sit in the middle of the orchestra for every performance if they would let him, and she wasn't far off base. He preferred to be part of the action—and tonight, so did I.

Hardly anybody was seated yet, apart from a few older folks, and a small man in the third row wearing press credentials. Simon Wilkerson.

As I walked to Dad's seat in the front row, his eye caught mine, and he shot me a barely perceptible nod. It could have just been a hello. But it did strike me as interesting that he wasn't out there in the lobby, interviewing Nora and guests, almost as if he had his story already and was waiting to see how it would play out.

He wouldn't be disappointed.

The orchestra filled the stage like the tide sweeping over a beach, then sounds began to percolate, small adjustments before the big tuning. Somehow, those notes pierced me more than composed music.

The choir filed in, taking their seats along the side of the stage, and the sight of them cut me like a brand-new wound. It was silly to have hoped. But I *had* hoped—recklessly, fully, with every part of me.

I mourned belonging to this. I probably always would . . . unless there was still another role I could play. I thought of the tech people, the ticket takers, the back-office staff, the hit-the-ground fundraisers, the people who made the instruments, the people who built the talent.

I thought of Mrs. Swenson, all those years ago, helping me position my hands over the keys like clouds—*Let the rain fall, drip-drop, one finger at a time.*

I missed her. I owed her a visit.

Chatter joined the instrumental din as the audience took their seats. Someone behind me was going to a wedding at Elon Musk's house. Another was deeply concerned about a real estate deal in Arizona. Another was so busy, never a moment to rest, insane really . . .

I tuned them out. Breathed. Waited.

A couple passed me in the front row, then sat in the two seats to my right. I heard an "Oh" and turned to see that it wasn't a couple at all—it was Liz Trombly and Emil Reinhardt.

Liz looked mortified to be next to me, but got out, "You look lovely tonight."

"You too," I said, trying to put her at ease. "I'm so excited to hear the piece."

Emil Reinhardt leaned over her to shake my hand. "Everybody's in for a treat."

A flash of blue and blond dropped into the seat next to me. Jules's cheeks were flushed with excitement. "This is my first classical music experience, *do not let me fall asleep.*"

"I promise. You won't."

The orchestra quieted, house lights dimming but not all the way—enough to cue the audience to wrap up chitchat. Nora walked onstage, shimmering in her long blue dress. Everyone applauded. She pressed her hands to her face like she was blushing, then waved for everyone to stop.

"It is my *great honor* as chairwoman," she said, "to open this season of Amberley concerts with . . . something extraordinary."

The entire hall went perfectly silent.

"A new voice. And a new era for our school."

Applause, everywhere, a smattering of whistles. I clapped along, smiling through my panic. How was I going to do this with Liz and Reinhardt right next to me?

"Diversity is not just a buzzword," she went on. "It is a reflection of life—exactly what the greatest works of classical music strive for. So tonight, I hope you will join me in opening, not just your wallets . . . !" She paused for laughter, and was rewarded. "But your hearts and minds as well."

I tasted something sour. Kept clapping.

With a grand gesture to the orchestra, she started offstage.

This was it. My moment.

Think about the cause. It really is everything.

I stood and turned toward the audience, purse raised high like Nora at the park tea. I remembered that one quick lesson with Odile, drew a breath from the diaphragm, and let my voice ring out loud and clear.

"I'd like to pledge twenty thousand dollars to Amberley's diversity fund."

A gasp rippled through the audience—not at the amount, a modest sum to many of them—but at who I was, whose child, how young, the breach of decorum I'd committed in talking cold, hard cash before a cultural event. The gesture was still enough to bring forth a round of applause, and to draw Nora back center stage, hands clutched eagerly together.

She sought me out, mouthing *thank you*, and I could tell from the triumph in her eyes that she was actually *moved* right now. She saw my mother in me—and herself. I'd become all she'd hoped I would be.

But I wasn't done.

"Just as soon as they *establish* a diversity fund."

The audience went quiet, apart from a near-silent "*Suh-nap!*" from Jules. I kept my eyes on Nora, watching as her face locked solid and a thought-bubble appeared above her head: "RUBY KNOWS."

Then I turned away, heart pounding so hard I swore it was going to knock me over. Amid the dizzying crowd, I saw Simon Wilkerson leaning forward. I trained my eyes on him, refilling my tank of courage.

"As soon as I've seen paperwork establishing the fund, along with the rest of this year's financials, I'll be glad to carry out my pledge. In the meantime, I've donated an additional ten thousand dollars to the Sphinx Organization, which works to develop the talents of young black and Latino classical musicians."

I was met with confused applause. This would be over soon.

"And tonight, I also bring Amberley one more donation . . ." I reached into my bag, brandishing a printout from an online gift confirmation. "From the parents of Oscar Bell, in the amount of twelve thousand dollars."

Now the applause was even more scattered, low conversation rumbling underneath. Somehow, nobody had realized he even had parents, let alone ones with means. Amberley's PR campaign had been remarkably effective.

I turned back to Nora, so she could see the page too.

"Should be enough to cover Oscar Bell's tuition. Plus a little extra. For *emergencies*."

I'd decided *emergencies* was subtler than, say, *the lawsuit that's about to hit your desk*. Amberley would hear from the Bell family's attorney soon enough. And judging by Nora's wild laugh, she already knew exactly what I meant.

She clapped her hands. "Thank you very much. The next generation, ladies and gentlemen!"

Her face started to crumple, that shield of a society smile finally failing her, and for a moment I felt sharp regret that I was the cause of it. But she hurried off the stage before her composure deserted her completely, and I remembered the way she'd run yesterday too, right after Dad's heart attack.

To the far left of the front row, I saw a man slowly, robotically open a fire exit door and glide through it. Bill Rustig.

If somebody told me tomorrow that he'd been spotted fleeing with Nora to the Bahamas, I wouldn't be at all surprised. Despite it all, I clung to that image—Nora and Bill, in some dingy tropical bar, in permanent exile—instead of her being led away in handcuffs. But why?

Shouldn't she face justice? People like her were born with a heaping stack of free passes. This should be the moment those passes ran out.

Still . . . I couldn't pinpoint how I felt. Criminal or no, caring, phony, she was someone I'd known all my life. Someone who'd at least been present, holding my hand when others didn't. Some part of me would always care what happened to her.

I melted back into my seat as the orchestra started its last tuning, disparate rivers of sound converging into one clear A.

"Congratulations," Jules whispered. "You are officially a badass."

Liz leaned forward to shoot me a nod. *"Brava,"* she said, while beside her, Reinhardt coughed to cover his wild giggles.

I relaxed, *finally,* and all of me crumpled, arms and legs shaking, teeth chattering, in physical shock at what I'd had the guts to do. But I no longer cared how I looked, even to my apparently approving seatmates.

My part was played, that final *hell no* delivered, the lights were dimming to nothing, and the great Oscar Bell was finally taking the stage.

43.

Oscar's arrival induced an instant standing ovation, the kind given to living titans, even though he was as of this moment an unknown entity, a human question mark.

He stood before the podium, hands pressed in thanks as he took a bow, gestured to the audience. Then he faced the orchestra—and froze.

No. He was locking up. Taking too long to get going. Losing his momentum at exactly the wrong time.

I racked my brain for a way I could communicate to him what this was, not a wave of pressure, but one of support. The glass wall was there, yes—the patrons in full regalia, here to gawk—but cracks were spreading all over it, and not just because of my speech. This room, filled as it was by some of the toughest, most sophisticated music aficionados in the city, felt warm as a family gathering as we stood applauding what he was about to do. A seventeen-year-old kid. It really was amazing.

I willed him to turn—look at me—but then my eyes drifted to the students in the orchestra, the choir. They were grinning up at Oscar with sparks in their eyes, primed and ready, and I started to laugh. I'd thought I was infallible, that I knew what he was feeling, but I was wrong, *completely* wrong. He wasn't losing his mojo. He was sharing it.

He turned, finally, and the last of my fears evaporated. There was his foppish posture, his grin, his charm, his stately elegance, *the maestro* fully merged with himself.

His eyes scanned the front row and found me—and at his tiny wink, my hands laced themselves together and dropped.

He waved for the audience to sit, but didn't turn back to the orchestra. First, he had something to say. Even I wasn't sure what it would be.

I clutched the velvet of my seat while Oscar beamed at the crowd.

"Ladies and gentlemen, I know your program advises everyone here to turn off their cell phones during the performance." He gestured to a woman in the crowd holding one such program. "But . . . I'm going to ask you to do something different."

The audience started rumbling. In the row behind me, I saw people leaning forward, taking out their cell phones and turning them over in their hands as if they were brand-new tech.

"First of all—let's keep the ringers off, that was a good plan." Oscar raised his hands, laughing, the audience chuckling back. "This is *not* a ringtone symphony, sorry to get your hopes up."

That joke got a full guffaw out of Reinhardt. I grinned at him, liking the man better by the minute.

"No, here's what I'm going for."

Oscar drew a breath, glanced back at me, then kept going without a hitch.

"Amberley wants tonight to be an exclusive event. I get that. You fine people—and have I mentioned how *lovely* you're looking tonight?" They laughed louder this time. "Seriously, take a selfie while you're at it. No shame at all."

He took his own cell phone out of an inner pocket of his tuxedo jacket. Where was he going with this? I had no idea!

I pressed my knuckles to my perfectly made-up lips, mussing them, way too riveted to care.

"You've paid for the privilege of hearing this symphony played for the very first time." He held his phone to his heart. "I am *honored* by that. Beyond words. *I* feel privileged to stand on this stage, alongside these truly incredible musicians . . ." He made a sweeping gesture to the orchestra and choir, met with a rapid wave of applause, my own claps the loudest. "And in front of a crowd like you. But I wrote this piece—this *symphony*—for everybody. For people who would love to be here but can't afford the ticket price. For people who don't *get* classical music but are willing to give it a try."

His eyes darted to Jules. She gave a salute.

"For . . ."

He lifted his phone to show that it was dialing.

"*My mom!*" He pulled it to his ear. "Hey, Mom, I'm gonna put you . . . here."

He positioned the phone on the podium, while the audience audibly melted.

"I wrote this for my buddies back at Farnwell Prep, my two brilliant sisters, my unbelievably loving and *patient* parents, my cousins in North Carolina, my new friends here in New York—um!—and for . . ." He turned, gesturing to me in the front row. "For my girlfriend."

Joy shot through me, an electric shock.

"You get the gist." He twirled his baton with a grin. "So everybody who's up for it—let's open this concert up to the rest of the world. If you know how to connect to a livestream, go for it, if not, take a video, post it for your friends when you get back home. Let's share this with anybody who's interested. Sound good?"

A few seconds of confusion, then someone started to clap and everybody followed suit, young and old, even Liz and Reinhardt lifting their phones excitedly.

"I am *so* streaming this," Jules muttered, adjusting her framing while little smiley faces and hearts started to flutter up her screen.

I hesitated a moment—then set my own phone to silent, video-dialed Dad's cell, and positioned it against my knee, praying he would answer. Whether Dad deserved it or not, Oscar would want his mentor to be here.

"Ah, one more thing." Oscar spun back around. "As you well know, proceeds from tonight's benefit concert will go toward Amberley's diversity initiative."

The audience's applause started nervously, unsure, given my little speech, then grew, several people shouting their approval. Oscar nodded along, then added, loud enough for his voice to be heard over the cheers,

"Yes. It is so important. *Make sure it happens.* You're Amberley's donors—if your dollars matter, so do your voices. Hold them to their promises."

Oscar's hands were pressed together, bowing to the room, all graciousness, so his words came across as thankful rather than critical. But in the context of what I'd stood up and said, his real meaning couldn't have been missed.

"Hear, hear!" shouted some old man in the back of the room.

Oscar grinned. And turned to face the orchestra, letting out a long, slow breath.

"Okay, then," he said, lower.

He picked up his baton, with a mischievous wiggle of his fingers. The orchestra leaned forward, lifting their instruments.

"Let's go."

A swoosh. They were off, the room exploding into sound.

I had to brace myself to keep from swaying loose and flying away as I watched Oscar ignite, electric bolts shooting from his fingers, his eyes, his smile, his every movement music itself.

And the music was *immense*. That flirty first movement, the Latin-tinged second, worlds warring, flirting, sinking into one another. I knew it by heart, I'd heard it fleshed out in rehearsals, but never as confident as this, swirling like a hurricane. It felt concrete now, a day-dream turned solid matter, a life in a song.

The third movement was familiar until the last few bars. And the last—*allegro con brio*—was a revelation.

Not Mozart. Not Ravel. Not Tchaikovsky or Handel or anybody else Oscar's mimetic tricks had touched. It wasn't even Chertok.

This was one hundred percent Bell.

I could recognize Oscar in every lilt, every strain, every unresolved chord . . . his humor, his heart, his pain, the way he split himself, the way he tried and blustered and suffered and hid it behind a smile—his courage. I heard all of him because I *knew* him but there was even more there than I'd ever imagined.

I stared up at his face in profile, slack with joy at the podium, and my heart swelled and broke and healed to break again, because oh my God, *I knew him,* this quickly, and he knew me, and there was still so much left to know, to be wrong about, surprised by, to marvel at, this separate person who somehow loved me.

Forty minutes passed—a summer, years, a lifetime. And all of it *his* now, in every sense, all rights reserved in perpetuity throughout the universe. I listened, silent, but inside I was singing along at the top of my lungs.

The orchestra played the final bars with the golden exhilaration of sunset burning over the city's horizon. One more flourish of the baton—and silence fell.

My heart rested, but only for a second. Because then the world started to roar, a volcano erupting as everyone flew to their feet, cheering for Oscar. Not for what he *might* accomplish. For what he had.

He didn't turn to face us yet. He nodded, set down the baton. A quick whisper into his phone before he pushed to hang up, and even then, he didn't turn.

I scrambled to my feet, too overcome to clap. Oscar pivoted, numb, like he was in shock, and found my face in the crowd. I shot him a smiling nod, encouraging him to take his bow.

Instead, to the whoops of the audience, he hopped from the stage into the front row and headed straight for me.

I took his hand. It was trembling again.

He stepped closer, his mouth resting just past my ear. "I'm not staying for the meet and greet."

I laughed. "I think that's okay!"

Oscar leaned past me to slap hands with Reinhardt and whisper a heartfelt thank-you to Liz. Jules shot him a thumbs-up, mouthing *Whoa,* and he clutched his heart, grinning.

But before any of us could urge him back onstage, he took my hand.

I glanced at Jules.

"Go go go!" She winked. "I've got potential clients to gawk at. See you back on the block."

With that, Oscar was in motion. He led me swiftly away, toward our closest fire exit, all the while motioning gratefully to the orchestra and giving a hasty wave to the shouting audience.

As soon as we were through the doors and out of sight, we ran—fleeing together through the back rooms of Lilly Hall, like we'd pulled off a heist, me in pristine silver shoes, his glossy ones squeaking with every stride, laughter bubbling, then bursting out of us, wild.

We hit the stage door and erupted into the humid night. Oscar swung us left, away from the press, past the side of the plaza where limo drivers stood smoking, then down a flight of steps and into the wild, steaming clamor of the city.

Where were we heading? Oscar seemed to know. He had a full tank and a map in his body, and we drew closer with every step until we were jogging clumsily with hands clinging, fingers locked together tight.

He turned us onto West Sixty-seventh—and only then did I know.

In the hazy streetlight, the optical illusion between buildings was even harder to spot, but Oscar wasn't fooled. He pulled us into the courtyard.

The apartments around it were all lit up. White fairy lights glittered along the top of the fire escape. I'd never seen this place animated by night before, people washing dishes, laughing at dinner tables, flipping on televisions.

But the courtyard itself was as mystifyingly quiet as ever.

He pulled me slowly in until my cheek rested against his warm chest, my hands traveling around his back to pull him even closer.

I closed my eyes and listened—to our gasps. Our heartbeats. A percussive two-voice melody.

"You asked me to pick one song to listen to for the rest of my life," Oscar whispered.

I smiled at the memory. "You couldn't choose."

"How about this one?"

I peered up at him, every cell jumping, dancing, jittering, terrified. *Happy.*

"That's quite a promise."

He leaned back, eyes burning into mine. "It's quite a song."

I lifted my chin and kissed him, listening hard to the rich, full silence, marveling at the change in this place. In the person I was here.

Any mental picture I could form of my life—two, five, ten years from now—was as unclear as it had been at the beginning of this summer. But ambiguity no longer felt like a failing. Just a natural law. A space where wonders could occur, sparks and surprises and things I never thought I could do and people I never thought could be real.

There were things flittering in the back of my mind even now. Facts.

He would go back to Bethesda in two days, reunited with his family, missing me desperately. I would plan a visit and meet the Bells. We would call, text, video chat in honest conversations, raw with longing. We would compare college application notes. His fame would skyrocket from tonight, my own path would form in unexpected directions, and then . . . I didn't know.

I only knew that our future wasn't blank. It was a crisp, clean composition page, waiting to be written on.

Oscar kissed me and I kissed him, every touch a note, while just past the silence, the city kept time to the heartbeats of eight million extraordinary lives.

Acknowledgments

Writing *Night Music* was a bit of an odyssey, both mentally and geographically, since I relocated from Florida to England while working on it! There is no way I could have steered this book home without the help of an incredible crew of brilliant minds and enormous hearts helping me along the way.

First, I want to thank my heroically tireless editor, Jessica Dandino Garrison, whose brainstorming and fine-tuning and pushing for depth and spark and fullness of story filled this book with life. Your faith in my writing and dedication to these characters invigorated me even on days when it was hard to return to the page. I am a happier writer for having embarked on this journey with you.

Thank you to my wonderful agent, Katelyn Detweiler. At a school visit once, I was asked to name my favorite part of being an author, and on the spur of the moment, I said, "My agent." And it's true! You unfailingly make me feel that I truly belong in this industry, that my words matter and my stories are important. I can't tell you how happy I am to have you as my champion and friend. Thank you also to the whole JGLM team, especially Cheryl Pientka and Denise St. Pierre, whose cheerleading and thoughtful notes have always been incredible boons.

And speaking of invaluable mood-boosters, thank you so much to all my beautiful, spectacular, gifted, honest, inspiring author friends, who read and commented and encouraged and distracted and laughed and commiserated through all my many drafts. Extra love to Virginia Boecker, Lee Kelly, Candice Montgomery, Amber Hart, Jay Coles, Lauren Gibaldi, Kim Liggett, and Mackenzi Lee—you mean the world to me.

394

My endless gratitude to the team at Dial Books and Penguin Young Readers Group, especially Ellen Cormier and Lauri Hornik for their keen support and insightful feedback, and Regina Castillo for her dazzling eagle eye. Thank you to Dana Li and Theresa Evangelista for their endurance and creative thinking in creating an utterly delightful cover, and to Cerise Steel for her elegant and industrious work on the design of the interiors. I'm especially indebted to all those who provided incredibly helpful thoughts along the way, particularly Amber Nicole Salik, Christina Colangelo, Bridget Hartzler, Elora Sullivan, Kara Brammer, Courtney McAuslan, and Lizzie Goodell. Extra-jumbo thanks to the brilliant Felicity Vallence for her encouragement, expertise, and boundless ingenuity. And an enormous, heartfelt, so-long-it's-awkward hug to the lovely Lindsay Boggs, who is *basically* my fairy godmother. A million thanks for the magic you weave every day.

Thank you to my family, especially my dad for consistently steering me toward the career I was meant for, even when I really didn't want to hear it. Oliver and Henry, my brilliant boys, I love you "infinity"— thank you for being patient with me when my mind was wandering and I had to leave LEGOs to go write something down real quick. Rob, you're a marvel. Your faith and love and logistical wrangling are what make my writing possible. I will forever be grateful for all you've done to make my dream real.

And one final shout-out to everyone who creates music. Whether you're playing on an elite stage, studying at a conservatory, doing eight p.m. sets at a dive bar, working through your first song in your neighbor's garage, struggling to master the pennywhistle you bought at a roadside stand, singing badly and loudly along with your car radio—the world is far better for having you in it.

About the Author

Jenn Marie Thorne graduated from NYU-Tisch with a BFA in drama and realized she was having more fun *writing* plays than performing in them. What followed were her acclaimed YA novels, *The Wrong Side of Right* and *The Inside of Out*. Jenn lives and writes as an American expat in Gloucestershire, England. Connect with her on Twitter @juniperjenny.